THE BOOK OF HEROES

Miyuki Miyabe

TRANSLATED BY ALEXANDER O. SMITH

Haikasoru
San Francisco

The Book of Heroes (EIYU NO SHO)
by MIYABE Miyuki
Copyright © 2009 MIYABE Miyuki All rights reserved.
Originally published in Japan by MAINICHI NEWSPAPERS CO., LTD., Tokyo. English
translation rights arranged with OSAWA OFFICE, Japan, through THE SAKAI AGENCY.

Cover Illustration by Dan May
Design by Courtney Utt

HAIKASORU
Published by
VIZ Media, LLC
295 Bay Street
San Francisco, CA 94133

www.haikasoru.com

Library of Congress Cataloging-in-Publication data has been applied for.

*The rights of the author of the work in this publication to be so identified have
been asserted in accordance with the Copyright, Designs and Patents Act 1988.
A CIP catalogue record for this book is available from the British Library.*

Printed in the U.S.A.
First paperback printing, November 2011

THE BOOK OF
HEROES

TO STUDY THE SELF IS TO DIE.

The Prayer-Song
or

Amidst the mists and clouds of ashen blue that blur the line
between Heaven and Earth. They drift along and together,
hanging over all, cold and silken as a funeral pall.

In this land, here since ancient times, here still in distant future.

A stillness near to nothing its only master. Cast
from time's grace, free too from time's yoke.

No country, nor village. We who live here call it simply this land.
Those whom fate brings here read, in that eloquent silence, a truth:

This is the nameless land, they say.

To you, who for reasons unknowable glimpse here these words.
Good people, do not mistake the terms of the agreement:

Do not ask men for the story of the nameless land.

Do not move lips and tongue in an imitation
of the tongue of the nameless land.

Do not treat as men those who are
imprisoned in the nameless land.

The story that shall be told for all time, henceforth, is the cursed
tale of two children, one monk, and one traveler without a soul.

We weavers have glimpsed these cursed lives time and
time again swimming in time's eternal flow. We record it, we

The Lament of the King in Yellow

repeat it, we revere it as we revile it, and so does the shaft
of dark brilliance that this cursed tale travels from world to
world, from age to age, from the old gods to the new.

We are the inculpated.

All stories are the sin of their weaver.

Good people, may you know peace in your dreams.
The light in the window of the house where you rest
shines in a paradise that does not suffer us to tread.

Do not wish for this cursed life to visit your light.

Do not extinguish your light and wait by the window in
silence to hear the footfalls of this cursed life as it passes.

Do not do these things, and your path will not lead you
to the nameless land. This story will not echo past the
words upon its pages, never barring your swift progress.

This cursed life is called the Hero.

At times, the King in Yellow.

Prison Break

Halfway up the long slope to the Threshing Hill, the youth heard the sound of a tolling bell.

He stopped and looked around. The sound came thickly through the chilled ashen-blue mist that rose all around him, yet he heard it as sure as he felt the vibrations in the ground beneath his feet.

The First Bell was ringing in the bell tower.

The youth remained standing still, uncertain of his next step. He knew all too well what the tolling of the First Bell meant, though it had never been sounded in his living memory.

He could continue to the top of the hill, but there he would only find his brothers standing still as he was standing now, their hands stopped from their work of pushing the Great Wheels. He should run to them, join them, become one of their number. That had to be better than standing here, frozen to the spot while this unspeakable unease rose inside him.

But is there not more here than just unease? he wondered. The youth put the palm of one hand to his black-robed chest.

As a nameless devout, the youth had no word with which to refer to himself. He had no self. He was a part of this place, the nameless land—a fragment, made to express its will and nothing more.

He had no soul.

Yet still, perhaps because of this, in these eternal lands free from the yoke of time there was something that settled in those vessels, an essence that lodged in the hollow voids where their souls belonged. There were people, besides the devout, who had in this past visited this land from other worlds. They came from the stars or other countries, full of life and possessing both color and names. These visitors called this thing that filled the nameless ones by many names. Some called it *emotion.* Others simply *heart.* Others called it the very stuff of humanity.

Regardless of what it was called, the youth knew it resided here, beneath where his palm touched his chest.

There was no time in this place. No time meant no daily routine. For the nameless devout, there was only the work to be done on top of the hill and the guarding of the Hall of All Books; that was all. They did not rest, but also they did not tire. The only unpredictable elements of this place were the ebb and flow of clouds and mist, and the coming of visitors.

Once a visitor had asked whether the devout found their lives boring.

What does that mean?

It means tiring of something. Becoming weary or jaded, the visitor had explained.

Anyone who has to perform the same task over and over tires of it eventually.

But the devout aren't anyone. They aren't "one." How then could they tire?

But that was not the whole truth.

The youth felt a shivering well up from inside his sparse frame under his black robes. It was a fact that he did not feel boredom. Yet now, he had to admit, he was feeling the exact opposite emotion.

Where there are opposites, there is also truth.

The youth realized that somewhere inside his body, inside this hollow vessel lacking even a soul, something had been waiting for that first bell to ring.

Something is happening. Events are happening.

Soon a new visitor would surely arrive.

This pleases me!

The youth clenched his hand upon his chest into a fist. Closing his eyes, he let himself feel the trembling inside his body.

The First Bell continued to toll. The mist brushed against the youth's shaven head, condensing into tiny droplets of dew before collecting to run in a rivulet down his temple. He exhaled deeply, his breath a plume of white in the air. The soles of his bare feet were caked in mud from the trek up the hill.

At length, he heard something else through the mist: the faint sounds of the invocation. The youth opened his eyes to look up toward the top of the hill. He still couldn't see anything. Then the mist shifted, and he heard through it again the chords of the song. *My brothers.*

The youth squinted, and eventually he was able to make out the lights of their torches, soul-wisps darting aimlessly through the mist. Now going to the side, now up or down, drifting through the air, yet definitely coming closer.

A group of the devout was descending. The youth was one of them, a part of them, as they were a part of him. The black-robed devout.

Their heads were shaven, like his. Their feet were bare, like his. Their voices were the same. Their faces were the same. There were too many of them to count, and yet there was only one.

The youth unclenched his fist and began to walk, his voice joining the chorus as he slipped in among them.

They, his brothers, who were also him. Yet the youth felt that he held within his chest a note absent from the melody of his brothers' prayer-song.

As they descended the slope, the tolling of the First Bell grew clearer and more fierce. The mist thickened, swallowing their invocation, even as the peak of the roof over the Hall of All Books cut through the mist's gray veil. The youth drifted back toward the tail end of the procession, and again he stopped, looking up, a whisper on his lips.

It is free.

Soon, there would be war.

CHAPTER ONE

Something Important, Which Was Broken

It was a lazy, warm spring afternoon, the kind that would make anyone sleepy.

Fifth period. Pencil in hand? *Check.* Eyes open? *Check.* Awake? *Not really.*

She was full of lunch, and besides, she hated science class.

"Yuri. Yuuuuri!" Kana whispered at her from the next seat over. Part of an eraser flew through the air and bounced off her desk.

"Your head's swaying! He's gonna see!"

Yuriko Morisaki sat up with a start. Mr. Katayama was in the middle of writing something on the blackboard, his back turned to the class. Yuriko hurriedly rubbed her eyes.

Kana held a hand to her mouth, stifling a laugh. Yuriko grinned at her. Their seats were in the middle of the classroom. She looked around behind her. At least half of her twenty-five classmates were either already asleep or soon would be.

Yuriko glanced at the clock hanging above the blackboard. Twenty minutes till class was over. She had to find some way to stay awake. She glanced down at her notebook. After the third line or so, her writing had become an almost illegible scrawl. *That must have been when I dozed off,* she thought.

"Share your notes later," she whispered to Kana at the very same instant Mr. Katayama turned around. Pushing his glasses up with one finger, his gaze wandered across the room before coming to rest on Yuriko.

"Morisaki?"

Kana immediately looked down at her desk and began moving her pencil furiously.

"No talking during class."

"Sorry, sir."

Yuriko sank down in her chair. *What about the kids who are sleeping, sir? Don't I get points just for being awake?* She hadn't actually said anything, only thought it, but the defiance must have shown on her face. Mr. Katayama put down his chalk, wiped his whitened fingers together, and put one hand on his hip. "Are you aware that the average grade in this class on last week's science test was the lowest of any fifth-grade class in the district? *In the district!* I know not everyone is fond of science, and I'm not asking you all to get one hundred percent, but still—"

This latest lecture had the effect of rousing several of the students from their naps. Yuriko hurriedly began tracing the garbled letters in her notebook with her pencil as though she might somehow be able to decipher them.

There was a light knock on the door at the front of the classroom. Mr. Katayama stepped away from the blackboard, a frown on his face. Yuriko busied herself with tracing letters, so she didn't see who it was or what was being said. She looked up only when the door closed with a loud slam. Mr. Katayama was looking in her direction.

No, he's looking right at me. Or so she guessed. His eyes were hidden behind the light reflecting off his glasses.

"Ms. Morisaki," he said, still standing by the door, his voice cracking strangely, "I want you to get your things and go home."

All at once, every student (at least, every student who was awake) turned their eyes toward Yuriko. She could almost feel their gazes hitting her. Yuriko was not used to being the center of attention. Not because she was boring or didn't stand out, but because she had cultivated a certain protective anonymity.

"Um, what?"

Yuriko looked around to see if anyone else understood what was going on. *What did he just say?*

Mr. Katayama jerked into action like a windup toy that had just been released. He walked down the aisle between the desks toward hers. His motions seemed rigid and unnatural, like a robot's.

He stopped by Yuriko's desk and placed one hand on the desktop and another on her shoulder. "Your mother called. Something's happened at home. You need to go now."

Now the other students started whispering to each other. "Someone bought it, someone bought it," she heard them say. *What does that mean, bought it?*

Someone died, Yuriko realized.

Kana was staring at her, worried. But then, when the teacher went to the back of the room toward the student lockers, she stood up before Yuriko could say anything and shouted, "Mr. Katayama, I'll help."

Mr. Katayama had been just about to open Yuriko's locker, but now he turned. A boy named Sato, who sat in front of her, also got up from his desk and went to stand by Yuriko. A few of the other students looked like they were going to get up too, so Mr. Katayama quickly returned to his desk at the head of the class and shouted loudly for everyone to sit down, his voice cracking.

Yuriko crammed her textbooks and notebook into her bag that Kana brought to her. Her face was flushed, but a cold chill had begun to spread through her chest.

Schoolbag under her arm, she went out into the hall. Mr. Katayama joined her. She was surprised to see her class's head teacher Mrs. Kiuchi waiting outside. She looked relieved when she saw Yuriko come out.

"You're all packed, great. Let's go."

Yuriko felt her teacher's hand on her back. Mrs. Kiuchi was as old as Yuriko's grandmother, fat and short, and sweaty as usual. She could feel the warmth of her hand through the back of her shirt.

"Thank you," Mr. Katayama said, bowing as they left. He stood there in the doorway until Yuriko had gone down the hall and around the corner.

"Mrs. Kiuchi, what's happened?" she asked as they walked. Her teacher was looking down at her feet. She was walking fast, so fast Yuriko had to trot just to keep up. Though she had her hand on Yuriko's back the whole way, she hadn't looked at her once.

"Don't worry. Your parents are waiting for you." Her voice sounded as stilted as Mr. Katayama's had been. "Let's just get you home quick."

Someone bought it. Someone's died. The words she had heard in the classroom echoed in her head. *Who died? Dad? Mom? But didn't Mrs. Kiuchi just say they were waiting for me—*

If her escort so far had been a National League surprise, what was waiting for her outside was Olympic. A taxi was idling right outside the school gates, and the principal and head teacher were standing by the door.

"Miss Morisaki!" the principal called out. Yuriko wondered if he remembered the names of every student in school, even the ones who didn't stand out. Ones like her. "Now, I don't want you to worry. Mrs. Kiuchi will see you to your home, all right?"

Miss Morisaki. He called me Miss Morisaki.

Yuriko got into the taxi with her teacher. It wasn't far to her house. She could walk the distance in ten minutes. It was crazy that they would call a taxi for that.

Yuriko's home was on the fifth floor of a ten-story apartment building. The building had a name written on a placard out front: Angel Castle Ishijima. It was an unassuming place, built a decade ago of gray concrete and steel. Certainly nothing like where Yuriko would imagine an angel lived, and not much like a castle, either.

When she got out of the taxi, Mrs. Kiuchi took Yuriko by the hand. *Holding hands with my teacher?* That was even more unlikely than riding in a taxi with her.

"Mrs. Kiuchi?" Yuriko tried again, looking up at her. "What was the principal saying to you when we got into the taxi?" She had heard the principal say something like, "Maybe you can talk with them."

Mrs. Kiuchi blanched. "Don't worry, just school business." Her smile looked like a jigsaw puzzle left leaning against a wall without a frame, ready to collapse at any moment.

"There's nothing for you to worry about, Morisaki."

Yuriko was in fifth grade. She might have been a child still, but she wasn't an infant. Wasn't she "standing at puberty's doorstep" or some such? She remembered the principal telling them that in one of his talks to her class recently, so she was pretty sure it was true. *So why is everyone telling me there's nothing to worry about, like I'm some kind of baby? What's going on?*

When the elevator doors opened, Yuriko shook off her teacher's hand and ran down the hall to her apartment. The door was unlocked.

"Mom! I'm home!"

She ran inside, practically leaping out of her shoes. Her mother was coming out of the living room.

"Yuriko—"

Mom's okay. She's alive. She wasn't the one who bought it.

Her mother ran to her and hugged her tight—Yuriko's third surprise of the day. This was bigger than the Olympics. *What would that be? The Football World Cup?*

"What's going on, Mom?"

Her mother was shaking. Her face was pale, her eyes watery and red.

"I'm Kiuchi, head teacher for Yuriko's class," Mrs. Kiuchi introduced herself. Yuriko's mother let go of her at last and welcomed her teacher.

"Thank you so much. I'm sorry you had to come all the way out here. I'm so sorry about all of this—"

Okay, first she thanked her, now she's apologizing? I wish someone would tell me what's going on!

"Have you heard anything more from the school?" Mrs. Kiuchi asked.

"No, nothing yet..."

A single tear dropped from her mother's cheek. "They still haven't found him."

Haven't found him? Found who? And why are they talking about my school?

None of it made any sense.

"What's going on?" Yuriko asked her mother again. Her only answer was a fresh round of tears.

"Mrs. Morisaki, you'd better tell Yuriko what happened. I'll answer the phone if it rings. I think it'd be better if you talked with her, just the two of you." Mrs. Kiuchi smiled a crooked smile at Yuriko, the puzzle pieces finally coming apart and falling to the ground. "Why don't you two go to her room?" She put a gentle hand on her mother's shoulder, urging her on. Her mother grabbed Yuriko's hand firmly and stood.

They left the living room and went directly into the room on the left. This was Yuriko's room. A small stuffed bear hung on a loop around the doorknob.

And next to her room was—

My brother's room. Every morning when they left for school, he always made a point of closing his door firmly behind him. He was in eighth grade and had been making a big deal about his "privacy" lately.

His door was open. She could see his desk and chair inside. A jacket was hanging over the back of the chair.

Yuriko's brother. Hiroki Morisaki. Age: fourteen.

Yuriko silently gasped. *They weren't talking about hearing from my school, they were talking about hearing from his school!*

They went into Yuriko's room, and her mother quietly closed the door behind them. She motioned for Yuriko to sit at her desk, while she sat on the floor. She looked weak, like she might collapse on the spot.

Yuriko jumped out of her chair and grabbed her mother. "Mom, what happened to Hiroki?"

When she had heard something had happened at home, Yuriko hadn't thought of Hiroki for a second. Her brother was one of the most self-assured, safety-minded people she knew. He got the best grades. He excelled at sports. They had picked him for the Little League team when he was only in first grade, and he was in regular rotation as a pitcher by fourth grade. Hiroki had joined the swim team in middle school—someone had told him swimming would make his pitching arm stronger—and was already breaking records.

The only thing she could imagine happening to him was some kind of accident. *Maybe a traffic accident, or a freak drowning at the pool.* Except it was too cold for the school to be still using the pool. *So it must have been a traffic accident. Maybe a car hit him.*

"Mom? Did Hiroki get run over?"

Her mother grabbed Yuriko's hands in her own. Her face was streaked with tears. She had been crying so hard she could barely keep her eyes open. She hiccuped. It made Yuriko feel like crying too. She didn't think she had ever seen her mother look so stricken by grief. Or any adult, for that matter.

"Is...he dead?"

Her mother shook her head, her eyes still closed. Yuriko felt the fear that had been stabbing at her chest suddenly slip away. The echoing words in her head faded. *Whew. So he didn't buy it.*

Then why is Mom crying?

"Your brother—"

"Yeah?"

"At school, during recess..."

"Yeah?"

"He got into a fight with some friends." Her mother's voice was hoarse. "And...he hurt them." She took a breath and hiccuped again. "The whole thing must have scared him, because he ran from the school. They don't know where he is now. His teachers and some men from the local fire department are looking for him."

Something else lifted off Yuriko's chest. This time, she wasn't sure what it was. She wasn't even sure if it was something she had wanted to keep.

"Don't worry," her mother said, sobbing as she stroked Yuriko's hair. "I'm sure they'll find him soon. Once he's back, we'll go to his friends' houses and apologize, all of us together. That will settle things." She spoke gently, but her face betrayed her feelings. She didn't think that would settle things at all, not really.

"Where's Dad?"

Her dad and her brother got along famously. Recently, Hiroki had made a show of stepping out on his own to assert some independence from the family, but he was still his proud father's son. "He must be really worried! Is he out looking for him with his teachers?"

Her mother nodded, then a fresh round of sobs erupted from somewhere deep inside her.

Her mom wasn't lying, Yuriko was pretty sure about that. But she also wasn't telling the whole truth. Finally, Yuriko found out what had happened that evening.

Hiroki Morisaki had taken a knife with him to school that day. Not a cooking knife from home. A long knife he had bought somewhere. Someone who saw it said the blade was almost fifteen centimeters.

Hiroki had stabbed two other boys in his class.

One in the stomach, the other in the neck.

The boy he'd got in the neck was dead even before the ambulance arrived.

It had happened during recess after lunch. The boys had been out behind the gymnasium, where there was no one else to see them. No one even knew it had happened until the boy who was stabbed in the stomach came crawling into the school looking for help.

By the time the news spread and the school had erupted into chaos, Hiroki Morisaki was nowhere to be found.

He'd taken the knife with him.

No one had seen him leave school. They didn't know whether he'd run or walked away. Whether he'd been crying or laughing. They didn't even know if he had been angry.

Or frightened.

All kinds of people came to their house: parents from the PTA, Hiroki's middle school teachers. The police came too, and the firemen. And then there were the neighbors. Most of their relatives lived far away, so none of them made it there that day, but the phone was ringing off the hook.

All Yuriko and her mother could do was wait at home. Occasionally, her father would call her mother's cell phone. Once, she had given the phone to Yuriko, but all she could do when she heard her father's voice was nod quietly. There was nothing to say.

The day waned and night came. They still hadn't found Hiroki.

The incident was on the news that evening. They were calling Yuriko's brother "Boy A." With a grave look on his face, the newscaster was saying that the police were looking for any information that might help them find Boy A as quickly as possible.

Yuriko sat still while all around her time marched on.

Yuriko wanted to wait in Hiroki's room. She felt like if she waited there he might come home. But they wouldn't let her. Adults were in and out all day and evening, examining his things, probing for clues.

Her mother called Hiroki's cell phone over and over again. The automated message said that it was turned off. She kept calling.

Yuriko didn't have a cell phone of her own. She thought about her friends—Kana must be worried sick. Of course, even if Kana tried calling the house, she'd never be able to get through with all the other people calling. If Yuriko couldn't go into Hiroki's room, then she wanted to at least be able to talk to Kana, but neither of those things was going to happen anytime soon, so she sat silently in her chair and did nothing.

It was almost as though everyone had forgotten she existed.

And in "everyone," she included herself. Even though Yuriko was right there in the room, she felt like she wasn't. She felt like she was just as lost as her brother.

Maybe I am. Maybe my soul's off somewhere with Hiroki. She had heard somebody on television saying that human beings had this kind of ability. Anyone could do it. Their body would sit still while their mind traveled freely, seeing things, hearing things, feeling things, even talking to people.

Hiroki! Yuriko tried calling in her mind. *Hiroki, can you hear me? It's me, Yuriko. Come home. Everyone's so worried.*

If she thought it loudly enough, she was sure that her soul or whatever it was would transmit her voice to her brother. If she only wanted it badly enough.

Yuriko called all that night, but there was no answer.

She was sure she had eaten something and probably gone to the bathroom. Maybe she even slept a little. She couldn't be sure though. Everything felt so distant, like she was looking at her own life backwards through a pair of binoculars.

Her mother had worn herself out crying.

Now the harsh light of the morning sun was spilling into her room through the lace curtains. Yuriko always slept late, but her brother was an early riser. He said it was because he always had sports practice to go to in the mornings. Wherever he was now, she bet he was already awake.

If only she knew where that wherever was.

The reality of the situation had finally taken concrete form in Yuriko's heart. It was as hard as stone, and heavy. She felt like she might be crushed under its weight. Crushed so completely she would no longer be able to feel that she was being crushed. She would no longer be able to feel anything.

Two days passed. Hiroki Morisaki's disappearance was the top story on every news channel. BOY A STILL MISSING went the headline. They mentioned that the boy with the stomach wound, who had been unconscious in critical condition for a while, was now showing signs of recovery. The television had been on constantly since Yuriko had come home from school, but when the news started reporting fears that Boy A might have committed suicide, everyone in the room rushed to turn it off. Yuriko wasn't sure who hit the switch first. It might've been one of her grandparents from Kyushu, who had finally gotten there the night before. Or it might have been one of her grandparents from Mito, who had been squabbling from the moment they walked through the door.

A frenzied crowd of journalists and cameramen hovered near their apartment building. Yuriko and her mother were moved to a hotel. She packed all of her clothes into the backpack she had used for summer camp the year before. Her mother asked her grandparents to come with them, but her father, who only came home long enough to change clothes before disappearing again, thought there was no point in them being there anyway, and told them so, which only served to worsen the mood.

The police escorted them to their hotel so that the reporters wouldn't follow them. It wasn't like the resort hotel Yuriko had been to once on a family vacation. They told her it was called a business hotel. Inside, the rooms were small, and there were more vending machines in the lobby than there was hotel staff.

She hadn't gone back to school once since she had left early that day.

Yuriko sat on her bed, which smelled faintly of laundry detergent, and gazed absentmindedly at a cheap print of an abstract painting that hung in the middle of a white wall. The frame was slightly askew.

They had fled their home to seek refuge in the hotel.

Everything around her that she had always taken for granted was gone.

Her brother had taken it all away.

Her mother was in the bathroom with the door closed, talking on her cell phone. When she finally came out, leaning on a wall for support, she looked up at Yuriko. "Yuriko. Some of the police are going to come, okay?"

Yuriko looked at her mother.

"They say they want to talk to you. It might help them find Hiroki. Don't worry; I'll be with you the whole time. That's okay, right?"

There was no point saying she didn't want them to come. If there was anything she didn't want, it was everything. All of it.

The police were there in less than half an hour. There was one man wearing a suit and a female officer in uniform. Yuriko wondered how they would all fit in the tiny room and where they would sit—there were only two chairs. But the police took her to their patrol car and brought her down to the police station.

Everything that had happened since the taxi ride home seemed like a tremendous waste of time.

They didn't bring her to one of those questioning rooms you always see on TV. It was more like a meeting room, with nice chairs and a big table. A woman from the child counseling center, the same age as Yuriko's mother, was waiting for them there

Yuriko tensed when she heard who the woman was. Why did they need a counselor? Had her mother asked for one? If her brother did something bad, did that automatically make her a problem child too? Someone they needed a counselor just to talk to?

Her mother bowed to them, saying she'd do anything to help.

The counselor began talking to her in a soft, easy tone, but Yuriko didn't reply. She looked out the window.

The view from the police station window was no different than what you could see from a taxi. For some reason, that scared her. It would make more sense if the city looked different from here somehow. Wasn't the police station a special place? Weren't the people they brought in here, like Yuriko, special?

"I was wondering if you could tell us a few things, Yuriko," the man in the suit said. He was smiling gently enough, but there was a strange sadness to him. *Why should he be sad about Hiroki? Isn't he trying to catch my brother?* Then she thought it might just be the way his eyebrows arched toward the middle. *Like a clown's.*

They asked all kinds of questions, using all kinds of words, but Yuriko immediately understood there was really only one thing they wanted to know.

Had she noticed anything unusual about Hiroki lately?

There was nothing unusual about her brother. Ever since the time she had first realized Hiroki was her brother, that was all he had been. He hadn't been sad about anything. He hadn't been in a bad mood. He had just been her brother.

Just her brother. Nothing else.

Yuriko said as much in as few words, and as quietly as possible. She thought she should talk a little louder, but she just couldn't summon the strength.

"I see," said the sad clown, and he tapped his chin with the end of his ballpoint pen. "We talked to Hiroki's teacher at school, and he said that ever since Hiroki started the eighth grade, he'd been having trouble getting along with his classmates. Did he ever say anything about that to you? Even something little in passing?"

Yuriko was sitting wedged between her mother and the child counselor.

When she didn't respond to the man's question, the counselor looked her in the eye. Then the police officer asked, "You got along well with your brother, didn't you, Yuriko?"

Yuriko didn't answer. Her mouth was closed, and she looked down at her hands where they rested on her knees. She had woven the tips of her fingers together.

"You talked to your brother about school sometimes, didn't you? Did he ever tell you about his school?"

Yuriko still didn't respond, so now the counselor looked up at her mother. "Maybe you heard something?"

Her mother was looking down at her lap. She reached out and held Yuriko's hand. Her skin was cold. *Why is Mom's hand so cold?*

"Well they *are* brother and sister, and three years apart besides…and he's in middle school…" her mother said. Her voice sounded even weaker than Yuriko's.

"Is that so? Yes, of course," the counselor said, answering her own half-asked question. She looked at the policeman.

Everyone sat in silence, waiting for someone to speak.

The policemen's words were echoing in Yuriko's head. *You got along well with your brother. You got along well with your brother.*

Well, yeah. But she couldn't help feeling that that didn't quite describe it.

They did get along. Yuriko was fond of her brother. And she was pretty sure he didn't dislike her. He would help her with her homework sometimes, and they would always joke around. He'd call her "little Yuri" or sometimes just "squirt."

When she did well on a test, he'd give her a pat on the head. And on nights when they'd seen a scary movie, and she was too afraid to go to the bathroom by herself, he would wait for her in the hall.

All that seemed different than "getting along well." They had a thing worked out. Her brother was the big one; she was the small one. He stood tall, and she was comfortable being at his feet.

"Hiroki was always very protective of her," her mother whispered, gripping Yuriko's hand even tighter. "I don't think he would have told her anything to make her worry."

That's right. That's the word. "Protective." That was their relationship. That was how it was, and how it was supposed to be until they were both grown-ups.

"He never said anything about troubles to us…" her mother said. Her voice broke, and she turned away.

The child counselor stood up from her chair surprisingly fast and went over to her mother, putting an arm around her for support. It was a kind thing to do, and her mother looked so frail with the counselor holding her that for the first time, Yuriko was glad the counselor had come. Not for her sake, but for her mother's. *Thank you.*

Her mother was nodding and saying she was all right.

"Right," said the policeman. "Well, there's nothing we absolutely *have* to hear from you today, Yuriko. Just, if you think of anything, even the tiniest thing, that might help us find your brother, contact us."

The two police officers bowed their heads and apologized for the trouble.

"Can we go home now? I mean to the hotel," Yuriko said. "Mom, you look really pale—"

"Yes, of course. Thank you, Yuriko. Ms. Morisaki, we'll escort you back to the hotel now."

Her mom sat in the patrol car with her eyes closed the whole way back. She wasn't sleeping. She looked more like she had gone unconscious. Still, she gripped Yuriko's hand tightly and didn't let go. Yuriko squeezed her hand back, trying to warm it up with hers.

Life at the hotel was uneventful. A week passed, then ten days, and still they hadn't found Hiroki.

Gradually, the news stopped talking about him. Yuriko's grandmother called and said that the reporters weren't around their apartment building anymore, so she and her mother decided to go home.

When she saw her father again he looked like he had lost several pounds, and his hair was whiter than it had been only a week before.

"Sorry about all this, Yuriko. It must have been tough for you in the hotel. We'll just live here like normal from now on, until Hiroki comes home. Don't worry, Yuriko," he added, "he'll come home. I'm sure of it."

Yuriko knew her father was trying to cheer her up. Her mother sat nearby on the couch, nodding. *Let's all be as cheerful as we can be.*

That's impossible, Yuriko thought, but she swallowed her words. There was no point telling her parents something they already knew. And she knew they were only trying to make her feel better.

One small relief was that the grandparents had all gone back to their homes. If they were there, there would be more crying and shouting and siding with her mother and annoying her father. That was how it had always been, before any of this had even happened.

I wish our relatives wouldn't shout all the time.

Hiroki had said that once.

And Mom's and Dad's parents don't get along with each other at all.

Yuriko was probably still too young to understand, he had told her.

But Hiroki understood. So why did he do something that was sure to bring them around to grumble and whine?

Just living here "like normal" meant that Yuriko would have to go back to school. She should have expected it, but still it was a shock when her mother asked if she was ready to return the next week. No, maybe not a shock *per se*; school was just a totally foreign concept. It was as if her mother had told her she was going to the moon. She couldn't imagine herself sitting at a desk in a classroom, taking notes.

How would her friends act?

How should she act?

Back in reality, time marched on, and on Friday afternoon, Mr. Katayama paid a visit to their home. He flashed an exaggeratedly large smile when he saw Yuriko. "Everyone's worried about you. I had some of the other girls in class take notes for you, so don't worry about that. You won't fall behind."

Then Mr. Katayama started talking to her mother. Yuriko was asked to go to her room.

"I'll just be talking to your teacher for a bit."

They closed the door to the living room.

Yuriko was walking toward her door, when she changed her mind.

Hiroki's room.

She hadn't been in there once since they had returned to the apartment. Her mother was always there, and when Yuriko was watching television or reading a book, her mother would slip off into his room and cry. She tried to hide it, but Yuriko still knew. So she had stayed away. She didn't want to see her mother like that, and she knew it would be worse for her if she knew Yuriko had been listening.

Hiroki's room looked exactly the way it had when Yuriko peeked in on the day of his disappearance, with one difference. Someone had taken the jacket off his chair and folded it on the bed. It was like trying to spot the difference between two seemingly identical pictures. Hiroki's room before, and Hiroki's room now. The biggest difference, but also the easiest one to miss, was that Hiroki wasn't there.

Yuriko sat lightly on the coverlet next to the folded jacket. The bed sank only a little bit beneath her.

A car drove by outside the window, loud music belting from it. It was a sunny day. Just like the day when Hiroki had disappeared.

Yuriko sat by herself, listening to the music.

It was then that it suddenly occurred to her—the way you suddenly realize that you've left something important behind—that she hadn't cried once. She had *almost* cried any number of times, but never like her mother cried. Not even when she had seen tears in her father's eyes.

Why? I'm sad. So why can't I cry?

Maybe, she decided, *I'm in shock. Don't people go all hollow inside when they're in shock?*

Yuriko fell back on the bed, lying on the quilted coverlet her mother had made. The bedsprings squeaked.

The coverlet smelled of her brother.

How could someone disappear, leaving nothing behind but a jacket hanging on a chair and a smell? How could they not find him no matter how hard they looked? Things like this weren't supposed to happen.

Yuriko looked up at the ceiling and slowly closed her eyes.

I don't believe it. It can't be true.

How could something like this happen to her family? How could a life she had taken for granted get smashed to smithereens in the blink of an eye? She never knew how important it all was to her until it broke.

Something welled up inside. Yuriko got ready, steeling herself for the sobs that were to come. Part of her had been waiting for it. Crying would save her. With each gasp she could spit out a bit of that black lump she felt inside her chest.

But nothing came. Yuriko gritted her teeth.

Why?

What came instead was this question. *Why? Why? Why?* Why did her brother stab his friends? If he was having some kind of trouble, why didn't he say anything about it? If he ran away, why didn't he tell even his family where he was going? Why didn't he call them now?

I'm mad, Hiroki. I'm really mad.

Yuriko lifted her feet off the floor, rolled over, and curled up in a ball on the bed. She felt suddenly sleepy. *That's right. I'll just go to sleep. When I wake up, maybe this nightmare will be over. This has all been a really long nightmare.*

When she closed her eyes, the smell of her brother from the coverlet filled her head and her mind. She breathed in deeply. It felt good. Yuriko was more tired than she had imagined. Her body needed rest. *I'll just sleep. Sleep…*

A scene spread out before her closed eyes, dimly at first.

This was a dream too. Or the fragments of a dream. The feel of the fabric beneath her, the warmth, and the sleep that filled her head brought back a dream she had dreamt before. The scene was familiar—like a breeze flipping through the pages of a book, giving her just a glimpse, then receding.

When did I last see this place in my dream? A week ago? Ten days ago? It might have been longer ago than that. Her brother was in the dream. She saw him in his room through a crack in the door. Yuriko stood in the cold hallway outside. The door was open only a few inches—

The lamp on the bedside table is on. Hiroki is over by the window, kneeling. There's someone standing next to him, facing him, a large black silhouette. He's curled up at the figure's feet.

It must've been the middle of the night. She had wanted to go to the bathroom, so she had dreamt of going there, and on the way, by accident, she had looked into his room. It almost felt like spying to see him and the shape in her dream.

The silhouette was large, looming. Bigger than a regular adult and round and swollen like a balloon. There was something on its head. A ring of pointed spikes—like a crown. That was how it looked to Yuriko in her dream. She'd thought it a very strange dream at the time. Or maybe it was a very strange thing to see, and that was why she remembered it as a dream. She was half asleep anyway.

Wait. If I was half asleep, does that mean I wasn't sleeping?

I was dreaming, wasn't I?

She remembered how the hard floor had felt cool beneath the soles of her feet. She had walked with her toes curled. The bathroom seemed impossibly far away. And she had to leave.

Now he's kneeling before the big figure with a shape like a crown on its head.

That's right, he's awake. Maybe he'll look in my direction. Maybe I should tell him I'm going to the bathroom. Because I drank too much milk before going to sleep.

He's bowing up and down now, bumping his forehead on the floor. Now he's whispering something. He's singing. He's talking to the silhouette. He's making an offering.

Then Yuriko heard the song again, except this time it was coming out of her own lips as she lay curled up on the bed. It was an unfamiliar song with a strange melody, in a language she had never heard. Yet she found she could sing an entire verse.

Her lips stopped moving. The song ceased. Yuriko, still lying on her side, opened her eyes wide.

What was that?

It was the song her brother had sung in her dream.

Why do I know that crazy song? Why did my mouth just sing it like that?

"Little miss—"

She heard the beating of faint wings, soft and delicate—like the wings of an insect in late summer when the nights are chilly. Except it was spring, so maybe it was the sound of a newly hatched insect beating its wings.

"Yes?"

Funny. The wings sound like they're saying something.

"Little miss. Oh, miss? Get up."

Yuriko shot up from the bed. For a moment she sat there, perfectly still. Nothing was moving in the room. The window was closed, so not even a breeze rustled through the curtains.

Yuriko looked up at the fluorescent light on the ceiling. The light made a faint buzzing sound. *Maybe that's what I heard.*

"I'm not up there, miss."

Now the beating of the wings was growing louder and sounding more and more distinctly like words.

"Miss, look over here," the beating of the wings said. "The bookshelf. I'm on the bookshelf."

Yuriko sat perfectly still, turning only her head, very slowly, in the direction of her brother's bookshelf. The bookshelf stood against the wall next to Hiroki's desk.

"That's it...right over here. Come over."

That's not the beating of wings. That is a voice. It's talking to me.

Frozen like a painter's model, Yuriko moved only her lips. "Who's there?"

There was no answer. Yuriko sat still, her ears straining to hear the voice. Outside, a car drove by.

"Who are you?" she asked again. Another car passed.

There was no reply. Yuriko began to relax. *I was dreaming again.*

"That's...a tough question to answer," beat the wings.

This time, Yuriko jumped off the bed and ran straight for the door, but her socks slipped on the flooring. She lost her balance and slammed into the door with a crash. Stars exploded behind her eyelids.

"Miss! Don't be frightened. I'm not scary, really."

The beating of wings returned, and now Yuriko's head was throbbing. The voice sounded like it was laughing, and kind of in a hurry. But it was right. It didn't sound scary.

"You're a ghost." Yuriko sat on the floor rubbing her head where she had hit the door.

"I am most definitely not a ghost," the beating wings replied quickly. "I don't have a single thing about ghosts written in me, either."

"Written in you?" *What does that mean?* Now Yuriko was growing even more confused. The voice wasn't making any sense. *Maybe I misheard it?*

"It means I'm a book, miss. So stop loafing around there on the floor and come over to the bookshelf."

It did say "written." It means actual writing in a...it's a book?

Yuriko found she lacked the courage to stand, so instead she crawled over to the foot of the bookshelf. She crawled with her back arched, rather gracefully looking up.

The shelves were packed with all kinds of books. There were reference books and dictionaries, picture guides to animals, and comic books. Her brother liked manga about sports heroes. There were a few mysteries tucked in there, some of which Yuriko had borrowed, but she'd found the type to be really small and hard to read. She didn't understand a lot of the stories, either. When she told her brother this, he laughed and said it was probably too early for a shrimp like her to be reading mysteries.

"Second shelf from the top," the mysterious voice said. "Pull out the books in front. I'm hidden behind them."

The books on the second shelf included *Space from the Hubble* and *Stargazing* and things like that. Yuriko remembered that her brother had gone through an astronomy phase the year before. He'd begged their parents to buy him a telescope. Though their father usually bent to this kind of request from him, this time he hesitated. Telescopes were pretty expensive, he'd said, and besides, her brother was busy with baseball practice, and didn't have any time. If he started stargazing every night, when would he sleep? Dad had wanted to know. That had been the end of her brother's future career in astronomy.

Yuriko pulled out one of the books, a colorful photograph on its cover, then pulled out another, placing them in a neat stack on the desk beside her. Behind them she found another row of books about sea life. (Her brother's interests, with the sole exception of baseball, tended to be fleeting.)

She had pulled five books from the shelf when she found between *Dolphins: Sages of the Sea* and *Let's Go to the Aquarium!* a worn-looking book, bound in red leather. It looked entirely out of place, which was why she noticed it. The spine was about an inch thick.

"That's right, miss. The red book. That's me." The mysterious voice sounded relieved, and brighter, like it was trying to cheer Yuriko on.

Yuriko extended an index finger and went to touch the cover of the red book, but stopped just before her finger made contact. *I wonder what the title is?* The letters on the cover—if they were letters—looked like some kind of code. They were stamped in gold and were pretty worn. In places, they seemed to have been rubbed away entirely.

"What's your title?" she tried asking. Her finger trembled in the air.

"If you have to ask, I'm guessing you can't read it. But if you want to know what's inside me, I'll tell you. I think you'd call me a...a dictionary. That's right. I'm a dictionary with a very special means of employment."

"A special what?"

"A special way to use me."

Yuriko's finger hovered.

"Didn't I just tell you I'm not scary? I mean, I guess I understand why you might be startled, but scared? Still, I couldn't just sit here and watch you..."

Yuriko lifted an eyebrow. *Watch me what?*

"Look, pick me up. It'll be a lot easier to talk that way."

Yuriko withdrew her finger. Her hands clenched tightly into fists. She was trembling. She heard herself swallow. *Gulp.*

She closed her eyes, then opened them and quickly yanked the red book off the shelf.

A second later, she tried to toss it to the floor. In her hand, the book was light as a feather, and slightly warm. It felt like...like human skin! As she jerked her hand, trying to toss it, she felt the cover warp, wrapping around her fingers, clinging to her.

It felt disgusting.

"Eeeeew!"

"Gentle, please! I'm an old book, you know. I don't even want to count the cracks in my binding these days. And don't even get me started about the glue."

Yuriko looked down at her hands and found that the book was still there, cradled gently between her fingers.

"Why don't you have a seat?" the book suggested. "You can just put me on that desk over there. Then open me and put your palm flat on my page."

"Open you to where?"

"Oh, any page will do."

Yuriko sat down in her brother's chair as she was told and placed the red book on the desk. It did look pretty beaten up.

She opened the book to the very middle; the pages settled to either side. They were covered with letters—the same code-like writing as the faded letters on the cover. The paper was yellow with age, with a few holes here and there.

"What an old book," Yuriko whispered. After wiping the palm of her hand on her jacket, she gently placed it on the page.

She felt a sensation like the page was stroking her palm. Just like the cover had, the paper felt warm.

"I see," the red book said. "You're younger than you look, ain't you, little miss?" Now the voice sounded normal, a plain human voice, not like the fluttering of wings she'd heard before.

"H-how can you tell?" she stammered.

"I can tell."

"I'm eleven years old, you know."

"As you count the years, yes, I suppose you are. Tell me, how old is your brother?"

"Fourteen."

"He's pretty young too, then, isn't he?" It sounded like the book was scoffing.

Yuriko frowned. "My brother's not a kid. Maybe he's not grown up, but my parents said he will be soon. He's…" She searched for the phrase. "He's a young adult."

A *difficult age*, she had heard her parents say once. But then they smiled. Nothing bad would ever happen to Hiroki.

"No, no, he's young enough. Believe me."

The book's voice was coming to her through the palm of her hand. It wasn't like she could hear it with her ears. More like the voice was echoing in her mind.

"Are you a book fairy?"

A *book fairy. A book spirit.*

"Fairy? That's an interesting word. Where did you learn that one?"

"In movies and folktales and stuff."

"Ah, yes. Stories. I'm a story too, you know."

"I thought you said you were a dictionary."

"I'm a dictionary and a story. There's a story in everything written in me. Of course, the stories came first."

The book's voice vibrated gently to her through the page. Even though the book was old and dirty and falling apart, she found to her surprise that it didn't bother her in the slightest to touch it. Or touch *him*—the book was definitely male, though Yuri wasn't sure how she knew this.

"Look, miss, I'm sorry. I hadn't meant to talk to you at all. I knew nothing would come of it, see? But you sang the song, so—"

"I did what?"

That strange song. The one that my mouth sang all by itself.

"I'll bet you don't even know what that song is."

Yuriko nodded. "I heard my brother singing it in a dream," she explained. She described the dream and what she'd seen.

The book trembled beneath her fingers. "Oh, so you did see it. Then maybe I *was* right to talk to you. Yes, that was definitely the move to make."

The book sounded a bit too satisfied with himself. *Or maybe "itself,"* Yuriko thought. She was talking to a book, after all. "It was a weird dream," she told the book. "And it's even weirder that I remember the song."

"But you don't know what the song means?"

"How could I?"

"I suppose it's just as well that you don't."

The red book stroked the palm of her hand again. Yuriko wasn't sure exactly how he could do something like that, but that was how it felt.

"Little miss. Never sing that song again. You'd be better off if you just forgot it entirely."

Now it is true in every place and age that the surest way to fire up a child's curiosity is to tell them that something is forbidden. Yuriko leaned forward. Her palm pressed down on the page of the book. "Why? Why can't I sing it?"

"Please, you're pushing kind of hard."

Yuriko hurriedly lifted up on her hand. She felt the book tremble, like he was catching his breath and shaking himself off after having the wind knocked out of him.

"Because," the book said after a pause, "that's a bad song."

Yuriko was silent for a while. In her mind she was replaying the scene of her brother singing the song while that strange figure towered over him. Because she was now fully awake, she felt like she could remember the scene in much better detail.

Again, the book shivered. Yuriko felt as though she was touching human skin again.

"That's right. That's *it*."

"That's what?"

"*It*," the book muttered and fell silent.

"Wait. You could see what I saw just now, couldn't you? Are you reading my mind? Do you have ESP or something?" Then Yuriko laughed at her own question. If anyone had ESP, it was she. After all, here she was talking to a book.

"Something like that," the book said.

Wait, Yuriko thought. *He sounds frightened now.*

"Is *it* something scary?"

"You mean you weren't frightened?"

She remembered her brother tapping his forehead on the floor. The giant silhouette looking down at him. Back arching, proud.

Suddenly a phrase sprang into her mind. "I alone am king of the castle."

"Huh?" said the book. "What's that you just said?"

"I said 'king of the castle.'" Yuriko stared at the book. "That big shape I saw—he was dressed like a king. Like the ones you see in picture books and the movies. He was wearing a crown."

"Did you see his cape? All tattered and torn, wasn't it?"

That's it! She had thought the silhouette looked swollen in places, like a balloon, but now she realized it had just been a billowing cape that swept from the shape's neck all the way down to its ankles.

"It was too dark to see it clearly."

"Then, did you see *its* face?" The book sounded so forceful, like this question was very important, that Yuriko reflexively pulled her hand away from the page.

"It was too dark."

"So you didn't see the face at all?" the book confirmed, his voice soft and whispery again.

Yuriko quickly replaced her hand on the page. "No, I didn't."

"That's good then," said the book. The book seemed to relax, the tension in his pages easing.

"So is this *it* all that scary? Is *it* a king of some place?"

The book was silent, almost as if it had decided to go back to being a regular book. But Yuriko could still feel him breathing against the palm of her hand. He was breathing like grown-ups did when they were worried about something. The book inhaled deeply, exhaled, then waited for what seemed like forever before remembering to breathe in again.

Once, two years before, her father had failed to pass a routine health check-up at his company. He had gone in for more tests, failed again, and was sent to a big hospital for even more tests. While this was going on, her mother would sit at the kitchen table by herself, breathing just like that. With each breath out, she was imagining all the terrible things that could go wrong, and it took her until the next breath to shake them out of her head. Luckily, in the end it turned out to be nothing serious, and the deep breathing stopped. Still, its rhythm remained etched in Yuriko's memory.

How terrible could it be?

Why was Hiroki bowing to it?

A dim light began to flicker in Yuriko's head.

"What if that's why he did it? What if Hiroki hurting those boys had something to do with that king?"

The red book jerked beneath her fingers.

34

Yuriko's eyes went wide. "That's it, isn't it?"

The book didn't answer, so Yuriko grabbed him with both hands and gave him a good shake. "Tell me! Tell me!"

"M-m-miss! Gently, please! Just calm down."

"And how am I supposed to do that?"

The book grumbled. "You're right, okay? *It's* bad. Evil."

And it makes people do evil things—

Yuriko felt her knees go all wobbly. She slumped back into the chair, clutching the book to her.

From the day her brother had disappeared up until this very moment, Yuriko hadn't heard one single explanation that made sense of what Hiroki had done. Not from her parents, her teachers, the police, or even herself. Every time she had gone looking for one, she had been told not to worry, or that she didn't need to know. What the book had just told her as it quaked with fear (probably because she had shaken it so roughly) had been her first real answer.

Uh-oh, I think I'm going to cry.

"I knew he wouldn't have done something like that. I knew it." She really did begin to cry now. One drop, then two drops splattered on the cover of the red book. "It's not like him. I know him."

"Of course he wouldn't," came the red book's gentle assurance. "Your brother's a good kid. He would never hurt his friends, let alone take a life."

Yuriko looked up. "You know him?"

"Sure I know him. Not for very long, mind you, but I was always nearby."

Yuriko wiped the tears from her face. *Of course. The book was on Hiroki's bookshelf.*

"Believe me, miss. I tried to stop it with all my might. I told him to be careful. But he didn't hear me until it was too late. *It* moved too fast... And *it's* much stronger than I am," the red book added, bowing its head in shame—or at least, that was how Yuriko imagined it.

The book sighed. "I'm no match for *it*. It is the Hero, after all."

"The hero?"

Yuriko was surprised to finally hear the dark figure's name. But the name didn't fit. A hero was noble and strong. In history books, the heroes always saved the day. In sports, the one who set a new record was a hero. And in stories, the hero was always the main character, the good guy. How could a hero be something so evil?

"Wait, you're joking, aren't you. A hero can't be bad."

"I'm sure that's what they taught you, yes."

"Nobody *taught* me that. It's just common sense."

"Common sense?" The red book sighed again. "Fine, whatever you like. Oh, and it's not 'a hero.' It's 'the Hero.' It's a title, not a name."

Suddenly, the book felt different under her hand. He was no longer warm, and she couldn't feel him breathing. It was as though the strange talking being in her hand had become nothing more than a dusty old *book*.

"Hey, wait!" Yuriko shook the red book. She tried holding it upside down by the cover, so the pages fluttered in the air. She tossed it and stomped on it and did everything she could think of short of ripping out the pages, but the book was silent.

"I don't believe it!" Yuriko cried out loud. "That's not fair. You—you're mean!"

Sadly, she soon found that books are not easily swayed by little girls' tears. Yuriko gritted her teeth, and summoning all her strength, she flung the book hard across the room. It opened in midair before slamming into the wall and dropping onto the floor face down, its pages bent beneath it.

There was no cry of pain, no angry shout. The book didn't glare at her. It didn't do anything.

Yuriko left the book where it lay and walked out of Hiroki's room, her head filled with the rush of victory, but her feet dragging in failure.

She didn't tell her parents about the red book. What would she say? It seemed like a dream even to herself, though she knew she had been awake. That evening, all they talked about was Yuriko's return to school the next day, and how her mother would be bringing her in for her first day back, and how she was to play with her friends just like she had before—and nothing else.

The red book was left abandoned, crumpled on the floor by the wall.

The following day, Yuriko went to school as planned. When she got there, the head teacher, the principal, Mrs. Kiuchi, and Mr. Katayama were all there to greet her in the principal's office. Her mother must have bowed to them a hundred times. The teachers all bowed back. Then Mr. Katayama took Yuriko to class.

After first period ended, during the first break, Kana ran over and hugged her. She looked like she was going to cry. *I was so worried. I'm so glad you're back.*

The other students in class were smiling, or looking sympathetic, or just pretending not to notice she was back—but no one was cold or angry, as she had feared they would be.

Whew, she thought. *Everything's back to normal. Except for the fact that my brother's gone, nothing's changed.* Yuriko felt the tension in her heart ease.

But it was all a sham.

After third period, Yuriko joined Kana for a bathroom break. That was where it happened. Some girls from the next class over walked into the bathroom just as they were about to leave—she had seen their faces before, but didn't know their names. One of the girls saw her, then did a double-take. Her eyes sparkled. Not a bright sparkle, but a dull, dark sparkle, like the twinkling of a lantern at the bottom of a deep well. *Here's something fun,* her eyes said. *Here's something freakish. Let's play with it and see if we can make it cry.* Yuriko could feel hands reaching out of those eyes, grabbing for her. The feeling was intense.

Let's get out of here!

As they passed, Yuriko's hand lightly brushed one of the girl's hands. So lightly, she almost didn't notice—the kind of contact that happens all the time in a crowded school. But the girl leaped away from her like she'd been burned.

"Whoa! S-sorry!"

All the other girls around her squealed with terror.

"You're Morisaki, aren't you?" the girl she had touched said. "I'm sorry. I'm so sorry! I didn't mean to run into you, honest! *So please, pretty please, don't stab me!*"

Her voice echoed off the cold walls and ceiling of the bathroom. The girls continued screaming, like they were under attack, rushing to be the first out of the bathroom. The swinging doors to the hallway burst open. The girls ran out into the hall, where their screams quickly changed into whooping bouts of laughter.

Yuriko stood still in the doorway.

She glanced over at Kana. Her friend was so pale, Yuriko thought she might faint.

Fourth period rushed by and Yuriko barely even noticed. Whenever she took her eyes off Kana, Kana would be staring at her, and when she turned toward her friend, Kana would look away, an apologetic look on her face.

The next incident took place during lunchtime.

Mr. Katayama was helping the students pass out lunch trays, when a woman about the same age as Yuriko's mother came up to him in a hurry. She wasn't a teacher at the school, and she wasn't dressed like one of the assistants either. It took Yuriko a while to realize that she was the mother of one of her classmates.

She wasn't just in a hurry, she was *angry*. She grabbed Mr. Katayama and started talking rapidly before turning and calling her daughter—a girl named Fukuyama, whom Yuriko hardly knew—to her, pulling the girl close to her side. Every so often she would turn and find Yuriko in the room, then glare icily at her. Mr. Katayama grew red in the face, and he managed to coax the woman out into the hallway, but not before everyone heard what she was saying.

Criminal.

Murderer.

My child. No explanation. Unconscionable.

What is the school thinking? What about her parents?

Even in fragmented snippets, her point was crystal clear.

It was then that Yuriko first noticed several of her classmates were absent that day. Far more than usual.

I'm not a criminal.

I'm not a murderer.

But Hiroki was. He had killed another boy. And she was his sister. Who would want their own child to sit in the same classroom as the sister of a murderer? That was what Fukuyama's mother was saying. She hadn't heard that Yuriko would be coming back to school today. If she had, there was no way she would have let it slide. What was the school thinking?

Fukuyama's mother had been trembling. Her daughter too. They were scared of Yuriko. And Yuriko thought she detected the faintest trace of something else in the mother's eyes. Disdain. They were mocking her. How could she be so stupid to come back to school? Did she really think everything was going to be just the way it was before?

Yuriko looked up to find every head in the room looking in her direction. Kana was one of them.

Then, one by one, they turned away. They looked off to the side. They looked down at their lunch trays. There was the sound of clattering dishes. But not a single student in the entire room was talking.

All conversation in the room had been sucked into the tiny black hole at its center. A black hole named Yuriko.

Yuriko threw her books and her pen case into her bag and left school before Mr. Katayama could come back into the room.

I'm going home. I'm going home. I'm going home. A little music box was playing a dark tune over and over in Yuriko's mind. *Go home. Go home. Never go back to school.*

There's no place for you there anymore.

Her knees buckled, her jaw sagged. When she ran, the world seemed to sway around her, and the pavement turned to wet sand beneath her feet.

Back home, she ran into the living room and grabbed on to her mother. Then she cried and wailed louder than she ever had. Louder than Fukuyama's mom.

For a long while, the two of them sat there, hugging and crying.

Yuriko wouldn't be going back to school. She would never go to that school again.

Late that night, Yuriko went back to her brother's room. She didn't want her parents to know she was in there, so she left the light off. The light coming in through the window from the streetlamp outside was enough.

The red book was back on the bookshelf. It was sitting at the edge of one of the front rows. Her mother must have come in here and picked it up. The bent pages had been smoothed out.

Yuriko stepped closer and gently touched a finger to the book.

The magic was back, she could tell that instantly. The jacket felt warm to the touch.

"That you, little miss?" the book asked in her head. Yuriko nodded silently. She began to cry as quietly as she could. The more she cried, the more tears came.

She grabbed the book off the shelf and hugged it to her chest.

"Y'know, that kinda hurt the other day," the book said, pouting.

"I'm sorry," Yuriko said, the tears rolling down her face.

The book sighed. "Sounds like you got hurt too." A gentle vibration came through the book's cover. Yuriko nodded, hanging her head, and she slumped down against the wall with the book in her arms.

She told him what had happened that day at school. She kept backtracking, adding details, and crying in between parts of the story so that in the end it must have sounded like a tangled mess, but the red book seemed to understand. The whole time she talked, he said only one thing. *It's okay. Don't cry.* No matter what she said, no matter how much she cried. *It's okay. Don't cry.*

"It's like that for everybody, you know," he told her when Yuriko had finally finished her story and her tears had dried. "Everyone feels the same thing you do, little miss, when the Hero takes someone."

When the book spoke, it sounded almost like a song. There was a melody to his words. It was a song about the river of tears that people had cried over the ages, over countless sorrows.

"No one can do anything about it. I'm sorry, but no one can undo what has been done."

You can't turn back time.

"You'll be at home for a while now, won't you, miss? You should take it easy. Time may be your enemy now, but in a while, it will become your ally."

"You mean I'll forget?"

"Maybe. Probably."

No I won't. How could I?

"But my brother is gone." Her brother's absence had stopped the clock for Yuriko. The whole Morisaki family was frozen in time. "Remember what we were talking about yesterday?" Yuriko asked, holding the book up in front of her face. "You know more than you've told me, don't you. If you know why my brother did what he did, I'll bet you know where he is now."

The red book hesitated.

Bingo, Yuriko thought. "Where is he? Where's Hiroki? What happens to people taken by the Hero? Does the Hero bring them somewhere? Is he in some kind of prison?" Her questions came out one after the other, with barely a pause between them. "Hiroki didn't stab his friend because he wanted to, right? The Hero made him do it, right?"

After a pause, the book answered. "That's correct. That's in *its* nature. It manipulates people, starts wars, turns the world on its head."

Yuriko had to think hard to understand some of the words he was using.

"The Hero starts wars? That's weird. The heroes I know about are always ending wars."

That was how it was in all the stories. That was how it was in her textbooks.

"Beginnings, endings, they're all the same, miss. They're the head and the tail of the same beast."

This she understood even less. She wished the book would stop talking in riddles and just get to the point. "So my brother isn't bad, then. He's not the evil one. Something evil grabbed him and made him do those things."

Hiroki is a victim.

"I have to help him!" she said out loud, and then she had the strange sensation that the words took shape as she said them and floated up in the air of the darkened room, glittering as they rose.

"I have to go help him. You have to tell me where he is." Then a light went off in her head. "Wait, the answer is written inside you, isn't it? All of this is written inside you. That's how you know so much about the Hero!"

Even before she had finished talking, Yuriko tried opening the book. But to her surprise, he resisted.

"What? You can't do that!"

The book tensed, dug in its heels (or would have if it had them), and fought against Yuriko's grip. Yuriko tore angrily at the book. Still, the pages wouldn't open. *You opened up easily enough yesterday!*

"You can't do that!" she fumed. "You're...a...book!"

"You can't save him," the book said. His voice wasn't singing anymore. There were no more gentle vibrations either. "No one who the Hero takes can be saved. Not by a person."

"Well I can. Just tell me where he is and we'll save him! I'll get the police and the firemen, and Dad and Mom!"

"Ridiculous! What can adults do? They can't get near the Hero. They can't even leave this world!"

There he goes again. Talking in riddles.

"Fine, whatever, I don't care. Just let me read you. What I need to know is written in you, isn't it?"

Yuriko struggled with the book there in her brother's neatly tidied-up room, in the pool of pale white light that spilled in through the window from the streetlamp outside. When she thought about it later, she couldn't

40

remember exactly *how* she had struggled with the book, but she had. At the time it felt more like she was fighting not with a book but with a boy—a boy just about the same age as her brother.

Of course, that was a losing battle. She had never actually fought with her brother, but her arms were shorter, and her feet were slower. Luckily for Yuriko, though, girls have a secret weapon when it comes to fights.

Yuriko bared her teeth and bit into the book's jacket. She heard the red book yelp and slip out of her hands, turning over in the air to land, pages up, on the floor.

Out of breath, Yuriko scooped up the book. The book looked like it was sagging in shock. She could clearly see her own teeth marks on one corner of its cover. A perfect little semicircle. She had always been proud of her teeth.

"Now that was a very mean thing to do," the book moaned.

"You're the one who's mean!"

"Look, even if you got me open, you still couldn't read me. You can't even read the letters on my cover."

She had to admit he was right.

"I never took you for someone so fierce, little miss. I guess it's true what they say. Don't judge a book by its cover." The red book chuckled and then groaned. He sounded less surprised by the whole thing than hurt. Just like a real person. "You may have very sharp teeth, but you're just a little girl. You can't save your brother. Now be good for a change and dry your tears and blow your nose, and get to bed. You'll feel better in the morning, and pretty soon you can go back to school. That's how you do it. Just live life the same way you always have. It'll be hard at first, but that's what you have to do."

That was the last thing Yuriko wanted to hear. She might have had her temper back under control, but she was still just as angry, and it was bubbling up inside her.

"I can't just pretend everything is normal."

"You have to try."

"If I go back to school they'll pick on me again."

"You'll find some who won't. They'll be your allies."

"Oh what do you know? You're just a book."

For a moment it was quiet in the room. Then the book spoke again, his tone somewhat different than before. "I get it. You just don't want to go back to school. That's why you wanted to go help your brother. It was just an excuse to play hooky."

Yuriko went to throw the book on the floor again, but her hand stopped in midair. She stood there, holding the book over her head. An unbearable sadness washed over her, and her eyes burned with shame. Yuriko lowered her hand and gently slid the book back onto Hiroki's bookshelf.

"There, there. That's the way," the book said, sounding satisfied. "Good night, miss. Get some rest."

I'll let go of the book and just walk out of the room. We're done here. Wait. No we're not.

"Is there really no way I can help my brother? Are you sure none of the grown-ups can do it? My parents and the police can't help?"

"That's right, they can't."

"And I can't help either because I'm a little girl? So who could? Who else is there? Isn't there anybody who could help my brother?"

"What would you do if I told you?"

"If there is, I'm going to go to them and ask them to help my brother."

I would go and ask, and they would listen.

"If you know, you have to tell me. Where can I find someone who can help my brother?"

Yuriko wasn't looking at the clock, so she didn't know how much time passed before the book answered, but it seemed like an eternity. "Nowhere here. An *otherplace*." There was something in his voice that sounded sterner, more solemn than before. "You would have to leave your world in order to find someone who can help your brother, little miss."

How am I supposed to do that?

"Is that what you were talking about when you said adults couldn't even leave this world?"

"That's right."

"But I'm a kid...so I can?" *If I can, I'm going.* "Where is this other place? Is it in another country? Would I have to take an airplane?"

"Not just any other place, an *otherplace*. A place outside this *Circle* you're in."

The book began to explain. *Circle* meant this world. And not "world" like in "world history," or even "world map," or the other worlds that Yuriko was familiar with. It meant something bigger, much bigger.

"You could walk to the farthest corner of Earth, or the most distant star, and that would still be inside your *Circle* as we see it. Your world, or to be more precise, the story of your world is all inside this Circle, and nowhere else."

This wasn't very helpful. But Yuriko had found one thing to seize hold of.

"But if I really, really want to go, um, outside my Circle, I can, right? Would you take me there?"

"Well, you are a child..." the book muttered. "And because you're a child," the book said, a little more loudly, "you can make this kind of immense decision. The kind of decision that might change your life. The kind you can never take back."

She couldn't tell whether the book was rolling his eyes or was genuinely impressed with her.

"But I suppose there's no helping it, after all it was my fault for talking to you in the first place. I have a responsibility."

Something deep in Yuriko's chest tightened, but for the first time in a long while it wasn't thanks to sadness or anger.

"Thank you! Thank you so much."

"Don't thank me yet. This isn't going to be easy. And I won't be able to do it by myself," the red book admitted. "That's why I need to take you to my friends first. And besides," the book added quietly, "that's where the Way In is, anyway."

"So we have to find your friends? Where? A bookstore, maybe? A library? You're pretty old so...maybe a used bookstore?"

The red book chuckled. "You're pretty funny, miss. Maybe you've forgotten?"

Forgotten? Forgotten what?

"Do you really think your brother picked up a book like me, with all the strange things written inside me, at the local bookstore? Think about it. Try to remember. How long ago was it? It was still cold outside. You and your brother were all wrapped up in your thick coats. Remember going to a place where there were books like me, so many you could hardly count them?"

Yuriko picked the book back up off the shelf and sat down so she could think better. *When it was still cold? Wearing coats? With my brother—*

"And all of us went, our whole family?"

"That's right."

White breath puffing in the air. A place with so many books you couldn't count them.

Yuriko's mouth hung open. "You mean my uncle's cottage!"

"Well, to be precise, he's your father's uncle, which makes him your great-uncle."

It had been the first Sunday of December the year before. The whole family had piled in the car.

"I remember he had this incredible reading room there—it was like a whole library inside."

"And that's where I was," the red book said softly. "The Hero was there too."

But Yuriko was too busy thinking and remembering to hear his whispers. Where was her great-uncle's vacation home, anyway? It couldn't have been far, since they went there and came back in the same day, but it had been in the mountains—she remembered that well. And they had driven on some dirt roads to get there. She remembered her mother gasping at every bump.

"How am I supposed to get all the way up there by myself? I don't even know the address or the road."

"Well then," the red book said, and she imagined a twinkle in his eyes. "This is your first test."

CHAPTER TWO

The Hermit's Library

Kids can think up great lies. They're just not very great at telling them. In order to tell a really good lie, Yuriko knew, you first have to believe in it yourself. Emboldened by the red book's encouragement, Yuriko spent the next thirty minutes getting ready. It was easy to come up with a suitable lie, but hard to make a convincing performance of it.

It didn't take much for her to wake her parents. Neither of them had slept particularly well since her brother's disappearance. It was only recently that they even bothered with sleeping in their bedroom. For a while, they had just nodded off wherever they happened to be—in the living room, in a chair, or on the sofa. They had left the front door unlocked and would jump up and run outside at the slightest sound in the hope that Hiroki had come home at last. Finally, the police had told them they couldn't keep on like that forever, and they had begun sleeping properly again.

When Yuriko began her lie, her mother's expression changed almost immediately. She wasn't surprised or angry. A mix of joy and regret crept over her thin features. Why hadn't she thought of it herself sooner?

"I completely forgot about it myself, Mom," Yuriko was saying. "He could hide out at our great-uncle's summer cottage for weeks without anyone knowing."

"That's right. Yuriko's right," her mother said as she shook her father by the shoulder with her left hand. Her right was around Yuriko's shoulder. "I'll bet Hiroki's at the cottage!"

"How would he get all the way out there?" her father groaned, wiping the sleep from his eyes. "He doesn't have a car. He's only in middle school." He wasn't buying it, but Yuriko detected a glimmer in his eye. He *wanted* it to be true; he just wasn't letting himself get his hopes up.

"Hiroki's always done what he wants to once he sets his mind on something. And he's smart too. And clever. I'm sure there are lots of ways he could have gotten out there. He could've hitchhiked."

Her mom was sitting on the edge of the bed, ready to leave that very instant.

"Just wait," her father said. "It's the middle of the night."

"Well I can't just sit around here doing nothing. Can you? What if he's out there?"

"Shouldn't we tell someone we're going?"

"Who would we tell? The police?" A dark cloud passed over her mother's face. "Not if I have anything to say about it," she practically shouted. "We're finding Hiroki ourselves, as a family. We can tell the police later!"

Gradually, her mother's enthusiasm nudged her father into action. It was the usual pattern of events whenever big things got decided in the Morisaki household.

"Fine, okay. We'll go. Yuriko—"

"I'm going too!"

"Of course. We have to take Yuriko," her mother agreed. "I won't split up this family again," she added, the words catching in her throat.

Forty-five minutes later, the three remaining members of the Morisaki household had piled into the car and driven out into the quiet city streets. Packing had taken them all of fifteen minutes (her father had to stop her mother before too long, as she packed a change of clothes for her brother, and food, and cold medicine in case he had caught a cold, and medicine for diarrhea...). The remaining half hour they had spent figuring out the exact address of the cottage and how they would get there.

They had only been to her great-uncle's place once. They hadn't thought they would have a reason to go back. When her great-uncle had died, the family had decided to leave the handling of his affairs to the lawyers. So her father couldn't remember where he had stashed the year-old memo with the cottage's address on it. At first, when he couldn't find it, he'd suggested they call his father to find out, but Yuriko's mother refused. She didn't want to have to explain to him why they wanted to know. "He'd probably call the police. I know he would," she said. Yuriko's grandparents on her father's side of the family had always been cold to Hiroki, she explained. When her father started defending them, Yuriko had to butt in to stop them. In the end, it was Yuriko who found the memo tucked away in one of her mother's many places where she was in the habit of "keeping things for just in case."

Her parents sat in the front. Whenever they went out someplace in the car, her brother always sat behind the driver's seat, and she would sit behind the passenger seat. Now it was just her in the back seat. On her knees, she carried a pink backpack inside of which was the red book.

—Good work, little miss.

Yuriko stuck her right hand into the top of the backpack and laid her palm across the book's cover. She could hear his voice like she had in Hiroki's room.

You know, she aimed her thoughts toward the book, when I was telling them, I started believing it myself. I really started to think maybe he was out there in the cottage.

—Unfortunately, that's impossible, the book replied. *Your brother's disappearance has left a hole in you, I know, but don't fill it with empty hope. What matters now is whether my friends are still there in the cottage or not.*

What do you mean? You said that's where they were.

—Try asking your father. Ask if any of his relatives came to the cottage and did something with the books.

Yuriko pulled her hand out of the backpack. She leaned forward.

"Dad? Remember when we went to visit the cottage? Do you think anyone went in there after us to clean up?"

Her father's eyes darted to the rearview mirror. "If they have, I haven't heard about it."

"So it's all there just like it was? Remember all those books? It was like a library…You think they're all still there?"

"I should think so, Yuriko. If somebody did anything, my father or your Uncle Takashi would have told me."

Takashi was one of her father's two brothers, the oldest in her father's family.

"Weren't they saying that they couldn't find a buyer for the house?" her mother asked. She had a hand on the dashboard, like she was trying to push the car to go just a little bit faster. "It's just so remote out there. There wasn't even a proper road. And the building was getting pretty old."

Yuriko remembered Uncle Takashi saying that if the location were just a little better, or the place in a little better shape, it might make sense for them to put money into renovations and make it a summer cottage the whole family could enjoy. "But not like it is now," he had said. "The place is a bona fide ruin."

"Those books, though—Takashi was talking about showing them to a specialist at some point. There were so many of them there, one or two might actually be worth something," Yuriko's mother said. "Did your brother ever say anything about them, Yuriko?"

Her mother was sharp. Yuriko shook her head. "Nope. But I remember he was pretty impressed with how many there were, and how our great-uncle must have collected them all by himself."

That was true. When her brother had seen the reading room at the cottage, he had wanted to stay in there for hours. He said he thought there must be books from all over the world there. *Check it out, little Yuri. Here's one in English, and here's one in French, and I've never even seen this language before. This one looks like it might be hundreds of years old.*

"Hiroki always was fond of reading," her mother said in a soft voice.

"Come to think of it, it's been almost five months since we were there. I wonder if the place is locked?" her father muttered, suddenly worried.

"If it were locked, he would've just broken in through a window," her mother said, urging Yuriko's father to drive faster. He shifted his grip on the wheel. Yuriko stuck her hand back inside her backpack.

Mom really thinks he's there waiting for us.

—*There's nothing you can do about that. She's his mother.*

But it's my fault.

—*If you're going to wimp out now because you're afraid of hurting your mother's feelings, you'll never make it where we're going. Besides,* the red book added, *you should get some sleep.*

How can I possibly sleep? I'm not even sleepy.

—*Then tell me what you know about the owner of the cottage, your great-uncle.*

You mean you don't know? Didn't my great-uncle buy you?

—*I want to know what you know. So I can put what you know and what I know together. You don't have to explain it to me, just try to remember by yourself. I'll hear.*

Yuriko leaned back in her seat and started to remember everything she could about her great-uncle.

The first time she had even heard about him had been about a year ago, in the summer, when the weather was still warm. They had been sitting around the dinner table when her father suddenly said, "You know, it seems I have an uncle."

Her father's father—Yuriko's grandfather—was an only child. He had no siblings. So how could a great-uncle suddenly appear out of nowhere?

"The circumstances are a little complicated. My parents never mentioned it to us until now," her father explained to her mother, who was just as shocked as the children were.

Apparently, from the time Yuriko's grandfather was in fourth grade to the time he was in eleventh grade, he had an adopted brother.

"He was the son of a man who had helped out my father's father at work."

Though Yuriko's father had made the announcement to everyone at the table, when it came to talking about the details, he spoke only to her mother. As it always was with talk between adults, Yuriko couldn't follow a lot of what he was saying. Her brother just kept eating like he wasn't particularly interested, but Yuriko knew he was listening because when she shot him a glance to ask what something her father was saying meant, he would give her a "you don't need to understand" look back. *If you really need to know, I'll tell you later.*

"There was all kinds of trouble," her father was saying. "The child had been passed from relative to relative. No one wanted the burden, and so in the end they came to my grandfather, begging him to adopt. He had a reputation for his generosity, I guess."

Her mother started asking lots of questions. *Was the child legitimate?—Yes.* (Whatever that meant.) *And the mother?—She ran off, saying she couldn't raise the child alone.*

The questions went on, but Yuriko quickly lost track of who had done what to whom, and why.

"How old was he when they adopted him?" she finally managed to ask, during a lull in the conversation.

"Just a year younger than my father."

"So they were like brothers then."

"Had everything gone well, yes."

But everything hadn't gone well. The adopted brother hadn't been a good fit with the Morisaki family.

"Though I suppose it was a better place for him than anywhere else. They did make it for several years, after all."

"The poor child," her mother had said.

Apparently, the adopted brother and Yuriko's grandfather had never gotten along.

"My grandfather put him through school," her father said, "but he quit as soon as he got to high school. He left home soon after."

The adoption hadn't been formal, so there were no certificates or papers to deal with. The boy had simply disappeared.

"My grandfather was pretty put out for a while—I think he expected the kid to be a little more grateful. And my grandmother was sick with worry about it, but there was not much either of them could do in the end."

Yuriko's grandfather had completely forgotten about his adopted brother by the time he was an adult. Pretty soon he was a father in his own right, and then a grandfather. His own parents were long gone by then.

The adopted brother's name was Ichiro Minochi. "Minochi" because he had never officially taken the Morisaki name.

"What an unusual name!"

"His mother's maiden name, apparently."

And Ichiro Minochi had died.

"Happened just last month," her father had told them. "The lawyer they put in charge of managing his affairs contacted me—that was the first I'd heard of any of it."

Ichiro Minochi had left a will specifying that part of his estate was to go to the Morisaki family, who had taken care of him when he was a child.

"His estate...was he rich?" Yuriko's mother had asked, eyes wide, chopsticks still in her mouth.

"He had some luck with the stock market. Was an investor of some standing, it sounds like. Never know where life is going to lead, do you? He had no family and I don't think he ever graduated from high school, but here's this success story."

Except Ichiro Minochi had died alone, with no family or relations. The bulk of his estate had been earmarked for a charity.

"My dad was sure impressed when he heard. Said he wished his parents were still alive. They'd have been happy to hear that Ichiro made something of himself."

"So do we just get the money? What about taxes? I've heard about people getting an inheritance and ending up owing more than they get," her mother had said.

"Don't worry about that. The lawyer's taking care of everything. We'll only receive what we're actually due."

"Wait, but *we* won't get it, will we? Doesn't it go to your father?"

Yuriko's father had laughed. "Yeah, but that just means it will be mine and my brothers' before long."

It was about a month later that Uncle Takashi paid them a visit. (*My, you two have sure grown! How's the baseball coming, Hiroki? Hitting any home runs?*) Her uncle and her father had talked together for a while. She remembered her father hadn't looked pleased.

"Oh well. I guess it was too much to hope for," she had overheard her father saying.

"That's what Dad told me," her uncle had said. "No such thing as a free lunch after all, eh?"

According to the lawyer, after all the paperwork was finished and taxes were paid, all the Morisaki family was due for their inheritance was an old cottage up in the mountains north of Tokyo.

"It was a summer cottage, but apparently Mr. Minochi spent most of his time there."

"That's where he died?"

"No, he died on some trip. In Paris."

Yuriko's great-uncle had passed away in a used bookstore along the River Seine. He had just keeled over between two stacks of books and was dead before the owner even had time to call an ambulance. The cause of death was a heart attack.

"His heart had been giving him trouble from before. I guess that's why he took the trouble to draw up a will."

He had been to Paris several times, it seemed. And many other places around the world.

"Makes sense, seeing as how he was living alone with money to burn. When he wasn't out traveling, he was holed up in that cottage. Didn't much care for other people. No friends or even acquaintances, really. The only person he had talked to in the last two years was his lawyer. And that's only because he had to, most likely. The lawyer said they hadn't so much as gone out for a drink in all the time he knew him."

So Yuriko's great-uncle had been a rich hermit. That was how Mr. Minochi introduced himself, the lawyer had said.

"So his only hobby was traveling abroad?"

"No, actually. The trips were merely a means to an end. His real hobby was books, books, and more books. Old ones."

So he'd gone around the world visiting used bookstores. When he found something he liked he bought it. Money was no object. (He spent money like it was water, Uncle Takashi said.) He bought, and bought, and bought some more. "Apparently, he had built three other houses besides this cottage just to store his finds. But those he didn't leave to Dad."

The cottage, too, had been left filled with books, the ones their great-uncle had loved best.

Uncle Takashi had said he was going to go check the place out. "Dad's really not interested now that there's no money involved. Said he wanted me to deal with it."

"Well, thanks then," her father had said.

"Hey, even if the place is a little run-down, if it looks usable, we should all share it. Could be a great place to get together in the summer and do barbecues."

"If he was rich, he might've had some nice furniture," her mother had said then. "Be sure you take a look."

"Your wish is my command," her uncle had replied.

Uncle Takashi contacted them about the place several times after that. Each report only dampened hopes further. The cottage wasn't just old—it was a miracle the place was even standing. There was hardly any furniture, and most of the rooms were filled with junk. To say her great-uncle hadn't ever hired a maid would be an understatement. It wasn't even clear how he had lived there by himself. When Uncle Takashi had turned on the water, nothing but rusty brown sludge came out of the tap.

But there were books. Mountains of books. The walls of the largest room on the first floor—the reading room—were covered with shelves. That hadn't been enough to hold all the books, though. There were piles on the floor too, Uncle Takashi told them.

"I took a look, but almost all of them were in foreign languages. Don't even have an idea how much they're worth."

That was when the idea of selling them had first come up.

"We should probably get an expert to come take a look at them. I just wish the location were a little better. It's not even a vacation home spot. Just a house sitting by itself in the middle of nowhere, nothing around at all. And once you're halfway through the mountains, the road isn't even paved. I don't think it's a public road, either, because no one seems to have been taking much care of it. The first time I got there, I had to turn around and find a hardware store in the nearest town to buy some weed cutters and a shovel. Man, that was a lot of work."

"Guess we'd better deal with that before we try sending some book expert out there," her father had said. "They might charge us double for the inconvenience," he chuckled wryly. Their inheritance was looking grimmer by the moment.

How had her adopted great-uncle lived in such a place, in such a house, surrounded by so many books? What had he thought of his life? Hadn't he been lonely?

"Hey, we should go take a look ourselves." It was her brother who first suggested it. He worked on Dad until their mother got on board too.

"You know, I don't trust your brother and his wife when it comes to assessing the value of things. They're just not greedy enough. They might have completely overlooked some hidden treasure. I should go take a look at the place too. See what I can see."

"Yeah, but Isamu and his wife went too, and they came home just as depressed as Takashi."

Isamu was Yuriko's other uncle, her father's second oldest sibling. He had been married once, had gotten a divorce, and was now living with his second wife. They didn't have any children. Since both of them worked, they were by far the most well-off of any of his siblings. "Though they do tend to spend too much," her mother had said. "And they might have an eye for quality, but they're so trendy. I'll bet they wouldn't know an antique if it bit them."

When it came to matters of any importance, Mom's opinion held the most weight. So when December of that year rolled around, Yuriko's family went on a survey expedition to the cottage. It was thankfully too cold by then for snakes or much vermin, but they had still needed grass clippers to get to the place. The memory jolted Yuriko back into the present.

❦

"You think we'll be able to get through on that road?" she asked her parents in the front seat. "I hope it's not totally overgrown already."

"Don't worry," her father replied. "I still have your uncle's clippers in my trunk from the last time we went. Good memory," he added.

"I'm sure your brother's cut a path," her mother added quickly.

Her father had nothing to say to that.

They were driving on the expressway now. The road was empty, save for the occasional trucker. For a while, they were driving alongside a truck with pictures of all kinds of fish on the side, until it left on the next exit ramp.

The red book spoke to her.

—Sounds like my friends are still there in the cottage.

Yeah! We're in luck.

—I remember the one your father calls "Takashi." He was in the reading room. His wife too. But no children were with them.

Uncle Takashi had kids—Yuriko's cousins.

They're older than me and my brother. I doubt they go places with their parents much these days.

Her brother had been heading in that direction himself. Ever since he'd started middle school, he would make faces whenever talk came up of a family trip. Usually, he'd come up with some excuse so he wouldn't have to go, and even when there was no escape, he made it clear he didn't want to be there...though he always seemed happy to go out with the baseball team or friends from school.

"Daddy," her mother said, impatient. She sometimes called Yuriko's father that. "What happened to the cottage after all that, anyway? Does your father own it now?"

"I suppose so. I kind of lost interest myself."

"And the paperwork is all done?"

"I think so."

"That's good. If Hiroki is there, at least he won't be breaking and entering. It's family property, after all," her mother concluded, sounding pleased with herself. Her father looked like he was about to say something, then abandoned it and focused on driving.

—*That's funny,* the red book said. *Your family seems to know hardly anything about the man who owned the cottage.*

Well, how could they? They never met him.

—*But they call him your great-uncle. Doesn't that seem strange to you? It seems strange to me.*

Yuriko thought about that for a bit.

It's probably just because they don't feel comfortable calling him "Ichiro" or "Mr. Minochi," that's all.

—*That would sound like they were even more familiar with him though, oddly enough.*

I guess so.

That reminded Yuriko that her grandfather had said once that they should consider his late adoptive brother to be family. It was the least they could do, seeing as how there was no one else left to remember him. Her grandmother had been worried about the grave. Who would wash it and make visits? she asked.

—*He was a very solitary man.*

My great-uncle, you mean?

—*Yes. I was only in the cottage for three years myself, but it was immediately clear he lived alone. But,* the book added, *he didn't seem lonely.*

Even though he lived alone?

While she was waiting for his reply, Yuriko remembered something important.

Wait, didn't you say the Hero was there at the cottage with you? Does that mean the Hero is a book too?

The book answered, his voice so faint Yuriko felt she had to press her hand harder against the cover just to hear it.

—*That's right.*

So it was one of the books my great-uncle bought?

—*Yes. I don't know where he got it, if that's what you want to know.*

Though one of my friends probably does.

Then how did my great-uncle manage to escape it? How come the Hero didn't take him?

They had left the expressway and were now on a city street, under the light of streetlamps and shop signs. Though they were indistinguishable from the night sky now, Yuriko knew they were surrounded by little hills, and in the distance, mountains. The little building indicators on the car's GPS screen had grown few and far between.

—*It's difficult to explain.*

This was hardly a surprise for Yuriko by now.

—*See, what we call the Hero isn't even in this Circle. It's in another place, imprisoned.*

A police car pulled out of a side street, turned toward them, and passed by. Yuriko saw the officer in the passenger seat craning his neck to look inside their car. Her father drove smoothly, and her mother didn't even seem to notice the police. Her eyes were fixed on the road ahead, like she could already see the cottage in the mountains before them, her son huddled in a dark room, only a flashlight or a candle for light, an old blanket or jacket draped over his shoulders.

—*The Hero has a power other books lack. And the copies of the Hero that exist here, in your Circle, act as a conduit for that power. They're not the Hero itself, but they're a part of the Hero, in a manner of speaking.*

So the book that Hiroki had found in Ichiro Minochi's cottage had been a copy. Yuriko had never heard of anything so strange, or so intriguing.

So what's the point in throwing the Hero in prison if there are copies all over the place? Yuriko asked with all the indignant fury a fifth grader could muster.

The red book didn't flinch. *If the Hero were free to roam, it would roam throughout the Circle, its copies multiplying freely. That we have as few copies to deal with as we do now is thanks to the fact that the Hero is imprisoned in the nameless land.*

The *"nameless land"?* Yuriko was pretty sure she hadn't heard of any place like that yet. She was about to ask the book about it when the car bounced suddenly and her backpack slid off her lap. Her hand lost contact with the book.

They had just run out of paved road. Her father tensed in the driver's seat, and her mother pushed with renewed intensity on the dashboard.

"Almost there now. Up this road, right?"

"I'm pretty sure there's only one way to go."

Yuriko caught herself so she wouldn't hit her head on the back of the seat, and managed to reach down and pick her backpack up off the floor.

Outside the car, beyond the beams of the headlights, the night was pitch black. The wavering lights made it look like the trees that came looming out of the darkness were swaying their branches and dancing along the sides of the road. *Who goes there, bringing light into our mountains at such an hour? Who is it who needs light to enter our woods?* The leaves rustled. The branches swayed. Without realizing it, Yuriko shrank away from the window, her whole body tensed.

Abruptly, the silhouette of the cottage appeared in the headlights. It was like it hadn't existed until that very moment. Like it had been an animal, sleeping until the sound of the car's engine woke it and sent it lumbering into the light.

Where the night sky and the mountains and the forest had seemed dark, the cottage was darker still as if it had trapped inside it all the darkness from all the nights it had been left abandoned. Though the darkness in the air around it was free to leave at dawn, the darkness within the cottage was permanent. In the days and weeks it had sat there, the darkness had piled up, condensing. It looked like the weight of all that darkness had pushed Minochi's cottage even closer to collapsing than it had been the last time they visited.

The car stopped. Her father turned off the engine.

"Time to get out, Yuriko."

Yuriko was clutching her backpack to her chest as if it were a bulletproof vest. The last bit of overgrown road up to the house was short, but very steep, keeping them from just driving up. Her father had to use the clippers just for them to get to the cottage door. The grass and weeds and brambles had all grown tall. There was no sign that anyone had cut a path.

Yuriko had tripped walking up it the last time they were here and found a chunk of old pavement stone in the grass. There had been several of the smooth flat stones lying here and there. Her brother had noticed them when he came to help her to her feet. He hadn't said anything at the time, but later when he was telling their parents about it, he suggested that Mr. Minochi might have once been rich, but had since fallen on hard times.

Her mother and father had looked at one of the smooth cobblestones, then at each other.

"Must've been hard for him to keep this place in shape," her father had said.

"If he needed money, why didn't he sell his books?" her mother had wondered.

How had he gone all the way to Paris in search of old books, but not been able to pay for the upkeep on his own cottage?

🌱

"Hiroki! Hiroki!" Yuriko's mother called as she waved her flashlight about and tried to push past her husband.

"Hey, watch it. I don't want to catch your hand with this thing," her father warned, swinging the cutter, but it seemed like her mother couldn't even hear him.

No matter how many times her mother called, nothing stirred. She searched, looking for some light that wasn't there. It seemed to Yuriko that her mother's eyes burned with an intensity so bright, she half expected them to reflect in the windows. But the windows were dark.

The front door was locked, and with more than just an ordinary lock. Someone had attached a light green-colored metallic plate to the door and the frame just above the knob, from which hung a large padlock. Both looked brand-new, like someone had slapped them on by magic just moments before.

"Who did this? The lawyer? Your brother?" Mother asked in a panic.

"How should I know?" her father snapped. "Get a handle on yourself, Yoshiko," he said, grabbing her by the shoulder and shaking her. Her eyes seemed to lose their focus. The burning intensity in them went dull. The hand gripping the flashlight lowered to her side.

In the end, they decided to break in through one of the windows on the first floor. Her father cut his wrist a little when he reached in through the broken pane to undo the crescent-shaped lock on the window frame. Yuriko, with her small size and light weight, had the easiest time getting through the window once it was open. Inside, the place smelled like dust. The darkness pressed in on her. Yuriko sneezed and had to press her face into her backpack to stop.

"Hiroki! Hiroki?"

Her father and her mother moved through the cottage, shining flashlights into every corner.

Yuriko heard the red book whisper to her where it touched the tip of her nose through the thin fabric of her backpack.

—Little miss, the reading room.

The only light Yuriko had was a tiny pencil flashlight—the kind you got for free when you bought something else. She had to skid the tips of her shoes along the floor as she walked in order not to trip on anything. She was glad she hadn't taken off her shoes. Lots of stuff was scattered around on the floor, so she repeatedly trampled over unseen objects as she walked. In the next room, she pulled the red book out of her backpack and held it to her chest with one hand, then dropped the backpack on the floor.

—Go right here. Down the hall.

Her memories from her last visit to the place came slowly drifting back to her. The large room ahead would be the reading room. Just through that door.

The doorknob turned easily, and the door opened toward her. A light breeze blew past, wafting through her hair as she stepped through. Even though it should have been as dark as pitch in the room, she could clearly see the books lining the walls well outside the tiny circle of light cast by her pencil light.

They're shining!

The books in the room *were* shining, glittering faintly like stars in the sky, winking and blinking, each of them in a slightly different shade. There was white, yellow, blue, gold, purple...a faint light was coming from the red book clutched to her chest now too. The glow reached up to her chin.

"Aju?"

"It is Aju!"

"Aju's come back!"

Voices rained down on her from the walls and the ceiling. She almost jumped when she heard a voice coming up from near her feet.

"Welcome back, Aju."

Yuriko turned to run, when the red book in her arms flared even brighter, giving off a warm light.

"It's okay, little miss," the book said. "Don't be frightened. They're my friends."

You mean those voices...are coming from all those books?

Lit by the glimmering light of the countless books surrounding her in the reading room, Yuriko felt like she was watching a show in a planetarium.

"Who is the child, Aju?"

"Why did you bring a child here?"

I'm not even touching them, Yuriko thought. *How can I hear them all talking so clearly?*

"Because you stand within the boundaries of a sanctuary we created, little miss," the red book told her gently. "You don't have to hold me quite so hard to talk to me anymore, by the way. You must be exhausted. Have a seat. We've finally made it."

Bewildered by all of this, Yuriko couldn't move for several moments. The books fell silent, waiting to see what she did next. In their light, she spotted a small stepladder on the floor by her right foot. Her great-uncle must have used it to reach the books on the higher shelves.

The ladder had three steps on it, though the second step was mostly occupied by a teetering pile of books. Yuriko sat on the lowest step, taking care not to lean too far back. The red book she put on her lap, unwilling to lose contact with it just yet.

"I need a spell, if you would," the red book was saying to his friends. "This child's parents came here with her."

Just then, Yuriko heard a beautiful voice singing from the bookshelf just by the door. It was only a snippet of a refrain. No words, just humming.

Suddenly, she could no longer hear her parents moving through the cottage. Their cries of "Hiroki!" didn't just trail off, they stopped cold.

Yuriko jumped to her feet. "What did you do? You did something to my parents, didn't you?"

She dropped the red book on the floor and made for the doorway. The door slammed shut before her eyes.

"It's all right, little miss," the red book said, chuckling from where it lay on the floor. "They're just taking a little rest, that's all. You wouldn't want them to worry while you're talking with us, would you?"

Yuriko grabbed the doorknob. It rattled in her hand but wouldn't turn. The door was frozen shut.

"Really? They're just asleep or something? That's all?"

"Of course."

"How can you do that? How did you make them sleep?"

"Books have the power to lead people into dreams," the red book explained. "You've fallen asleep while reading a book before, haven't you?"

In fact, she had fallen asleep several times at her desk while facing a particularly boring textbook. "I don't fall asleep if it's interesting," she said, pouting, though she realized that didn't exactly counter his argument.

"Who is the child, Aju?" a voice asked from behind and above Yuriko, up near the ceiling.

"She is the sister of the one who took the Book of Elem," the red book answered. Yuriko realized she could tell the red book's voice apart from the others. Each of the books' voices was slightly different—just like people.

Yuriko warily returned to the stepladder. She couldn't see where the red book had landed among all the scattered shimmering volumes on the floor.

"Little miss, turn off the device in your hand. Its light is harsh to us."

Yuriko didn't see any point in protesting now, so she did as she was told. When the light flickered off she inhaled deeply, getting dust in her nose, which made her sneeze. Moving her feet to keep her balance, she stepped on something on the floor. When she looked by the light of the books, she saw it was a piece of cloth. She reached down to move it so she wouldn't step on it again, and found it velvety to the touch and surprisingly heavy.

"You know what has happened, don't you, Aju?"

Around her, the books began to talk to each other.

"I know. This child's brother touched the Book of Elem. His name is Hiroki. Hiroki was a vessel. Thus was he possessed." The red book's voice sounded earnest and full of regret. "I did everything in my power to stop it, but it was not enough. I am sorry."

When the book said, "I am sorry," Yuriko finally spotted its red glimmer. It had fallen on the floor on the other side of the stepladder.

"You're called Aju? That's your name?" Yuriko asked.

"More or less," the book replied. "It's a short form of my real name."

Aju explained he was a dictionary, compiled around 3000 BC. "Of course, I didn't look like I do now when I was first written. There were no leather-bound books in this Circle back then."

Yuriko didn't follow most of these details, but she understood one thing: whatever was written in the red book was very, very old.

"Where were you made?"

"In a land called Babylonia."

The red book explained it was a beginner's dictionary of spells. Yuriko laughed out loud at the thought of there being a beginner's dictionary for something like that. "This is all starting to sound like some kind of fairy tale," she said, but the red book—Aju—didn't join in her laughter. The sound was swallowed up in the silent glimmer of the books.

"Aju," one of the other books said. "This child Hiroki was not merely a vessel. He was the last vessel."

"What!" Aju practically shouted. Yuriko had never heard him raise his voice like that before.

The books all began to talk at once.

"The child Hiroki was not merely possessed."

"He has become the Summoner."

"It is free."

"It has escaped."

"The First Bell rings in the nameless land."

"The Hero is free."

"The prison has been broken."

Everywhere, all around her, the books were speaking. It was like she had been thrown into the middle of a flock of birds, all squawking in whispers. All the books were talking, winking and blinking like stars. Yuriko grew dizzy. She felt sick. Her stomach rose in her throat. She screwed her eyes shut and was about to clap her hands over her ears when one of the books said, "The end is coming."

All the books fell silent.

Her fingers were already loosely over her ears, but Yuriko could still hear the words creep in.

The end is coming. The end of the world!

She looked up to see the books in the reading room glittering like gemstones at the bottom of a pool of water. She stood in the middle, bathed in their eerie light.

"What does this mean?" a familiar voice asked. Yuriko stretched out a hand, snatching up Aju from the other side of the stepladder.

"What are they talking about? Tell me! Explain it so I can understand!" Yuriko whirled around, the book in her hands, and opened it to the very middle, pressing her face into its pages. She could see the tight lines of its code-like letters.

"Miss. Oh, little miss," Aju said, its voice trembling, dizzy from the quick motion. "Please calm down. Hurting me won't help anything. I want you to talk to them. Tell the books here what you saw your brother do."

"No, I want you to explain this to me first!"

What was this Book of Elem? And the nameless land? Whoever heard of a place with no name? What country was *that* in?

"The Book of Elem is one of the copies in which the story of the Hero is written. It's the name of the book your brother took from here the same day he took me. He thought he needed me to read it."

The letters written in the Book of Elem and the letters written in Aju were very similar at first glance, the book explained. They looked the same, but their formation and their history and the people who made them and used them were entirely different.

"Still, your brother was very smart to realize that I am a dictionary." However, the book explained, he didn't think her brother had planned to decipher the books all by himself. "He was probably planning on showing me to one of his teachers."

"No, Aju. That was not the way of it," said a weighty voice from behind Yuriko. "From the moment the child touched the Book of Elem, he was defiled."

"Then why did he need me?" Aju retorted. "No, he was simply curious, that's all. He flipped through the pages of several other books, comparing the writing within, before choosing me. You all remember that."

"The vessel is only a vessel, nothing more," another voice said, coldly.

"Don't talk about him that way. Hiroki is this little girl's brother," Aju replied, his voice sad. Though she couldn't follow their entire exchange, Yuriko realized Aju was trying to protect her.

She lifted her eyes, facing the books in the room. "My brother—" she thought she could feel the books turning toward her, listening. "At school, he..." Then Yuriko told them. She told them about her brother Hiroki. She told them what kind of a person he was, what he liked to do, and about what had happened at school. She then told them about coming home early from school and her mother crying, and what her parents talked about in the car on the way to the cottage, and everything else she could think of. She jumped backward and forward in her story, until everything was so tangled she was sure she wasn't making any sense.

But the books listened to every word.

"My brother doesn't fight with his friends like that. He would never stab someone," Yuriko told them. Now it was her turn to protect her brother. "Aju told me my brother had been possessed by an evil book. The book he took from this room...the Book of Elem, was it? That's the evil book's name, right? It can possess people, right? The book is this Hero you all talk about, isn't it? The book made him hurt his friends, and made him kill a boy even though he didn't want to."

I saw the Hero. I saw his shape, even if I couldn't see his face. His funny pointy crown and his tattered cape. And my brother, bowing his head to the floor in front of him.

"The Hero was standing in front of him, like he was proud. He tricked my brother, I know it. There's no way he would do what he did otherwise. No way. No way!"

Yuriko was out of breath, and her story was finished, even though there was so much more she could say, so much more she could tell them.

"This girl," Aju said when she had fallen silent, "wants to help her brother. She wants to go find him."

The books began to blink faster, their light waxing and waning.

"I told her it was impossible, reckless. Of course, I didn't yet know what I know now."

About it being free.

About Hiroki becoming the Summoner.

"Now that this has come to pass, someone must go recapture the Hero. Is this girl not qualified?" Aju asked the books.

The room was silent. There was only a faint glow and more blinking. For the longest time, no one (that is, no book) said a word. Yuriko was tense at first, but she had almost grown bored by the time the weighty voice from the top shelf broke the silence.

"If we are to speak only of qualifications, then you are most likely correct. But, Aju, do you truly believe it proper to further burden this young child who has already suffered so much?"

Yuriko found the book that was talking, a large tome that winked with a deep green light. She was able to spot it easily because when it talked, the light from the other books dimmed, as though they were holding their breath.

"It's not about whether it's proper or not," Aju insisted. "She's saying she wants to go look for her brother. She's begging to go."

"Only because she does not know how hard a path it is to walk."

"You can handle it, can't you, little miss?" Aju asked her. "You don't care how hard it is as long as you don't have to go back to your life the way it was, right?"

Aju told the other books how the students picked on Yuriko at school. "Which is why you decided to go look for your brother, right?"

It was true that was what she had told Aju before, but now, in this bewildering place, hearing all the books talking and faced with the prospect of even more hardship, Yuriko's resolve was shaken. She was ready for some difficulties, sure. But how much could she take?

"Will it be that hard to find him?" she asked.

"Don't tell me you've lost your nerve already!" Aju wailed. "Or...have you not made up your mind yet?"

"No, I made up my mind. But..."

More than anything else, it was the words she had just heard that bothered her. *The end is coming.* That sounded hundreds of times more important than a missing middle school student, even if that student was her brother. She couldn't just pretend she hadn't heard it.

"Be quiet a moment, Aju," the dark green book commanded. "Child. Tell us your name."

"Yuriko. It's Yuriko," she answered, looking up at the dark green glimmer high on the shelf.

"Yuriko, you may call me the Sage." The book's voice was raspy, like an old man's. "I was friends with the master of this house."

"With my great-uncle? With Mr. Minochi?"

"That's right. There are many here who have sat upon this shelf far longer than I, but none were as close to him as I was." Then the Sage asked what had become of Minochi.

"You mean you don't know?"

"It has been a long time since he left us. Too long for one of his regular trips. You must tell me. Has Minochi died? He has died, hasn't he?"

Yuriko nodded. She told the books about the used bookstore in Paris and the heart attack.

"It is as I feared, then."

"But," Yuriko said, "I've been here to this cottage since then. And so have my aunts and uncles. Did no one talk about Mr. Minochi dying?"

"I did notice the people visiting. They were surprised to find us all here, I recall. But they spoke little of Minochi, and as he was not one with many connections in this world I thought perhaps he was merely feigning death for the sake of solitude somewhere. And yet now I hear he has truly died." Yuriko detected genuine sadness in the Sage's voice. "Minochi and I had a falling out. I believe that is why he departed to Paris."

So people and books can fight with each other. Yuriko supposed that was possible with books like the ones here.

"I could not fulfill Minochi's wish. It was an impossible wish to begin with. Over the years I was here, I tried to explain this to Minochi, to convince him, but he did not accept my reasoning. He grew angry with me, denying what I had to say. He went on that trip to find another sage to replace me."

Yuriko wondered what kind of wish her great-uncle—a rich hermit who collected old books—might have had.

"Minochi searched for a way to raise the dead."

Even despite her amazement at everything that had happened up to this point, Yuriko found herself surprised anew.

"The dead! Who?"

"A woman who was important to him. The only person who ever was. She died a long time ago."

Ichiro Minochi had lived a solitary life. But there had been a woman. *I wonder if he truly loved her?* "And he bought all these books, just searching for that?"

"Yes, he did. He believed that if he could only collect all the knowledge there is in this world, he would find a way to raise the dead."

Yuriko looked over the countless blinking lights there in the dark room. It *was* a tremendous collection of knowledge.

"I told Minochi his efforts were in vain. There is no book possessing a technique by which one can raise the dead. Certainly not the way for which he searched. I urged him to choose a different story, but he would not listen."

Yuriko raised an eyebrow at the word *story*. Even to a young girl, the way the book had used the word seemed strange. Didn't he mean *way*, or *path*, or even *spell*?

"Story?"

She meant it as a question, but the Sage did not explain himself. His light wavered slightly. "Yuriko," the Sage said. "Compared to me, Aju is as young as you. I can appreciate why he seeks to support you, but he is inexperienced and has brought you here without giving you sufficient knowledge."

"That's not true," Aju said. "And I'm no youth, so don't treat me as if I were."

Apparently, books could also fight amongst themselves.

"Still, it is clear you have confused this child Yuriko."

Aju sighed but said nothing.

"Mr. Sage, please don't be angry with Aju. He was there for me when I needed him. He let me know that I wasn't all alone." Yuriko didn't know what she would've done after getting picked on at school if the red book hadn't talked to her.

"Then I will scold him no further," the old book said gently.

"Thanks," Yuriko whispered, and she smiled. Then she remembered she was speaking to someone very old and wise, and she said, "I mean, thank you very much, sir."

"Yuriko. Before we speak of anything else, there is something which you must decide." She had a choice, the book explained. She could either wake up her parents now and go home, or stay here and listen to what the book had to say.

"Of course, you may listen to me, then depart after that if you wish. But it will be a tale long in the telling. I'm afraid you will worry for your parents. This house is cold."

It was true. Yuriko was shivering herself. If she left her parents out there sleeping, they might freeze to death.

"Can't you cast a spell to make it warmer?" she asked.

"It is not impossible," the Sage said, a hint of laughter in his voice. "Do I take it from your question that you do not intend to leave us now?"

Yuriko nodded. She would stay.

"You are a strong-minded child," the book said. She wasn't sure whether that was meant as a compliment or not. "Are you afraid of being picked on at school? Is being picked on so frightening?"

"Well, yes...But it's more than that. Mr. Sage, I'm curious," Yuriko said. "I mean, it's amazing just being able to *talk* to a book, and I've learned so much from Aju already. But I feel like I've only heard a tiny part of the whole story."

Then she thought she heard the Sage sigh.

"Curiosity? Yes, the desire for knowledge. You have your brother's eyes."

Yuriko's heart tightened, then it leaped. *I'm like my brother?*

The Sage called to one of the other books, which replied in turn by singing another song—a spell to warm the cottage. This song was slightly longer than the one for sleep and with a different melody entirely.

Moments later, Yuriko felt warm air rising from the floor. *The book's magic. Real magic!*

Not wanting to let on how amazing she found all of this, all Yuriko said to the books was a polite "Thank you, that's great," and she sat back down on the stepladder.

"First," the Sage said, "I will speak of the Hero. Of all the stories in your Circle," the Sage explained to Yuriko, "the most beautiful and treasured is the story called 'The Hero.'"

"That sounds more like the heroes I've read about," Yuriko said.

"But the Hero is no person, Yuriko. It is a *story*."

"But—"

"Consider a person's life," the Sage continued over her objection. "No matter what great deeds they might accomplish, they are merely creating a reality, nothing more. Only when we have thoughts, and the telling of thoughts, and those thoughts become stories is the Hero first born. What we think, we tell, and are told—all are stories. But the Hero is the story that is the source of all the greatest deeds. The heroes who exist in your Circle all spring from this original story. They are like copies. The story called 'The Hero' came first.

"When people in the world do something great or upstanding, they are called heroes," the Sage went on, "and when their stories are told over the years, it means a copy of the Hero has been created. Because these copies of the Hero are themselves stories, they in turn feed the strength of the original story.

"Now, stories run in a cycle. As history progresses, all manner of heroes are born and their great deeds are told of, and told of again, increasing the Hero's power. In this way, a more beautiful, more noble story is formed, larger and stronger with each retelling."

"Well, what's so bad about that?" Yuriko interjected. "Wouldn't a bigger source of the Hero make better copies? Wouldn't there be even more heroes in the world then?"

"If that were all of it, it truly would be a wonderful thing," the Sage agreed. "Yet," he continued, his tone darkening, "if a beautiful, noble story shines very brightly, then the shadow it casts must also be very deep. This shadow too is the Hero. Like a coin, a story must have a front and back, right and wrong. Light and darkness always exist together, and there is no one who might separate them. It is impossible."

If the light is strong, the shadow is deep.

"In the original story of the Hero, there is darkness and evil in equal measure to light and good. Both sides grow together in a contest that continues to this day. This," the Sage said with a sigh, "also holds true for the copies produced by the source. The heroes of your Circle are ever a combination of light and dark. And if the dark side of the source should deepen, so too does the dark side of the copies deepen and grow stronger. The light leads to all that is good, and the darkness presides over all that is evil."

The Sage winked slowly once, looking down at Yuriko. "Now," the book asked her, "what do you think happens when the darkness grows stronger? What do your thoughts tell you?"

Yuriko spent a while listening to her thoughts. "I think," she said after a moment, "that more bad things must happen."

"Correct," the Sage replied. "In this Circle, there are many strong shining lights, and just as many dark, stagnant pools of malevolence. It is overflowing with both."

Which was why the original story, "The Hero," had been placed under lock and key.

"Stop the source, and you stop the cycle. While you cannot sweep away the light and the dark that already exist in this Circle, you can prevent them from further increasing."

So they had stopped the great cycle, keeping it small, and hopefully, more manageable.

"Like turning off the faucet so no more water comes out?" Yuriko ventured. "And then you just use what you already have, in a bucket or whatever, over and over again?"

To Yuriko's surprise, the Sage laughed. An old man's dry chuckle. "That is a most interesting comparison. I believe you have understood me well."

Yuriko felt like she had just scored a hundred on a test. "But," she addressed the Sage, "there's something I don't get. What's this Circle you keep talking about?"

Aju had used the word too. She had already figured out that it meant the world and everything in it, but she couldn't understand why they had to call it a special word, and something told her that was important to know. "Why don't you just call it 'the world'?"

"Because the world is not a Circle. Because the world is only what it is, and nothing more."

Yuriko frowned. *I'm not sure that made a bit of sense.*

"This world in which you live was here before the world of men was born," the Sage continued, heedless. "And this world is more than just the world of men. It is the skies, and the earth, and all living things. Everything around you is part of this world. Not so a Circle. A Circle is born of words. It only begins to exist the moment men first attempt to understand the natural world around them. It is power, it is a desire, it is hope, wishes, and prayer. It is all of these things."

This was starting to get difficult. Yuriko's brain had to work overtime to follow what the Sage was saying. "So the Circle is the world of people?"

"People are a part of the Circle, yes."

"But aren't all those things you talked about, like praying and wishing, things that people do? How can we just be one part of the Circle?"

"Do people not try to understand things that cannot be seen? Some of these things are far larger than the world of men. That is why the Circle, Yuriko, is much vaster than anything you can experience directly. Your Circle in particular has grown much larger than your world."

The world that is only what it is.

And the Circle *had grown even larger than the world it was trying to understand?*

"It is within this Circle that stories cycle, you see," the Sage concluded.

Okay, that's it. I give up. Yuriko raised her hands in defeat. "I'm sorry, I just don't get it."

"That is to be expected," the Sage said, still gentle. She had half expected a scolding. "You are still young. What you must do now is listen. Knowing that someday you will understand is enough."

So that was her homework. This was starting to feel like school.

"Tell me, are there not others who live in your world? Creatures other than man?"

"You mean animals, like dogs and cats?"

Yuriko had always been fond of cats, but her brother was decidedly a dog person. The memory of an argument flashed across Yuriko's mind. "It's got to be a dog," her brother had said, putting his foot down. She couldn't even get him to budge on his position—a rare thing between them.

"That's right," the Sage said, snapping her out of her reverie. "Now, do dogs and cats tell stories? Do they attempt to understand the world as you do? I think they do not. Dogs and cats all live in this world, yet they do not create the Circle."

"But there are lots of stories about dogs and cats. Sometimes they're even the heroes of stories."

"Yet these stories do not belong to them. These are stories created by people in an attempt to understand their companion animals. That Circle does not belong to the dogs and cats. It belongs to you."

Only people create stories, only people tell them.

"Now, Yuriko. I would like you to consider something. Tell me, where do you think stories come from?"

That seemed simple enough. "Well, if people are the ones thinking up stories, then don't they come from inside us?"

"Inside you? Where exactly inside you do you think that power to create stories lies?"

"In our brains," Yuriko said, pointing at her head. "Up here."

"Are you sure?"

Yuriko hesitated a moment, then pointed to her chest. "Okay, maybe they come from here. The heart." *Yeah, that sounds right.*

"The heart? You can point to this with your finger?"

"Yeah, it's right here, in my chest."

"Your heart is there, surely, but is that not merely an organ? A device for circulating blood through your body?"

Yuriko could feel her pulse beating now in the palms of her hands.

"All stories must have an origin, Yuriko. An origin born the moment the Circle is born, when man first attempted to understand his world. All stories were born there, and from there they flowed out into the Circle, where their cycle began."

An origin. A source.

With a faucet on it?

"But that doesn't make sense. People think up stories, right? How could their origin be some other place?"

"Their origins are in some other place. There are many origins—as many as there are people."

"Doesn't that mean the same thing?" Yuriko accused the Sage, jabbing a finger toward the shelf. "Aren't they coming from people after all?"

"There are as many origins as there are people," the Sage continued, in a tone of voice that demanded silence, "yet they are all the same. There are as many origins as there are people, but there is only one. That is because there is only one desire—to try to understand the world. For one Circle, there need be only one origin."

Now, Yuriko thought, *he's deliberately not making any sense.*

"This single origin lies in the nameless land."

There it was at last. *The nameless land.* Yuriko looked up, determination on her face. She might not understand everything, but she wanted to get a few things straight at least.

"That is where all stories are born, and the place to which all stories must return. This was also the place," the Sage explained, "where the great story known as the Hero was imprisoned. The ones who guarded that prison were the watchers, known to us as the nameless devout."

"Devout?" The word sounded familiar.

"Are they monks or something?"

There was a long pause before the Sage replied. "In form they appear to be, yes. But in truth there is no way to call them, for they have no name. The 'nameless devout' is a convenience bestowed upon them by one from the Circle who visited that land. He must've thought they resembled the devout monks of a religious order."

"Do they pray at a temple?"

"No, for there are no gods in the nameless land," the Sage said. "Only the story which gives rise to all gods is there. Along with the origin of stories, and the Hero."

Yuriko had wanted to ask more about the nameless land, but the Sage had already returned to a previous topic.

"As I said before, there are stories of the Hero already flowing through the Circle. They cycle and multiply, creating copies." The Sage paused. "I would speak to you of two things. The first is human memory. The second is human record. Do you understand the difference?"

She did, sort of. Yuriko nodded.

"Record and memory work together, augmenting each other. Sometimes records are created from memories, and sometimes memories serve to complete that which the records lack. Other times, records can sometimes create wholly new memories, even though there may be nothing worth remembering about them at all." Which was why, the Sage told her, even if they turned off the faucet at the source, it was impossible to mop up all of the stories that had already escaped.

"As long as the original story was imprisoned, the shadow did not darken too dangerously. Nor could the light reach as far as it had when the Hero was truly free." This, the Sage explained, was a mechanism for maintaining peace within the Circle.

"Yet, it is the way with men that, no matter how much time one gives them, they cannot understand this simple yet vital truth," the Sage lamented. "Since time immemorial, men have searched for the Hero. When the Hero was imprisoned, they searched for it all the more. They dug, they looked, and they sought to claim it. In this, the copies acted to guide them toward their originator."

The copies were the books Aju had told her about: not the Hero itself, but a part of the Hero, possessing part of its influence.

"Some copies are about the Hero, others are about the Hero's deeds. Still others are the records left by those who have encountered the Hero."

"And the Book of Elem?" Yuriko interrupted. "What sort of thing is that supposed to be a copy of?"

"The third kind—a record, and not a very good one. Yet enough of one to influence a child," the Sage muttered, pain in his voice. "As a book, it has only existed for one hundred years. A young book, fit for a young reader."

Yuriko glanced at Aju. She felt the red book return her glance. They too were a pair: the child and the young book.

"Through these copies, men glimpsed a part of the Hero's power. They experienced a fragment of what the Hero is."

And it takes them.

"Of course, not all who touch the copies are so possessed. In order to be possessed, one must have the necessary qualifications. These are the ones we call 'vessels.'"

"So what about the Summoner? How is he different from an ordinary vessel?"

Yuriko remembered someone had called Hiroki the "last vessel."

"You are bright, Yuriko, but impatient," the Sage scolded her. "You must not jump ahead like this. One has to walk through the fields of knowledge to pick its flowers. Run, and you will miss the best blossoms."

Yuriko sat quietly, so the books wouldn't think she was trying to run ahead again.

"What does a person need in order to become a vessel, you ask? Only one thing, and they must have it at the moment they touch the book, or it will not take them. They must have anger. The shadowy parts of the Hero favor human anger above all other emotions."

"So, you mean my brother was angry at someone?"

The room was silent.

Maybe I'm running ahead again, Yuriko thought to herself, despondent. When the Sage spoke again, he did not answer her question directly, but instead observed, "Those who live in this Circle, including yourself, seem to always think of the Hero as something good and beautiful. They point at the Hero's light parts, and call it so. Which is why, when it falls to us to explain the truth of the Hero as I do to you now, there is always this confusion, this inability to understand at first."

He was probably right. Yuriko felt like things had only gotten more and more confused in her head since she started talking to the books.

"Yeah..." she agreed.

"Then let us call it by a different name. The good of the Hero shall be called the 'hero' as you have always thought of it. And the dark side of the Hero, that which is evil, shall be called the 'King in Yellow.'"

The King in Yellow?

Next to her, Aju repeated the words. *The King in Yellow.*

Suddenly, an image sprang into Yuriko's head. The strange silhouette she had seen in Hiroki's room did have a crown like a king's, and a cape—though it had been too dark for her to see what color it was.

"A long while before you were born, more than a century ago, there was a weaver in this Circle."

"That's a person who writes the stories," Aju explained.

"You mean an author?"

"Something like that."

"This weaver, his name was Chambers, got as close to the truth of the Hero as a human being can get," the Sage continued, "and he wrote about it in a book titled *The King in Yellow.*"

It wasn't a novel, as Yuriko had expected. In the book, the weaver had described a play.

"Those who knew of the play shunned it, saying it would lead any who read it to their ruination. But while there were those who feared it—and rightly so—there were many others who sought it out."

"So this *King in Yellow* book was another copy of the Hero, right?"

"Correct. One of the most powerful copies of all."

Then she sensed that the Sage was smiling. He was pleased with her. *He's tough when he's scolding me,* she thought, *but sometimes he can be nice.*

"That is why, when we talk about the darker side of the Hero, we sometimes call it the King in Yellow."

Yuriko made a mental note of this. It certainly would be easier having two ways to talk about the Hero, she could tell.

"Notice, Yuriko, that the Hero changes its shape depending on who views it. In a sense, it becomes that for which they search. That is why the Hero will not always appear as a king. Nor will he always be shrouded in yellow. The Hero appeared in royal regalia when you saw it because that is what your brother wished to see. Your brother must have felt that a cape and a crown were appropriate garb for something of great power."

Yuriko thought back, trying to remember the comics and books and movies her brother liked. "I think you're right," she told the Sage.

It was difficult for Yuriko to imagine some powerful person who *didn't* look like the king she had seen in Hiroki's room. He certainly wouldn't look like the prime minister—that would just be a regular old man in a suit. What about a general in a uniform? No, the king sprang to mind much easier than that. Now that she thought about it, kings were everywhere. In the picture books their mother used to read to them, in the video games her brother always played.

"I think I get it," Yuriko said slowly. "So the King in Yellow was what made my brother do what he did."

The King in Yellow and its evil, terrible power.

"Now, Yuriko, I want you to consider something else for me. Imagine you were stripped of your freedom, locked in one place for an impossibly long time. What would you want the most?"

Yuriko didn't have to think about that one too hard. "I'd want to be free," she answered almost immediately.

"This too, the King in Yellow wanted. Yet to become free, it needed more power. Power to break the bonds that held it. The King in Yellow gets this power by using its copies throughout the Circle to possess a vessel. Not even the nameless devout can prevent this from happening."

"Why not? Can't they just gather up all the copies?"

"All of the copies in the entire Circle?"

"Sure."

"That would take an unimaginable amount of time. And it would be in vain."

"Why?"

"Men hide the copies," the Sage said. "And make copies of the copies. Over and over."

Yuriko frowned. A wrinkle crossed her pale forehead as she sat there in the darkened reading room surrounded by mountains of books. "Then can't you just pick up the Hero wherever it is? Not just turn off the faucet, I mean, but pick up all the water and the bucket with it?"

There was a pause, and then the Sage replied, his tone soft again, "But that would mean taking all the good that the Hero had done out of the Circle as well."

"Then, can't you just collect the bad ones?"

"What is good, and what is evil? Where do you draw the line between the two?"

Now Yuriko was getting a little upset. *I'm just in fifth grade, you know. They haven't taught us difficult things like that yet.*

"There are some who, even though they may touch a copy, do not become vessels. Some who are entranced by a copy, and yet do good by it. Others realize the danger that a copy represents and roam the world, seeking to find them and hide them away."

Yuriko looked to Aju, hoping he could make some sense out of this, but her friend was silent. If the red book had eyes, they were looking away.

"In any case," the Sage was saying, "it is impossible to stop the stories from cycling through the Circle. What did I tell you at the beginning? The Circle and the story are one. Lose the story, and the Circle will disappear. To put it another way, it would mean that all culture and civilization would vanish from the world."

Leaving only the world as it is. With people, living as animals.

Once she had figured it out, Yuriko agreed that sounded like a very bad thing.

"So the King in Yellow gathers power through its copies," the Sage continued, "and so it has for a very long time. One vessel leaves, and another appears to take its place. All of them work to give more power to the King in Yellow."

"What kind of work?"

"What do you think?"

To be honest, Yuriko was having trouble thinking of anything. Her heart and her head were so full of thoughts and emotions tugging her this way and that, she was having trouble picking one to follow. Anger rose in her, then left just as quickly, leaving her feeling like she wanted to cry. She was exhausted.

From behind her, another book said something in a soft, sweet, feminine voice. Yuriko turned around.

"What was that? Could you say that again?"

"Battle," the voice said. "Conflict."

War, thought Yuriko. *She means war.* "You mean the people who the King in Yellow possesses want to start wars?" Yuriko asked loudly, looking between the deep green glow of the Sage and the faint purple light of the book with the soft, sweet voice.

"There are many wars now in your Circle," the Sage pointed out.

"Not in Japan."

"I said in your Circle."

Yuriko knew that much. It was in the newspapers and on the nightly news.

"And by conflict, I did not mean only wars," the female voice said. "People take lives. They fight with other people. All of these are forms of conflict."

"So are crimes conflict too? Like murder?"

"They are," the female voice said, trembling with sorrow. "There is conflict even in the taking of a single life."

Like Hiroki had done when he stabbed a boy to death and wounded another.

"Whenever a vessel creates conflict," the Sage said, "The King in Yellow's power increases. It grows over years, decades, centuries—until it has enough to break free. Enough power to destroy an entire planet."

To generate such power took a very long time, the Sage explained, and a very great number of vessels were used and discarded along the way.

"No matter how high the tower, if you continue to climb, eventually, you will reach the top. No matter how deep the chasm, if it keeps raining, it will eventually fill to the brim."

Yuriko finally understood. The last vessel was the one who gave the King in Yellow the final bit of power it needed to break its bonds.

"Yes, that is the last vessel. The Summoner. And when its bonds are broken, and it is free, the King in Yellow borrows this last vessel's body that it might manifest itself within the Circle. Your brother," the Sage said softly, "has become the King in Yellow."

Yuriko buried her face in her hands. Her body was trembling, even in the magical warmth of the reading room.

"So, Hiroki…"

All around her, the books winked and blinked, their many shades of color covering her like a blanket, protecting her.

"…Where is he? If he's in the Circle, does that mean he's here, in this world?"

No one answered.

"You mean you don't know?" Yuriko asked with a sigh of despair. "You have no idea? Not even a hint?"

"I'm sorry," the sweet female voice whispered.

"We cannot be sure that the King in Yellow still uses your brother's form," the Sage said quietly. "As the last vessel, the boy may already have been consumed."

"Aw, you didn't have to tell her that," Aju protested. "Think of the poor girl."

"As you thought of her when you brought her here, Aju?"

Aju fell into a sullen silence.

"You asked about a hint?" the Sage said. "A hint, we do not have. But I know where you can find one."

Yuriko looked up so quickly her ponytail made an audible slap against her back. "Really?"

"Were you to visit the nameless land, the devout there might be able to teach you something. Perhaps they will even aid your cause...and perhaps you will be able to aid theirs."

Yuriko remembered something Aju had said. "I'm...qualified, right?"

"Yes, because you are of the same flesh as the last vessel."

And because I'm a child.

"Why can't adults leave the Circle, again?"

"Because adults carry within them the stain of too many stories. Were they to step into the nameless land, they would not be able to maintain their current form. They would likely not even be able to remain as people."

Yuriko didn't understand all of this, but the gist of it seemed clear enough—it had to be her. Her mother or father couldn't go. Neither could the police or the army.

"Or, you could just leave it be, Yuriko, and do nothing."

Yuriko's eyes went wide with surprise. *What did he just say?*

"You are still young. And weak. You need not take on this burden."

"But if I don't, won't the world be destroyed?"

"No, this Circle will be destroyed."

"What's the difference what you call it?"

"If the Circle is destroyed, another will take its place. And Yuriko, this Circle will not die immediately. It still has time. Enough time, perhaps, for you to become an adult, grow old, live a full life. You must not forget, Yuriko, it is the Hero that has broken free of its bonds. A story that combines both the good hero, as you know it, and the King in Yellow. When the Hero appears in your Circle, it will not appear only as the great evil that is the king. There will be a great good to match it."

So her Circle wouldn't be destroyed just like that. "There's going to be a war, isn't there. A war between good and evil."

The Sage winked twice as if to nod. "Yes. And many people will be involved in that war. You will not be fighting it alone. Even if you do fight, you can wait until you are grown to do so."

Then Aju glimmered brightly in the darkness, trying to catch her eye. "Little miss. I thought you should know that there are people in the Circle who have already sensed that the Hero is free. Grown-ups too, not children. It won't be long before they act."

"Who? What kind of people?"

"People who have traveled the world looking for copies. Remember what the Sage said? They are those people who seek out the copies so they can hide them."

"And those who seek to study the copies and learn the true nature of the Hero," the Sage added. "And those who would use that knowledge as a fortress to defend this Circle from the King in Yellow."

These people would follow the Hero's every move, the Sage told her, and acquire the knowledge they needed to hunt down the King in Yellow. "We call these people the 'wolves.' Because they have keen noses, sharp fangs, and swift legs that never tire."

"So," Aju added as brightly as he could muster, "you could just leave the fighting to them, little miss. You don't have to do this."

Yuriko mulled over what the two books had said, weighing their words against each other. Her heart was racing so fast, she found it hard to even think clearly, but she did what she could to focus. She combed the tangles out of her disheveled hair with her fingers and sniffled. Somewhere along the line, she had gotten a runny nose.

"Will these 'wolves' save my brother?" she asked at last. That was where all her thoughts led—to her brother.

Neither the Sage nor Aju replied. Even the book with the sweet female voice was quiet.

"They won't, will they," Yuriko said, answering her own question. "Why would they go out of their way to do that?"

And besides, if they waited any longer, they might run out of time.

"I have to go. I have to go save my brother," she said with finality, and a shiver ran through her. At the same time, a shiver also ran through every book in the reading room, like a collective sigh.

"So, that is the way of it, then," the Sage said, his voice echoing. Yuriko looked up. "You're already part of the Hero's story."

Me? Part of the Hero?

"Do not forget, child. Make yourself remember. Say it to yourself in the morning when you wake and at night when you lay down to rest: the Hero and the King in Yellow are two sides of the same coin."

"Are you sure about this?" Aju asked, his earlier confidence gone. "She's just a little girl."

"We will send Yuriko to the nameless land."

"But—"

"It's okay, Aju," Yuriko said, gently stroking the book's cover. "I'll do my best. And I won't be alone. I'm sure I'll find someone to help me in the nameless land, and even if I don't, I'm sure I'll come across the wolves while I'm looking for my brother. They'll help me for sure."

Even if I have to start my journey alone.

"Wait, I know!" Aju shouted. "Why don't you look for the wolves here first? I'm sure that Minochi had encounters with wolves. Maybe some of them even visited."

"You think so?" Yuriko asked, feeling a light of hope go on inside her. "You mean one of Mr. Minochi's friends?"

"Yet we do not know who might be, or where," the Sage responded. "Minochi was wary of the wolves. He would not have invited one here to his home." There had been some visitors who might have been wolves, the Sage explained, but her great-uncle had always turned them away at the door.

"Maybe he took down an address or something," Aju suggested, unwilling to give up so easily. "He might have gotten a phone number!"

"Like in an address book?"

"Right! Seen one anywhere?"

Yuriko had not. If her great-uncle did have anything of the sort, she supposed he'd probably have had it with him when he collapsed in Paris. Yuriko had no idea who might have it now.

"Then you should start by trying to find that. You could wake up your parents and ask them."

Yuriko hesitated. It seemed like a good idea. But if she woke up her parents, she would have to try to explain the whole story to them. That would take forever.

"Aju, do you think you could explain it to my parents for me?"

"Of course!" Aju said enthusiastically, but the Sage cut him off.

"Even were the girl's parents to see the truth with their eyes and hear the truth with their ears, they would not believe it."

"Why not?"

"Aju, calm yourself and think about it for a moment. I believe you already know why."

Placed in the same position as Yuriko had been, adults would doubt before they believed. They would doubt their own eyes and ears—and their sanity.

There was a long pause before Aju glumly agreed. "You're right."

It was as the Sage said.

Yuriko closed her eyes and then stood up from the stepladder. "I haven't come this far just to sit around and do nothing."

"Then first, Yuriko, we must fashion your replica."

"A replica?"

"Were you to leave your parents here alone, would they not be worried about you?"

They sure would. But how...? "What exactly do you mean by 'fashion your replica'?"

"It is best you see it for yourself," the Sage replied. He then called out "Vagesta?" and a book answered from Yuriko's left side, from a shelf at just about the height of her head.

"Step toward me, miss," said a soft female voice, "and hold out both hands in front of you, if you would. I will fly to you, so please catch me."

Yuriko stuck out her hands, and a black, velvety book fell into them.

"Let us begin," the book said. "First, I'll need a strand of your hair."

CHAPTER THREE

The Nameless Land

Before she even opened her eyes, Yuriko felt a slight breeze against her skin. It brushed across her forehead, lifting up her bangs.

And the smells—there was dirt and grass, and something else. A smell she had never encountered in the city where she lived. An unfamiliar smell.

The ground felt soft beneath her sneakers. *It's a field. I'm standing on grass.*

That wouldn't be so unusual, if she hadn't, until moments before, been standing in the reading room of Ichiro Minochi's cottage.

She had done everything as the Sage instructed her. She caught the book that fell from the bookshelf and flipped through the pages until he told her to stop. Then she read the words there—she couldn't actually read the letters herself, so she had to repeat them after the Sage. Apparently, it was important that she hold the book and say the words herself.

Then she had to search the cottage until she found a piece of white chalk in order to draw a strange circular pattern on the floor of the reading room— based on the diagram in one of the books the Sage showed her. Before she did that, she had to clear a space on the floor, and that meant moving stacks of heavy, dusty books which made her sweat and sneeze terribly.

Even still, the moment she saw an exact copy of herself emerge from the strand of her hair she had placed in the middle of that strange magical circle, the aching in her shoulders and back and the burning in her bleary red eyes all vanished. She was so surprised she forgot to breathe. Everything about the girl standing in the middle of that circle was just like Yuriko. The girl grinned and took a step closer.

"Do not be frightened. While you are away, your replica will serve in your place," the Sage explained.

"I-I'm not supposed to touch her, right?"

Yuriko recalled a science fiction movie her brother had rented once. The main character in the movie got into a time machine and went back in time to meet his past self. She remembered the scientist who invented the time machine telling him sternly that whatever he did, he wasn't to touch his past self. If he did, not only he, but the entire world, would disappear in an instant.

The Sage chuckled softly. "It will do no harm. Your replica is yours to command."

"Really?"

"Try giving her an order."

So Yuriko had her replica help her erase the circle she had drawn on the floor. It was harder then she'd expected to get the chalk off the wood floorboards, so she asked her replica to find a mop somewhere, and the replica walked out of the room, only to reappear five minutes later, mop in hand.

"The next circle you will draw is far more complicated than the last," the Sage warned. "You must draw it carefully, so there are no mistakes."

This second circle would serve as the gate to send Yuriko to the nameless land.

After a few false starts, and with lots of corrections, she drew the circle. Yuriko stood up to get a better look at her work. Part of her wanted to stride boldly into the magic circle's center, while another part of her was afraid and wanted to run away. So Yuriko stood still, breathing raggedly. Then she heard the Sage speak.

"Yuriko, do you always wear your bangs down like that in the front?"

They were hanging down now. Yuriko had always been a little embarrassed about her forehead, which she felt was far too large for its own good. When she combed her hair forward, her mother would always scold her, saying it would get in her eyes, and make Yuriko press her bangs back with pins or hair gel, but over the course of a busy day her bangs would naturally fall forward anyway.

The question seemed so out of place, for a moment Yuriko didn't know how to respond. "Is this another test?"

"Lift up your bangs with one hand so we can see your forehead. Now, turn toward me and lift your chin. Ah! Don't step on the circle yet!"

Yuriko put her back against one of the bookshelves and looked in the direction of the Sage.

The Sage began to cast a spell. His words had the rhythm of a song, but he was not singing. His voice rose and fell like a Buddhist chant, but it was not a prayer. Yuriko had never heard such a strange sound in her life.

The Sage's voice grew suddenly clear and higher, then stopped abruptly. A moment later, the white chalk circle she had drawn on the floor began to burn with a pale light. Yuriko jumped. Then she felt something like a cold fingertip running across her brow. Unconsciously, she lifted her own hand to touch it. On the floor, the magic circle went dark.

But something was still giving off light near Yuriko, shining in her eyes.

"I believe there was a mirror in the hall," the Sage said, ordering Yuriko's replica to fetch it. The replica left the room again and came back carrying a small square mirror in her hands. The frame was covered in rust, and about a third of the mirror's face was clouded and cracked.

"Look into the mirror," the Sage told Yuriko, but she didn't hear him. She was too busy being surprised at the warm touch of her replica's hand when she took the mirror from her.

"Yuriko, look at your face in the mirror," the Sage repeated.

Hurriedly, she held up the little square mirror.

A small magic circle had been drawn in the middle of her forehead about the size of a large coin. This was the source of the light that was making her squint. The little magic circle glowed a peppermint color and was an exact miniature of the magic circle she had drawn on the floor. It was like someone had drawn graffiti on her face with a fluorescent marker.

"What is it?" she whispered.

"That mark upon your forehead is a glyph. It allows you to travel freely between this Circle and the nameless land. It shows that you are permitted to pass through the gate between worlds."

All she had to do to move between the nameless land and her own world was place her hand upon the mark and wish it, the Sage explained.

"Wait, so when I want to come back from the nameless land, do I show up here, in the cottage? Or can I go anywhere?"

"Anywhere you like, but—" the Sage's voice grew louder, "should the magic circle in this reading room be erased or destroyed, the glyph upon your forehead will lose its power. You would do well to return here frequently to check on the parent circle, for it is your lifeline home."

So if one of her uncles or the lawyer came here and tried cleaning up the magic circle, she'd be in trouble.

"Could you use your magic to keep everyone out of the cottage while I'm away?"

"We could."

"Then will you?"

"We may, but we cannot stop the people who try to come here from wondering why they fail time and time again."

So their magic wasn't all-powerful.

"Right, I guess that would be a little strange."

"Indeed."

Yuriko nodded firmly. "Okay, I understand. I'll be careful."

"You're forgetting something important," Aju said to the Sage. It was good to hear the red book's voice again. "Little miss, try not to go showing that mark on your forehead to everyone you meet. Better keep your bangs down over it when you can."

So that's why the Sage was asking about my bangs.

"You are impatient, Aju," the Sage grumbled. "I was just about to tell her that. And besides, you forgot an important part. There will be no need for you to hide your glyph in the nameless land. You only need conceal it here, in this Circle. And you'll need to conceal it should you cross over to any other region within this Circle."

"Any other region?"

"You'll understand once you go there."

"Oh, oh, one more thing," Aju cut in. "There will be people who know you bear the mark, even if you hide it. Those are the wolves, Yuriko. Their knowledge allows them to sense the glyph's presence. Don't worry about them, for the most part. Except, wolves tend to be a little *unusual* sometimes—so come to think of it, you might want to watch out for them after all."

Yuriko wasn't sure how she would do that. "Do these wolves all collect old books like my great-uncle did?"

"Many of them do, yes."

"So they're scholars. That doesn't sound too dangerous."

"Well," Aju said, "just be careful. There are some real weirdos out there."

"Once again, Aju, you leave much unsaid," the Sage scolded the red book in a harsh tone. "The wolves are pursuers of the Hero, child. They are hunters. And now that you bear the mark, you are one of them."

"Me? A wolf?"

"You leave now on a journey to find the Hero, to find the King in Yellow, do you not?"

He's right.

"And, Yuriko, the King in Yellow knows. It can sense that you have received the mark. You are an *allcaste*."

"*Allcaste*," Yuriko muttered to herself.

"That is the word the devout in the nameless land use. That is your identity now."

Yuriko swallowed. "So the enemy knows about me already?" Her knees started to wobble. It didn't seem fair. She just wanted to find her brother, not get mixed up in all of this. *I think that maybe I started something big without really understanding what I was doing.*

"Now that the King in Yellow is free of its prison, it is also free to collect more power. It will come to this Circle, intent on adding to its strength, and perhaps not notice you at all. But should it feel you are a hindrance to its plans, it will quickly move to eliminate you."

No one said anything about this!

"We cannot know how it will act, or react. But Yuriko, be wary, for the King in Yellow has many familiars, and while not as powerful as their master they are nothing to laugh at."

Familiars? Like the animals witches are always sending to do their dirty work? Yuriko swallowed again.

"Are these nameless devout guys strong? Can they fight?"

The Sage did not answer, so she turned to Aju.

"Do you think the wolves will help me if I ask them?"

Aju too was silent. Yuriko stepped forward and picked up the red book. "Will you go with me, Aju?"

The book's red glow flickered weakly, like its batteries were going dead. "The time for me to be summoned to the nameless land has not yet come," the book replied after a moment.

Yuriko sighed and placed Aju back on the shelf. The book mumbled an apology, and she felt it shiver sadly as her hand left the cover.

"Now then, are you ready to go?"

She almost said *no*.

She wanted to cry.

Next to her, Yuriko's replica stretched out a hand. Yuriko grasped it and held tightly, but the replica slowly shook her head.

"Hand that mirror to your replica," the Sage instructed her. "You will not be able to bring anything with you from this Circle to the nameless land but that which you wear. You must pass through alone."

Shoulders sagging, Yuriko handed over the mirror. But she still held the replica's hand, not letting go until the replica had to gently pry off her fingers.

"Do you wish to see your parents before you leave?"

She had found them lying in the hall and on the entrance mat when she had gone looking for the chalk. They had been sleeping like babies. It had taken all her willpower to resist the urge to shake them awake.

"No. I'm okay. I'll just go like this."

Yuriko gave up trying to control things. She would just have to go for it, she decided. Even if what she was about to do sounded a whole lot scarier than getting picked on at school.

What was that line again? "There's no turning back now."

"Take care of them for me, will you? My parents, I mean," she said to her replica, and her replica smiled and nodded. "Don't worry. Leave them to me."

She can speak! With my voice! It was obvious, when she thought about it—she was an exact replica intended to take her place after all. But it still startled her to hear her own voice like that.

"Won't it be weird if there are two of me here when I come back?"

"Don't worry about that, either. There's a way to make it so no one will notice. I'll explain when the time comes."

Yuriko thought the replica sounded a little older than she did. Like a seventh grader, maybe.

"Good luck," the replica said, and Yuriko wondered if a piece of her hair had somehow managed to turn into a more grown-up, confident person than she was.

"Then let us open the gate," the Sage said solemnly. "To the center of the magic circle, Yuriko."

Though her knees were still a little wobbly, Yuriko stepped into the very center of the circle and stood. The Sage began to chant again. Soon the other books joined, until the voice of every book in that reading room was raised in a single chorus. She could make out Aju's voice among them.

Once again, pale flames rose up from the magic circle. The flames arced in the air, wrapping around her legs and arms. Though Yuriko closed her eyes against the glare, the image of her replica standing just outside the circle, waving her hand, still floated on the inside of her eyelids.

And that was how she had come here, wherever *here* was, standing on the soft grass.

She didn't feel like she had moved since stepping on the magic circle. She hadn't flown up into the air or tunneled through the ground or had to duck through any sort of opening.

She was just here.

Yuriko slowly opened her eyes, steeling herself for whatever might be waiting. She had already imagined several possibilities. She felt ready for just about anything. Anything at all.

What she saw dashed all pretense of readiness from her, scattering her resolve to the wind.

She was looking out over a dry grassland, bleached of color, as bleak as the gray sky that hung low above it. There was no one else in sight.

She noticed the light above her eyes again. The glyph on her forehead was glowing. She lifted her own hand and saw its pale light reflected on her fingers, and then it went out. Like a signal announcing her arrival extinguished when its purpose was served.

The sky seemed oppressively close. The clouds hung heavily over her, and beneath them floated a layer of mist. The mist had a slight bluish tint, making it look cold, as though tiny particles of ice flowed through the air currents above her head.

The gray grass that covered the ground was surprisingly soft to the touch, supple even, and moist. *Maybe it's not dried-up at all. Maybe this is its natural color.* She held up her hand to her face and sniffed it. It smelled of soil. Drops of dew glistened on her fingers.

For 360 degrees around her, as far as she could see, there was only the sky and the grass. The ground was slightly uneven, like the ocean on a calm day, lifting and falling in gentle curves. The high parts weren't quite high enough to be called hills, and the low parts not quite low enough to be called valleys.

She thought for a while before she remembered where she had seen something like it before. *Sand dunes. They look like sand dunes made of grass!*

So this is the nameless land.

Maybe they should've called it the colorless land.

For no particular reason, Yuriko pursed her lips and whistled. It made a weak trill that the wind quickly swept away and carried across the plains.

So, which way do I go?

Just then, she heard the sound of a bell tolling from far away through the mists. Yuriko took a step back, hunching low to the ground. When she stepped back, it sounded like the bell was coming from behind her, and when she stepped forward, it sounded like the bell was somewhere in front of her. The deep, booming sound seemed to bubble up from the ground and rain down from the sky all at once.

Then the mist ahead of her split in two like an unbuttoned collar. It was as though the bell had been a signal telling the mists to open the way for her. Far beyond the gently rising and falling plain, Yuriko spotted the silhouette of a giant building, and her eyes opened wide. The wind in her face made her eyes water, but she found herself unable to look away, even to blink.

Was it a temple or some kind of church? Could it even be a mountain that she was just mistaking for a building? She had seen mountains something like it, with pleated edges and high ridgelines towering straight toward the sky, on a family trip to the Japanese Alps. It looked like some kind of massive folding screen. But the color was all wrong. From here she could see dark grays, darker even than the clouds, and tiny spots of something glimmering like violet crystals, and other spots that were as black as night. The way the colors were arranged reassured her that whatever it was, it wasn't natural. *It must be a building.*

Now the mist cleared further, and she could see a roof, triangular at the top, with columns like horns standing to either side of it. Actually, it was less a rooftop than it was a tower. Below it, the building was divided into stories. She counted three before the base of the structure disappeared below the horizon. What had looked to her like folds in the mountainside were rows of decorative columns lining the walls. And the spots of pitch black were windows. *The violet crystals must be light shining out from some of the windows.*

The sound of the bell was coming from that building, she was sure of it.

And then, suddenly, it stopped.

The wind whistled in her ears. And then she heard voices carried on the wind, people talking. *No, they're not talking. They're singing.* Someone was out there, singing. Their refrain seemed to echo low along the ground, creeping across the grassland, coming closer.

Suddenly, a torch flared up in the mist, startlingly nearby. The flame trailed sparks behind it in the wind. Then another torch appeared, and another, and three torches soared over the rising curve of one of the grass-dunes. Heads appeared, one head by each torch.

The three people climbed to the top of the dune, and she saw that they were all dressed in the same black robes. The robes went down to just above the knobs of their ankles, and the hems were wrapped tightly around their calves. They were barefoot.

The trio approached. They walked evenly, all at the same pace, not in any hurry, but steadily. Yuriko took a few steps toward them, then stopped. She stood up straight, fixing her posture, though no one had told her to do so. It just seemed the thing to do in the presence of the nameless devout—and she was sure that was who they were.

The three came down the slope. When they had reached the bottom of the swale, they were only thirty feet or so away. The wind whipped across the grass between them. Sparks danced from the torches.

The three stopped. It had been they who were singing, but now their song ceased.

Then one of them lowered his torch from his face. Another, torch still held high, took a step forward. Before he or Yuriko could say a word, the glyph on Yuriko's forehead glimmered brightly, then faded again.

"Young child," said a youthful man's voice, "new *allcaste*, we greet you."

Yuriko looked at the monklike figure and then up at the giant building distant in the mist behind him. For a moment, it seemed to her as though it had been the building that spoke, not the man.

"Hello?" Yuriko ventured. Even though her throat was too tight and her voice too soft, the word seemed to ring through the air. Then the gray sky and chilly mist echoed her word back to her. *Hello. Hello...*

"We are the nameless devout, guardians of the Hall of All Books," the young man's voice said. Then the one who had stepped forward bowed deeply, still holding his torch high. Behind him, the other two joined his bow.

Unsure of what to do, Yuriko merely stood as straight as she could.

The three nameless devout lifted their heads. "This is the nameless land," the one in front said. "The sound you heard was the Second Bell ringing to mark the arrival of an *allcaste*. We have come to greet you."

Come, one of the monks motioned with his head, turning sideways to her to open the way. To Yuriko, it felt like an eternity passed before she could summon the nerve to take that first step. It took more courage than it had to step into the magic circle that had brought her here. *Now I really can't turn back. Once I go with them, it's started.* Though, in a corner of her mind, she still felt like there was time for her to apologize and just go home. She was sure they would forgive her—

Yuriko stepped forward.

"There's nothing to be frightened of," the lead devout said in a gentle voice as she approached. "There is nothing in this land that threatens you, *allcaste*. Come, let us take you to our hall." The two devout in the back now led them, and the devout who had stepped forward matched Yuriko's pace to walk beside her.

"Is that big building the Hall of All Books?" Yuriko asked, indicating the silhouette on the horizon with her eyes. Somehow, she felt it wasn't appropriate to point.

"That is so."

"So that big building is filled with books? Like a library?"

For moment, the nameless devout walking next to her seemed to not understand the question, then he smiled and said, "Ah yes, a library. That is what you call them in your Circle. It is something like that. A very large library."

The nameless devout's features matched his youthful voice. He was a boy, and not a very tall one—Yuriko's head came up to his shoulder. His head was perfectly hairless save the thick brows over his eyes, and he wore no clothes, jewelry, or any adornments other than his black robes.

Yuriko imagined them to be scholars watching over the staggeringly large library as if it were a church. It made her smile to think of them as librarians. Except the people who worked at the library near her school all wore colorful aprons, even the men. She wondered if the nameless devout would look good in aprons.

I'm just trying to calm myself down by thinking silly thoughts—and it's not working. Yuriko sighed and put the mental image out of her mind.

They walked steadily onward, but the hall on the horizon didn't seem to get any closer. The way it loomed up into the sky made Yuriko jittery, and she racked her brain for something she could talk to her escort about.

"You were singing before, weren't you?"

"Yes."

"What was the song?"

"It is the invocation," the devout replied, explaining before she could ask that it was a song of prayer.

So they do pray, sort of. "I couldn't understand the words—what language was that—" Yuriko clapped a hand to her mouth. Not understanding the lyrics to their song was one thing. But how could she possibly be talking with them now? *What language am I speaking?*

Again, the nameless devout answered her question before she could ask it. "We of the nameless land can understand the words of the *allcaste* and employ them ourselves. But the words of the invocation are something else entirely. That is why you are unable to comprehend their meaning."

"Well, what language were the lyrics in?"

"In the words of the nameless land."

So the nameless land had its own language. *Guess I'm not in Japan.*

"I was wondering," she began, "if you...if you could tell me what the words to your song meant?" She hesitated halfway through her question when it seemed to her that a dark look passed over the nameless devout's face.

"It is a song about the King in Yellow, and the weaver."

"Oh," Yuriko said simply, then shut her mouth. She had lots of questions burning inside her now, but she didn't want the monks to think of her as an annoying little girl.

She looked up to see that the building loomed even closer now. *Funny, it doesn't feel like we've walked that far*—of course, she thought, maybe it was the lack of any reference points whatsoever that was throwing off her sense of distance.

Again, a bell began to ring, but with a slightly different tone, and at a different pace. Where the bell she had heard earlier was slow and booming, this one was light and up-tempo.

"This bell tells the nameless devout that the *allcaste* will soon arrive at the hall, calling them to gather at the Dome of Convocation."

How does he always know what I'm just about to ask?

"Are there lots of you?"

"We are a thousand, and we are ten thousand," the boy monk told her. "Yet we are only one."

Yuriko frowned. How could "we" be one? It took at least two people to make a "we," as far as she knew. And weren't there three of them with her right now? The path curved gently downhill until they were close enough to the Hall of All Books that Yuriko could make out some of the details.

It's a castle, was her first thought, *like they have in Europe.* She had never seen the real thing, but she had seen plenty of buildings like it on television, and in movies and pictures, sitting on the tops of mountains or cliffs, rising from a forest by a lake in Germany or France.

Yet at the same time, it seemed different from those castles—though she couldn't put her finger on why it did.

Was it a church, or maybe an abbey? That would make sense, if monks lived there. *But no,* she thought, *it's something else. Something that every castle has, but the Hall of All Books lacks.*

Then it hit her. There was no wall around the building, not even a court-yard. It just rose abruptly from the surrounding grasslands. Because there were no walls, there was no gate. There was only a small, pointed roof over the main entrance directly in front of them. The double doors in the entrance were fashioned of some dark material, though she couldn't tell whether it was metal or wood. Carved figures and shapes covered their surfaces.

Three semicircular steps led up to the doors. To either side of the steps stood two torch poles, each as high as a two-story building, their flames giving off plenty of light and smoke. Yuriko and the three devout approached, and the doors opened inwardly, seemingly by themselves. They moved like they were very heavy, yet made not a sound.

The two devout who had been walking in the front split off to the left and the right, opening the way for Yuriko and the one who walked with her. It was the first time she had gotten a good look at their faces.

So great was her surprise that she almost hiccuped. *At least,* she thought, *I didn't shout out loud.* The two in front looked identical to the one walking with her. *All three of them look exactly the same!* Now that she thought about it, she realized they were all the same height too.

Are they triplets? If they don't have any names, how am I supposed to tell them apart?

Then the devout standing by her side bowed lightly and walked ahead of her. Yuriko looked around, then followed him into the hall. It was dim inside, and the air smelled faintly of something pleasant—though not flowers or incense. It smelled like the air smells after a thundercloud has passed. A moist, pure smell.

When a lot of rain falls in a short amount of time, it releases negative ions. That's why the air smells different after a thunderstorm. Her brother had told her that once.

The place she was standing in now was more like a town square than a hall. Looking up, she could see a vaulted, six-sided ceiling high above her. Thin light streamed through small windows that had been cut out of the walls in each corner. Yuriko lowered her eyes and found that the floor of the hall was also six-sided, with six pillars standing around the edges.

The nameless devout in front turned to the left. Yuriko squinted her eyes to look at the carvings and statuary around her. Some of them sat on the floor, others had been carved higher into the walls themselves, and some were part of the columns.

All of them were shaped like people. It was like a Greek temple she had read about once. Gods in robes and sandals. But then she noticed one wearing long stocking-boots, like a character in an old samurai movie. Another statue, across from him, looked just like a general in the old Chinese warfare video game her father was always playing.

The floor was covered with overlapping patterns made from tiny, intricately arranged tiles.

Not just patterns, they're letters! Letters, letters, and more letters. Letters of all kinds, woven together like a puzzle, stacked on top of each other. Some of them looked like jumbles of random lines, and others looked like some foreign language, and they were all mixed together. She recognized Roman letters here and there, and something that looked a lot like Korean. *I wonder if there's any Japanese?*

She was so busy looking down at the tiles beneath her feet that she walked into the back of the nameless devout in front of her. Yuriko jumped back, mortified, but the monk didn't seem to mind.

"We'll be entering this hallway."

Ahead of them, a long hallway led away from the room, curving gently to the right. The right-hand wall was solid all the way down, but the left-hand wall was broken up by tall, narrow windows every six feet or so. The light coming in through the windows made the hallway much brighter than the giant chamber they were leaving.

"You'll want to watch your feet through here," the devout warned her. Yuriko nodded and began to walk, but before she had gone very far, she stopped short and jumped.

Japanese! It's a Japanese character! She found it on the dark black wall on the left-hand side, between two of the window slits.

It was only a single character, carved in relief—and large, about the size of a car tire.

円

"*En!*" she shouted, a little too loudly. "That's the character *en*, isn't it?"

The two nameless devout behind her said nothing, but the one in front smiled gently and nodded.

"I'm sorry. I was just surprised to find something I could read here."

She was surprised at how relieved it made her feel. She felt happy, and homesick. And it was also a little funny. She had never seen this particular character written so large, not even in the lobby of a bank.

"Did you know that this is the word for the money we use?"

The nameless devout nodded. "We do. Yet it also means 'circle.'"

And by circle, he means "Circle." *Like the Circle I live in. Of course. I always thought "en" just stood for money.*

"I'm sorry, I talk too much, don't I? I'll be quiet." She was embarrassed. *Why am I so flustered?*

The nameless devout walked on in silence, a little quicker than before. In order to avoid further distractions, Yuriko kept her eyes off the walls and walked as straight as she could. But she stopped when she realized that the wall on the right side, which she had assumed was just covered with sculpture like all the rest, was actually divided into shelves stacked full of books. Their spines ran in tightly packed rows as far as she could see.

"These are all books?" she asked before she could think to stop herself.

Yuriko reached out and touched one. It felt strangely hard beneath her fingertips.

It's like they're made of stone. These aren't books. More sculpture.

One of the nameless devout was looking at her. She mumbled an apology and pulled back her hand. The young monk didn't scold her, but he wasn't smiling either.

They walked on slowly down the curving hallway. It occurred to Yuriko that maybe she had been wrong when she thought there were no walls around the Hall of All Books. Maybe the hallway she was walking down now wasn't the *inside* of the building. In other words, what she could see from the outside wasn't actually the Hall of All Books, but something like a thick wall that surrounded it. Its immense size had made it look flat, like the side of a building, when she'd gone in, but they had been walking around a curve for so long, she imagined it might have been part of a much larger, circular structure.

If that were true, then the castle, or abbey or library, would be further inside. But it didn't seem like that was where Yuriko was heading.

Finally, the end of the hallway came into view. Straight ahead was a dead end, but the right wall was open to another room, though a portcullis of thin bars blocked the way. Yuriko caught a glimpse of green grass through the bars.

The nameless devout walking behind her stepped ahead and pulled the lever on the wall next to the portcullis, causing it to creak open to one side.

If Yuriko could trust her sense of direction, going through this door should bring her behind the wall. She looked behind her and saw that this exit also had metallic double doors, though this pair had been pushed open to stand flat against the wall. It wasn't exactly a sunny day outside, but coming out of the darkened hallway she had to blink against the brightness. Yuriko squinted her eyes—and gasped.

She had been right. The towering edifice Yuriko had first seen from the plain was only an outer wall, and only a part of it at that. It *had* been like a folding screen. One bigger than she could have ever imagined. And behind it was this: More buildings than Yuriko could count on both her hands. There was one like a long, low hall. Another like a giant's bowl turned upside down on the ground—possibly the dome of something-or-other that the devout had mentioned. A bell tower stood next to that.

In her short life, Yuriko had never seen a bell tower other than the one on the low stand in front of her neighborhood temple, but she knew this was a bell tower immediately thanks to the three bells hanging in the belfry near the top. They were huge, these bells, each as large as a house. *Monster bells,* thought Yuriko.

The buildings were gray for the most part, though she spotted slight differences here and there. Some seemed to have a faintly purpleish hue, others were darker, and some were blue. There were wide, low buildings and tall, narrow buildings. Though each building seemed to be of its own unique design, they nevertheless looked like they belonged there together. Perhaps it was because the buildings were connected by long exterior hallways and stairs hewn from stone. Not one stood entirely apart from the others—yet the way they had been connected was bizarre. In one spot, two buildings stood so close together there didn't seem to be any point in running a hallway between them, and yet a hallway zigzagged through the narrow gap, with stairs going up and down so that to walk along it would nearly quadruple the actual distance between one building and the other. In another part, two buildings at the very edges—as far away from each other as they could possibly be—were connected by a long aerial walkway about three stories off the ground.

The manner of their linking seemed complicated and random, following no discernible pattern. She tried following the hallways with her eyes, and it still wasn't immediately clear what connected which building to which. It was like one of those picture puzzlers. In part it seemed like they had just kept adding buildings, linking them however they felt like at the time, even if it didn't make any sense—but at the same time there was a certain joy to the way it looked. Yuriko felt like she had just opened a toy box filled with wondrous things. The buildings were huge and dark, towering and giant, weathered and gray, yet they were each so different and curious and strangely cute in places. Even though it was so big, and she was so little, Yuriko found herself growing quite fond of this strange and tangled town.

And there was something familiar about it too, though she couldn't imagine how that might be possible. There was nothing particularly Japanese about the buildings, nor was there anything that seemed quite like the scenes of Europe that Yuriko had seen in movies. It wasn't American or British either. Still, it felt curiously familiar—*and all of it was hidden behind that wall,* thought Yuriko, impressed anew with the wall's sheer magnitude.

Green grass, cobblestone plazas, and brick roads filled the open spaces of the town. Like the buildings, none of these were the same. The first thing she realized when she saw the roads was that the steepled entrance and long hallway she had come in through were only a side entrance to the town.

Directly opposite from where Yuriko had entered, there was a two-story-high gap in the external wall, with a giant gate. The doors of the gate were reinforced with strips of ancient iron, with sharp spearlike adornments running along the top edge. *To keep out intruders? Or to keep people from escaping?*

Not that she could see anyone who might try. The place was deserted.

The main gate was closed, and Yuriko imagined the chilly mist pressing against the far side. A large road passed under the gate, though Yuriko couldn't begin to guess where it led.

One of the nameless devout noticed her looking. "We will take you beyond that gate later, but now we must hurry to the convocation."

As she had expected, they began to walk toward the building that looked like a giant's bowl turned upside down on the ground. The exterior walls of the dome were covered with what looked like bronze plates. They were rusting in places—here and there, splotches of vivid green stood out on the dull surface.

It was like the giant who owned the bowl had taken a paintbrush to it and made a grand mess of the thing. *Perhaps it was the giant's child,* Yuriko thought, *playing with the paint.*

At the top of the dome was a small protrusion—a handle on the kettle. It was round, like the little onions her mother used to put in her stew sometimes, or like a dollop of whipped cream on a shortcake.

Then it hit her. *This is a picture-book building. In a fairy-tale town.*

A place that existed only in the imagination. A place that belonged in stories. A town that was nowhere.

Yuriko walked, her sneakers squishing across the damp cobblestones. The feel of the stones must have been just as strange to her sneakers—which were accustomed to walking on the pavement by her school, the shopping street, and the sidewalk near her house—as this town seemed to Yuriko.

I wonder if the nameless devout are cold with bare feet like that. She could see the lines of their bones clearly where their feet stuck out from the bottom of their robes. She hadn't even known it was possible for people to be so thin.

She wondered if life was hard in this place.

She began to think that the giant's child had a hand in building the whole, strange, marvelous town—perhaps with a little help from its father. But the town was filled with these barefooted, terribly thin guardians who watched over all the books in the world.

Protecting the books.

Protecting the books from something.

Protecting something from the books.

One part of the domed roof straight ahead of them was curled back, like a dancer's fingertips, creating a gap between the roof and the ground beneath it. This was the entrance. Now that she was close, Yuriko realized that the dome alone was not connected to any other building.

Steps rose in layered semi-circles from the cobblestone path toward the entrance. They were made of bronze and looked slippery. The doors at the top were surprisingly small, hinged in the middle so they folded like an accordion to one side. These too were covered with letters. Letters, letters, and more letters, all carved in relief.

A nameless devout stood to either side of the doors. Yuriko looked up at them and gasped.

They all have the same face!

The monks bowed silently, and the doors opened. When one set of doors opened, she saw behind them another set of doors identical to the first. And beyond them, another set. And another. *Wait a second. That doesn't make sense. Are the walls to this place that thick?* It didn't seem like there would be any space at all inside once she had gotten through all those doors. One by one, the doors opened. Yuriko passed through them as though pushed by an invisible hand from behind. No, she was being sucked in toward the center of the dome. Her feet had left the floor and she flew through the air. The black robes of the nameless devout in front of her drew closer, then farther away. She was having trouble focusing.

Then the smell of incense brought her back to her senses.

This place was toying with Yuriko's sense of distance and space. The dome had seemed large enough from the outside, but inexplicably, the inside seemed even larger.

It's a coliseum—an arena. The thought occurred to her suddenly. *Or maybe it's some kind of round theater?* She noticed the round dais that sat in the very middle. Steps circled the dais, rising up like an inverted cone. Some kind of low walls ran down the steps, or maybe they were actual seats—she couldn't tell, because every inch of open space on the steps was filled with black-robed nameless devout.

"To the center, please," the one who had walked with Yuriko said as he drew off to one side. Yuriko walked toward the circular stage. No one in the entire place so much as sniffled. It was perfectly quiet, but Yuriko could feel the gazes of the nameless devout on her.

Her legs felt shaky again, and she found she had trouble lifting up her feet. Her toes wanted to trip on the floor and send her sprawling. She almost did fall, but still, no one said a word. She couldn't hear a single voice, just the gentle squeaking of her sneakers on the floor.

Directly above the circular stage hung a glass orb that looked like a large light bulb. It was high above the floor, yet still looked big—so it must have been very large indeed. Yuriko walked slowly beneath it, afraid that if she were to make some mistake here, the giant light bulb might come crashing down on top of her.

A chill ran across her forehead.

At the same time, the bulb above the stage began to shine.

Now her forehead was shining too. It seemed like the light from her forehead was aimed directly at the glass sphere above her. Like a spotlight was emanating from her own head, illuminating the bulb.

She saw the magic circle appear on the side of the giant sphere. That light reflected back down onto the stage, making the floor glow. It was another giant magic circle.

"*Allcaste*!" the masses of nameless devout said as one, "step into the circle."

Though her teeth were chattering so loudly with fear she was afraid they might fall out of her mouth, Yuriko walked into the circle upon the floor.

When she reached the center of the circle, it shone more brightly than before; then the light subsided, trapped inside the whorls and eddies of the pattern again, flowing along the lines of the circle. The lines went dark, and only the corners where two lines met sparkled. Then it seemed like a strip of light began to snake its way along the lines of the pattern, tracing out a figure eight.

"Lift your eyes. There is no need for fear." It wasn't a chorus. The thousands, no, tens of thousands of nameless devout were talking to Yuriko with one voice, and the sound was deafening.

Yuriko looked up. She was in the middle of the dais, the lowermost part of the amphitheater, surrounded by the nameless devout. The top row was so distant from where she stood she could barely make out the monks sitting there. But it was enough for Yuriko to see the faces of the nameless devout standing in the rows closest to her.

They all looked the same. They weren't triplets, or quintuplets, or anything like that. They all had the same face, the same body.

All thousand of them, all ten thousand of them.

All one of them. *So that's what he meant.*

Yuriko's internal surprise meter was completely overloaded. The needle spun around so fast it broke. Yuriko stood with her mouth hanging open, looking up at the sea of black robes. *Is this what it's like to be a rock star playing the Tokyo Dome?* Except her Tokyo Dome was filled with monks. And she wasn't singing. Though some kind of hymn might have been appropriate.

"Um…hi?" Yuriko said, her voice cracking. "N-nice to meet you."

As one, the sea of nameless devout bowed in reply. The robes made a sound like waves rippling. *This isn't some kind of hallucination. They're all really there.*

"M-m-my name is Yuriko Morisaki."

The nameless devout bowed again, sending a shudder through the air of the dome.

"What's, um, your name?"

"We are the nameless devout," they replied.

It was her against thousands. She felt like the strength of their voice would crush her.

"S-sorry. Would it be okay if only one of you spoke?"

The room fell silent. *Maybe that wasn't the right thing to say.* She hoped she hadn't inadvertently insulted them.

Then, a single of the devout broke from one of the rows directly in front of her. Cutting down through the rows, he walked toward Yuriko. Yuriko waited in the perfect silence of the dome for him to get to her. She could hear the faint *slap, slap* of his bare feet on the floor as he got closer.

The nameless devout stopped a short distance away from her and lowered his head, addressing her as "*Allcaste.*" She noticed his feet had stopped short of touching the magic circle on the ground. "Will this make it easier for you to speak with us?"

The devout had the same face as the one who had brought her here, with the same dark brows. His voice was the same too.

Yuriko nodded. "Yes, thank you."

The nameless devout smiled a smile that had a far more powerful effect on Yuriko than she had expected. The tension seemed to drain from her body. She felt like she could breathe normally for the first time since she had entered the dome.

She looked up and saw that the masses of nameless devout were all looking down at her with the same face, the same smile.

"We who have no name have no true individual form," the nameless devout said, spreading the sleeves of his robes. "We can change our appearance to make your dealings with us easier, if you wish. We are very young now, I fear. You were surprised to see us this way, weren't you?"

Yuriko nodded.

"I believe that when you heard we looked like monks, you pictured someone far older—like this, perhaps."

The nameless devout rubbed his face with his hand, and like that, he changed. His head was still bald, but now his brows were long and white, and wrinkles lined his face. His back was slightly bent, so that he stood no taller than Yuriko.

She looked up, and sure enough the thousands of nameless devout looking down at her had all become the same old man.

"Th-thank you," she stammered. "I think I can get used to this face."

I shouldn't look up at them. I should just focus on the one here in front of me. I'll think of the rest of them as...as scenery.

Not that it wasn't an unusual and interesting experience to have tens of thousands of old men staring down at her so intently.

"I suppose you know why I've come here?"

The nameless devout nodded. "You seek your brother."

"Yes. My brother, Hiroki. He has become the last vessel."

When she said it, she felt something inside her harden. One astonishment after the other had thrown her completely off balance, but now she felt like she was finally starting to get her feet back underneath her. *That's why I'm here. That's why I've come to the nameless land. The place where the Hero was imprisoned. The place from which it escaped.*

"The book who sent me here said that you might be able to help," Yuriko said, taking a step back and bowing so low her face almost touched her knees. "Please, you have to help me. Tell me what I need to do in order to find my brother."

There was silence. Yuriko closed her eyes tight.

Nothing happened. Slowly, she opened her eyes again. Then she saw the old monk's withered feet stepping onto the magic circle on the floor.

The nameless devout put a hand on Yuriko's head. "I am sorry for your plight," he said in a voice that was low and gentle. "Most of the *allcaste* who come here are young. For only the young souls are able to find their way to this land."

This confirmed what she had heard from Aju and the Sage.

"Yet even among their number, your soul is particularly small and lacking strength. You are but a girl. Your cheeks are soft, your arms thin, and your legs so weak they are barely able to hold your own weight. Yet still you would go on this quest to find your brother?"

Yuriko looked up, and the old nameless devout stroked her head once before drawing back his hand.

When she looked up at him again, she saw in his eyes that he was sad for her. He was truly sorrowful for her plight. All the words of sympathy and consolation she had received up to that point added together couldn't match what she saw in the monk's eyes that instant. It was a look more gentle than his hand on her head.

They know about the Hero. They know about the King in Yellow. They know about the vessels. And what happened to my brother. They won't laugh it off, they won't not believe. I don't have to explain anything to them. They know it all.

The thought gave Yuriko great courage. "I am a little girl, but that doesn't mean I'm weak," she told the devout. His thinking was clearly a little behind the times. "We can do everything boys can do. Sometimes better. I'll be okay. With your help, I hope!"

She would find her brother, rescue him, and help them find the King in Yellow again—but the old nameless devout raised a bony hand to stop her.

"*Allcaste*. I believe you are mistaken."

"Mistaken? About what?"

"It was we who bound the Hero here in imprisonment."

"Yes, I know. That's why—"

"But now the Hero has broken free from its prison and escaped into your Circle. We do not have the power to hunt the Hero there. We are bound just as it was to this land. We are not warriors."

"So then who's going to capture the Hero? Don't we have to capture it in order to imprison it again?"

The nameless devout shook his head. "No one can capture the Hero."

For a moment, all Yuriko could do was stand there, gaping.

"All one can do is sap its power in order to pull it back into the flow. Because the Hero is a story it can be absorbed within the flow of the great story and placed upon the Great Wheels of Inculpation, which will bring it back here of its own accord. Only then might we seek to imprison it again."

The great wheels of incul-what? What's that?

"This land is the origin of stories," the nameless devout continued, his eyes firmly on hers. This was a lecture. "Here, stories are born, emerge, and fade. It is from here that stories leave, and to here they return. The Great Wheels of Inculpation are those that speed the birth of stories—devices, if you will."

It was their job, the nameless devout explained, to keep pushing the wheels; their "duty" was the word he used.

"But Aju and the Sage—and all of the books I met—they said you could help me."

"If it is wisdom you seek then help you we can. We might also find the map which you seek. Yet we cannot give chase to the Hero, nor hunt it down. In truth, we cannot even stand up to the Hero, for we are the inculpated."

There was that word again, but Yuriko didn't have time now to wonder about what it meant. What the nameless devout was telling her was not what she had expected to hear.

"So I'm all alone? Nobody will come with me?"

There are so many of you!

Though her distress was certainly clear to him, the old monk spoke just as calmly as before. "*Allcaste*." He stepped forward and placed a hand on Yuriko's shoulder. "You have many allies other than us. The books are your friends. They know that the Hero has escaped, and even now they begin their hunt. The wolves too will make their presence known to you before long. And in regions you do not yet know of there are swordsmen and sorcerers who might aid in sapping the Hero's power."

Swordsmen? Sorcerers?

Yuriko had begun to shake her head—she was starting to lose track of what he was saying—when the nameless devout shook her lightly by the shoulder. She looked up.

"You must not despair. There are as many regions as there are stars in the heavens."

"What are these 'regions'? Are they like the world where I live? There are no swordsmen and sorcerers in my neighborhood, that's for sure."

The nameless devout smiled. "The place where you live is a region, yes. But there are many other regions. It is these of which I speak."

The nameless devout explained to her then that all of the countless stories that flowed through the Circle were each in themselves a region. "Each has their own place within the Circle, closed to the others."

Yuriko frowned, not quite getting it. *Stories moving through the Circle?* "You mean like books?"

"Not only books. Though that may be their original form, many regions appear in different forms as well."

"Like movies? And comic books? And games?" Yuriko asked, her voice rising higher with each question. "You mean I have to go into those regions to find help?"

"Wherever your brother's trail leads, you must follow. Whether it stays in the real or strays into fantasy."

"How am I supposed to do that?"

"You can, because you are an *allcaste*."

Yuriko touched the glyph on her forehead. Her head was swimming. The mark felt heavy against her skin. *I've been branded.*

"You look tired. You should rest."

How do they always know what I'm thinking? One more comment like that and I might just lose my temper.

"I will show you to your quarters."

Then the old nameless devout lifted a hand, and another came down the stairs to the amphitheater floor. This one's face was young, the same as the one she had first met. When she looked around, she saw that all of the nameless devout, save the old monk who had been talking to her, were young again.

"I alone will stay in this form, so that you may know me and take comfort in it," the lone old devout said. Then he smiled, the wrinkles deepening at the corners of his eyes.

CHAPTER FOUR

The Great Wheels

Following the twisting paths and corridors that led from the Dome of Convocation, Yuriko passed through three stone buildings, each one a different shape and size. For a moment, she was walking outside through a garden under the weak sunlight; then she was back inside yet another building. This was the lodge where the nameless devout lived. Yuriko was to be appointed a room here with them.

From the outside, the lodge also appeared to be made from stone, but inside she noticed rafters and posts carved from ancient, thick logs. Boards ran across the floor, the wood stained dark with age. The furniture was all wooden as well, with nothing resembling the intricately wrought metal fixtures she had seen inside the other buildings.

Following the young devout, Yuriko climbed up the stairs to the third floor—at least she guessed it was the third floor, based on the windows and stair landings she passed on the way up. The wooden stairs creaked under her feet, but the railing was made of a cold metal that resembled the smooth black material of the portcullis at the side entrance.

There were very few windows in the lodge, making it rather dark inside. The stairs were steep, and each step very high, so that Yuriko's calves ached by the time they reached the top.

"This way."

The nameless devout opened an iron-framed wooden door to a cell. The room was small, with a right wall made of what looked like clay. The ceiling slanted up to a triangular window at the top. The left-hand wall was a bookshelf, packed full of books.

A simple wooden bed sat flush to the wall on the right. On it, she saw a thin pillow with a white cover, and next to that, a folded blanket the color of camel's hair. A desk and chair about the same size as the ones they used in her classroom back home sat at the foot of the bed. Atop the desk sat a lamp small enough to fit in the palm of her hand. A white wick, its lower end suspended in translucent oil, stuck out of it.

"Make yourself at home."

The young nameless devout bowed once, then left. He left the door open behind him, however, making her think that he would be back. Yuriko sat down on the chair and waited.

The monk soon returned. He was carrying a tray in both hands and another blanket draped over one of his arms. "Please eat," he said, placing the tray on Yuriko's desk. The tray held a white dish with a piece of white bread next to a glass of water.

"Thank you," she said, and the monk bowed silently in reply. Every time he bowed, he would straighten his back first, placing his feet together. *Very formal.*

"Should you need anything, please ring." The monk indicated a bell shaped like an upside-down lily on the tray next to the cup of water.

Yuriko looked closer at the monk's hand and noticed with a start that it was criss-crossed with scars. His fingernails were chipped and split in places.

"I'm sorry. I can't just sit around here," Yuriko began. "I have to—"

"First you must rest," the young monk interrupted her, placing the blanket he carried at the foot of her bed. "The rooms here are chilly. Use this blanket should you need it."

This time, it seemed like the monk was leaving her for good. He put a hand on the door and was straightening himself to bow again, when Yuriko stood. "The books here are all fake too, aren't they?"

She had noticed it the moment she stepped into the room. Every book on the wall across from the bed were sculptures, like the ones she had seen in the long curving hallway. With one small difference: these were made from wood, not stone.

"If this place is the Hall of All Books, then why are all the books fake?"

The young nameless devout stared back at Yuriko, unblinking, his thick brows lifting over jet black eyes. "They are not fake," he replied. She was able to hear him clearly, though his voice was little more than a whisper. "These are what you might call emblems—or perhaps, remains."

Emblems? Remains? Neither of those words seemed particularly appropriate for books.

"The Hall of All Books is both the origin and the final resting place of every story. So you see, it does not matter what form the books take here. All that matters is what they hold."

While Yuriko was thinking about this, the monk bowed. *Uh-oh, he's leaving!* Suddenly, Yuriko didn't want to be left alone in this place. Quickly, she asked him the first question that came to mind. "But don't you read them?"

All librarians read books. They were experts. She expected most of them took the job because they liked books. Why would the nameless devout be any different?

The young monk tilted his head, thinking. His gentle expression did not change. "No, we do not read books," he said. Then, as if to prevent Yuriko from asking yet another question, he quickly added, "We are, in a way, like books themselves, so there is no need for us to read them."

This was confusing, and Yuriko made to ask another question when the nameless devout patted the air with his hands lightly, as if to say there would be time for that later. "Rest now, *allcaste*, for you are far more weary than you think."

"But I—"

"Once you've rested and regained your strength, you'll have plenty of time to think on what you must do and the path you must take. The Archdevout will wait until you are ready."

"The Archdevout?"

The monk smiled faintly. "The old nameless devout you met earlier. You may call him that. We seek to make it easier for you to speak with us—who are many and who are one."

So they're keeping one of the nameless devout looking old and calling him by a special name for my sake. Even if there are a thousand of them, or ten thousand, they all have the same face.

Yuriko wondered what that felt like. *What would it be like if all my classmates had my face?* No, it was more than just looking alike—they would all actually be the same person. They would all do the same things, talk the same way, think the same thoughts. There would never be any fights or bullying. They would never disagree.

It sounded nice, easy.

But how would I know which was the real "me" if everyone was *me?*

Yuriko pondered how she might ask the nameless devout about that when he stepped into the hall and shut the door behind him. Yuriko was alone.

Suddenly she yawned. *Maybe I'll lie down,* she thought, when her stomach rumbled so loudly the sound echoed off the ceiling. Yuriko laughed.

She ate the bread and drank the water. The sounds of her own chewing and swallowing were unnaturally loud in her ears. Then she started to feel lonely, like she might cry, so she swallowed her sobs down with the bread.

The bread and the water were both unexpectedly tasty. She finished them in a few moments, and a wave of drowsiness hit her. She kicked off her shoes, flopped down on the bed, and managed to pull the blanket over her before curling up and falling asleep.

It was a deep sleep without dreams.

She had no idea how long she slept, but when she awoke, the room was much darker. Someone had lit the lamp on her desk. Yuriko lay there awhile beneath the blanket, watching the lamp's tiny flame flicker in the darkness. The flame cast a warm circle of light on the desk. The wall of books across the room looked dark and solid in the lamplight.

Even though she was now completely awake, she felt like she was dreaming. It didn't matter where she was or what she was doing. Somehow the feeling of it being out of her hands was a comfort to her.

Maybe I'll just sleep here forever. It felt like something she might actually be able to get away with here in the nameless land. In time, she would lose her name too, and her identity. She'd become another nameless part of the place.

It was like a strong desire had suddenly materialized inside her. *I want to become nothing.*

Then an edge of the darkness moved near the door, just outside the circle of light cast by her tiny oil wick lamp.

Yuriko shot up in bed. She could hear footsteps pattering away.

Somebody had been outside her chamber.

Sliding off the bed, she tiptoed over to the door to find it had been left open a crack.

Were the nameless devout spying on me? No, why would they do that? Then she thought that maybe it was the one who came to light her lamp.

They might have run away when they saw me waking up, so as not to frighten me. That seemed far more likely than a peeping Tom.

She rubbed her eyes and gradually realized there was another source of light in the small room. She looked up. The light was coming from the triangular window near the ceiling. The light fell on the floor where it wavered slightly. It seemed to Yuriko that the light was coming from not one source, but many at once.

It's coming from outside the building.

Yuriko quickly drew on her shoes. She stood, and noticing a chill in the air, she took one of the blankets and wrapped it around her shoulders like a shawl. Then she slipped out through the door into the hall.

Small candles burned in sconces set at intervals down the long hallway. By each pool of light, she searched for a door that would lead out, checking both sides as she walked.

She intended to follow the route she had taken when the nameless devout first brought her here, but it soon became apparent that she had taken a wrong turn. Yuriko went around a familiar-looking corner only to find a life-size bronze statue that she was certain she hadn't seen on her way in. She leapt back in surprise, clapping her hand over her mouth to keep from shouting.

The statue itself wasn't particularly scary. It was the figure of a monk much like the nameless devout, wearing robes and carrying a book in one arm. His eyes were lowered, his head bowed as though praying. Still, in the flickering light of the candles, what was probably intended to be a work of art ended up looking like some pop-up bogeyman in a haunted house. Yuriko blushed, ashamed at her own lack of nerve.

Calm yourself. She looked around and found several other statues nearby. She was in more of a small chamber than a hallway now. The ceiling was vaulted, and the candles here were set much higher up on the walls. Double doors stood in the wall to the left, slightly larger than the single door to her room, and reinforced with the same iron frame. *That must be the main entrance.* The doors were open slightly, and a sliver of light spilled in from outside.

Yuriko put both hands to the door and slowly pushed. The door opened smoothly outward, and light spilled in from the widening crack.

"Whoa!"

It's the Milky Way!

Except it was below her.

Thousands of points of light were flowing by like a river below, quietly, solemnly. She squinted and saw that each point of light was the torch held in the hand of a nameless devout. It was a procession. She was standing above them, somehow, looking down.

She could now hear their bare feet slapping against the hard-packed ground, even from her distant perch. Each of the devout wore a hood over his head, their darkened forms blending with the darkness around them. In the wavering torchlight she caught a glimpse of a narrow shoulder here, a thin back there.

Where could they all be going?

"We go to fulfill our duty," a voice said from below. The Archdevout, a torch in his hand, was coming up toward her. One of the nameless monks—the young-faced devout with dark brows that had shown her to the lodge—followed close behind him.

For the first time, Yuriko realized she was on a veranda of some sort, up on the second or third floor. The Archdevout and the young monk with him were climbing a flight of exterior stairs. Yuriko decided to give up trying to figure out the layout of the place. Everything in the nameless land was too convoluted, it seemed.

"So they're going to work?"

The Archdevout reached the veranda and stood next to Yuriko. The young monk stepped behind her and opened the doors wide.

"They're going to work even though it's so dark out?"

"It is the changing of the shift."

So it's like a factory?

"What kind of work do they do?"

Sorting books, maybe? Or maybe they make the fake books to put on the walls? She supposed there would be maintenance to do on the buildings, and cleaning too. *But why did they need so many of them, and why are they heading away from the buildings?*

The Archdevout held his candle off to the side so that the light would not hit Yuriko directly in the face. Even in the dark of night, she could see the thin wisp of smoke rising from the candle flame. The burning wick made a faint sizzling noise.

"Well then," the Archdevout said with a smile, "will you come watch us at our labors?"

It seemed a plain enough invitation, but Yuriko sensed something else in his tone. It was as if watching them work would require no small effort on her part, and the Archdevout wanted to know if she was truly ready.

Yuriko looked at him more closely, marveling at how he seemed more like a little old man than any little old man she had seen in her entire life. He was a champion among little old men.

Of course he seems that way, she thought. *That's what I was expecting, after all.* But now, in the light of the candle, she noticed something else. There was a severity in the Archdevout's eyes. She certainly hadn't ever met an old man back home with eyes like his. She'd never met another person with eyes like his, period.

Yuriko felt her back straighten. Her improvised shawl pulled taut around her shoulders. "Is it all right if I watch?"

The Archdevout nodded. The eyes of the young devout with him were pointed firmly at the ground.

"When you see, you'll understand why this land exists."

Well, then I have to see it, don't I? "Every *allcaste* sees you at your labors, don't they?"

"Yes," the Archdevout replied, then fell silent. Yuriko heard the sizzling of the wick. "Though there are some," he continued, "who after seeing what you are about to witness, leave our land and never return."

Yuriko's heart shuddered in her chest. "Is...it scary?"

"Well now," the Archdevout said, smiling gently. "That depends on what you find fearful, what you find joyous, and what is in your heart. These things are yours alone."

While they were speaking, the Milky Way of torches had passed them by and was now receding into the distance. The tail end of the procession was even with the balcony now, and the head of the line had already gone through the central gardens. The devout appeared to be heading toward the single large gate she had seen earlier that day.

And what lies beyond that?

"I'll go. Please show me."

Without a word, the Archdevout turned and went down the stairs. The young monk waved a hand indicating she should follow. She did so, trying to keep her knees from buckling beneath her as she went down the steps.

Now she could hear a song echoing from the ranks of the nameless devout ahead. It started quietly, like a whisper, but soon swelled louder.

"That song—"

It was the same song the three nameless devout who had come to greet her had been singing.

"That's the invocation, right?"

"You are correct."

When they had caught up with the procession, the Archdevout and the young devout with her both joined in the chorus. Yuriko passed through the large gate, enveloped in their echoing voices, and with the nameless devout she left the Hall of All Books.

There were no stars in the nighttime sky. The line between the gray-black of the sky and the jet-black of the land was the only indication of her surroundings. The wind blew, carrying with it the scent of grass. The night dew wet her shoes. There was no road to speak of—certainly nothing paved. They were stepping on the grass, cutting along a natural course through the same rolling dunes she had seen upon her arrival. The grass was bent down where they walked—pushed into the ground by the passage of countless bare feet.

The wind tugged at the torches of the nameless devout walking in front of her, sending sparks up into the sky. One spark whirled high, then fell back down, making a sharp pinprick of pain where it landed square on Yuriko's forehead. She lifted her hand and rubbed, noticing the pale light of the magic circle on her forehead reflecting off her fingers.

She glanced at the Archdevout walking next to her. He didn't seem to notice it was glowing, or perhaps he didn't care. *Maybe they're used to seeing people like me.* Yuriko wondered how many *allcastes* had come to the nameless land.

Eventually, the path began to climb, a steady rise though not steep.

"This is a path we use often," the Archdevout began, leaning toward Yuriko. "It leads to the Threshing Hill where we perform our labors.

"Of course," he went on, "nothing in the nameless land has a true name. One of your kind—an *allcaste* who visited here—named the hill when he departed, having fulfilled his task."

The nameless devout had been calling it that ever since, he told her. Yuriko detected something like reverence toward this *allcaste* in the Archdevout's voice.

"He was a boy only a few years older than you, with golden hair."

Not Japanese, then. "Why did he come here?"

"Like you, he was searching for someone close to him."

And he fulfilled his task. "So it went well? He was able to find who he was looking for?"

Someone from his family, his girlfriend maybe—someone taken by the King in Yellow.

"Yes," the Archdevout replied simply.

Yuriko found herself a little short of breath from the walking, but the Archdevout and the other devout with her never slackened their pace or seemed to breathe any harder than normal.

Yuriko considered this story of the golden-haired boy who had named the Threshing Hill. It was a bit like giving your blessing to a place, Yuriko thought—to give a name to something that had no name. The boy had given this hill his blessing. A moment later, the thought struck Yuriko as incredibly odd, coming from her. It wasn't the sort of thing she ever would've thought about before. *Why, it's like I'm a little more grown-up all of a sudden. What if, when this mark got pressed into my forehead, I became another version of myself—a better version?*

The Archdevout spoke again, his voice as calm and steady as his pace. "The *allcaste* I spoke of said that the view from this hill was much like a place where he had grown up. All it lacked, he said, was a river flowing by it and a waterwheel and millhouse."

A millhouse? Yuriko didn't think they even had those anymore. *Maybe the golden-haired boy came here a long time ago?* Yuriko tried to think when they would have last had millhouses. *A hundred years? Two hundred?*

I wonder if I'll get to name something here. She could find her brother, and the two of them could leave the nameless land together. But just before she left, she would give the land her blessing. *That,* she thought, *would be a fine thing to do.* As she walked along through the dark, the dew clinging to her feet, Yuriko felt her determination grow. Her hands clenched into little fists. Next to her, the Archdevout remained silent. She wanted him to say something like "good luck," or "I pray for your success." She had turned to him to tell him about her plan when she felt the ground tremble slightly beneath her feet.

An earthquake? No—it didn't feel like that. But the ground was trembling. Maybe it had been trembling from a while before, but she just hadn't noticed it. She looked at the Archdevout, but he seemed not to have noticed anything unusual. Ahead of her, the processions of nameless devout were still singing their invocation, their pace unchanging.

As they continued climbing the hill, Yuriko noticed a faint squeaking noise that seemed to match the vibrations she could feel beneath her feet. Something large was moving on top of the hill, hidden in the darkness ahead of them. *That's what's making that noise,* Yuriko finally realized.

"What is that?"

The Archdevout looked up, squinting into the flurry of torch sparks. "This is our task, *allcaste.*"

♆

Atop the Threshing Hill, Yuriko saw a scene that staggered the imagination. The top of the hill was a wide plateau thronged with black-robed nameless devout.

They were moving, undulating. Countless black robes turned in dark circles under the dark sky. When the dark circles moved, the ground shivered. She could feel it in her gut and in her bones. The sound seemed to vibrate up from her kneecaps, passing through her entire body before shooting out into space from the top of her head.

The nameless devout were turning a pair of giant wheels lying flat on either side of the plateau. They were enormous. Yuriko immediately thought of the Tokyo Dome. Her father was a Yomiuri Giants fan, and he took the family to the ball games a couple times a year. They'd watch games in the dome, eat hot dogs and ice cream, and cheer along with the other fans through tiny megaphones they sold in the stands. Once you were inside the dome, you hardly noticed its size—but Yuriko remembered being impressed when she saw it from the walkway outside, or when she saw the great arc of the dome from the train window on the way there. She often wondered how people had managed to make such a giant building.

The Tokyo Dome is big, but these wheels are even bigger!

On closer examination, Yuriko noticed that the giant wheels had no rims. A pillar about the size of a small building stood in the center of each, and from there radiated incredibly long spokes—too many for her to count. The nameless devout stood along each spoke, pushing them to turn the wheels.

For some reason, the wheel on the right and wheel on the left were turning in opposite directions. The left appeared to be going clockwise, while the right went counterclockwise. Where the two wheels met, the spokes seemed so close together that the sleeves of the nameless devout's robes brushed against one another as they passed.

The invocation had stopped somewhere along their journey up the hill. The devout pushed in silence, their only accompaniment the rumbling in the ground and the creaking of the two giant wheels. The nameless devout pushed with their hoods back, heads bent low, arms extended ahead of them to grip the spokes.

The torches she had seen them carrying had been placed into simple stands set into the ground, tracing two larger circles of light around the dark circles of the wheels.

As Yuriko stood there, dumbfounded, first one nameless devout then another broke from their positions at the spokes, retrieved torches from the stands, and began to walk toward the path leading down the hill. Nameless devout from the procession that had come here with Yuriko stepped into their places, setting their torches in the empty holders. It was a changing of the shift, yet the wheels never stopped their turning. There was no break in their work.

Before Yuriko had fully realized what was going on, the departing monks had formed a full procession heading down the hill behind her. She heard their song rise again, snippets of verse reaching her ears over the relentless creaking of the wheels.

"What's this all for?" Yuriko asked, her voice dry with shock. Next to her, the Archdevout stood silently watching the rotation of the wheels. Yuriko tried raising her voice. "What are they doing? Are they creating power for something?"

The Archdevout pulled back his hood, turned to Yuriko, and bowed. "*Allcaste*, these are the Great Wheels of Inculpation."

The Great Wheels, Yuriko whispered to herself, though she could not even hear her own voice through the rumbling.

The Archdevout's black eyes reflected tiny pinpricks of light from the torches floating in a sea of darkness. "The right wheel sends stories out into the Circle, while the left wheel receives those stories that have lost their power. All stories leave from here, and to here return. It is our duty to ensure that the motion of the Great Wheels never ceases."

The Archdevout lowered his head once again. He was not bowing to Yuriko, but to the wheels.

"But where are the stories?"

From what he was telling her, she half expected the stories to pass through the spokes like thread on a spinning wheel.

"Stories cannot be seen by the human eye—not as they are," the Archdevout added with a smile. Oddly enough, Yuriko had no trouble hearing him, calm and quiet though he was, over the noise of the wheels. "It is only those people living within the Circle who can give form to the stories sent from here. It is the power of humans that brings the stories toward a true existence. All we do is maintain the flow."

Yuriko couldn't believe it. The picture books she had loved when she was little, the things she and her classmates thrilled over now—schoolgirl romance manga, the blockbuster movies her family went to see—all the stories that had touched her life came flooding back to her. Her head was full of them. The characters she had fallen in love with reading late into the night. Those great lines that had brought tears to her eyes. The fantastic CG scenes that came back to visit her dreams.

And all of them, every single last one, began here, at the source, these two wheels that creaked as they turned. And the countless nameless devout kept it going. They kept the flow of the stories constant, their bald heads glistening with sweat, the black hem of their robes bound tight to their calves as they silently pushed the spokes. Each with the same face, the same pointed chins, in their simple clothes and bare feet slapping against the ground.

How could something as beautiful, fun, and lively as a story have its origin here?

"No way..." Yuriko breathed, her lips curling into a lopsided smile. "No way. I don't believe it. This is some sort of joke, isn't it? You're playing a game with me?" Stories were fun. They were beautiful things. Things of value. "People make stories themselves! We create them, imagine them, write them! I can't believe they come from *this*!"

Yuriko's shouts were lost in the grinding of the wheels. Only the sparks of the torch flames seemed to react to her at all by dancing even higher into the night sky.

The Archdevout cupped his aged hand lightly on Yuriko's shoulder. "You may recall that I told you some of the *allcastes* choose to leave this land after witnessing the nameless devout at our task. They all said the same thing that you say now."

Yuriko could feel the Archdevout's gaunt hand on her shoulder. A wizened little old man.

"Will you leave us too? If you wish to, no one will stop you."

It was a serious question. Should she go forward or go back? A difficult choice offered in gentle words.

The question was easy to answer. *This is ridiculous. I'm out of here. I'm going home!* All she had to do was shout that and it would be over. The Archdevout wouldn't stop her. But something inside Yuriko wouldn't let her do it. She couldn't just turn away. A voice from deep in her belly told her not to jump to conclusions, and above all else, not to turn her eyes away from what she saw here.

The pair of wheels rumbled on. She could hear the slapping of innumerable bare feet upon the ground. The creaking of limbs as they pushed against the heavy spokes. There was the smell of sweat and of the earth and the cool night air.

They're doing penance.

Another thought I never would have had before a day ago.

"You *are* human, right?" she managed to ask. "You work in shifts, and rest, eat, and drink, right? So how can you do all this? Why do you have to do this? Isn't it hard on you?"

The Archdevout turned to look directly into her eyes. His eyes looked softer now, and not just on account of the weathered lines and wrinkles around them. He shook his head. "We are no longer human as you think of it."

No longer human? But you look human. Then what's different? Is this another word game? Yuriko bit her lip.

"It is true. We rest, and we eat—though we have no physical need to do so. It would be easy enough for us to go without, and yet, by going through the motions of our former selves, it helps us retain some vestige of our humanity."

"But how can you go without food or sleep?"

The Archdevout smiled consolingly at Yuriko. "Because our forms as you see them are borrowed things—temporary vessels."

Then he spread his arms, letting the sleeves of his black robes flutter in the night air. The fabric of his long sleeves clung to the bony arms. Yuri thought it looked like laundry caught in the branches of a withered tree.

"When we were human like yourself, we each had our own individual appearance. Yet these we lost when we became the nameless devout. Rather, we abandoned our individuality in every way. Now we are one and we are many. We are many and we are one.

"Yet it is true that when one loses one's self, one is also likely to lose one's sense of duty. So it is with men. That is why we sleep, and eat, and rest:

to remind ourselves of our past humanity and maintain some vestige of it within. This is how we perform our roles and do penance for our sins."

Doing penance for sins. That reminded Yuriko of something she had heard soon after her arrival in the nameless land. "The inculpated," she whispered. Hadn't one of the nameless devout said that? "An inculpated means a sinner?"

The Archdevout and the young nameless devout behind her nodded their heads in unison.

"Why are you sinners?" She took a step toward the Archdevout. "What sin did you commit?" Another step.

The Archdevout stepped back and turned to face the mass of nameless devout pushing at the great wheels. "These wheels are called the Great Wheels of Inculpation. They send out the stories and receive them back, maintaining the flow of narratives. You see, *allcaste,* the stories are our punishment."

But that's ridiculous! "But stories are fun. They're beautiful. They make people happy!"

The Archdevout turned back around, fixing Yuriko with his eyes. "And yet it is also stories that gave birth to the King in Yellow."

Yuriko was shaking. It was cold. She pulled the blanket tighter around her shoulders.

"Let me ask. What are stories, *allcaste*?" The Archdevout answered before she could. "They are lies."

Yuriko stood there, shivering, next to the line of nameless devout pushing, the great wheels turning.

"It is the creation of things which do not exist. And the telling of these things. The lies become record, from which memories are born. But they are still lies."

So making up a world and telling about it was a lie. And putting together the pieces of old records to tell a story about things that happened a long time ago—like in a history book—that was lying too.

"Yet without these lies, men could not live. Their world could not stand. Stories are vital to your kind. They need these lies to be who they are. Yet lies are lies, and to lie is a sin."

And when there is a sin, someone has to do penance for it.

"By turning the Great Wheels of Inculpation we provide the lies that the world of men seek. We work always, that the flow never be interrupted. It is both penance for our sins and the creation of new sin. So, as you see, our task is great," the Archdevout added with a sigh. "This is the task set before man as well. Those of us who have become the nameless devout are guilty of committing the sin of storytelling when we were men ourselves. That is why we now serve to bear the burden of story's sin for all those who live in the Circle."

The young devout standing with them stepped forward quickly and grabbed Yuriko by the arm. It wasn't an act of aggression. He was catching her because he had seen her legs begin to buckle.

"I'm sorry. Thank you."

Yuriko straightened herself out, making sure that her feet were firmly planted beneath her. The young nameless devout gently released her arm.

His hand had been warm—it the warm hand of a person.

Yuriko felt a tightness in her chest. "It's not fair," she said, her voice choked with tears. "Why do you have to be the ones to do this? If telling stories is a sin, aren't we all guilty?"

A broad smile spread across the Archdevout's wrinkled face. "You are kind. A kindness such as only children possess. Thus may only children visit the nameless land." There were others as well who bore the guilt of telling stories in the Circle, the Archdevout told her. "I'm sure you will encounter them in your search for your brother."

"You mean people who make stories? Like authors or historians?"

"Not only these people. And not all of them are even aware of their own sin. The wolves too are among their number. And those who hate the King in Yellow and gather up dangerous copies in order to protect the Circle are inculpated. All of them do penance for their sins in their own way."

Yuriko didn't understand. She didn't want to understand. Even while her head strained for comprehension, her heart pushed it away. "But what about all the good that's in stories?"

"Yes, there is much good in stories. They fill the Circle with light. But," he went on, "it is not so here. Not in the nameless land. Because this is the origin of all stories, the origin of lies."

"So why didn't all of you stay in the Circle like the rest, doing penance for your stories there? Like the wolves? Why did you have to become the nameless devout?"

Yuriko felt her own questions getting narrower. She was retreating into specifics. Or maybe she was going forward, searching willy-nilly for comprehension, wherever that might be found.

"What bad thing did you do when you were people to become the nameless devout?" Yuriko asked. She was as fearful as she was curious. *What sort of people could have done something to deserve* this?

The Archdevout thought for a while, his heavy eyelids closed, until Yuriko actually thought he had fallen asleep standing up. A considerable amount of time passed.

What is he doing? Why isn't he answering me? Yuriko's fear doubled inside her. She trembled.

Then, finally, the Archdevout opened his eyes. His soft gaze fell on Yuriko's face. "If I tell you now, my words will not reach your heart. Yet I will offer them to you, all the same." He spread his arms. "We are the remains of those men who sought, in their lives, to live a story. We are guilty of the great sin of living lies and trying to make those lies real. That is why we lost ourselves and became the one that is many and the many that are one—the nameless devout in our black robes, living here in this nameless land."

They tried to live a story?

Now an even sharper need pierced Yuriko's chest: a question that demanded an answer. "When will you be forgiven?"

"Who would forgive men of the sin of living a lie? The gods? The gods are themselves no more than a story made by men, and lies cannot forgive lies, let alone absolve us of them."

"You mean you're all stuck here forever? For eternity?"

"There is no time in this land. An eternity is like moment, and a moment like an eternity. We are only here *now*. There is no *then*."

Yuriko shrank back, but the Archdevout's thin hand gently reached out and grasped hers. "Come this way. I will show you the wheels from a higher vantage point."

The Archdevout led Yuriko by the hand, their feet swishing through the dew-laden grass. Though she had thought the plateau where the wheels turned to be the top of the Threshing Hill, she found that it rose even further beyond. They walked upward, moving against the wind. A stiff night breeze brushed Yuriko's face, tossing her hair this way and that. The glyph on her forehead was glowing softly. The creaking of the great wheels grew slightly more distant.

She looked back to see, below her, the throng of black robes whirling, rustling as they moved around. From this height, she could no longer hear the footsteps and ragged breathing of the nameless devout. Though she could still feel the heavy creaking of the wheels in her feet, the sound did not reach her ears.

What she could hear was the creaking of the pillars at the center of each great wheel as their spokes rotated around them.

Yuriko's eyes opened a little wider.

The sound was pretty. It was high in pitch; a light, clear sound—like the ringing of tiny bells or the lilting refrain of a child's song.

Next to her, the Archdevout smiled wryly at the surprise in her eyes. "Yes. You are hearing the song of the heart-pillars. The right we call the Pillar of Heaven, the left we call the Pillar of Earth."

Yuriko realized that she and the Archdevout were standing alone atop the mound overlooking the plateau. The young nameless devout that had joined them on their first ascent had stayed down by the wheels where they left him. He wasn't even looking in Yuriko's direction. He had his back to them, standing as still as one of the torch posts.

"Is it the invocation?"

"No, it is not. The invocation is not so full of joy as that. It does not soothe the heart as their songs do."

"The Pillar of Heaven, which sends out the stories, offers joy with its song, while the Pillar of Earth, which winds the stories back in, offers solace," the

Archdevout explained. "Both are invaluable functions of stories."

At the same time, the Archdevout told her, these two songs bore a wish: that the stories they sent out might bring as much joy into the Circle as possible. They also praised the stories that returned for fulfilling their roles in the Circle, and wished for them peace.

"Your brother is in one of the stories sent by these wheels now."

Along with the Hero, the King in Yellow.

"Now that the Hero is in the Circle, there will soon be a modulation in the songs of the Pillars of Heaven and Earth."

"You mean the songs will change? How?"

The Archdevout's reply surprised her. "They will grow stronger."

Released into the Circle, the Hero would seek energy for more stories. Naturally, this would increase the amount of story energy used. The more energy used, the higher and louder the song of the heart-pillars would become.

"If the Hero is not bound, and the heart-pillars are allowed to sing higher, and many stories are returned here, then in very little time, the Great Wheels will become much more than we nameless devout can handle." The surging flow of the stories, the Archdevout explained, could gain wills of their own. They would fly from the wheel to join the Hero. Soon, the Hero would begin to tug at the right wheel—the Pillar of Heaven—causing it to move whether the nameless devout pushed it or not. In time, it would spin so fast that the devout could not keep up.

"We would trip, fall to the ground, and be hit by the spinning spokes. The spokes would crush our bones, and we would return to nothing."

Meanwhile, the rotation of the Pillar of Earth would slow. This was because the Hero would use up all the stories within the confines of the Circle. A story devoured by the Hero would not return to the nameless land.

"No matter how hard the nameless devout pushed, eventually, the Pillar of Earth would not move."

And that, the Archdevout told her, would be the end of her Circle.

"The moment before the Circle stopped, the Pillar of Earth would shriek, singing its song louder than any song heard before. This cry is a message to those who live in the Circle that their world is ending. Some have likened it to the sounding of the angels' trumpets."

In the end, once the Great Wheel of Earth had stopped spinning, the free-spinning Great Wheel of Heaven would also slow, eventually joining it in stillness. When that happened, those nameless devout who had not already been returned to nothing would be left alone here in this land.

"Where they would wait for the next Circle to be born."

"What about the Hero?" Yuriko asked.

"The Hero has already descended into the Circle. Should the Circle end, the Hero will end with it."

"And the Hall of All Books?"

"It shall remain," the Archdevout told her. As he spoke, his eyes flickered in the direction of the hall. Yuriko followed his eyes out into the void of night.

The great silhouette of the hall was lost in the darkness. Only tiny points of light from the windows were dimly visible in the distance.

"While we waited for the next Circle to be born, we would go into the Hall of All Books and take from there every last one of the carven books—they represent all the stories of the lost Circle—and we would destroy them, leaving the hall empty, awaiting the arrival of new stories whenever they might come." So would her civilization disappear, and another civilization be born, the Archdevout explained. "That is the history of this nameless land where time does not exist."

But then—

"So what am I supposed to do?"

"Whatever you wish," the Archdevout replied. "You are free to follow your heart."

She could return to the Circle, the Archdevout explained, and watch the Hero at work and be destroyed together with her world. Of course, that destruction would take time. It might not even come within her lifetime. It was more than likely that Yuriko could live out the rest of her days in relative peace.

"The books in Mr. Minochi's reading room said the same thing."

The Archdevout nodded. "Yes, that way is still available to you. What you do not see and do not know of does not exist, after all. You can forget about this land if you wish it."

"But I can't forget about my brother." Yuriko had meant to shout the words, but they came out weakly, no stronger than a sigh. "And I can't forget all of you either."

How could she erase what she had seen, what she had learned? She could not. That was Yuriko's choice. "But I can't fight the Hero—the King in Yellow—either. I can't save the Circle. I'm just a kid. How can I do something so huge? I just want to save my brother. I just want to see him again."

"*Allcaste*," the Archdevout addressed Yuriko, bowing his head deeply and taking both her hands in his. "You speak of two goals, yet they are one and the same."

Saving the world is the same as saving my brother? That's impossible. One was the destiny of, well, everything. The other was just a boy. How much more different could that be?

The Archdevout squeezed her hands more tightly. "Think on this. Your brother has become the last vessel. Now, do you remember what the last vessel is?"

"Yes, the last container for the power that the Hero needed to break free from its prison. The last drop to fill the chasm."

"If this is true, then take away that drop, and the chasm will not be completely filled."

Yuriko's eyes went wide. "Take away the drop?"

The Archdevout nodded. "Should you take your brother from the King in Yellow, then the Hero will lose power equal in measure to that which it gained from him."

So I have to undo what Hiroki did. He added the last drop. I have to take it away.

"Should the Hero lose the power contained within the last vessel, it will lose its strength until it flows back into the greater story of its own accord. Once it has returned to the flow, the Great Wheel of Earth will pull it back here to the nameless land where it will return to being only a story—a very powerful one, but simply a story and nothing more."

"Is that true?" Yuriko asked, still unable to believe what she was hearing. "That's all? I just have to take my brother away from the Hero and that will save the world?" It sounded too good to be true. Or rather too small an act to really make a difference.

The Archdevout smiled. "Tell me, in the region where you grew up, what did they teach you about the value of a person's life?"

Yuriko was nonplussed. *What kind of question is that?* "I'm not sure I understand what you mean."

"Then let me ask in a different way," the Archdevout continued gently. "In your region, what does one compare a person's life to? What do they say a person's life is worth more than, or worth as much as?"

Yuriko thought a moment. "My teacher once said that a person's life is more precious than the whole world."

The Archdevout let go of Yuriko's hands and lifted one index finger. "So we might say that a human life has the same value as the world, yes?"

Yuriko frowned. "Okay."

"Therefore it shouldn't be strange to think that saving one person's life could indeed lead to saving the world, should it?"

Yuriko frowned again. *I'm not sure I'm buying this.*

The smile faded from the Archdevout's wrinkled face. When he spoke again, his voice was solemn and severe. "Imagine a world in which a single boy, by his own free will, does not hesitate to take the life of another. This is no different from a world in which one thousand men might take the lives of another thousand, or ten thousand the lives of another ten thousand."

Yuriko's eyes opened wide as she looked at the Archdevout. The Archdevout met her gaze, unwavering. In that moment, it was as though a fog had lifted. Suddenly, things were starting to make sense.

"We are one, but we are many. Many, but one," Yuriko whispered. "That's what you mean?"

The Archdevout nodded deeply. "If you truly wish to save your brother, then you truly can save the world. Yet..." he stared intently at the girl, "do you know how great your difficulties will be in saving your brother? Do you know what great fears you must overcome along this path? In order to save your brother, you must meet the Hero. A single misstep, and you too will be taken and swallowed whole.

"Though they do you credit, your feelings for your brother may also be your undoing. You may wander, despair, and fall into self-pity. For the Hero is very strong. It is a complete story, possessing unparalleled power. It can bewitch men and take them hostage. And the dark side of the coin, the King in Yellow, is always there."

Yuriko wasn't the type to argue the finer points of things, but something the Archdevout said put a question she wanted to ask into perspective, and it came bubbling out of her. "You know, something always struck me as strange."

The Archdevout nodded lightly. "Yes?"

"You all talk about the Hero and the King in Yellow as being two sides of the same coin, right? Which is just a way of saying they can't be separated, right?"

"This is true," the Archdevout agreed.

"Well then, why don't people just look at the good side? At the 'hero' and not the 'king.' Then the King in Yellow won't lead them astray, and they can just take the good parts of the story. You wouldn't even have to imprison it."

People just had to be careful how they handled the Hero, that's all, Yuriko thought. *Keep their eyes on the front and never look at the back.*

The Archdevout stared at Yuriko for some time. Yuriko stared back. After a while like this, the Archdevout sighed—a curiously human gesture. Yuriko wondered if it was for her benefit. "You are still a child. And while I admire your faith in humanity, you seem to misunderstand the coin," he said, shaking his head. "It is a metaphor. There is no coin."

"I know, but—"

"The Hero and the King in Yellow are one and the same thing, *allcaste.*"

Two sides of the same coin, I know that! But there has to be a way...

"Let me put it another way," the Archdevout said, sighing again. "Were the nameless devout or the people in your Circle to see the Hero's face, we would not know it. Nor would we know the King in Yellow. We would not be able to tell them apart."

"Well then shouldn't we try to figure out *how* to tell them apart?"

The Archdevout fell silent.

Maybe I said too much. "I'm sorry, I don't mean to say your system here isn't working, it's just..." Yuriko swallowed. *This isn't making things any better.* "Just, I don't feel like I can really chase down something I know nothing about, let alone fight it alone."

Yuriko had meant it as a confession, but somehow it came out sounding more like a complaint. *I'm even starting to get on my own nerves.*

But the Archdevout seemed to understand what she meant. "You're not alone," he offered gently. "The many books in the Circle are your allies."

But books can't fight. They can't hold swords.

"And there are the wolves. They are true warriors, *allcaste.* They will protect and serve you until your mission is complete."

"But where do I find them?"

The Archdevout's sour face brightened. "They will find you."

There were many wolves within the Circle, the Archdevout told her. They were already aware that the Hero had broken its bonds and would be moving to discover who had become the last vessel, and where he was. "They will find you because in order to free the last vessel from the Hero's enchantment, and thereby weaken the King in Yellow, they will need the strength of an *allcaste* who shares the last vessel's bloodline."

"I can't believe people would do something so dangerous like that just because they wanted to..." Yuriko began, then she remembered what the Archdevout had just told her. The wolves, like nameless devout, were inculpated. They too were doing penance for the sin of storytelling.

That's why they'll help me. Until my mission is complete. My mission for one—getting back my brother—is also for many. Saving the world.

"Come." The Archdevout extended a hand to Yuriko. "Let us return to the Hall of All Books. We must show you the Book of Heroes."

"The Book of Heroes?"

The Archdevout nodded as they walked down the hillside hand in hand. "In the Hall of All Books there is one volume alone that retains the shape it holds within the Circle. This is the book in which the Hero was imprisoned."

Though now that the Hero had escaped, the Archdevout explained, the book was nothing more than an empty cage, awaiting the return of its prisoner.

"Until the blank Book of Heroes once again holds that story within its pages, it is called the Hollow Book. It bears upon its cover the same glyph that you now wear upon your forehead. And on the day that you release the last vessel, the glyph upon your forehead and its sister upon the Hollow Book will burn more brightly than ever before, and then fade."

"A great deal depends on me." Through her glyph she was, in effect, responsible for bringing the Hero back to its prison. "Not only do I have to find my brother, I have to fix what he's done, don't I?"

It was more of a complaint off the top of her head then a revelation sprung from deep thoughts. Partially, she was saying it to herself. Though when she said it, she couldn't help but notice that the young nameless devout who was again following them as he had on the way to the hill broke stride for a fraction of a second.

Yuriko felt suddenly embarrassed. *He thinks I'm blaming my brother for all of this. He thinks I'm blaming him for putting me in this position.*

"If you find this path too difficult," the Archdevout said quietly, "then you may remove the glyph upon your forehead and leave this place."

Yuriko walked toward the Hall of All Books in silence. She had reached the foot of that impossibly massive folding screen of a wall before she stopped and took a deep breath.

"I will not run away from this."

Yuriko resumed walking, her pace faster and more determined than before.

Telling her to wait at the Dome of Convocation, the Archdevout bid Yuriko farewell at the entrance to the hall. The young nameless devout accompanied her to the middle of the Dome, so that she wouldn't get lost. When they reached the dais, the young nameless devout bowed and left, leaving Yuriko to wait by herself.

Something odd had happened on their way to the dome. As they walked, the young nameless devout looked over his shoulder several times as though expecting to see someone following. Each time, he did it so quickly that Yuriko didn't have time to ask him what the matter was. Still, it made her nervous.

Now that she was alone, she grew even more nervous. What if something was there? Something waiting in the darkness. Why would a nameless devout act like that?

A rat, maybe? Yuriko made herself picture it until she laughed. *Imagine a rat being here. It'd eat all the books. That is, if they weren't made of stone.*

Sitting alone in the middle of it, Yuriko felt that the Dome of Convocation seemed immensely vast. It seemed as though she could hear her own breath echoing off the ceiling high above.

Eventually, she heard light footfalls approaching, and the Archdevout reappeared. Behind him came four devout bearing a large silver chest between them. The chest was covered with carved letters of all sorts on all six sides. *It looks like a casket*, she thought. The casket had four metal rings attached to the corners of its lid, two in the front and two in back, through which ran two long metal poles that the nameless devout carried upon their shoulders.

The Archdevout joined Yuriko on the stage in the center of the dome. Meanwhile, the four nameless devout set down their burden and removed the metal poles.

The Archdevout approached the casket and placing his hands together, bowed. Then he took a step back, knelt down upon the floor with both hands out in front of him, and brushed his head to the ground twice. Then he stood. The four nameless devout approached, one at each corner, and at a nod from the Archdevout, they opened the lid.

Yuriko braced herself, but nothing happened. No lights streamed from the casket. There was no loud noise, no noxious plumes of smoke. The Archdevout knelt reverently, then walking on his knees, slowly slid up to the casket where he bowed a final time before reaching inside.

He pulled out something small wrapped in dark black cloth. It was shaped like a book. The Archdevout shuffled back on his knees to his original position, where he sat, straight-backed, and began to undo the black cloth.

"The Hollow Book," the Archdevout announced simply.

The black cloth fell away, revealing an old, leather-bound tome. It was large, very large, and yet surprisingly plain. Yuriko could see no markings upon it whatsoever.

Maybe that's because it's blank? It must've been beautiful when it was still the Book of Heroes... Yuriko snapped out of her train of thought. Something was wrong.

The four nameless devout who had carried in the casket stood motionless, rooted to the spot. They were staring at the Archdevout, who in turn was standing so still he might have become a statue. His eyes, almost hidden by his wrinkles before, were open wide, and his whole body was trembling. Yuriko heard a strange noise; his teeth were chattering.

"What's wrong?" Yuriko asked, taking a step toward him.

"Stay there!" the Archdevout practically shouted at her. Yuriko shrank back as though stung by a whip.

He wasn't even looking in her direction. His eyes were fixed on the empty book in his hands. His hands shook as he gripped it, and the jet-black cloth slipped and fell to the floor.

"What is this?" Yuriko thought she heard him say, though his voice was more a moan than proper words.

The Archdevout began shaking his head. He shook it several times, then let it sink down until his forehead touched the cover of the Hollow Book.

Fear crept over Yuriko. *Something's not right. Something happened that he wasn't expecting.* She had never seen any of the devout look so flustered. Or show any sort of emotion like this at all.

"Archdevout, what is it?"

Instead of answering, the Archdevout and the four with him looked up, their faces taut and pale. They looked poised to run, like frightened rabbits, looking back toward the entrance to the dome.

Something was very wrong. Yuriko stood, struck speechless at this turn of events. Next to her, the Archdevout shouted into the darkness.

"You there! Show yourself!"

Something in the darkness shivered. Yuriko blinked. She saw it again—a rippling in the gloom that gradually took the form of a small person.

Black robes, bare feet, a youthful face. *A nameless devout. But his face is different!* He wasn't old like the Archdevout, or like the four who had come carrying the caskets.

"P-please forgive me," the new arrival stammered. "Forgive me!"

With great speed, the devout ran down toward the center of the dome and before Yuriko knew what was going on had prostrated himself before them and began bowing to the ground, begging for their forgiveness. Yuriko stood for a moment, wondering what that strange slapping sound was, when she realized it was the sound of his forehead hitting the floor.

"Hey." Yuriko took a step closer. "Hey! Don't hit your head like that. Doesn't it hurt? You'll get a bump!"

At her voice, the new devout shrank back and looked up. The thin light streaming from the top of the dome reflected off his bald head.

His face did look a lot like the faces of the four nameless devout already standing there. This new devout looked very similar to the devout who had greeted her when she first arrived in the nameless land. Like him, this new devout had dark, bushy brows. But this new arrival's face was even younger than that. He looked no older than fourteen or fifteen. Maybe something like the other devout might have looked a few years ago.

Are they brothers?

The Archdevout stood, the Hollow Book in his hands, and walked over to the fifth nameless devout.

"You are before an *allcaste*. You will kneel."

The young devout prostrated himself again. Two of the four who had carried the casket stepped forward now, and each grabbed one of the young devout's arms and dragged him across the floor to the Archdevout's feet.

"There's no need to do that," Yuriko said, stepping over to the Archdevout. She knelt by the prostrated new arrival. She half expected the Archdevout to stop her, but he did not. The others stood by silently, saying nothing.

"Did he do something wrong?" She looked up at the Archdevout standing above her. "I think he's asking for you to forgive him—look how he's trembling!"

Yuriko put her hand on the young devout's shoulder, feeling a hardness beneath the cloth. *Why, he's all skin and bones!*

Yuriko barely had time to register her surprise when something most unusual happened. The glyph on her forehead glowed brighter than ever before. For a split second, the light was projected on the far wall of the dome, creating a perfect replica of the glyph there.

The light shone on the young devout's face, one arc of the circle reflecting across his forehead before it disappeared.

"What was that?" Yuriko whispered, looking at her hand. She tried touching her forehead. The glyph had gone out. Nothing happened.

With both hands, the Archdevout lifted the Hollow Book and pressed it to his chest directly over his heart. Standing still, he closed his eyes. When he opened them, he held out the book and pressed it to the forehead of the young devout, right over the spot where Yuriko's glyph had appeared.

"*Allcaste*," the Archdevout said, his voice sounding weak to her ears.

"Yes?"

"This one will be your servant."

Yuriko turned to the young devout. He was bowing again to the floor, thrusting his head in between his arms, as though he could hide from her sight that way.

"The Hollow Book has chosen him. You will take him with you," the Archdevout said, his shoulders slumped. The book shifted in his bony fingers so that Yuriko thought it might drop to the floor. But instead, the Archdevout sank to the floor so fast it looked as though the strength had left his legs. The book fell into his lap.

"Show us your face," the Archdevout commanded. "You will touch the Hollow Book with your hand," he ordered the young devout.

The devout stood, trembling slightly, and took the book. He held it gingerly, as though it were a hot coal that might burn him.

The Archdevout narrowed his eyes and frowned, peering into the young devout's face. He leaned forward, coming so close to his young double their foreheads nearly touched.

But then the Archdevout straightened himself. He spun around and walked away so quickly he might have been fleeing.

"Take him with you. He will serve you," the Archdevout said to Yuriko, facing away from both of them. "He is your slave. He will do as you ask and aid you in any way that he can. Take him with you!"

For a moment, Yuriko couldn't decide whether the Archdevout was commanding her or pleading with her.

"Wait, wait, please," the young devout said. His voice sounded both earnest and pained.

For a sliver of a moment, Yuriko looked into his dark black eyes. He blinked, then shuffled away from Yuriko across the floor, the book clutched to his chest. He bowed again, to her this time. "I will aid you, *allcaste*. This I swear. Please, take me with you."

The Archdevout stood looking away. The four nameless devout stood with their heads down, hands clenched into fists by their sides, as though at any moment they expected a great weight to fall down upon them from the sky.

"All right," Yuriko said at last. It didn't sound like the sort of request one refused. And besides, had she said no, she was afraid the young devout would burst into tears. "Maybe you could stand up?"

He stood, trembling, the Hollow Book clutched in his hands.

"Might I take a look at that?" Yuriko asked. She was about to reach out for it when the Archdevout shouted, "No!"

Whirling around, he snatched the book from the young devout's hands. Immediately, the four nameless devout rushed between Yuriko and her new servant, forming a wall between them.

"The *allcaste* must never touch the Hollow Book, never!" one of them said, grabbing her by the shoulder. Yuriko reeled.

"You may not even look upon it from too close a distance! Your glyph will be defiled!"

"Okay, I get it! I understand!" Yuriko shouted back, brushing off the nameless devout's hands. "I just wanted to see it, that's all. I'm sorry!" At the sound of her voice, the four nameless devout seemed to recover from their panic. One of them had pushed the young devout to the floor and was still sitting on him.

"Could you let him up? You're going to crush him," Yuriko said, catching her breath. The nameless devout stood, helping the younger to his feet.

"I apologize for this," the Archdevout said to Yuriko, his voice still shaky. "For you to see or touch the book is taboo."

"I understand. I'll be careful." Yuriko turned her back on the nameless devout. "I'll just look the other way so you can put the Hollow Book away—hide it or something."

She heard the rustling of robes and the soft padding of the nameless devout's feet as they moved across the floor of the dome. It took every ounce of her willpower to resist turning around. She knew what the word *taboo* meant, but it lacked any real punch for her. The pull of curiosity was far stronger, and heedless of logic.

She really did wonder about the book. *If only I'd gotten a better look at it.* It was just so different from what she had expected. For one thing, she hadn't seen anything on the cover, certainly nothing like the glyph on her forehead. It had just been a plain, leather-bound book.

And the way the devout had reacted...

"Archdevout?" Yuriko asked, without turning.

"Yes, *allcaste*?" the Archdevout replied. His voice had regained its calm.

"Is the glyph on the Hollow Book? It's supposed to be, isn't it?"

The Archdevout paused for breath before responding. "Yes, the glyph is on there."

"Are you sure?"

"Does it concern you?"

Maybe what I saw was the back of the book?

"Archdevout, why were you so startled when you saw the book the first time? You looked almost frightened."

Behind her, the rustling of robes ceased.

"Didn't you say something like 'What?' Like you were shocked?"

The Archdevout did not answer her question but informed her that the Hollow Book had been returned to the casket. "You may turn around again, *allcaste*."

Yuriko turned slowly. The Archdevout was standing next to the young devout, the other four a respectful distance behind them.

All trace of confusion was gone from their faces. Their expressions were soft and calm. In the gloom of the dome, their pale heads floated like white balloons over their black robes.

Only the young devout's eyes seemed ill at ease. His eyes darted back and forth.

"The Hollow Book is damaged," the Archdevout said then. "It reveals the violence with which the Hero broke its bonds. That is why I was so surprised. I apologize. It was most unbecoming of the nameless devout," the Archdevout said, hanging his head. "I beg your forgiveness, *allcaste.*"

The four nameless devout standing behind the Archdevout joined him in bowing to her.

Yuriko and the young devout stood there stupidly, like children unable to follow a grown-up conversation. A beat later, the young devout hurriedly bowed his head.

His eyes met Yuriko's on the way down.

Yuriko smiled at him, though she couldn't say why. It just seemed to rise naturally to her face.

The young devout's lips opened slightly. He was looking at her strangely. Yuriko couldn't remember anyone ever looking at her like that. It was as though she had become a rainbow. The young devout was looking up at her in awe, like she was a rainbow in the sky.

Yuriko blushed, then giggled despite herself. Behind the young devout, the Archdevout and the others stood.

"My servant," Yuriko said softly, walking over to the young devout. She bowed once before him, crisply. "Pleased to meet you. I'm Yuriko."

CHAPTER FIVE

The Hunt Begins

Yuriko found herself once again standing on the small knob of a hill overlooking the plateau where turned the Great Wheels of Inculpation. Next to her stood the Archdevout and the young nameless monk who had so recently become her servant. Dawn was beginning to break in the nameless land. Light crept warily over the eastern horizon as a wavy white line hovering in the distance.

"When departing and returning to this land, it is best you make this spot here your point of reference," the Archdevout counseled her. He had an air of dignified authority about him again. Gone was the momentary confusion she had seen in the Dome of Convocation. "The magic glyph upon your forehead will work to take you to other places, but you will be safest if you keep close to the Great Wheels, the origin of all stories."

"You mean there's a chance I might get lost?"

"Yes, though it is very slight," the Archdevout admitted with a faint smile. "Not that you would be in any danger, but I fear much time might be lost were you to find yourself on an accidental visit to some far-flung region."

The young devout had been silent, his mouth stuck in a crooked little frown. He was shining with sweat from the very top of his bald head down to the bridge of his nose, and seemed as stiff as a board. Whenever Yuriko happened to so much as glance in his direction, he would practically leap back and lower his head. Yuriko got tired just watching him. She decided to try to avoid looking at him at all.

The Archdevout handed Yuriko some black robes, much like the ones the nameless devout themselves wore, and told her to put them on over her regular clothes. "These are vestments of protection. They protect the *allcaste* and strengthen the workings of magic. They will be of much aid to you on your journey, I think."

Yuriko put on the inky black robes. They smelled of dust. The hem of the robes was long, reaching down to the knobs of her ankles. The sleeves went all the way down to her fingertips. When she put on the hood, it nearly covered her face, making her entirely incognito and very suspicious-looking.

Before she began her search for the Hero, the Archdevout explained, she must first return home. "You will look for clues. You must find what it was about the King in Yellow that bewitched your brother so."

So much that he swore allegiance to him. So much that he pressed his forehead to the floor.

"You must find out into which hole in your brother's heart the King in Yellow crept." In order to do that, the Archdevout explained, she would have to discover exactly what Hiroki had been doing before the incident and his disappearance. "You must find out what thoughts crystallized in your brother's heart in those days—they will be the clues that guide you toward him."

In other words, she needed a motive. "But how am I going to find that out?" Who could she ask? Who would tell her? Her father? Her mother? One of Hiroki's teachers at school?

The Archdevout nodded. "When you return to the Circle, the correct path will open before you. The books in the reading room will aid you of their own accord. Do not despair, your allies are many."

His voice was full of confidence, as though to drive all doubt from her mind. Yuriko found her mouth mimicking her servant's frown. *Oh,* she realized, *he's not unhappy. He's just tense.*

"Do not forget, you're not the same person you were before you visited our land. From now until the moment your role in the story is complete, you will not be the eleven-year-old girl Yuriko Morisaki. You are the *allcaste*. You are not bound by considerations of age, gender, or your former position in society. Thus, I think it well that you choose a new name. A name befitting your new status."

Yuriko brightened. Choosing a name sounded like fun. *I can pick something cool, like—*

The Archdevout interrupted her rising enthusiasm. "The soul resides in the name. You must not choose something too different from your original name or you risk alienating the eleven-year-old soul you have carried with you thus far."

Suddenly it didn't sound as fun.

"Yuriko, Yuriko, Yuriko," the Archdevout muttered thoughtfully. "How about U-ri?"

That's not so bad. It sounds like my old nickname.

Yuriko—now U-ri—turned to the young devout. "I think you need a name too. I can't just call you 'servant' all the time."

The young devout hesitated, glancing toward the Archdevout.

The Archdevout sighed. "The nameless devout must not be named while they set foot in this land," he explained. "You may name him once you have returned to the Circle. No, you *must* name him—for he is not permitted to name himself."

U-ri agreed she would.

An early morning breeze blew across the top of the hill. The hem of her robes fluttered. Some distance below them, the Great Wheels turned. "So, I should go, shouldn't I? No point in staying here, really." U-ri felt suddenly afraid. Her heart beat rapidly in her chest. "How do I do this again?"

Something about touching the glyph on her forehead...

"Take your servant's hand," the Archdevout instructed her, lowering his head reverently. "So that he may pass with you into the Circle."

U-ri glanced over at the young devout. He appeared to be drenched in sweat again.

"Your hand," U-ri said, offering her right hand to the boy. With jerky movements, the young devout reached out his right hand too, then hastily exchanged it for his left, which he then withdrew as well to wipe it on the black cloth of his robes over and over.

U-ri smiled. "It's okay. I'm sweaty too." She grinned and took his hand. It was dry as a bone—softer and warmer than she had expected.

U-ri placed her left hand on her forehead and closed her eyes. She spoke clearly, carefully enunciating each word. "Take us back to Ichiro Minochi's reading room."

The magic circle on her forehead shone with the cold light of the moon, instantly illuminating her face.

Then U-ri and her new servant vanished, leaving the Archdevout standing by himself.

For a while, the Archdevout stood there silently in the dim light of dawn. Tiny droplets of morning dew on the grass caught the brightening rays of the sun and began to sparkle like fragments of stars scattered across the ground. As they left, the torches around the turning wheels below burned down to stumps and flickered out one by one.

The Archdevout looked up. His aged body shimmered and then reshaped itself into the familiar appearance of the other nameless devout—the youthful monk U-ri had met first upon her arrival.

Without a sound, he began to walk down the hill.

❦

It happened just as it had when she first came to the nameless land. U-ri opened her eyes, and she was back in the reading room in her great-uncle's cottage, surrounded by stacks of books. She was standing in the center of the large magic circle she had drawn on the floor.

"You're back!"

It was Aju.

U-ri's heart leapt with joy. Even though she hadn't known the book for more than a few days, he already felt like an old friend.

"Aju! Aju, where are you?"

"Right here!" A red light blinked furiously from the corner of one of the stacks of books up against the wall. The book looked like he was practically jumping to get her attention.

"Aju!" Yuriko ran over and hugged the red book to her chest. "I was there, Aju! I went to the nameless land! I even went inside the Hall of All Books! And, and—" U-ri's throat burned and her voice choked with a sob of relief. "I saw the Great Wheels! I heard them turning, and their song. And the nameless devout were there, pushing them, pushing..."

Tears flowed down her cheeks, though she couldn't say whether they were of relief or sadness. U-ri pressed her face to Aju's cover and cried.

"We know. We know what it's like over there, all of us," Aju said gently. There was a warmth to his red glow. "I see you're wearing vestments of protection."

U-ri looked up, wiping her face with one sleeve. "Yes, the Archdevout said they were special."

"They are. They hold a very powerful magic. They'll protect you from danger, little miss. So you probably shouldn't blow your nose on them."

U-ri—who was indeed about to blow her nose—laughed out loud. "I have a new name, Aju."

"Yes, as an *allcaste*. What are you called?"

"U-ri."

"A good name. Has a nice ring to it." Aju glowed once brightly, making U-ri squint against the light. "And you have a servant, I see. Won't you introduce him to us?"

The young devout was still crouched in the middle of the magic circle, perfectly still though his eyes flashed like those of a captured beast. When Aju mentioned him, he jumped like a frightened rabbit, scurried over to the door of the reading room and knelt there, pressing his hands and face to the floor, and stammered, "Forgive me! I-I am the Lady U-ri's servant!"

His voice was shaking and squeaky. He was sweating again too. It was morning in this world. The early sun came in through the window, making his head glisten brightly.

"You don't have to be scared," U-ri said, turning to him. "These books here are my friends. Just like the Archdevout said—"

"That's right," Aju agreed. "Stand and greet us. If you insist on cowering every time you meet someone, you'll only be a bother to your master."

The boy devout managed to look up and immediately began to apologize.

Still holding Aju in her arms, U-ri found a place for the two of them to sit among the piles of books. "Here, sit down. Let's catch our breath for a moment." U-ri sat on the stepladder she'd used before. For the younger devout, she motioned toward a small stool hiding between two of the teetering stacks of books. He went over and sat down with a wary look at the stool, as though it might bite him.

"So, you have brought back a servant," said another familiar voice. U-ri turned around, looking for the Sage.

"Is that you, Sage? We're back," U-ri announced herself.

There was no response.

Even though the reading room was gradually brightening, the morning light did not completely drown out the paler light of the books. Except now the room looked less like a planetarium and more like a hidden cave filled with glittering jewels.

"Where is the Sage?" U-ri asked, standing. Eventually, she heard him speak from directly ahead of her, high up on one of the shelves.

"Lady U-ri, what will you name your servant?"

His voice sounded very somber to her, not that he was ever as lighthearted and easygoing as Aju was. But U-ri thought she detected something else in his voice—he sounded displeased. The young devout seemed to have noticed it too, for he ducked his head again and drew his legs up onto the stool.

"I'm still thinking about that," U-ri replied, her own voice growing more serious. "Is something wrong? Was I not supposed to bring him back?"

The Archdevout hadn't said anything like that. He said the Hollow Book had *chosen* the young devout. She had to bring him back—she didn't have any choice. U-ri explained all this, wondering what could be bothering the Sage.

Again there was no answer. The Sage's deep green light winked slowly, as though he were deep in thought.

"Are you angry?" U-ri stood and began to move the stepladder over toward the wall. She thought it might help if she could pick the Sage up and talk to him directly.

"I'm not angry. Please be seated, Lady U-ri."

She noticed that the Sage was even more polite than he had been before—it was almost embarrassing to have everyone calling her "lady."

"I am not angry. It is only that the nameless devout are, as a rule, never to leave the nameless land. That one would break away and join you as your servant indicates most unusual circumstances—circumstances of which I believe you have not yet been informed."

The young devout bowed his head even deeper. The collar of his robes shifted, revealing part of one emaciated shoulder.

"Circumstances?"

From U-ri's lap, Aju spoke. "If it was decided in the nameless land that he should go with her, then I don't see what the problem is."

"Silence, Aju," a female voice said. "You're still young. There is much you do not understand."

U-ri looked at Aju—she sensed that he returned her gaze, or would have, were he human.

"Tell us then," the Sage inquired of the young devout, "why is it that you have come here with the Lady U-ri?"

U-ri felt as though the weight of every book in the room had become a heavy silence, pressing down on her head. She heard a sound—the young devout's teeth were chattering. U-ri immediately felt sorry for him. *Why is the Sage being so harsh?* She felt like she was looking at herself a few days before. She remembered how frightened she had been, how sad, how she had curled up in a ball and clenched her fists and trembled.

"I-I was…" the young devout's throat was dry, his voice constricted. "I have lost the right to be one of the nameless devout."

U-ri's eyes opened wide. *Nobody told me anything like that!* "What do you mean?" she asked before she could think better of it. The nameless devout flinched back as though he had been pricked by a needle. U-ri's words seemed almost physically painful to him. "I'm sorry, it's okay. Don't be frightened. I'm not angry. It's just, I'm starting to feel like there are a great many things the Archdevout didn't tell me. And I'm starting to wonder what's going on. Aren't you all?" she asked the books around them, but there was no response.

"I feel the same way you do, U-ri," Aju offered at last. "And I'm not sure why everyone seems so put out." U-ri sensed him glaring at the Sage. "Let's hear what the boy has to say and make our judgments after that."

"That boy is an apostate," the Sage said curtly. "He has admitted as much himself."

"Yeah, but the Archdevout chose him. The same thing with U-ri—"

"There are no ranks among the nameless devout. Thus, there can be no orders given from one to another. This one who called himself the Archdevout was merely identifying himself as such for the benefit of Lady U-ri. He has no authority to choose nor recognize anyone."

This silenced even Aju. He and U-ri exchanged glances again.

"It's strange for an *allcaste* to have a servant?" U-ri asked the Sage. "Is this unusual? Is that why you don't like it? Didn't you tell me yourself that the nameless devout would help me?"

The Sage *hmm*ed thoughtfully for a moment before replying. "I did not mean they would aid you in this particular way, and since they have, there must be a reason for it, Lady U-ri."

Now they were getting somewhere.

"So let's hear what the reason is. Then we'll know, right? And I really think you're scaring him. I…I really don't want you threatening my servant."

U-ri hadn't intended it, but her voice seemed to have gained an air of authority. The Sage's green light grew duller.

"I have spoken out of place, and I apologize," the Sage said gravely. "Let us do as the Lady U-ri advises."

U-ri blinked. "Oh—I'm sorry. I didn't mean to go against you." *Now I've done it.* U-ri wondered what a grown-up would do in this situation. Maybe cough or something to change the mood? She tried coughing. It didn't seem to have much of an effect.

"Right, well, look—" U-ri turned back to the young devout. "You just said something that I hadn't heard before that sounded very important. Could you tell me more? Why were you no longer able to be a nameless devout?"

U-ri watched the young devout—who seemed completely unable to stop shivering—and remembered something she had heard in the nameless land. *Weren't the nameless devout supposed to be sinners of some kind? Wouldn't it be a good thing to lose your qualifications to be one, then? If you ceased to be a nameless devout, weren't you free of sin?*

The young devout looked up at her. He blinked and opened his mouth as though he meant to say something but couldn't figure out exactly what.

The weighty voice of the Sage cut in again. "I would inform the Lady U-ri that nameless devout can never truly be freed. Once a soul has become a nameless devout, they will never be anything but."

"But this one here—"

"If a nameless devout loses his right to be a nameless devout, then he becomes nothing. He *is* nothing!" the Sage practically shouted.

Yuriko jerked back. Her tongue curled up in her mouth. *He's scary when he's mad.* Mrs. Kiuchi at school could be scary sometimes, but it was nothing like this.

"If you will permit me—" the young devout began.

"Go on," U-ri urged. "Permit what?" She was about to go over and hold his hand again. He looked like he needed it.

"If you will permit me, Lady U-ri, I will tell you why I was cast out of the nameless land."

Cast out?

"You can have all the permission you want. But what's this about you being cast out? You weren't cast out."

He was chosen to follow me, wasn't he?

The young devout shook his head. He was trembling again, and his teeth were chattering loudly. "No, Lady U-ri, I was c-cast out. For to be chosen by the Hollow Book is to become an outcast."

"Well, nobody ever told me that!"

The young devout slumped, clutching at the collar of his black robes with tight fingers. He looked like a little lost child.

"Remember when the Archdevout told you to take me with you?"

"Yes?"

"Didn't it seem to you like he was in a hurry? Could you not hear the harshness in his tone?"

In truth, she had. The Archdevout *had* sounded very displeased with her new servant—just as the Sage had a moment ago.

"He was in a hurry because he had very little time to remove me from the nameless land...for I had been defiled."

"You were defiled? Why? Because the book chose you?"

The young devout bowed deeply. "Yes, but you have the order reversed. The Hollow Book chose me *because* I had been defiled."

"Then how were you defiled?"

The young devout clutched at his collar and swallowed dryly a couple times. "In the nameless land, the First Bell is rung to mark the escape of the Hero. The only other time that bell is rung is when the Hero is imprisoned. Yet the bell rings differently on each occasion so that any who hear it might know immediately what it means."

"So you heard it when the Hero broke out of its prison. Had you heard the bell ring before?"

The young devout nodded. His teeth had stopped chattering. "Yes, when the Hero was bound. I cannot say how long ago it was because there is no time in the nameless land. But I can say that when the Hero escaped, that was the first time I had ever heard the bell ring in that way. I knew immediately what had happened. The Hero was free—" the young devout closed his eyes.

"And the knowledge of that moved me," he said, shuddering as though he were deeply mortified by the admission. Around them, it seemed as though the books were holding their breath. "The Hero had escaped into the Circle. At the moment I knew that, I felt something in my heart—a heart I should not possess."

U-ri didn't know what to say to that.

"I knew there would be war," young devout continued. "A hunt would begin to chase down the Hero and bring it back to the nameless land. That is what the ringing of the First Bell told me. That is what moved me."

U-ri breathed out slowly. "Pardon me if I'm getting this wrong, but are you saying that you heard something big was going on, so you got excited?"

The young devout shrank back again, rooted to the spot. He was hugging himself with both arms. "Yes," he replied in a tiny voice. "Yes, that is what happened."

"Excited? So that's what you call it," the Sage said. U-ri thought she detected a hint of sarcasm in the Sage's harsh voice. "He admits that the escape of the Hero brought change to that changeless land, and his heart leapt, his soul stirred, he knew joy!"

Something else had crept into the Sage's voice as he spoke. *Fear.* The Sage was afraid. He was frightened by what U-ri's servant had said.

What's going on here? The Sage is just as frightened as the Archdevout was when he opened the casket and took out the Hollow Book.

A heavy silence descended upon the room. The only sound was the ragged breathing of the young devout. He seemed ready to cry or scream.

"Aren't you being a little hard on him?" U-ri turned to the Sage, trying to hide her own surprise at all of this. "I think I understand what he's saying. If I were forced to live in a place like that, doing the same thing over and over, I'd be happy about a little change myself."

She pictured the devout at their endless task. Day after day pushing those giant wheels. The only thing even slightly unpredictable in their world was the movement of the sparks that rose from their torches.

"But, Lady U-ri, the nameless devout exist solely to push the Great Wheels of Inculpation."

"Why, because they are sinners? Because they tried to 'live' a story?"

Once again, the books in the reading room held their breath. Only Aju seemed unperturbed.

"Look, what I don't get is, if they committed a sin and are being punished, why doesn't the punishment ever end? Maybe when my servant's heart leapt, it was a sign that he had already paid off his debt and was ready to become a human again!"

Nobody said a word. The young devout looked up, but before he could speak, Aju whispered to her. He was glowing very dimly. "Sorry, U-ri, but I don't think that's right. That's not like what I know about the nameless devout. Their labors are never supposed to end."

"So they're never forgiven? Ever?"

"There is no 'ever' in a place without time."

U-ri pouted, sticking out her lip. *That's just too cruel. How could that possibly be fair?*

"It is true. Our sins are never forgiven, Lady U-ri," the young devout said softly.

"Well, if you insist, then fine. You'll never be forgiven. I just don't think that's right." U-ri shook her head. "So what happened then? What happened after your heart jumped?"

"I waited."

"Waited for what?"

For the first time, the young devout smiled. It was such a faint smile that, for moment, Yuriko didn't trust her eyes.

"For you."

Had a boy said the same to her a week ago, she would have blushed bright red, but with her new name, wrapped in the vestments of a nameless place, it seemed entirely appropriate. She understood how he had waited, full of hope and fear.

U-ri lifted an eyebrow at the young devout. "You were the one who put the blankets on me when I was sleeping in the Hall of All Books, weren't you. You lit the lamp in my room."

The young devout blanched.

Gotcha! "So you were watching me!" He'd been waiting for the *allcaste* to arrive, and when she did, he had watched her. Not like a policeman tailing someone, or a stalker—he just hadn't been able to keep his eyes off her. "So you were there the whole time—until the Archdevout called you out of the shadows in the dome."

The young devout nodded slightly. "My brothers realized this, and thus knew that I had been defiled."

So things like curiosity and wanting change are considered defilements in the nameless land?

"It happens only rarely," said a voice. It was the Sage. He spoke only with great difficulty, forcing the words out. "You might call it an accident." The tinge of fear in his voice grew stronger.

"An accident?" U-ri echoed. *That reminds me.* "When the Archdevout first pulled the Hollow Book from its container, he was surprised at how damaged it was. You say the nameless devout aren't human and don't have hearts, but I don't think that's true. They can be surprised, and frightened, and even a little angry. Just like you can."

The Sage was quiet. His green light winked slowly, at great intervals, as though he were taking deep breaths.

"If the Archdevout was so surprised at seeing the book damaged, it must not happen very often—could that be connected to what happened with my servant? If both are such rare things, I'll bet it's not a coincidence."

"Is that what the Archdevout told you?" the Sage asked quietly. "He said that the book had been damaged? Is that how he explained his dismay when he retrieved the Hollow Book from the casket in the nameless land, Lady U-ri?"

"Well, yes."

The Sage fell silent once again. His green glow began to flicker more rapidly, like a sprinter's heartbeat, then slowed again to the pace of a meditating monk.

"I find it hard to believe that the book was damaged," the Sage said at last. "But if the Archdevout said it, it must be so."

He's choosing his words pretty carefully.

"And I think that the Hero's violent escape from its prison is somehow connected to the birth of your servant, as you say, Lady U-ri."

Okay—kind of a roundabout way of agreeing with me, but okay.

"Have you never met an *allcaste* with a servant?"

"This is my first. Though I did know of the possibility."

"So it's not the first time ever?"

"It is not."

"And...it's not a good thing?"

There was a pause.

"It is not."

"Which is why you scolded me when I showed up with him."

"I was not scolding you," the Sage hastily clarified. "If my words sounded harsh, then I must apologize."

U-ri smiled. "It's okay. I was just surprised; I'm not upset. And, the book being damaged sounds pretty bad, but I don't see what's wrong about me having help. And think of him." She looked at the young devout. "If I hadn't taken him out of that dismal place, he would have been stuck there forever. That *has* to be a good thing."

U-ri turned to face the young devout. "The Hollow Book chose you to help me. What could be bad about that?" U-ri was practically shouting, happy with her own idea. "I'll bet the book figured the *allcaste* would need some help after it saw how violently the Hero broke free of its prison. That's why it chose you!" *And if he helps me fight the Hero and rescue my brother, so much the better.* "Think about it! You'll be freed! I'm sure of it!" The book was giving him a second chance. U-ri felt a warm strength swell inside her. She stepped closer to the young devout and took his hand in hers. "So stand straight, and keep your chin up! You're here to help me, after all. And you're here to help yourself."

"O-okay."

"Um, excuse me?" It was Aju. "I hate to interrupt this heartwarming scene you've got going here, but I'd like you to try something for me."

"What's that?"

"Take off your robes."

U-ri shrugged and took them off. She staggered. The strength went out of her knees. Her whole body felt heavy, and the room began to spin around her. She felt like the stacks of books were going to collapse in on her in an avalanche of paper and leather bindings. She fell to the ground, unable to stand, her elbows hitting the floor. She lacked even the strength to yelp.

What's wrong with me...

In the silent room, U-ri's stomach growled.

"You're starving, that's what!" Aju said with a laugh. "And you're completely exhausted to boot."

Oh...really? U-ri lifted her head and looked in the direction of Aju's voice.

Then she panicked. The young devout was gone! *But he was right there just a second ago. He was holding my hand. Where is he—*

"Servant!" she called. "Where are you? Where did you go?"

"Now, now, don't worry," Aju said, winking at her with a burst of light. "Put the vestments on again."

It was ten times harder putting them on than it had been to take them off. But the instant the dusty black cloth fell over her shoulders, her strength returned. Her belly no longer felt empty and the room stopped spinning.

The young devout was right there, standing as he had been when they were holding hands a moment before. Except that his eyes were wide open. "Lady U-ri?" Hurriedly, he went to help her to her feet.

U-ri jumped up. "I'm okay. I'm fine." She spread the sleeves of her robe and looked at them. "I get it. So that's what they do."

"That's what they do, and more," Aju said brightly. "The vestments of protection have several features I'm sure you'll find handy. Best remember them." Aju made a sound like he was clearing his throat. "One. As long as you wear the vestments, you will feel no hunger or fatigue. Two. Inside the vestments, you will be invisible to anyone in this world."

"You mean like the Invisible Man?"

"No, you'd still be—" Aju began before realizing what she meant. "Ah, yes, that's the name of a story, isn't it? Yes, something like that. Still, though you'll be invisible, anything you touch or move with your hands will be visible to people, so be careful. If you want to make something else invisible, though, all you need do is slip it beneath your robes. Oh, and you'll be incorporeal inside the robes too—which means no one will be able to touch you or know you're there in any way."

Finally, Aju explained, when she took the vestments off, she would not be able to see her servant.

"So that's what happened!"

The young devout's head bobbed. "Yes, yes. You disappeared from my sight too, Lady U-ri. There was only space where you stood a moment before. I tried to reach out to you, but felt nothing."

"That's because nameless devout have no real form outside of the nameless land, right?" Aju said, directing his question toward the Sage.

"That is correct," the Sage confirmed, a lingering harshness to his voice. "The magic of the vestments works through U-ri to give her servant shape. His existence in this world is a borrowed one. Without the magic of the robes, they will not be able to see each other, and should they be drawn too far apart, they may never find each other again."

U-ri swallowed. What would happen to the nameless devout if they got separated? Would he wander through the world, unable to leave, invisible to everyone?

"He will return to nothing, for he is nothing," the Sage said, answering her unasked question.

"Then I'll have to be careful," U-ri muttered. She wrote a note as big as she could in her mind, sticking it where she would see it.

"Oh, and one other thing," Aju added, a hint of laughter in his voice. "The power of the vestments has given you the ability to use all kinds of magic spells—that is, it should have."

"Should have...?"

"Well, let me ask you then. Do you feel like you can do magic?"

Not at all. Yuriko tried to focus her thoughts into something, but nothing came. She didn't even have an idea of where to begin.

"As I thought. It's because you lack knowledge. You don't know the spells. Lucky for you," Aju continued, "there are lots of spells in the books right here. Each one of us has our own specialty. Which brings me to another question. Remember what kind of book I am, by any chance?"

"You're a dictionary! A beginner's dictionary of spells!"

"Very good!" Aju cheered. He was in a fine mood. "Just use me and you'll be able to learn all sorts of spells—if you make the proper preparations, that is."

"What sort of preparations?"

"Well," Aju said, "there is a limit to my knowledge. I won't be enough to cover all you'll need on your upcoming journey, for sure. That's why you'll want me to be able to communicate with my friends here in the reading room no matter where I am. That would be nice, eh? Then you'd just have to consult me to learn anything contained in any of the books in this room."

All she needed to do, Aju told her, was cast a spell of linking on him.

"So what's the spell of linking? Where do I find it?"

"That's one of the higher-level spells," Aju said with a wink. "I'll bet the Sage knows it."

U-ri looked up. The Sage's green glow strengthened, then faded—as though he were about to say something then thought better of it. "If the Lady U-ri wishes it, I will teach it to her," he said at last.

"Thanks!"

"I'll grab something to write with," the young devout suggested, dashing out of the room.

"I won't need anything—" U-ri tried calling him back, but he didn't seem to notice.

"It's okay, let him go. He probably won't like this part anyway."

"Won't like it? Why?"

"You are a bit slow, aren't you, U-ri," Aju said in a singsong voice. "Remember what I said about me being able to communicate with my friends *no matter where I was*?"

"Aju!" U-ri said, putting her hand to her mouth. "You mean you'll come with me?"

"You bet I will!" Then Aju really did break into song—a song about traveling with U-ri and his upcoming adventures with the *allcaste*.

"Should I carry you in my backpack again?" U-ri asked, suddenly wondering where she had left her backpack.

"Nope! Not this time."

"Why not?"

"Because there's a better way! You can turn me into something more convenient. Something smaller. Something that can move by itself."

"Like what?"

"I've got just the spell, take a look!" he said, not answering her question. His pages began to flip before U-ri's eyes. "Right here! That's the page. Now," Aju instructed, "hold me open to that page with both hands. Move your feet apart a little, that's right. You'll want to be steady. Now recite after me."

U-ri took a breath and began to repeat the words after Aju said them.

"*Quesaran, pasaran, altimidite! Uga, uga, ugachakaraka modistan*—what a ridiculous spell!" U-ri laughed out loud. In her hands, a bright red light suffused the book. For moment, it glowed so brightly U-ri was afraid he had caught fire. She closed her eyes.

When she opened them again, a red sphere about the size of a soccer ball was floating before her nose, bouncing up and down like a balloon in the hands of a happy child.

She extended a finger and gingerly touched it. The red sphere wobbled gently in the air.

"Hurry! Let me out!" It was Aju's voice, coming from inside the sphere. "Break it and let me out!"

Flustered, she grabbed the red sphere in both hands. It was like grabbing a giant blob of Jell-O. In fact, it even looked like Jell-O. *I wonder if it tastes like raspberry,* U-ri thought as she gave it a good squeeze. Her fingers sank into the blob. The sphere warped, then popped loudly.

"Ayeee!"

Something small came flying out of the sphere. It zipped up through the air like a spinning firecracker then zig-zagged about the room before returning to land atop U-ri's head. It felt soft against her hair, warm. She raised a hand to touch it.

A long tail dangled down in front of her face, hitting her on the nose.

"Aju? What are you?"

Something small was creeping through her hair. She could feel tiny feet, with even tinier toes. Whatever it was, it had four legs.

"Aju?"

"Frankly, I was hoping for something a little, well, cooler." It was Aju's voice. He sounded crestfallen. "Oh well, I should've known. The vestments of protection might be strong, but you're still pretty young."

Yuriko felt around gingerly with her hand until she found the little thing's neck, then she picked it up between her fingers and brought it in front of her face.

"Hiya!"

Two little eyes blinked at her above a twitching pink nose. Disproportionately long whiskers tickled U-ri's cheek.

"Aju! You're a...a field mouse!" U-ri said, startled—then the tickle of the whiskers made her sneeze.

"Hey! Watch it!" Aju shrieked, covering his eyes with two tiny paws.

"It is not the Lady U-ri's fault. You are but a small collection of knowledge. This size suits you," the Sage commented, and all of the other books blinked with laughter.

U-ri smiled. It was good to feel the mood brighten around her. Everything had been doom and gloom for too long.

"Well, Aju, I think you're kinda cute." U-ri smiled and pressed her nose to Aju's tiny pink nose. "It's nice to meet you again."

U-ri looked down at her vestments. They were older than they had seemed at first and showed signs of having been mended several times. In one place, the inner lining had a large tear in it that someone had patched with a square of cloth. But the thread along the top side of the patch had come undone, making a perfect pocket for Aju to slip into. Inside the pocket, he was right over her heart, and when he stuck his nose out, he could look around from the split in her front collar.

"That's comfy," Aju squeaked, sounding pleased with this arrangement despite his earlier protests.

By the time the young devout had returned from his search of the cottage, an old marker in hand, U-ri had already finished casting the spell of linking on Aju.

"Sorry, we don't need that anymore," Aju told him. The young devout's eyes opened wide like he'd seen a ghost—or rather, a talking mouse. Everyone laughed.

"Thanks," U-ri said. "Maybe I can use it for something else."

"You know, U-ri did tell you she didn't need that, but you didn't hear her—pay more attention next time," Aju scolded.

"There is no need to be short with him, Aju," U-ri said, examining the marker. It looked ancient. She tried scribbling something with it, but no ink came out. It must have all dried up, even though the cap was on tight.

U-ri frowned. "You didn't find anything else that looked like it could write?"

"Nothing at all." The young devout shook his head.

That was odd. She knew her great-uncle had lived alone, but it seemed strange for there to be only one pen in the entire cottage. Pens and pencils were the sort of thing that collected when you weren't looking until you had a whole pile of them, weren't they? That, and she knew Mr. Minochi had been a collector of books, which meant he did research. *Which means he must've taken notes. Unless he did everything on a computer?*

But then he still would have needed a pen or pencil to jot down memos and the like.

"What is it, U-ri? Let's get going," Aju said. He tickled the bottom of her chin with his long whiskers until she feared she might fall to the floor giggling uncontrollably.

"All right, all right—that is, where are we going, anyway?"

"Your house, of course. We'll need to go searching for clues eventually, but first let's see how your double is doing. And you want to see your parents, don't you, U-ri? It's been a while."

"Yeah..."

She wondered what it would be like meeting her parents now that she was an *allcaste*.

She wondered if she could get used to it.

U-ri walked into the center of the magic circle on the floor. "You come too," she said to the servant. "I think we have to hold hands again."

The young devout stepped toward her but hesitated at the edge of the magic circle.

"Where exactly will you go to, U-ri?" Aju asked from her pocket. "It's teleportation, so you can be really specific."

My room, maybe. No—my mom might be in there. Even if she can't see me in these robes, I'd be able to see her and I might freak out.

"I think the road out in front of the apartment building. We can cross the street and go in through the front door."

"Are you sure that's a good idea?" Aju asked. "You remember exactly how wide the road is? This teleportation business is more difficult than you might think. Maybe somewhere inside the house would be safer for the first try—"

"Nah—we'll be fine! Let's go!"

U-ri put one hand to her forehead. The young devout took her hand and swallowed nervously.

"Take us to the road in front of my house, next to the electrical pole with a sign for the Onoda Clinic on it!"

Then U-ri and the devout and the little mouse Aju disappeared, leaving the blinking and winking books behind.

"Sage," said a quiet voice seemingly as old as the Sage himself. "Are you sure about this?"

The Sage winked once, slowly, before answering. "I am. And besides, we don't have a choice about it now."

The winking of the books in the reading room stopped briefly, as if they were all taking a moment to silently pray.

The teleportation was different—maybe because she was traveling through the real world this time. U-ri felt a sense of motion, and she knew it when she had landed. She bent her knees and crouched, as though she had just hopped down from some higher place. Across the road stood a familiar gray building. *Angel Castle Ishijima. Home.* Her eyes went up to the fifth floor.

Wait a minute, the building looks closer than it should—

"U-ri, look out!"

With a tremendous rumbling noise, a giant truck, its bed piled to overflowing with steel girders, came thundering down on them—and *it passed right through them.*

Stunned, U-ri watched the back of the truck race away. Its exhaust swirled through the air around them.

"We're in the middle of the street!" Aju cried.

Not that U-ri needed him to tell her that. The electrical pole she had been aiming for was to her back. There was the sign for the clinic on it.

"I told you, it's hard to get the distances just right at first."

"What's the matter? It's not like the cars can hit us."

The young devout got his footing and spread his arms wide. Blinking, he looked down to make sure he hadn't been crushed. Then he looked up, and his eyes opened wide. His jaw went slack and he gasped.

"What is it?" U-ri looked up. Dawn had broken and it was already well into morning. The spring sky was blue, with a few puffy clouds bobbing peacefully along like bits of dandelion fluff. "What are you looking at?"

The young devout didn't answer, so U-ri reached out and touched his arm. He still didn't look at her, so she gave him a gentle shake. He stood there, still, looking up into the sky. "What—what is it, Lady U-ri?"

"What do you mean? It's the sky. What's so strange about that?"

"The sky..." the young devout muttered. "No, it is surely the heavens! But why is it such a blue color?"

U-ri blinked. "Don't they have a sky in the nameless land—"

Oh, that's right. It's always cloudy there. And covered in mist. "You've never seen a blue sky before, have you!"

Eyes still wide, he looked at U-ri. Then he jabbed a finger above her head. "What do you mean 'sky'? Is there a blue sky up there? All I see are the heavens, Lady U-ri."

U-ri finally realized what the problem was. *They must not use the word* sky *in the nameless land.* Now that she thought about it, she realized that the pillar in the center of one of the Great Wheels and the clouds over their heads had both been called "heaven."

"Here we call the heavens *sky*," she told him. "This is a blue sky." She pointed upward.

"It's so...beautiful," the young devout breathed, enchanted by the scene above him, its blue reflected in his eyes.

Of course, they were in the middle of the city, full of trucks and cars going this way and that. *That's not a* real *blue sky*, U-ri thought, frowning at the brownish haze that clung to the horizon.

It reminded her of something her brother had said once. There was a sky color they called "azure blue" in more difficult books than the ones she read. It was the kind of deep, rich blue she and her brother would never see in their city—maybe not even in their country. There was probably only a few places in the world left where you could see a real azure blue sky.

Still, the sky here seemed to be more than enough for her servant. Even standing here in the exhaust from the big truck, this smoggy sky was enough to impress someone who had been trapped for so long in the nameless land.

"I've got it," U-ri said suddenly. "Sky!"

"What's that?" Aju asked. The nameless devout was still too busy staring up, the springtime sun in his face, to notice. His eyes were closed and he had begun to gently sway back and forth.

"That's your name now, servant."

The young devout blinked and looked at her. "What? Did you say something, Lady U-ri?"

"Yes, your name will be Sky. I can't keep calling you 'servant' forever."

She thought it might be nice to shake his hand and make a formal occasion out of it, when another giant truck rumbled *through* them. Exhaust swirled around their heads.

"U-ri? Sky?" Aju whimpered. "Can we please get out of this road?"

The front door was locked. U-ri didn't have a key. It was in her backpack, which she had left somewhere in Mr. Minochi's cottage.

"So what do we do now?"

U-ri ignored Aju's question. She bit her lip, then pressed the button on the intercom by the door.

Ding dong.

She heard footsteps approaching from the other side. Someone in slippers was running for the door.

"Let's step back a little," U-ri said, pulling Sky back with her.

"Yes?"

The door opened. It was her mother. There was a video camera on the intercom, but she hadn't bothered looking at it. *That hasn't changed at least. She still thinks my brother might be coming home.*

"Who's there?" Still in slippers, her mother walked to the door and leaned out to look down the hall. "Who's there? Hiroki?"

Now she was outside, running down the hallway. That too was the same as always. She would go all the way down to the elevators to check, hoping that Hiroki had finally come home.

"Now's our chance," U-ri said, slipping inside the apartment. The door began to close slowly behind her. Sky hurriedly followed her in.

"Does your mom always run out like that?"

"Yeah. Her eyes were pretty red again too. I bet she's not sleeping much."

U-ri felt the pain in her chest, but she gritted her teeth against it. She couldn't cry now. That wasn't why she came back. She hadn't become an *allcaste* for this.

"At least she got a lot of rest at the cottage," Aju said, trying to make her feel better.

She went inside and peeked into the living room. The television was on but no one was there. *Maybe my double is at school?* She decided to check her own room first.

Behind her, Sky was looking wide-eyed at everything. Even his pupils seemed bigger than usual. Everything was new to him, the colors, the sounds, the furniture—and above all, the electrical appliances. He shrank away from the TV, cowered by the refrigerator, and jumped when the washing machine clunked as it switched cycles.

"You'll get used to it in no time," Aju told him. "It's not magic, but it's almost as useful."

"I see…" Sky said, his voice a reverent whisper.

U-ri knocked on the door to her room. Even though she was still wrapped in the vestments, her knuckles made a satisfying noise.

"Yes?" she heard her own voice say. The door opened, then, "Welcome home!"

U-ri's double bowed when she saw her. She didn't seem surprised at all to see Aju and Sky. *Maybe she can't even see them—*

Wait, how can she see me? Maybe because she's magic, she can see through the magic of the vestments?

"Hi," U-ri replied, feeling like she should say something more to mark the occasion but unable to think of anything appropriate.

Her double was standing by the desk. One of U-ri's textbooks and a page of notes in someone else's handwriting sat side by side.

"Are you—" U-ri began, then stopped. "I mean, am I going to school?"

Her double shook her head. "You didn't want to go back, so neither did I, Master."

"Master? Oh, right. You can just call me 'U-ri.'"

"Right, U-ri."

"Where did those notes come from?"

"Kana and Sayuri took them for us."

Just hearing her friends' names made U-ri's eyes burn with tears, but she held them back. "Right, Kana's my best friend. And Sayuri and I are really good friends too. Did you thank them?"

"You didn't want to see them, so we did not meet. Your mother brought the notes home for us."

That sounds like something Yuriko would have done, U-ri thought. Her double was right. "Okay. Just, I might change my mind in the future and want to meet them. I mean, could you meet them for me?"

"Of course."

Suddenly, U-ri felt uneasy. "I don't want you getting too close to them, though. They're *my* friends."

"U-ri, U-ri, U-ri," Aju cut in. "She's your double, a magical puppet. She can't really be *friends* with another person, not like you can."

U-ri figured he was probably right, but somehow she couldn't make herself feel it. U-ri plucked Aju up in her fingers. Extending her arm, she held him out, away from the folds of her robe. "Can you see this?"

"That's a book, transformed by magic."

So she can see it—and she knows what it really is.

"How about Sky, can you see him?"

Her double smiled. "Of course I can see him. U-ri, I am your double—a true duplicate. Until the enchantment on me is broken, I am you. So you don't need to tell me anything you know—because I already know it."

That's why nothing surprises her.

"And Aju was a little wrong. Even though I cannot be friends with another person, I am close to one person—you."

Her double reached out a finger and gently rubbed Aju's tiny head. He squeaked just like a mouse.

U-ri felt the strength go out of her. Placing Aju on her shoulder, she sat down on the bed. Sky stood at the foot of the bed, his back straight. The perfect model of a servant.

"So, what happened after I left?"

It had been three days in the real world since Yuriko and her parents had come home from Mr. Minochi's cottage in the mountains. "Your parents told the police about it. They said they had gone to take a look but hadn't found Hiroki. And there was no sign he'd been there."

Even so, the police had agreed to keep an eye on Mr. Minochi's cottage in the future.

"Well, I'm grateful for that, I guess—but that will make protecting the magic circle a little harder." As soon as U-ri said it, it struck her as a particularly grown-up sort of thing to say. —I have *changed*.

Yuriko hadn't been going to school. She studied at home from the notes that her friends had taken for her. Her parents had been talking with the teachers about possibly switching schools, but nothing had been decided yet.

"Everything is the same at home. I think your mother's a little tired."

"She still cleans Hiroki's room every day?"

"She cleans it and sits in there for about an hour. She's usually crying, so I go in there sometimes and give her a hug, and cry with her."

"Thank you—" U-ri began, then she laughed. "Why am I thanking myself?" she wondered out loud.

"That's quite all right, U-ri," her double said with a smile.

She's awfully nice for a magical puppet. U-ri was glad. When she thought about it, it made sense that she should get along well with a copy of herself. She wondered if anyone had ever tried it before. Maybe she was the first ever in this world.

"Well," U-ri said after a while, "I suppose I'll be making this room my headquarters from now on."

She stood up from the bed, crossed her arms, and looked around. *I'm home. I'm finally home. This is my world.*

"You know, I could really use a bath. Even a shower."

"You're not hungry, or tired?"

"I got magic for that—and I don't have a whole lot of time. But I really need to clean up."

Aju had been keeping quiet while the two talked, but now he piped up. "Let's magic you up so you're bright-eyed and bushy-tailed first," he suggested. "Then you can let your double wear the vestments while you take a bath. Sound good?"

"Yeah, but we normally don't take a bath in the morning in my house. Mom will wonder what's up."

"That's okay—I went to sleep early last night with a headache," her double told her. "I didn't take a bath—she'll just think you're making up for that."

"Great—could you go talk to Mom for me?"

Her double left the room, and Aju scrambled up higher until he was sitting on top of U-ri's head. "All right, repeat after me!" the little mouse said in a chipper voice.

U-ri began reciting the spell quietly so her mother wouldn't hear. The spell to get rid of hunger and weariness was a happy-sounding one, with lots of *pa*'s and *pi*'s that made her giggle.

Her double returned. U-ri wedged her chair under the doorknob just in case anyone tried to open the door, then took off the vestments of protection.

She wasn't weak like she had been before. In fact, she felt better than ever.

Except she stank of sweat and was covered in grime. Even her fingernails had dirt under them. *Dirt from the nameless land,* she thought, and her heart thumped in her chest.

She finished taking off the robes, but now she quickly looked around— *that's right, I can't see Sky anymore.*

"Sky, where are you?"

Aju stuck his head out from beneath the vestments of protection draped over her arm. "He's standing right by the bed. Quick, cover up your double before someone sees both of you standing here like this."

❦

"You don't often get headaches—are you sure you don't have a cold?" Her mother put her hand on U-ri's forehead. "You don't feel like you have a fever."

No, stop. Don't cry. It was everything U-ri could do to keep from bawling on the spot. How could she tell her mother she was sorry? Why did she have to apologize anyway? Because she was hiding something? Because she wasn't Yuriko anymore?

U-ri shook her head. "I'm sorry, Mom. I—I didn't mean to make you worry."

Great. Why did I say that? Now she'll suspect something.

"What are you talking about? You're a silly girl, Yuriko. Go on, the bath's all hot. I'll bring a change for you, so just jump in. You need it—" her mother added, holding her nose and laughing. She pushed U-ri in the direction of the bath. Her mother's hand on her back felt soft and warm.

U-ri stood in the bathroom under the shower and cried. *This is it. I'm not crying again after this one time, I swear. Just let me cry now and get it out of my system.* She sank down in the bath and poured hot water over her head, and felt herself relax a little. The door to the bathroom opened. She could see her mother through the fogged glass.

"It's warm today, but you'd better wear a long-sleeved shirt, just in case."

"'Kay, Mom."

Light was streaming in through the window—*it's still morning*. She usually took baths at night, and the bathroom was never this bright. Her mother was a bit of a neat freak, especially when it came to the kitchen and the bathroom, so every surface was sparkling clean. But the apartment was old enough that there were still cracks in between the tub and the wall where a little mold had grown, stubbornly resisting her mother's attempts to flush it out.

U-ri traced one crack with her finger, then let her hand splash back into the tub.

Splash.

Seeing the bathroom in the daylight reminded her of something. —*When was that again?*

Yuriko had just gotten home and was getting ready to go to a playdate at Kana's house, when her brother had come rushing in to take a shower.

CHAPTER SIX

Digging Deeper

When was that exactly? A month ago? No, it was right after her brother entered eighth grade. U-ri was a new fifth-grader. She remembered now why he had come home early from school that day.

"Family visits this week. Classes are getting out early."

The after-school clubs were all on break, so her brother was going to go out with some kids from the neighborhood baseball team and practice.

"I'm just gonna take a quick shower before heading out."

The memories came back into sharper focus. Mom was out shopping, leaving U-ri alone at home. The front door had banged open, and her brother bounded into the bathroom before she even had time to say hi.

She looked in. He had already taken off his school jacket and was standing there in his shirt and pants. He quickly closed the changing room door.

"Sorry, U-ri, I was sweating like a pig in phys ed. I kind of stink," he told her before she had time to ask why he would take a shower before going out to practice again.

Soon she heard the sound of the shower running.

It hadn't seemed all that strange at the time. Her brother had always been fastidious about cleanliness. Even though they took baths at night, he would sometimes shower before leaving for school. She hadn't paid it that much attention. If she hadn't been taking a bath now, during the day like this, she would've forgotten about it entirely.

Something about it made her uneasy.

Maybe there was more to it than I thought.

U-ri sat in the tub, hugging her knees to her chest, thinking. Had he taken more showers during the day after that? Hadn't he come home a few times and run into the shower without even saying hi to their mom? *That wasn't like Hiroki. Why didn't I notice it before?*

The hot water from the showerhead beat down on her furrowed brow.

And what did the policeman with the eyebrows like a clown say?

"Ever since Hiroki entered the eighth grade, he'd been having trouble getting along with his classmates."

Now even what her mother had said to the policeman sounded ominous.

"I don't think he would have told her anything to make her worry. He never said anything about troubles to us…"

What hadn't he told them?

Was he being bullied?

Yuriko sat up straight, letting her hands fall down into the tub. The water splashed up into her eyes. It ran down her face and dripped off her chin as she stared at the wall.

Bullying? It didn't seem possible. *Who would bully Hiroki?*

Hiroki was tough. There was no better word to describe him. He was good at sports, good in school. He was perfect. Even the most dedicated schoolyard bully would have had trouble finding a weak spot to needle Hiroki about. If anything, *he* would have been the one doing the bullying—and that wasn't even remotely imaginable. Hiroki Morisaki was the top of the heap. Even as a middle school student, he had presence.

U-ri sighed. *What am I thinking? The hot water must be getting to me.*

She got out of the tub and twisted the shower knob until the water ran cold, and stuck her head under it to cool off.

So what did the policeman mean when he said Hiroki hadn't been getting along with his classmates if there hadn't been any bullying one way or the other? How was she supposed to interpret that?

And the fact remained that her brother had hurt two of his friends. He had gone out and bought a knife, and stabbed them. He was going for the kill, and he had succeeded with one of them at least. Those were the facts, and there was no getting around them.

U-ri chewed her lip. She realized she had been avoiding facing the facts of what happened for too long. *That was a mistake.* U-ri returned to the living room, drying her hair with a towel. Her mother was in the kitchen running the juicer. *Banana juice. My favorite.*

"I thought you might like some after your bath."

Her mother set a large cup on the counter and filled it to the brim. She always put a little ice cream in her juice, making it thick and sweet.

It was one of Hiroki's favorites too. U-ri savored the taste. Magically filling your stomach was certainly convenient, but there was nothing like the real thing.

"Hey, Mom?"

Her mother was still standing by the sink. She looked up from her own smaller cup of juice.

"Hiroki always liked your banana juice, didn't he?"

Her mother's smile twitched. Her hand gripping the cup shivered.

"He does."

"I hope he comes home soon," U-ri said, her voice suddenly choked. It wasn't an act. She really meant it. "Wherever he is, I'll bet he's missing that—and your Spanish rice too."

Her mother closed her mouth and set her cup down next to the sink. Her eyes wandered down to the faucet. She shook her head slightly and looked up. "Maybe I'll make some tonight then."

"Maybe he'll smell it and come home!"

"Yuriko," her mother said quietly. "Do you think about your brother a lot still?"

U-ri answered her with a question of her own. "Do you?"

"I do. Every day—no, every hour."

More like every minute. "Me too," she said after a moment.

Her mother sat down across from her at the table. "There's something I've been wanting to ask you. Don't feel like you have to answer if it's too tough."

"Okay."

"Are you angry at your brother?"

U-ri didn't have to think too long about her response this time. "I am, a little."

Her mother's eyes opened slightly wider. "What for, exactly?"

"I'm mad that he left home and hasn't come back." *Making us worry. Making us cry.* "That's why I'm angry at him. Other than that, I'm just worried. I worry about him every day."

Her mother closed her eyes. "You aren't angry with Hiroki for what he did to his friends?"

U-ri stared at her half-drunk glass of juice. "No. Because I don't know why he did it. I mean, he never even got into fights much before."

Her mother nodded silently.

"I think he did it because he got too wrapped up in his own thoughts—something was bothering him so much he didn't feel like he had another choice. I mean, of course he should have talked to you or dad, or one of his teachers, before bringing a knife to school, and I'm sure there are lots of other things he could have done that would have been better. I just think he would have realized that himself unless he was trapped in some really unusual circumstances. So unusual he couldn't really *be* himself, you know? And unless I know what the circumstances are, I don't feel like I can say he was entirely to blame. Sure, what he did was wrong, but I still want to hear what he has to say about it first. We're his family, after all."

At some point while U-ri was talking, her mother had started to cry.

A pain stabbed at U-ri's chest. She had seen her mother cry many times before. She had even cried along with her. But she had done those things as Yuriko Morisaki. This time was different. She was U-ri now. For the first time, she wasn't seeing the woman sitting across from her as "Mom," she was seeing a mother who was terribly worried about her son. Her son who had done something horrible.

It felt very strange. Her mother was right in front of her, in tears, and yet she felt completely calm. She didn't feel like crying. She felt pity, and more than that, she felt like she had to help—like she was the only one who *could* help. A sense of...*duty?* It ran through her veins, her heart beat with it. It was inside her.

Inside U-ri.

I'm not myself anymore.

I'm an allcaste, *on the hunt for the King in Yellow.*

And this woman, my mother—no, her name is Yoshiko Morisaki.

Poor troubled Yoshiko. Hurt. Sad. A little life spinning in the Circle. *Hear me now, Yoshiko. I will help you.*

Something swelled up inside U-ri, and her whole body trembled.

"Don't cry," she heard herself say. "You're crying too much, Mom. It's not good for you. Hiroki would worry about you."

Across the table from her, Yoshiko covered her face with her hands.

"Mom, did you know the two boys Hiroki hurt?"

Yoshiko shook her head, her eyes on the table. "I think they were friends of his."

For the first time, U-ri realized she didn't even know their names. That is, she was sure no one had told her on purpose. That had probably been for the best when she was Yuriko. She didn't need to know the harsh realities. But U-ri was different.

"I'm sorry, I don't know," Yoshiko said, rubbing her face with her hands and sniffling. Her eyes were red. "Neither of them were in his class until he entered eighth grade; I never met them."

"So they weren't in his swimming club?"

"I don't think so."

"No, you're right, they couldn't have been in his swimming club," U-ri agreed. "Otherwise they would have been with him from first grade."

After-school activities at Kibogaoka Middle School were on a strictly voluntary basis. Hiroki had told her once that many of the students chose not to participate in any clubs at all, and most of them went home right after school was over.

But you should definitely join a club when you get here, little Yuri. You'll make a lot of friends. There's a lot you can't tell about somebody just sitting next to them in class.

Hiroki had never complained about anyone in swimming club. If he had, U-ri hadn't heard about it—which brought her back to the main problem here, that Hiroki wouldn't have told any of them if he were having difficulties at school. To the contrary, he would have kept it to himself and tried to solve his problems on his own. That was just the way he was. And that was why so many people liked him. He was popular. Which made it even harder to imagine someone picking on him in any serious way. So if he really had been backed into a corner, how did it happen?

That's the key. What would it take to make Hiroki Morisaki lose his cool, to make him cry, to make him ashamed? What could have upset his groove so much?

Certainly not schoolyard teasing. Maybe he was jealous of someone? Or someone was jealous of him? No, he must have been used to that already, being at the top of his class or near it all the time. He would have long ago learned how to brush that sort of thing off. It wasn't anything like that. *So what was it? What was it?*

U-ri's mind raced as she swallowed down the last of the juice. Her teeth clinked on the edge of the glass, snapping her out of her thoughts.

With a start, she realized that somewhere along the line, she had started thinking of her mother as Yoshiko and her brother as Hiroki Morisaki. And her father—

Shiro Morisaki. Yoshiko's husband.

And Hiroki had never confided in them about any problems he was having at school. If he had said anything at all, things would've played out very differently, she was sure.

U-ri shook her head and put her empty glass down on the table. She stood. "Thanks, Mom. The juice was great. I'm going to go study a bit in my room."

"Okay, just don't overdo it," Yoshiko said. But she meant *Don't worry too much about your brother.*

U-ri dashed back into her room, shut the door, and locked it behind her. Her double peeked her head out from the vestments.

"Are you all right?"

"I'm not," U-ri said, trembling. "I think something's wrong with me."

How can I think of my own family like that—as if they were just strangers to me?

"Nothing's wrong with you at all," Aju chirped from the desk, his little pink nose twitching reassuringly. "You're going to have to be able to keep a cool head about things from here on out, or you might lose your way. It's a good thing."

"You'll get used to it, really," her double said gently. "And don't worry. Yuriko is still in us, safe. I'll protect her. And when you're done, I'll give her back."

U-ri grabbed her double's hand. "Look after Mom while I'm gone, okay?"

"I will. I promise."

Her double offered U-ri the chair and placed the vestments on her. U-ri started when she saw Sky standing at attention by the door. *That's still going to take a little getting used to.*

Aju scurried up her arm to sit on her shoulder. "What do we do next?"

"We have to find out who the two boys Hiroki hurt are. We have to find out what happened that day."

"Are we going to his school?"

U-ri shook her head. "I don't think going there will do much good. The teachers won't tell me anything, that's for sure. Going to the police might be quicker."

Aju squeaked with laughter. "You weren't planning on going as yourself, were you? Even the police wouldn't talk to the suspect's sister."

"I know *that*." U-ri frowned. "You got any ideas?"

"Well," Aju said, "you could transform yourself to look like someone who the police would be more likely to talk to, for starters."

So what, a reporter? U-ri dismissed the idea. The reporters who swarmed to their house just after the incident might still be on the case. She didn't even want to think what would happen were she to make herself look like one of them only to run into the real deal at the school or the police station.

"How about someone who would have a reason to talk to the police or the teachers but wouldn't necessarily get there as fast as the reporters did?"

"That's a toughie," Aju grumbled. "Let me take a look."

The little field mouse's beady red eyes sparkled. His tiny feet beat a quick rhythm on U-ri's shoulder. He stopped.

"You're talking to the books in the reading room, aren't you? What did they say?"

"Hang on, hang on, I'm asking the Sage now. He says he has to talk to the infants."

"Infants?"

"That's right. He means the youngest books—the ones written during your lifetime."

The books in Ichiro Minochi's reading room were all one or two thousand years old, reckoned in human years. Of course, the physical books themselves were much newer than that, though they had been carefully copied from much older originals.

Compared to them, most modern books *were* really infants. Some of them had barely even been born. And, it turned out, her great-uncle had collected some of those too.

"Minochi did a little light reading on the side. He wasn't totally cut off from the modern world, you know," Aju said.

"But I didn't hear anything like an infant's voice in the reading room."

"No, you wouldn't have. The owner kept all of the younger books in a different room. And most infants can't talk yet, besides. They can't even glow properly yet."

Aju's red eyes winked again. "Oh? Oh…" he said, then a moment later, "Right, thanks." He looked back up at U-ri. "The Sage found the perfect book!"

The book was very new, first printed five years ago. There had been an incident much like the one Hiroki was involved in at a middle school out in the countryside somewhere. A ninth grader had stabbed a classmate with a knife, seriously injuring him. Except in this case, the teachers had grabbed him immediately after—and he had a motive. The police found out that the victim had been teasing the suspect about his grades.

"This author, a lady by the name of Shinako Ito, wrote a book about the boy. See? Maybe she'd come here to write about your brother, seeing as how the cases are so similar. We can call ahead and see if she actually did come or not, and if it sounds like she didn't, that's our ticket in."

Sky, who had been standing in the corner doing an admirable impression of a statue until now, spoke quietly. "An author?"

"Yeah. Someone who writes things," U-ri explained.

"A nonfiction author, according to her profile," Aju added.

Sky blanched. "A person who writes books? But that is a weaver."

"That's right. We call them authors here. I guess they're called weavers in the nameless land 'cause they weave stories," U-ri added, even as she remembered something else she had been told. "Maybe you think of them as sinners, but this one's a nonfiction author, Sky. They write about things that actually happened. They aren't just making things up. I don't think that counts as the sin of storytelling."

Sky slowly shook his head. "Any tale that is told is a story, Lady U-ri."

"But she's not making it up—" U-ri began, then stopped herself. Hadn't the Archdevout said that history was just another kind of story? Even though it was supposed to be a record of things that had actually happened, it was still a story.

"If you'll allow me," Aju cut in. "Not all stories are woven from the imagination. Anything that can be told is a story, the same as any other. And before there was paper and writing people maintained their records and their stories and their histories by telling them to each other."

"But when they did invent paper, they wrote all those stories down in books and scrolls, right?" U-ri said. "As long as someone remembered it."

"That's true, but they didn't write down every story they heard." Aju's nose twitched.

U-ri smiled. *Here I am discussing the history of writing with a mouse.*

"There are lots of stories that continued to be told only by word of mouth, and were never put onto paper," Aju continued. "We call those stories 'unattached.'"

U-ri raised an eyebrow. "But if they weren't written down, wouldn't they disappear eventually? We're talking about a really long time ago, right?"

Aju poked his cold little nose into U-ri's cheek. "That's just it. Once told in the Circle, a story doesn't just disappear. Even if no one knows about it, it's still there, flowing this way and that."

Unwritten in letters, unimagined in pictures, banished from memory, but still there.

"That's why we say they're unattached. They're separate from everything and every place, just sort of drifting in the air. Of course, the unattached stories still end up getting pulled back by the Great Wheels for storage in the Hall of All Books. Then, eventually, the Great Wheels send them back out again. Funny thing is, some stories might get sent back into the Circle two or three times, and yet every time they remain unattached. Even if they happen into the Circle during a time when the methods for recording them are in place."

There were just some stories that were difficult to put into letters, Aju explained.

U-ri tapped Aju's head with her finger. "That's all very interesting, but aren't you getting off topic? Let's do some magic or whatever and go talk to the police."

"Oh, right, right!"

Aju recited the spell, and U-ri repeated the words after him. Sky stood as before, wrapped in his black robes, his pale face drawn.

U-ri found this very unsettling. *What's he so afraid of? If he is really scared, I wish he would just tell me why. Then I might be able to do something about it. And besides, isn't he supposed to be helping me?*

When she finished reciting the spell, a bright glow passed from her toes all the way up to her head.

"There you go!"

U-ri spread her arms apart. She looked down. She was still herself, in the same dusty old vestments of protection.

"I don't think it worked."

"You doubt my skill? Look in the mirror."

U-ri opened the closet door and stood in front of the mirror that hung on the back wall.

She was looking at a thirty-something woman with long hair. She was wearing a light blue jacket, perfect for early summer, and white pants. No jewelry. The woman's hair had been neatly twisted into a single knot on her head.

"That's how you look to everyone around you."

U-ri put her hands on her hips. "Impressive!"

Aju taught her the magic words that would make her change to and from her new form. Remove the transformation, and U-ri would once again be invisible. Useful for times when there were places she couldn't go, even in disguise—or when she didn't want anyone to see her for any reason.

U-ri uttered the magic word and slipped out of the apartment without Yoshiko noticing. In a corner of the hallway outside her door, she transformed into Shinako Ito and began to walk toward the neighborhood library. She had some research to do before anything else.

She was walking down the street, listening to her shoes click on the sidewalk, when she realized she was carrying a large bag over one shoulder. It was heavy too. She stopped at a light and looked inside to find a notepad, a digital voice recorder, a pen case, some business cards, a wallet, and even a cell phone.

"Does all this come with the transformation?"

"Sure. No investigative writer worth their salt walks around empty-handed," Aju squeaked from her pocket. "The bag's a copy of the real thing, so even if Shinako herself saw that, she'd think it was hers."

Yuriko opened the cell phone. The display showed it was getting a signal. "Wait, if I use this, will it charge her account?"

"I wonder. It is magical, after all, so I wouldn't worry too much about it. I doubt the phone companies charge for magical phone use."

Even still, U-ri made a mental note to avoid using it too much. It felt wrong.

The library was a familiar place for Yuriko Morisaki. She came here to get books with Kana all the time, and sometimes they would do their homework together in the study section. She went in and passed by the reception counter, so nervous she could barely walk straight. But the librarian at the desk didn't even glance in her direction.

That was unusual. Normally, when kids came in to use the library, the librarian would always say hello or good afternoon. Some of the kids wouldn't answer, but Yuriko and Kana had always made a point of saying hello back.

I guess because I look like an adult now, they don't bother saying anything.

Feeling emboldened, U-ri walked up to the counter and asked where the newspapers were kept. The female librarian politely indicated a corner of the room.

Hardly anyone used the library in the middle of the day like this. Even the study room was mostly empty. U-ri picked out one of the newspapers from the rack and sat down to read it.

Because the victims were both in middle school, all of the newspapers had withheld their names. To U-ri's disappointment, she found that most of the articles about the incident repeated the police reports almost verbatim, and added little else. She found only one newspaper that had gone any further and done a full investigative report of Hiroki's school.

The headline read INCIDENT AT KIBOGAOKA MIDDLE SCHOOL. It was the school where Yuriko would be going when she graduated from elementary school. *If I graduate.*

The newspaper had come to the school three or four times, asking if there had been any bullying involved—always a hot topic—but the school had denied it every time. "None of our teachers received any reports of the kind," the principal was on record as saying. And neither Boy A (Hiroki) or his guardians (Mom and Dad) had ever spoken to anyone at the school about it.

The school had maintained a constant line that there was no bullying—but, it turned out, they could offer no proof. They just hadn't heard of any bullying. Which is why, after the third or fourth article, the school began backing off from their position.

Sitting there in a thirty-year-old's body, U-ri thought she understood. *What else could it have been? There must have been bullying.* But it still didn't make any sense to Yuriko Morisaki. This wasn't a Boy A, this was Hiroki. Good in school, good at sports—Yuriko's perfect brother.

The tiny newsprint stung her vision. U-ri pressed the palms of her hands to her eyes. When her hand brushed her cheek it felt dry. *So that's what thirty-year-old skin feels like.*

U-ri realized that while transformed, she had access to her new body's knowledge and experiences. But her heart was still her own. She was an *allcaste* now, not Yuriko. So she was no longer a teary-eyed grade schooler, but her heart was young all the same. The newsprint hadn't been stinging her eyes. It was stinging her heart.

Whatever the details were, Hiroki's daily life at school hadn't been as spotlessly bright as it might've seemed to his little sister. There had to be some reason why Hiroki allowed himself to be tempted by the King in Yellow. U-ri had been telling herself all along that Hiroki's interest in the King had been a mere curiosity that, by an evil turn of luck, had run him straight up against the Hero and its incredible power. Now she understood that she had been wrong.

As the Hero searches for the vessel, so does the vessel call out to the Hero—to the King in Yellow. What had Hiroki wanted so badly? What did he wish for so much that he could only find it in the King in Yellow?

"You okay, U-ri?" Aju whispered to her from under her collar. U-ri wrapped her hand gently around his furry body. "I'm okay. What about Sky?"

She looked around and saw him standing near the entrance to the study area. He was facing away from her, his head cocked as though he were listening to something. He turned around first this way, then that. He looked very busy.

Oh, U-ri realized, *he's talking to the books.*

"Aju, are the books here saying something—"

Aju snorted a little snort. "They've been yakking it up since we walked in the place. Maybe you should talk to them a bit, U-ri."

U-ri hastily put away the newspaper. Hiding herself behind a bookcase, she uttered the magic word again. The moment she did so, a tidal wave of voices slammed into her from all sides.

"*Allcaste, allcaste!*"

"Um, I'm sorry I didn't introduce myself sooner," U-ri said, raising her voice to push back against the noise. "My name's U-ri."

"Lady U-ri!" One voice, that of a female-seeming book, rang out above the rest. "We thank you for visiting us. Please excuse the others. This is the first time anyone with knowledge of the nameless land has set foot inside this library—let alone an *allcaste.* I'm afraid we're all rather excited."

"Do you know why I'm here?"

"Yes, I do. I am connected to the nameless land. I know of the escape."

Hiroki came here a lot too. The books might know him. "The boy who became the last vessel is my brother. His name is Hiroki Morisaki. If you know anything about him, where he might be, please tell me."

"I am sorry, Lady U-ri," the female voice said, trembling. "There are many of us here, yes, but most are infants. They do not even know that the Hero is free. Even I only know of these things through knowledge gleaned from my elders."

Of course the books in public libraries wouldn't be that old.

"With the Book of Elem in his hands, your brother had no need for the likes of us. I doubt he visited here at all after its power came into his possession. And before he had the book, well, he would've just been one of many young boys who come here to read from our pages."

"You're right, I'm sorry. I hadn't thought enough about it."

"No, it is not your fault. And there is something I *can* tell you." The voice paused. "Two months ago, we books sensed the presence of the Book of Elem here, in our town."

That would have been right around when Hiroki snuck the book out of Ichiro Minochi's cottage.

"Even the youngest among us can sense it when such dangerous power is near."

The Book of Elem had come close, but never came inside their library. Even still, the books had spent many days trembling in the fear that it might.

"Then, one day, one of us was burned."

"One of the books burned? There was a fire in the library?"

"Yes, but no mortal flame," the female voice said quietly. "Magefire burned that book."

A single book on one of the library shelves had caught fire in the middle of the night, charring to a crisp in seconds. When one of the librarians found it in the morning and tried to take the book off the shelf, it crumbled, leaving a pile of ash.

"No normal fire would have burned a book so completely without catching fire to the whole place," Aju noted.

"Lady U-ri," said a voice behind her. It was Sky. He had been so quiet, she had forgotten he was there. "I found the place where the book burned. The stench of sorcery lingers in the air."

U-ri let Sky lead her to the spot. The sign at the end of the shelf read Home and Living.

At first glance she could see nothing strange, but when she got closer she found where a part of the shelf had melted, warping from the heat. The ash had left a faint black residue. She touched it. The surface of the shelf felt rough under her fingertip.

"Let me take a look," Aju squeaked, crawling up to her shoulder and hopping onto the bookshelf.

At once, all the books around them screamed. Loud—incredibly loud—a bloodcurdling chorus of terror. U-ri staggered away from the shelf. She had just been about to ask a question, and in her surprise, she bit her tongue.

"W-what is it? What's wrong?"

Even the female voice that had been talking to her before was shrieking. U-ri felt like her ears would burst. She clapped her hands over them.

In a flash, Sky stepped forward, plucked Aju off the shelf, and thrust him into his pocket. His eyes were as wide as hers.

Gradually, the screaming faded. The pitch dropped, the sound becoming thinner and more pointed, until it was finally over. Through the ringing in her ears, U-ri was just able to make out a sound like a frightened child, whimpering.

"What was that?" Quick as a whip, she turned to Sky. "What did you just do?"

Sky took a step back, his hand tightly clenched around the little mouse in his pocket.

"Stop grabbing Aju like that, you'll squish him! Let him out. Let him go now!"

"It's okay, U-ri," came Aju's voice, muffled by Sky's black robes. "I'm fine. And...I'm sorry. Sorry for scaring everyone like that! I wasn't thinking."

Sky released his grip on the mouse, and Aju scrambled up, poking his nose out from the pocket.

"What do you mean?"

It was the female voice that answered. "Lady U-ri. The King in Yellow has touched that one. He bears the Yellow Sign. He was in the presence of the Hero!"

So that's what frightened the books?

"Yes. I'm really sorry." The color had completely drained from Aju's pointed ears. "I knew I had to be careful—I just completely forgot. It's fine if I'm in the vestments or here in Sky's robes."

But it hadn't been fine when Aju jumped onto the bookshelf and touched it directly.

"But why didn't the books in the cottage seem to mind?"

"Because they're a tough crowd. Sages and sorcerers, the lot of 'em. But the books here, they're more like regular people. They can't take my, er, aura. The King in Yellow's aura, that is."

So what was that about the Yellow Sign?

Sky lightly touched U-ri's sleeve. "I will tell you about it later. Please forgive us. Both of us. I should have been more careful too."

He looked so apologetic that U-ri found she couldn't make herself get upset. Swallowing her unease, she looked up.

"Are you all okay?"

"Yes," the female voice replied, sounding short of breath. "I am sorry you had to witness that."

"Do you know what the book that burned was? Its title or anything?"

The books on this row of shelves seem to be organized by category—this particular spot held mostly how-to books and other practical guides.

She looked at some of the books near where the burned book had been with titles like *First-Aid Techniques You Should Know* and *Getting Healthy with Vinegar*.

"I'm sorry, Lady U-ri, but most of these books do not have names."

"What do you mean? They all have titles, don't they?"

"Yes, but for the most part, we do not know each other's titles. They have little meaning for us. Nor does a book's title have anything to do with its name," the book told her, sounding a bit surprised—as if this were supposed to be common knowledge.

U-ri resisted the urge to make a snappy comeback. "Okay, well, I guess I'll just look it up."

U-ri checked the catalog numbers of the books to either side of the gap on the shelf. The one in between would be the missing book. She could search for it on the library computer. U-ri cut across the aisles, heading for one of the booths where computers had been set up for visitors' use.

It didn't take long for her to find it.

Hidden Dangers or Hidden Rewards? Making the Most of Household Cleaners.

That's a funny title, U-ri thought. *At least the subject matter's pretty clear.* "Why would anyone go out of their way to burn up a book like that with magic?"

"I wish we knew," the female voice lamented. "Yet I can tell you with absolute certainty that it *was* the Book of Elem that burned it. I sensed its presence when it happened."

Which meant that Hiroki had burned it. Or the King in Yellow acting through him.

"It was Hiroki," Aju whispered from Sky's pocket. "I bet he just wanted to try out his magic."

So he had been testing his newfound power, given to him by the Book of Elem? That was certainly possible, but it still didn't explain why he had chosen a book about household cleaners.

"If he wanted to do a test, why didn't he do it on a book at home?" Yuriko muttered, clicking on the terminal keys, trying to find out more about the book. She scrolled down to view the rest of the entry.

Sky touched U-ri's sleeve. He was gesturing with his eyes toward the booth next to her. A middle-aged man was standing there frozen, like he was about to sit down. His eyes were open wide, and he was staring at her booth.

Oops! I forgot—I'm still invisible. He must've seen the keys typing and the screen scrolling all by themselves!

U-ri stood up and stepped slowly away from the booth. The man stared at the computer, frowning. Then, gingerly, he took a step closer and lightly touched the keyboard with one finger.

"Yikes. That was close! I totally forgot."

"It's easier than you might think," Aju squeaked merrily. It seemed his mood had recovered from the excitement before.

U-ri hid behind a nearby shelf and crossed her arms. "I think we've found out just about everything we're going to from this place."

"I am truly sorry we could not be more of a help to you, *allcaste*," the female voice apologized.

"That's quite all right," U-ri said, smiling. "I'm still figuring this whole thing out myself."

"Will you go to the library at the school?" She meant the library at Kibogaoka Middle School. "You may yet find books there that can aid you in your search. Though I am afraid many of them are infants yet, they may well know something of your brother, or at least the other students."

"You're right. I'll check it out. Thanks!"

She left the library. Just outside the front lobby there was a public phone which she used to call the police station. U-ri gave her name as Shinako Ito. When there was no reaction, U-ri breathed a sigh of relief. She was half expecting something like, "What, you again? Weren't you just here a week ago?" *Looks like my disguise just might work after all.* She told the person who answered that she was investigating the murder of the boy at Kibogaoka, and after she had been transferred several times, someone told her to come down to the station.

U-ri was increasingly aware that her disguise was more than just that—it was a complete transformation. She never would have been able to talk to people on the phone like this a week ago. It was incredibly convenient, as she needed access to the grown-up world to get things done, but also kind of scary. With all this business of being other people, she was afraid again that she might lose her real self.

"We can teleport there," Aju suggested. "I'll say the spell."

U-ri walked over to hide behind some bushes outside the library. Aju slipped out of Sky's pocket and hopped over to U-ri's shoulder. "You ready?"

"No, I'm not ready. You have to explain something to me first. What was the book in there talking about when she said that most books don't have names?"

Aju glanced back at the library, his nose twitching. "Well, for one, we books usually don't need to tell each other apart, really. See, there's not that many kinds of stories out there, when you get down to it. Only ten, to be exact. Of course, there are many more times that number of books in the Circle. Still, you can trace any of the stories in them back to the ten basic types we call the 'originals.'"

Aju stroked his whiskers as he got into telling his story. "Now people give books titles 'cause it's helpful for them to sort books, and they can use the titles to talk about what's in them. But all those titles have absolutely nothing to do with the ten originals. Which is why we don't bother keeping track of them. Knowing what original story type a book is fashioned after is enough for us, and we can tell that just by looking.

"Now," Aju mused, "it might be a different story if all the books got some kind of official numbers when they first appeared in the world—but that's not how the system works. And frankly, we books could care less. It's not like we have to introduce ourselves to each other like people do. We could just float namelessly through the Circle and never be the worse for it. And there's another reason why most books don't bother with names."

It turned out that most of the books written, collated, and printed by human hands—about 99.9 percent—had extremely short lives. They did not remain in the Circle for long. The Great Wheels of Inculpation dragged them back to the nameless land, then sent them back out into the Circle, where they found a mind or a heart willing to make another book of them. And of those new books, 99.9 percent wouldn't last long either. And it wasn't just books. Anything that had a story to it was subject to this endless recycling.

It occurred then to U-ri that people were much the same. They all had names, but for 99.9 percent of them, it wouldn't matter in the long run. *Because they just don't make any difference, and another would be there to replace them as soon as they left.*

It was a troubling thought. *That has to be wrong,* U-ri told herself. *Human lives were each valuable, weren't they?*

U-ri humphed loudly—loud enough, she hoped, to drive the thought right out of her head. "So, if you have a proper name, Aju, that means you're different from the other 99.9 percent of books?"

The Great Wheels wouldn't take him back anytime soon—his journey through the Circle was intended to be long. That was why he had been given a name.

"I am pretty old," Aju said with evident pride. Despite being a tiny field mouse, he was clearly capable of strutting. Aju's whiskers stuck out straight from the sides of his face.

"And you're forgetting to tell me something," U-ri said, her voice growing more serious. "What's this Yellow Sign the books were talking about?"

Aju wrung his little forelimbs together atop U-ri's shoulder. "Well, if I were to tell you honestly—"

"Which you will."

"U-ri, I could tell you but I don't think you'd like it. That is, I don't think you'd like *me*." The mouse stuck his nose into the fold at her collar, his pride deflating like a leaky balloon. Shivering, he explained, "You see, it's a story of my failure. How I was too weak to save Hiroki, too weak to stop them. How I couldn't fight the Book of Elem. And I don't mean that I fought him and lost. No, I barely even tried. I was no match for the book."

U-ri stood speechless for a moment, unsure of how to respond.

Sky walked over to her, his bare feet padding softly on the grass. "The Book of Elem is a copy containing a portion of the King in Yellow's hideous strength."

"Yeah, I know."

"Master Aju could not sway your brother's heart in the face of such power. That is to say, Master Aju's abilities as a book were impaired by the Book of Elem."

U-ri gently picked up Aju in the palm of her hand, placing him back in her chest pocket.

"I'm sure you did what you could, Aju."

"Only at the very beginning. It wasn't long before I couldn't do anything at all."

It had been like being stuck inside a giant glass box, he told her. He could see everything going on around him, but there was no sound. Nor could his voice reach anyone. He could have made all the noise he wanted to, and still he remained impossibly distant from Hiroki.

"Kinda chokes me up just thinking about it." Aju sniffled and began to mutter "sorry" again and again as he rubbed his forepaws together. It tickled. U-ri burst out laughing. "You're too cute, Aju."

Sky's expression softened. "This entrapment of a book's powers is what the books called the 'Yellow Sign,'" he explained. Its effect lasted a long time—and was enough to send younger, innocent books into fits of terror.

"This is partially due to the fact that a fragment of the King in Yellow's power remains in that mark and partially because it is believed that, through the Yellow Sign, the King in Yellow might continue to exert its influence on the book, changing it forever."

U-ri put a hand to her mouth, and gulped. "You mean Aju might be under the influence of the King in Yellow...permanently?"

Aju jabbed her cheek with his nose. "I was not! I'm fine. Totally fine. Absolutely! I'm no copy of the King and I never will be!"

If U-ri could have seen him where he was on her shoulder, she was sure she would have caught him baring his teeth. "The Sage gave me a clean bill of health. He guaranteed it. I talked to him while you were in the nameless land, you know. And he said I was just fine."

If it's good enough for the Sage, it's good enough for me, U-ri decided. The Sage was probably right, and worrying about it now would only be a waste of time.

"All right, all right. It's too bad, though. If the Yellow Sign had changed you, that might have given us some clue to help find the King in Yellow," U-ri said, half jokingly.

"It did not and it would not!" Aju shrieked. "I didn't change one bit, I swear it!"

"Okay, I'm sorry," U-ri said, more serious this time.

"Fine. Whatever. Let's get going," Aju grumbled, burying himself in the fold of U-ri's vestments.

As luck would have it, Yuriko was already familiar with the local police station. It was right next to a yummy Italian restaurant her family frequented.

The walls of the station were a faintly sooty gray, with old-fashioned-looking frames around old-fashioned-looking windows.

U-ri signed in at the reception desk on the first floor, and after announcing the reason for her visit, was made to wait for about fifteen minutes. Finally, a female officer in uniform arrived and leaned out over the reception counter. "Ms. Ito?"

The officer was about as old as U-ri's mother. She had big cheeks and a soft smile.

"Hello, I'm Kashimura. I've been in charge of the Morisaki family's affairs since last month. I hear you've come to do some research? I'm sorry, but the Morisaki family is refusing all interview requests."

Maybe they hadn't gotten the message she left when she called.

"Actually," U-ri explained, "I didn't want to speak to the Morisakis. I was more interested in hearing how the investigation is coming along."

Officer Kashimura blinked her round eyes beneath long brows. "I'm afraid that we're not releasing any updates to the press concerning the investigation at this time, as there's nothing new to report."

"Might I speak with a detective in charge of the case?"

"No, they're all out on duty right now. We're still searching for the boy, Hiroki."

So it wasn't an investigation. It was a search.

"Do you have any leads—"

"As I said, we don't have any new information."

Officer Kashimura reminded her again that she wasn't to bother the Morisaki family, and then she left.

"She was pretty cold," Aju complained when she had left. "Did you recognize her, U-ri?"

"I didn't, no. Maybe my double knows her."

Though it wasn't very helpful to her now, at least it sounded like they were properly concerned about her family's privacy. It sounded like her double and her parents were living in relative peace, at least.

Maybe it was a little optimistic of me to think that I would learn anything by going to the police. Maybe it was a little optimistic to think that being a reporter or writer would make this any easier. She wondered what the real Shinako Ito would do in this situation.

"So what next? Go invis and sneak in? Maybe we can find something out about the case."

It sounded like a good idea at first, but the reality of it was that U-ri had no idea where in the sizable police station something like case records might be located.

Next to her, Sky was looking around uneasily.

Some help he turned out to be. "I guess we'll have to think of another approach," U-ri said.

Sky blinked.

"What is it?" U-ri asked, looking into his eyes. For the first time, she noticed that his eyes weren't black like she had thought, but a very dark purple. Dark enough to be easily mistaken for black. It was only when light shone on his face just so that she could tell the difference.

He looked bewildered. "I'm sorry. My mind was elsewhere."

"First time seeing a police officer?"

"No—the clothing and uniforms do not surprise me. They're all part of the stories within this Circle, and as such, are familiar to me. It's just...so quiet," Sky added in a whisper.

U-ri looked around the station. There were people here and there, and the constant hum of conversations and ringing phones. It wasn't exactly quiet, but it didn't seem particularly busy, either.

"It is like there is nothing wrong," he said.

"Well, things are different here than in the nameless land," Aju said. "Most people in this region don't know about the King in Yellow, after all."

This was true enough, but U-ri didn't think that was what Sky had meant—because she too had noticed something missing.

They've all forgotten about Hiroki. It's just business as usual here. Time rolls on whether they find him or not.

"Why would it be any different?" U-ri whispered, when she felt a strange wrenching sensation in her heart. U-ri clapped one hand to her chest.

What was that? It felt like her heart had skipped a beat entirely.

"Is something wrong, Lady U-ri?"

She was about to tell him what happened when her heart skipped a beat again. She caught her breath. *That's strange.*

Walking quickly, U-ri left the police station. The automatic doors slid open noisily. She looked out on the street. A man in a suit was walking away from her on the other side of the road—some office worker on his way back from lunch, she thought. No one else was nearby at all. U-ri uttered the magic word and disappeared.

"Wait, U-ri! What are you doing?"

Maybe the transformation is putting some strain on me. Maybe it's the magic making my heart skip. But even now that she was no longer Shinako Ito, her heartbeat was still ragged. It was getting harder to breathe. U-ri fell to her knees. She had to stick her hands out onto the ground in front of her to keep from sprawling.

"Lady U-ri!" Sky reached down and slid an arm around her waist for support. Aju scampered up to her shoulder.

Something was ringing in her head. She could hear her own pulse throbbing in her ears—and something else. *Screaming. So many voices, screaming. Screaming at me. That's why my heart's skipping like this.*

The school.

Suddenly, it was as if a light had gone on in her head. *The school. Hiroki's school. I have to go. They're calling me. They're calling—*

The school library. The books there are calling to me. "Allcaste! Allcaste! Allcaste! Come quickly!"

"Aju, take us to Hiroki's school, now!"

"What? Why now? What's going on?"

"I don't know why! Just hurry, or we won't make it in time!"

"Make haste, Master Aju!" Sky shouted. "Do as the Lady U-ri says!"

Aju hurriedly began reciting the spell.

They cut across the sky, and U-ri found herself at Kibogaoka Middle School, standing in the school courtyard.

A line of students in gym clothes jogged past them, close enough to brush the hem of her vestments.

U-ri's pulse still beat ragged and quick. Her head jerked upward, looking for the source of the noise—the screaming books. *There, that window. On the third floor.* The window glimmered in the sunlight. *The library!*

"Run!"

U-ri took off. Sky followed close after her. Their robes fluttered in the wind. Aju clung to U-ri's hair for dear life.

She ran inside and up the stairs, taking three steps at a time. The closer she got to the library, the louder the screams rang in her ears, and the clearer they became. She could make out the words now. *"Allcaste, help! Save her!"*

U-ri bounded into the library. No one was sitting at the librarian's desk on the right. She looked around. The library was an almost perfectly square room filled with rows of shelves. There was no study space with chairs. Just a stepladder here and there for reaching the higher shelves.

The library was empty. It was still the middle of the day, so all the students would be in their classrooms. It was bright in there.

The room was at the corner of the building, so two whole walls were filled with large windows through which the sunlight streamed, making the dust in the air sparkle where the rays hit.

The books were screaming. *"Allcaste, allcaste! You must help her!"*

A light breeze brushed the side of U-ri's face. *There's a window open somewhere!*

She heard a clunk. U-ri whipped around in the direction of the sound. She was looking at a window, mostly hidden by a large row of shelves. The window was half open. A stepladder was positioned beneath it, and a girl in her student uniform was climbing up, over the sill.

U-ri dashed for the window. Sky ran with her. He grabbed the girl by the shoulders. U-ri grabbed her around the waist.

"What are you doing? Stop!" U-ri shouted as loud as she could and pulled back. The girl came tumbling down from the window. The three of them landed on the floor, limbs tangled.

U-ri hit the ground hard. Her head smacked against the floor making sparks fly in her eyes. *Huh?* she thought dizzily. *I guess the vestments of protection don't protect against this sort of thing.*

"Ouch!" U-ri rolled to one side, clutching her head in her hands.

"Lady U-ri!" Sky shouted from beside her. His thin frame was pinned under the girl.

Then the girl pulled herself up to one side, hands on the floor. Her eyes looked like they might pop out of her head. Her face was pale, her lips blue.

"Wh-who's there?" she stammered. At the sound of her voice, the books fell silent. "Who is it? I know you're there."

Did she hear me? The girl stuck her hand out, groping through the air. Her fingers came within a few inches of touching U-ri.

Sky sat up and helped U-ri to her feet. The girl was kneeling now, waving her arms around her. "Who's there? Someone grabbed me. Who is it?"

Of course—she can't see us. She can't even touch us. What do we do?

U-ri grabbed Sky's arm. Sky was staring at the girl. She was short and thin. Her close-cropped hair stuck up in places, like she'd just gotten out of bed. She was wearing a typical white school blouse over the kind of pleated skirt that (her brother often said) had "never been fashionable."

In other words, she was a typical middle school student—with one exception. She had a large scar over her right eye. It zigzagged like a centipede across half her forehead. The swelling was so bad that her right eye could only open halfway.

The girl looked frightened. *She's scared.* But when she spoke there was the unmistakable sound of hope in her voice.

"Morisaki," she said. "Is that you?"

CHAPTER SEVEN

The Knight and the Princess

The girl stood up and began to shuffle forward, her arms out in front and waving. Her left eye was opened wide and shining with excitement. "Is that you, Morisaki? Did you come back?"

U-ri wasn't the only one taken aback by this unexpected turn of events. Sky, still holding her, was stiff as a board, his shoulders rigid with tension. Confusion filled his dark purple eyes.

"You okay, Sky?"

She had to whisper to him several times before Sky blinked and finally looked at her, his mouth hanging half open.

"Lady U-ri. Are you injured?"

"No, not at all."

They stood. Waving her arms in front of her, the girl walked up to a shelf against the wall, then turned and called out to the empty library. "If you are here, Morisaki, you better answer me. I-I've been so worried!" she cried, clearly holding back tears.

She's calling for my brother!

"I can't do this by myself. I can't make it. I'm so lonely."

There was something in the way she spoke—maybe it was her complete lack of restraint or the tone of utter familiarity—that made U-ri realize this girl was in love with Hiroki. She extended her hands and searched through the empty air, fingertips trembling. A girl reaching out for her...*for her boyfriend.*

"Do you think she can see properly with that eye?" Sky wondered aloud, his voice uneven. He seemed to be in shock.

"I don't think so—" U-ri started to say when the girl stopped. Her eyes opened wide.

"Hey!"

Aju was sitting curled up into a ball on the carpeted floor a few feet in front of where the girl stood. He must have been thrown from U-ri when she fell and missed his chance to duck back under the vestments of protection. The tiny field mouse's entire body was quivering as if to say, *Now I've done it!*

164

Luckily, the girl didn't seem to be afraid of mice. She stood there for a moment, one eyebrow raised, and examined him from a distance. Then she knelt down and reached out a hand as though she were going to pick Aju up.

U-ri made a split-second decision. She threw off the hood of the vestments of protection and raised her voice. "I'm sorry if I've startled you."

The girl whirled around with the agility of a young deer. U-ri spread her robes apart, allowing the girl to see as much of her as possible. She shook out her hair that had been matted down by the hood and faced the girl. "It was I who stopped you from jumping out that window just now."

For the first time, a look of fear came over the girl's face. She stepped back without looking and hit her head with a loud *crack* on the shelf behind her.

Aju quickly scampered across the carpet, jumped onto U-ri's proffered arm and then climbed up to sit on her shoulder. The girl followed his movement with her good eye. She was hugging herself with both arms and trembling.

"Please don't be frightened. I do not intend to harm you," U-ri said, trying to make her voice sound as authoritative as possible. She had decided that this would get through to the girl better than gentleness or empathy. She was right.

The girl took a deep breath. "Who are you?"

U-ri raised her chin, straightened her back, and stared directly at the girl before replying. "I am a book-spirit," she said, consciously trying to mimic how the Sage talked.

Sky stared at U-ri dumbfounded, while Aju clung to U-ri's ear lobe with both paws.

"I am a book-spirit that resides in this library. You might call me an avatar of the books here." U-ri took a slow step forward. The girl was still glued to the shelf behind her. "I have appeared in this form because I learned you thought to throw away your life, and I would not have you do that."

U-ri brought her feet together and bowed—this time imitating the devout in the nameless land. "The white mouse on my shoulder is my familiar. But do not worry, I'm not a witch," U-ri explained, surprised at how confident she sounded. "He is merely a magical being that does my bidding. It is one of the powers we book-spirits possess."

The girl's shoulders slumped, and she sat down, her back still against the shelves. Her skirt lifted, revealing two round kneecaps. U-ri walked over to her and extended a hand.

"Please stand." Her eyes went to two chairs stacked at the end of the shelf behind her. "We can sit over there and rest a moment." U-ri tried smiling at the girl.

The girl reached out without hesitation and took her hand. *Now I've got her,* U-ri thought.

Even though it was a warm early summer day, the girl's hand was ice cold. U-ri took her by the arm and led her slowly to the chairs like a medic leading an injured person. She put one of the chairs on the floor and motioned for the girl to sit. The other she placed a short distance away and sat down herself.

Sky quietly walked over to stand behind U-ri's chair.

"How do you feel? I hope I did not frighten you too much."

The girl put a hand over her heart, as though checking her pulse. "No...I'm fine. I think I'm fine."

"That is good."

"Thank you."

Now that they were sitting closer, U-ri noticed the girl's fine features. Though the scar above her eyes looked painful, it did little to diminish her beauty. It was strange—like looking at the vandalized statue of an angel.

"You should not do such things," U-ri began. She was so flushed with the success of her newfound persona that she thought this might be a good time to offer some advice. "Your life is precious. There is only one of you in this world. And your life is not yours alone."

The girl looked up. "How can you say that? My life is my own, just mine. Nobody cares if I die."

The color drained from U-ri's cheeks. "What?" she said without thinking, all pretense of authority lost. "B-but what about your parents?"

"Mom and Dad don't care what happens to me. My dad wouldn't even come to the funeral."

Apparently, all was not well at the girl's home. U-ri hurriedly straightened her back again and thought as hard as she could. *Okay, what do I say now? Hiroki!* She had been calling for him, like a girl calling for her boyfriend—searching for him.

"Hiroki Morisaki would be sad."

The words had a bigger effect than U-ri could have imagined. The girl clutched at the neck of her blouse and slumped over in her chair. Her thin shoulders began to shake again.

"And we book-spirits would be greatly saddened were you to throw away your life," U-ri quickly added. "You loved us well, and because of that we love you." She was grasping for some kind of hold on the girl—any hold. If she wouldn't come to her, U-ri might as well go out and get her. "You came here to visit us often."

The girl nodded. *Score!* U-ri thought. For a second, she considered whether to add "with Hiroki Morisaki" when the girl saved her the trouble.

"Morisaki and I came here a lot to talk about books and stuff. We were both on the library committee."

U-ri smiled broadly. "Yes, I know."

Aju squeaked lightly in her ear. *I know, don't get carried away.*

It turned out to be a well-timed squeak. The girl smiled faintly, looking at the mouse. "He's cute. Does he have a name?"

"His name is Aju. He may appear to be a little mouse, but in fact he's quite ancient."

"No I'm not, U-ri!" Aju objected in his regular voice. He looked at the girl. "I'm a book-spirit too, actually. And, yeah, while we might live a lot longer than humans, I'm not old as my kind go. I'm just a youngling."

The girl's good eye went wide—even her right eye twitched under the scar. *So much for being the wise book-spirits.*

"Couldn't keep it to yourself, could you, Aju?"

"Hey, I can't be a mouse all the time. Howdy, little miss," he said to the girl with a wave of his tail and a twitch of his light pink nose. "What's your name?"

No, wait, U-ri realized, *on second thought he is playing along. Good for you, Aju!*

"Michiru Inui," she said immediately.

"You a classmate of Hiroki's?"

The girl began to nod happily, and then gasped. "Mr....Aju? Do you know Morisaki?"

"Yeah. And believe me, I'm just as worried about him as you are. Not just me. U-ri here is too. All the book-spirits are. Oh," Aju added, "and you don't have to call me 'Mister.' Just Aju is fine."

"And my name is U-ri," U-ri bowed again lightly. "That is, it is like my name—but to explain it would take too long. Think of it as a nickname."

Michiru frowned. U-ri looked at her, worried she'd said something wrong.

"I...never had a nickname," the girl said, pressing fingers to her mouth. "Everyone just calls me Inui. No one even calls me by my first name."

"Michiru. It is a pretty name," U-ri offered.

U-ri understood how lonely it must feel for a young girl not to have a nickname. It also helped explain why Michiru was often in the library alone like this while the other students were in class.

And why she had tried to commit suicide.

U-ri decided to ask, all the same. "Don't you have class now? Won't you get in trouble if someone finds you here in the library?"

"No—I snuck in. I'm...still not coming to school. But you knew that, didn't you?"

U-ri met the girl's gaze and nodded slowly.

"I've been out since Morisaki disappeared," Michiru explained, chewing at her lip. "But I still want to come to the library sometimes—I have to come sometimes—so I sneak in. The teachers don't mind. They know I'm here."

"They know?"

"Yes. They said I could come just to use the library even if I don't go to class. Of course," she added, "I can't stay for very long each time. I don't want to be here during break and have any of the students see me."

A look of fear quickly crossed the girl's delicate features. *She didn't want anyone to see her. She didn't want to see anyone.*

"Don't worry about that," U-ri said. "If anyone should come, I will hide you until they leave."

U-ri had barely finished talking when the bell rang to mark the end of the period. Michiru began to shake visibly.

"How long is the break?"

"F-five minutes."

Moments later, they heard the sound of students dashing out of their classrooms. Doors opened and closed, and laughter echoed down the halls. There was the sound of running feet.

U-ri quickly stood, walked over to Michiru, and wrapped the vestments of protection around them both. She lifted her index finger to her mouth. "You'll be safe here. Just close your eyes."

Michiru's entire body was tense and she was sweating. *She's breathing so fast. She must be really scared. Scared of her classmates, of everything outside these library walls.*

U-ri glanced at Sky, who still stood rigidly behind the empty chair. His eyes were fixed on Michiru, as if he were seeing something for the first time in his life and couldn't look away.

The bells rang again, and silence returned to the school. As luck would have it, no one had wanted to use the library during the short recess.

"There, now we can relax a bit," U-ri said, letting the vestments fall away from her again as she returned to her chair.

"You're shorter than I would have imagined," Michiru said. "You look like you're in grade school. Or...maybe you just made yourself look like that so you wouldn't frighten me?"

For a moment, part of U-ri wanted to tell her the truth—*I really am a grade school student. I'm Hiroki's little sister. Aju used to call me "little miss" too.* But the thought was gone as quickly as it had come.

"I like this form," she replied quietly. "And I fit well with Aju like this."

"That's true. Like a little girl with her pet mouse," Michiru said, smiling more broadly than she had before.

"You know," Michiru said, "Morisaki had a younger sister in grade school. He talked about her all the time. Yuriko was her name. 'My little Yuri,' he always called her. Yuri...kind of like your name."

U-ri gritted her teeth. *I'm not going to cry. I'm not going to cry.*

"I can't imagine how Yuriko feels," Michiru went on. "Losing a brother like that."

Then Michiru began to talk more rapidly. It seemed her smile a moment before had upset some delicate balance inside her, and now the floodgates were open and everything came spilling out. "I have to go apologize. It was my fault Morisaki did what he did. It's all my fault. I wanted to go apologize to her. But I couldn't, I couldn't..."

The sudden outpouring of emotion took U-ri by surprise, and she looked around for something to cling to so she wouldn't faint. She could feel the color draining from her face.

Then Aju batted at her ear with one paw. His long tail snaked down off her shoulder and tickled her neck. Behind her, Sky grabbed her shoulders, propping her up so she wouldn't sway.

U-ri looked up at Sky. He was still entranced by Michiru. She could see the girl's white school-uniform blouse reflected in his dark eyes.

Aju stuck his nose into U-ri's ear and whispered, "Stay with us, kid." It tickled so much, U-ri almost laughed despite the seriousness of the situation.

Across from her, Michiru's face twisted and she began to cry. She held her head in her hands and doubled over so fast she almost fell out of her chair. U-ri stood up, sweeping the vestments behind her, and knelt by her side.

"You bear a great burden. Is this why you wanted to end your life?"

Michiru nodded her head up and down, trembling uncontrollably. U-ri gently rubbed her back. Curiously, it felt like she was comforting herself at the same time. "Your burden is heavy," she repeated. "It must be very hard for you."

Michiru was sobbing out loud now. The tears she had kept dammed up inside came out in a great torrent. U-ri stood off to one side, watching it flow by.

"You have to put your burden down, Michiru. Talk to me. Tell me what it is you're suffering, why Morisaki did what he did. I—" U-ri shook her head. "Gah! Enough with the stuffy talk. Look, Michiru, I'm a book-spirit. I know a lot of things, but it's hard for me to see what's going on outside—in your world. I can't just walk off by myself and talk to people and look into things."

U-ri looked up at the library books lining the shelves. She could feel their silent support. She nodded to them, then turned back to the girl. "Michiru, please tell me. What happened? If we know that, we books might be able to do something to help you and Morisaki."

The girl sat up, hiccuping. Her face was streaked with tears, her eyes rimmed with red. It made the scar over her right eye look even more painful. U-ri gently brushed away the girl's hair where it was sticking to her forehead.

"We books are on your side. We are your friends. Please, you have to trust me. You have to tell me what happened."

Tears dripped from Michiru's chin. She pulled a handkerchief out of her skirt pocket and wiped at her face. The handkerchief was wrinkled and already soggy—she'd probably been using it earlier, before U-ri arrived.

"Morisaki..." She began speaking in fits and starts. It seemed painful for her even to breathe. U-ri rubbed her back again. "He saved me."

"Saved you?"

"He told them...told our class it wasn't right to pick on me. He told everybody."

Michiru and Hiroki had been in the same classroom in seventh grade.

"Some of the kids picked on me from the first day I got to school. But it wasn't anything too bad. It wasn't until the second quarter that more started doing it, and more openly. Probably when we started swimming in the pool for phys ed."

U-ri blinked. "So the other kids in your class were always picking on you? Why?"

Michiru's left eye opened wide and she stared back at U-ri. "U-ri, don't you notice my face?"

"You mean the scar above your eye?"

The girl nodded, lightly brushing the scar with one finger. "I fell from the second-floor veranda of our house when I was three. Someone had left a gardening hoe out on the lawn..."

The metal edge of the hoe had cut deep into her face. A little deeper and she would have lost sight in her right eye entirely.

"I had surgery twice. Once right after the accident, and once a year later. They took soft skin from my back and my inner thigh and moved it to my face. So...I have scars in three places now, instead of one."

When her class started using the pool, the other girls noticed. That was when the teasing really took off.

"I'm sure I looked ugly to them. I understand why. Even I don't like to look at myself in the mirror."

Some of the kids had already started calling her "monster" when the school year began, but only in whispers. When they found out about the other scars, they stopped holding back.

"Of course, not everyone was that bad. Some people never said anything at all. But they didn't protect me, either. If they had, they knew they would have gotten picked on themselves, so they just pretended not to notice."

U-ri screwed her mouth shut, afraid she might scream with rage. She understood how the other kids picked on her—that is, she understood the mechanism by which it had happened. But how could kids be so mean? She couldn't understand that. She didn't *want* to understand that.

"So they were picking on you about the scar on your face—that's all?" U-ri said, realizing she was sounding like a detective questioning a witness.

"Yes..."

"That's the only reason?"

Michiru flinched away. "I don't know. Maybe if I had just been able to laugh it off they would've stopped—"

"No. This isn't your fault. You did nothing wrong." U-ri gritted her teeth. "So who was the ringleader of all this? Who started it? Was it a boy or girl?"

"In the beginning it was mostly boys, but the girls started after the second quarter...there were five or six of them."

"Can you tell me their names?"

"U-ri," Aju butted in. "Maybe you should calm down a little."

"How am I supposed to do that? Have you even been listening to what she's been saying? I can't calm down, Aju!" U-ri practically shouted. Her hands clenched into fists. "I mean, those kids are just plain evil. You can't forgive something like that. Michiru, you have to tell me who they were. Aju, I'll need a spell."

"What kind of spell?"

"A spell to send the lot of them to the nameless land! We'll shave their heads and make them go barefoot and throw some old rags on them and *they* can push the Great Wheels of Inculpation for the rest of their lives! They're the real sinners here!" Midway through her fit, U-ri stood and caught a glimpse of Sky and his dark, sad eyes.

"Oh...sorry."

U-ri had forgotten that the real deal—a shaven head, barefoot, rag-wearing devout—was standing right behind her. He was a sinner. An outcast sinner, at that.

"Stop being foolish, U-ri," Aju said, his voice suddenly sounding much older and wiser than it should have coming from a tiny mouse. "You may be an *allcaste*, but you don't have that kind of power. And there is no such spell. You can't just grab somebody out of the Circle and cast them off into the nameless land!"

"Then who can?"

Aju paused a moment, his whiskers trembling. "The god of stories. Well, I guess."

"You guess?" U-ri rolled her eyes, though seeing Aju being so clueless did take the edge off her temper. She could feel her blood pressure dropping back down to normal. "There is a god of stories too? I thought the gods *were* stories."

"Yeah, well," Aju sighed deeply—surprisingly deep for a mouse. "It's an enigma. A mystery not for us to unravel."

"That what the Sage told you?"

Aju clapped his paws over his nose and squeaked "I guess" again.

"I think I understand what the Sage was talking about when he said you were still young."

"Lady U-ri," came Sky's gentle voice from behind her. "You're confusing the Lady Michiru."

U-ri glanced over at the girl who was sitting there with a look of utter confusion on her face. "You're right. I'm sorry. Thanks," she said to Sky.

Suddenly, Michiru unfroze and spoke. "U-ri? Who was it you said 'thanks' to just now?"

That's right—she can't see him.

"Oh, no one. I was just talking to myself," U-ri said, attempting to smile. Aju left her shoulder, ran down her arm, and hopped onto Michiru's knee.

"I think I'll hang with Michiru awhile. You scare me, U-ri."

Rude little vermin, U-ri thought. She was about to say something, but when she saw how happily Michiru was petting Aju's head she decided to hold back.

"So then this Hiroki Morisaki turned against the kids who were picking on you?"

Holding Aju in her palm, Michiru nodded.

"When was that?"

"Around October last year, I think. He stood up in homeroom and just started talking."

"You said that both of you were on the library committee, right? Then why didn't Morisaki notice what was going on sooner?"

Surprisingly, Michiru smiled at that. "Why would someone as popular and as busy as Morisaki notice someone like me at all? Besides, the kids didn't pick on me out in the open at first."

"Wasn't Morisaki a class officer too?"

U-ri remembered hearing Yoshiko and Hiroki talking about something of the sort. *"Weren't you elected to class office? Are you going to accept?"*

"No—he said he was too busy with clubs for that. He offered to go on the library committee because it seemed like the least amount of work."

"And you were elected because you like books?"

"No. The girl committee member was chosen by drawing straws. Because no one wanted to do it. Besides," she added in a quiet voice, "you really think anyone would've elected me for anything?"

"So...Morisaki joined the committee later?"

"Yes."

U-ri thought to herself for a moment. For Michiru, that might not have been an entirely good thing. She was sure some of the other girls had been jealous when they heard she'd be on the same committee as Hiroki. It would've only gotten worse as the year went on, until someone started to wonder why that "monster"—U-ri hated to even think the word, but that was probably what they'd said—got to be alone with him in the library all the time. *Yeah, there was definitely some jealousy going on there.*

"So he noticed when the teasing got worse."

And then he stood up for her. He called them all out in front of the class. Didn't they think it was wrong to pick on her? Weren't they ashamed? Didn't everyone else think they were wrong?

"When he did that, the kids who'd been pretending not to notice came out of the woodwork and agreed with him. It was easy to say teasing was bad when the great Morisaki was saying it first."

The worst teasing stopped—for a time.

"I came to school every day during the third quarter," Michiru said quietly, her eyes narrowing, her thoughts drifting back. "Things were good."

"What did the teachers do about all this? Were they also just pretending nothing was wrong until Morisaki stood up?"

Michiru shook her head vigorously. "No, not at all. Mrs. Kanehashi helped me a lot—and she would scold the kids teasing me."

Akiko Kanehashi was a young teacher. She taught English.

"But Mrs. Kanehashi was new at the school, it was her first time with a class of her own, and..." Michiru swallowed. Then, slowly, she began to explain that the mother of one of the kids who had been teasing her was a real loudmouth in the local PTA. When Mrs. Kanehashi punished her son, she came screaming to the school and called all the other board members.

"She hit so hard and so fast, and she lied about everything. Somehow she made it seem as though Mrs. Kanehashi was the one who was wrong all the time."

U-ri gritted her teeth again. "Didn't the principal have anything to say about this?"

Michiru was quiet.

"Let me guess. He didn't take Mrs. Kanehashi's side. And he didn't take your side. He just apologized on his hands and knees to the kid's parents and pretended nothing was wrong?"

Michiru slumped down in her chair and said, "I guess," in a tiny voice, just as Aju had moments before.

"What about your parents?" the mouse asked, his long whiskers trembling. "Weren't they worried? Didn't they notice you were having a hard time?"

Michiru's color had been improving while she talked, but now she went pale as a sheet. Her lips began to tremble and her shoulders sank. "My mom was there when I fell off the balcony."

She had just taken her eyes away for a second.

"My father blamed my mother for what happened. And his parents blamed her as well."

Things got bad between her folks, and shortly thereafter they had gotten a divorce.

"After that my mom raised me by herself and worked a full-time job. She was tired all the time. And grumpy. When I started going to school, she started working nights too...and drinking a lot."

It sounded to U-ri as though Michiru's mother had been so busy providing for her daughter she didn't have time to care for her.

"And your dad?"

Michiru grimaced like she was being squeezed between two giant hands. "Dad can't stand to look at my face."

He couldn't stand to see her. He didn't *want* to see her.

"I haven't seen him once since the divorce. I know he remarried and had more kids." Michiru's voice cracked, but she didn't cry. It was as if the pain was so great it had seared her heart and dried up all her tears. Her fingers twisted into claws, and U-ri half feared she would start ripping at her own face. "My mom blames me. She says—she says she and dad were in love when they got married. It was my fault that it all fell apart."

"Whoa, whoa, whoa, that is so not true!" Aju squeaked. He ran up Michiru's shoulder and jumped to where her hands rested on her face. He beat at her fingers with his long tail until she moved them away from her face. "Your mother blames herself, you know. But it's too hard on her—so hard she can't be kind to you. She doesn't really think it's your fault."

Michiru scooped Aju up in her hands and snuggled against his fur.

A cold thought crept across U-ri's chest. So cold, it felt like her heart had gotten frostbite. Pain stung at her.

What happened to Michiru could have happened to anyone. It was an accident, a tragic accident that brought her one unhappiness after another and made her life a living hell. How fragile happiness is, U-ri thought. *And how easily taken away. And we take it for granted when things are good.*

It was too easy for evil to seep into the cracks and turn a person's heart black.

Envy. Anger. Guilt. Regret over that which could never be undone. Sadness. Grief. By themselves, all of these things were harmless. Everyone had them in varying amounts at one time or another. One could hardly live without these emotions. But once evil got a foothold in a person's heart, everything changed. Evil twisted them, making their internal envy, anger, guilt, regret, sadness, and grief into something external—into energy. *Energy in need of a target.*

Michiru's face was scarred; her heart was scarred. Her father had abandoned her, and her mother treated her like a stranger. The teachers at school pretended not to notice. Only one young teacher took her side, but she was powerless to help. She couldn't hope to stand against the legions of evil that bore down on Michiru from all sides. Michiru had nowhere to run.

She was a princess, trapped in a high tower.

The metaphor occurred to U-ri suddenly, but it seemed very appropriate. She could see it in Michiru's slender form and lonely eyes—she was a princess taken from her home, driven from her palace, and made a prisoner of the enemy.

And Hiroki Morisaki was her knight in shining armor, riding forth to save his princess.

"A hero—"

The word came unbidden from U-ri's mouth. Aju looked up.

"Morisaki wanted to be your hero, didn't he?"

Michiru nodded.

U-ri noticed Aju's beady black eyes staring at her. His whiskers moved as though he were going to say something, but the mouse was quiet.

"But the hero and the princess are supposed to live happily ever after—once they've dealt with the enemies—isn't that how the stories go?"

The stories...!

"Why did Morisaki do it? And why now?"

Tears were welling in Michiru's eyes again. *No, those aren't tears. It's blood flowing from the latest, freshest wound in her heart.*

"It's my fault. He tried to save me. Just like a real hero—but once we got into eighth grade, they started picking on him."

In eighth grade, Hiroki and Michiru had been separated, placed in different classes. They had a new homeroom teacher as well.

"They took Mrs. Kanehashi away from our class after what happened with the teasing incident."

The charges were completely false, but for a time, things worked out—for Michiru at least. Her new class was much more laid back, and her new homeroom teacher kept an eye on things to make sure what had happened to Michiru the year before didn't happen again.

But things were different for Hiroki.

"When the kids were teasing me, hardly anybody knew about it—teachers or students. I doubt the students in the other classes heard a thing."

But everyone had heard about Hiroki Morisaki's heroic stand. And not everybody liked it. Not just students either; some of the teachers hadn't looked favorably on it either.

"When Morisaki called out the class, he called out the other teachers in school too, for not coming to help Mrs. Kanehashi."

Some of the teachers thought Hiroki had been out of bounds to criticize them. Gradually, opinion shifted against him.

The boy thinks he's a hero.

We've got to do something about this. It's disruptive to the class.

A student should know his place.

Of Hiroki's critics his new eighth-grade teacher was one of the worst.

U-ri's heart ached so much she trembled with fear that it would burst. She was almost afraid to ask the next question, but she had to. "You mean, Morisaki's teacher was actually encouraging students to pick on him?"

Michiru stared back at U-ri through her tears but said nothing.

"And the two boys that he stabbed, they were working for this teacher?"

At last Michiru nodded once, then twice.

It was getting difficult for U-ri to breathe. She paused, trying to calm herself down before speaking again. "What was his teacher's name?"

"Mr. Hata." Mr. Hata was an older teacher in his fifties. A sociology teacher, Michiru told her. U-ri felt her throat tighten even more.

"What happened to Mr. Hata after the incident? What is he doing now?" Aju asked.

"He's on leave. Like me."

Kibogaoka Middle School had descended into chaos after the incident. Some of the teachers wanted to deal with the matter head on, properly, while others just stalled, trying to make sure the blame didn't fall on them. Early on in the ensuing struggle, Mrs. Kanehashi had been suspended. That, it turned out, had been Mr. Hata's doing. He claimed that the teasing issue Morisaki had been involved in the year before hadn't been handled properly, and the principal and board had gone along. Mrs. Kanehashi was without allies—locked up in a tower of her own. She had clearly drawn the short straw in all this.

"Aju, I'd like to amend what I said earlier," U-ri began. "I think we should send the principal and Mr. Hata to the nameless land first."

"I already told you we can't do that!"

The mouse turned to Michiru. "Do Hiroki's parents know about all this?"

Michiru's face darkened and she shook her head. "I don't think Morisaki said anything to his parents about what happened last year. It didn't seem like the kind of thing he would go out of his way to say."

That made sense enough to U-ri. Hiroki wasn't the type to go home and tell his parents about what he had done that day—even if it had been standing up for a girl in class.

"And he didn't tell them about it when he started getting picked on?"

"I don't think so, Aju," U-ri said before Michiru could answer. "It's not the kind of thing you can talk about so easily."

U-ri closed her eyes. She finally understood. It made sense. When Hiroki had come home suddenly from school that day and run to the shower, it was because he'd been picked on at school. He was washing mud out of his hair, or dirt off his face, or blood from a wound.

Hiroki Morisaki was a tough kid. It would've taken a lot to get him down. But his situation at the time was anything but normal. Imagine getting picked on by half the class, with your own homeroom teacher as the ringleader. From under the bright shining flag of education, Mr. Hata had called his troops to battle and declared open season on bullying Hiroki. No wonder none of the kids had shown any hesitation. U-ri was sure there had been plenty of willing participants.

It was about as evil a situation as she could imagine. Certainly nothing a single middle school student could stand up to.

But Hiroki Morisaki hadn't caved. Something wrong was still wrong, no matter how many people were doing it. He didn't bow to the bullies. He knew he had to fight them.

That was why he went looking for more power. He was lured by the giant, shining coin of the Hero, and when he grabbed for it, there on the other side was the dark, bewitching glimmer of the King in Yellow.

Which is how the dark king looking for destruction and the young boy looking for power had met.

It was anger that led Hiroki to become the last vessel, after all. Not blind rage, but justified anger. Righteous anger.

Regret and sadness filled U-ri's chest to breaking. Somewhere buried beneath the vestments of the *allcaste*, Yuriko Morisaki was crying.

"So the two boys Hiroki stabbed were the main conspirators, er, the leaders?" Aju asked, carefully choosing his words.

Michiru showed no such hesitation. "They were Mr. Hata's flunkies. With their own teacher egging them on, they thought they could do anything—and they were right."

Aju clucked his tiny tongue. "Their kind always appears in times of war."

U-ri raised an eyebrow at Aju. "War?"

"That's right, war. This is a war."

The King in Yellow must have been pleased. The story of the Hero was always a story of war.

"Lady U-ri?" Sky called out hesitantly. As usual, U-ri had forgotten he was even there. "Might you ask if the Lady Michiru heard anything about the Book of Elem from your brother? About how he obtained it, how he used it. Perhaps she knows something?"

Sky was still looking at Michiru as if she were the strangest thing he'd ever seen in his entire life. His eyes were filled with reverence—or possibly fear. *Or maybe I'm just thinking too hard.*

"When we first saw her, Lady Michiru did something that troubled me. She turned to you—and you were invisible at the time—and called out for 'Morisaki,' yes?"

That's right. Didn't she ask if he'd come back? Which meant she had reason to expect Hiroki to return, invisible, to the library. More than expect. She had been waiting for him to come. That was why she had come to the library.

U-ri gave Sky a look to tell him that she understood. Then she turned back to Michiru, who was wiping at her eyes with the handkerchief that was by now so soggy it did her little good at all. U-ri lightly clapped her hands together to get her attention and leaned forward in her chair. "Michiru. I need to talk to you about something, something *very important* upon which Morisaki's life might depend."

Michiru jerked upright, nearly dropping her handkerchief on the floor.

"That's why," U-ri continued, "I need you to try to answer me as honestly as possible. Don't hide anything. All right?"

Michiru looked at U-ri with her bloodshot left eye and nodded.

"We book-spirits know that he had obtained a very powerful magical book as his ally."

Michiru didn't look startled by this. She only nodded lightly.

"It is called the Book of Elem. Do you know of it?"

"Morisaki talked about it, yes."

"But you never saw it?"

She shook her head. "He said it was very important—and besides, he had taken it without permission, so he kept it hidden."

"When was this?" Aju cut in impatiently, but U-ri tapped one finger on his head and went on. "You like books, don't you, Michiru?"

"Yes."

"And Morisaki also liked books?"

"Well, he didn't *not* like them, but he wasn't a bookworm like me. Still, I think I got him more interested than he had been. He always liked hearing me tell him about things I'd read."

U-ri nodded slowly. "All right, Michiru. Now did Morisaki ever tell you about a cottage in the mountains with a reading room? A place with many old books?"

A lump formed in Michiru's thin throat. She swallowed. "I know about the reading room. He brought us there once, the three of us."

"The three of you?"

"Yes, Mrs. Kanehashi drove us in her car."

It had been right after spring break started. They had gone out for a drive under a blue sky—a perfect drive on a perfect day, Michiru described it to her with watery eyes. Eighth grade had started. Michiru wasn't getting teased anymore, and the worst of it had yet to start for Hiroki. For the two of them, it was the most peaceful time they ever had together.

"Morisaki wasn't the type to be friends with someone like me, not really." Michiru crossed her legs and sighed. "When we first started out on the library committee together, we hardly spoke. I didn't know what to say to him, and he probably had no idea what to say to me."

But after he had declared himself her knight in shining armor, Hiroki's position had changed. Or maybe it was his whole way of thinking.

"He tried to be my friend. But we didn't have much in common—the only thing we could talk about was books. I think it was hard on him coming up with anything else at first. Then one day he told me about his strange great-uncle. That's when I heard about the cottage."

He had told her about the ramshackle place up in the mountains—like a haunted house—filled with rare books from around the world. Michiru had been intrigued, and midway through the third quarter, when the teasing had finally subsided, she had been happy when Hiroki mentioned it again.

"I told him I'd like to see it someday—I don't know why."

Hiroki had invited her to come. *"I've been wanting to go back myself."* He even remembered how to get there. *"You can't take a train, though. It's way up in the mountains—you need a car. Hey, I got an idea. Let's ask Mrs. Kanehashi!"*

Mrs. Kanehashi had been interested too. But being a teacher, she said she needed their parents' permission.

"Then Morisaki said that if they asked his parents, there was no way they would give the okay. The place was inherited, and until final ownership was sorted out they couldn't just wander in. He said we'd have to go in secret."

"It's okay, Mrs. Kanehashi. I checked it out when I was there last year— you could easily put your hand through one of the windows and open the lock. We'd be in and out and no one would know the difference. It's not like we're going to do anything bad."

U-ri was surprised. This was a side of Hiroki she never knew about. Though it was like him to remember details like where the windows had been placed—something she never would've noticed.

"Mrs. Kanehashi didn't get angry?"

Michiru grinned devilishly then, her good eye twinkling. "She said no way at first, but eventually, Morisaki wore her down."

"So he snuck out for a drive," U-ri muttered. "And here I thought he was always too busy with his clubs and baseball..."

Aju squeaked vigorously at her, and she realized what she was saying. Michiru was giving her a questioning look. *Uh-oh!*

U-ri coughed loudly. "So, Michiru, what did you think of that reading room you saw?"

"You know, I've been there myself," Aju hurriedly added. "Before I started hanging out with U-ri, I sat there for a good many years gathering dust."

"That's right," Michiru said, looking at the mouse. "You're a book too, aren't you!"

Whew, she's going to let it slide.

"When I first heard about it from Morisaki I had this image in my mind, but when I saw the real thing, I realized how far off I had been. I'd never seen books so old, and all in one place like that—more than even here in the school library." Michiru looked off into the distance. "The drive was a lot of fun. We listened to music, talked, stopped for lunch, enjoyed the scenery..."

Michiru lowered her voice and told them about their arrival in the mountains. The old wooden cottage with its fading paint and cracked windows let them in as easily as Hiroki had predicted, even if Mrs. Kanehashi had been sweating bullets the whole time.

"I remember feeling very cold the closer we got to the reading room. I think maybe I was a little queasy from the drive."

"Nah, the air in there's stale," Aju said. Michiru didn't respond. Her brows were furrowed with effort as she tripped back through her memories of the cottage.

"I remember Morisaki was all smiles. Mrs. Kanehashi was nervous enough for all three of us, but he was really excited—he was practically floating."

Flashlight in hand, he had urged them on toward the reading room. Mrs. Kanehashi and Michiru had to run to keep up with him.

"I was scared," Michiru said, and an actual shiver ran through her. "That reading room—it was like the room itself was made of books. And it frightened me. I remember feeling my body grow heavy when I stepped inside."

But Michiru hadn't said anything at the time. She hadn't wanted to ruin Hiroki's mood.

"Mrs. Kanehashi was sure surprised. She's great in English, of course, and she had also studied Spanish—but she said she probably couldn't read a single book in the place."

Hiroki had gone into the reading room and lost himself in the books, not even responding when Michiru or Mrs. Kanehashi tried to talk to him. Michiru found it hard to breathe in there; she had to go outside several times for some fresh air. Mrs. Kanehashi had joined her.

So Hiroki had plenty of time to himself in there. Time enough to grab the Book of Elem and Aju and sneak them out without either of the other two noticing.

"Lady U-ri?" Sky said from behind her, startling her yet again.

"W-what?"

"I was wondering if you could ask the Lady Michiru something for me. Ask her how your brother was looking at the books that day."

"Huh?"

"That is, was he merely plucking books off the shelves at random, or did he seem to have some purpose in his search?"

Michiru sat with her face pale, lost in her memories of the reading room.

U-ri glanced sidelong at Aju. "Wait. You were there. Can't you answer Sky's question?"

Aju blanched. "Er, maybe."

"What do you mean, 'maybe'?"

"See, until Hiroki actually touched my binding and pulled me from the shelf I was, er, asleep," Aju confessed, his eyes hidden behind his long tail. "Books sleep too, you know. When no one is using us or needs us, we kind of doze off."

"And the Sage was asleep too?"

"Well, the Sage is a special case, that old geezer, he—"

"Wasn't asleep like you were, then."

At least that explains why Aju's been mum about how he met Hiroki until now. He doesn't remember! It also explained why Aju hadn't recognized Michiru.

"The moment when Hiroki stuck me in his backpack and I realized I was leaning right up against the Book of Elem, boy, did I scream. But it was already too late."

U-ri called to Michiru. She looked up. Her lips were white.

"Did it seem like Morisaki was looking for a particular book in the reading room that day?"

Michiru thought about that for a moment. Her left eye wandered. At length, she shook her head apologetically. "I don't know. I don't remember. I just felt so queasy, and I didn't want Morisaki to know, see." Then Michiru's good eye opened wider. "But that reminds me. Morisaki did say something strange when we were planning the trip in the first place. He said that the reading room and all the old books in it seemed like something from another world. He said, *'I've been having this dream of that place since I went there with my family last year.'* He said that he had heard someone calling to him from the reading room. Just calling over and over. 'Hiroki, Hiroki.'"

U-ri felt an icy chill stop at each nerve ending along her spine.

When they had visited Ichiro Minochi's cottage together as a family in December of the year before, Hiroki had been right in the middle of playing knight in shining armor to Michiru's damsel in distress. He was being a hero, looking for allies, trying to defeat his enemies. And something in the library called to him. Something had called his name—

The King in Yellow. No, it was the Hero itself. Both sides of the coin.

"That good enough for you, Sky?" U-ri asked out of the corner of her mouth. He did not reply. She looked and saw he was lost again, staring at Michiru's face.

Aju lightly whacked U-ri's cheek with his tail. "I've got a question for Michiru too."

U-ri nodded. The girl looked up, her face drained of what little strength it had.

"Michiru, a little bit ago, you called out for Hiroki—you were groping for him with your hands. You asked whether he'd come back. What did you mean by that?"

Michiru's face twisted with pain. She must be exhausted—first an attempted suicide, and now this inquisition. But U-ri wanted to hear her answer as much as Aju did. She walked over to the girl and put her hand on her back.

"I'm sorry. We won't ask any more questions after this. We'll take you home, I promise. If you could just tell Aju—"

Michiru grabbed U-ri's arm. She could feel the girl's warmth through the vestments of protection. U-ri put her hand over Michiru's.

"When we got into eighth grade, and I heard that Morisaki was being picked on..."

"Yes?"

"I went to him and apologized...I apologized over and over again...I said that they could pick on me again if they wanted to, that I just wouldn't come to school, that he shouldn't protect me. I asked him not to."

Of course, Hiroki would never have done anything of the sort.

"It's okay, just leave it to me."

"But I think they were getting to him. He looked really tired. I was afraid if things went on like that, they might wear him out completely. I talked to Mrs. Kanehashi, and she said we should go talk to Morisaki's mom."

But Hiroki had found out somehow and insisted Michiru do nothing of the sort. He told her that if she did, he wouldn't ever speak to her again. Mrs. Kanehashi tried to convince them it would be for the best, but Hiroki wouldn't hear of it.

"It's all right. I can handle this. I know I can."

Of course he was confident, U-ri thought to herself. *He had the Book of Elem at home, and it was already starting to exert its influence over him. An influence that led to him stabbing two of his classmates soon after.*

U-ri stopped her train of thought. *That's odd. Why did he use any old knife? Not a knight's sword—a cooking knife. He didn't need the Book of Elem or the King in Yellow's power to use that.* It was something any kid in eighth grade could have pulled off.

Why would the King in Yellow bother possessing him if it was only to make him stab someone with a cheap old knife?

Then again, maybe it did make sense. After all, it was conflict. People injuring other people, drawing blood, taking lives. Maybe that was all you needed for there to be war.

"I...met Morisaki the morning of the incident."

U-ri was so deep in her own thoughts, she almost missed what Michiru said. Seconds passed before she looked up with a startled expression on her face. "You met him? That morning?"

"Yes. I ran into him at the cubbies on the way into school. He seemed... Morisaki seemed really happy."

"Get ready for a little surprise today," he had told her.

"A little surprise?" U-ri echoed. Michiru went pale and nodded.

"I'll fix everything. The teasing will end for good."

"And you believed him?" Aju asked. Michiru shook her head. "I was frightened. I guess I frighten easily. But I thought something was strange about Morisaki. He seemed so happy..."

Michiru had followed him into school, pestering him with questions. *"What do you mean 'you'll fix everything'? What are you going to do? Don't do this alone."*

Hiroki had laughed. *"I told you it's fine. Don't worry. I'm sure it'll go great."*

"You're 'sure'? What if it doesn't go great?" Michiru had pressed him, but Hiroki just laughed.

"It will go great, absolutely. And once it's all done, I'll explain everything to you, Inui."

"I still didn't believe him. All I knew was that he was going to do something he shouldn't."

She had confronted him. *"You're going to do something bad, aren't you?"*

"Something bad?" Hiroki had echoed back, suddenly sounding like a little boy. *"What do you mean, something bad?"*

Something that would get him in trouble with the teachers, something that they would take him out of school for, maybe even to jail.

Of course, she had been absolutely right.

But Hiroki had just smiled at her. *"If in the unlikely event they do take me away, I'll come back to meet you, Inui. I'll hide so no one knows where I am, and come to meet you, and explain everything."*

That just made Michiru even more frightened. But Hiroki was resolute.

"I promise," he had said. *"We can even choose the place where I'll find you. How about the library? Okay? No matter what happens today, I'll come meet you there. Even if you can't see me, you'll know it's me. All right?"*

Which meant that the Book of Elem had given him considerable power already—power far exceeding that of regular humans. Power like U-ri's.

"And you believed him?" U-ri asked.

She had, or rather, she had wanted to very badly. That was when she had given up trying to stop him.

"Which is why you thought we were Hiroki before, by the window."

Michiru's eyes were swimming in tears again. "I've been waiting since it happened. I knew he would come back to the library."

But he hadn't come back. Hiroki was gone without a trace. No one knew where he was. And how many days had it been since he disappeared, leaving Michiru in this lonely, frightening place.

She had come to the library with hope so many times before, but today she had come in despair.

"I don't know why I thought this, but it seemed that if I just had the courage to throw myself from the window, I could go to the place Morisaki had gone..."

U-ri knew just what she meant. She knew it so well it hurt. "Thank you for telling me. I know it must've been hard," U-ri said, giving the girl a hug. "You should go home and rest. Be good to your body and your heart. Try to get your health back." U-ri stared hard at the girl. "And I want you to promise me you'll not try to take your life again. Don't even think about it. You'd only make Hiroki very, very sad. All right?"

"Yeah," Aju added, "and we'll find Hiroki for you, I promise."

For all U-ri knew, they were just adding empty promises on top of empty promises, but that seemed to be enough for Michiru.

"I'll be waiting."

"You do that..." U-ri said, then she suddenly felt dizzy. A chill raced through her entire body. All around her, the books were calling to her in hushed voices. "*Allcaste!* Be careful! It approaches!"

U-ri tensed. Sky whirled around. Aju jumped on top of her head.

"What approaches?"

"Some *thing* that bears the Yellow Sign!"

"What, me?" Aju squeaked at the books. "You mean you didn't notice until now? Yeah, I've got the Yellow Sign, so what? It's all under control."

"This is not one of your followers, *allcaste!*" the books said, their voices rising into a scream. "It's coming closer. It's coming! You must leave here at once!"

Leave here? Where to?

Sky grabbed U-ri's wrist and began to run, leading her toward the exit. U-ri began to run with him, her arm around Michiru's shoulder, dragging her along.

"This way!" Sky shouted, throwing open the library door.

The three ran out into the hallway. Aju clung to strands of U-ri's hair, almost flying after her. Then U-ri came to an abrupt stop. Aju flew over her head, smacking square into Sky's back.

"What's the big idea?" Aju squeaked as he scrambled to dig into the devout's black robes.

Sky stopped too, rooted to the spot by the scene before him.

The library was positioned at the westernmost end of the school building. From the library door, they could see straight down the hallway, all the way to where the L-shaped school building's hall turned at a sharp angle. The hallway had been filled with sunlight coming in through the windows when they had first arrived. But now, unbelievably, it was dark—no, it was darkening.

The ceiling and two walls made a perfectly rectangular space that extended like a tube straight down to the corner. Except they couldn't see the corner anymore, because it was obscured by a veil of absolute darkness stretched across the hallway. And the veil was coming nearer.

What was left of the lit hallway was disappearing behind the dark.

Sky looked with eyes open wide, transfixed by the darkness. He spread his arms wide before U-ri and Michiru, as if to protect them. U-ri moved Michiru behind her, pushing her gently back toward the library. Then she ducked under Sky's arm and stood in front of him.

"Lady U-ri!"

"It's all right!"

In the time it took for their brief exchange, the wall of darkness had come closer—it was now only three feet away from the tip of U-ri's nose. And there it stopped.

U-ri threw back her shoulders, planted her feet firmly beneath her, and lifted her eyes to meet it.

CHAPTER EIGHT

The Man of Ash

U-ri braced herself. The glyph on her forehead shone like a star, illuminating the darkness in front of her. At once, the wall lost its solid appearance and recoiled like a living thing.

This did much for U-ri's courage. She steadied her feet, took a deep breath, and shouted at the thing. "What do you want of me?"

The darkness surged forward, filling the entire space of the corridor. U-ri strained her eyes until she saw something moving inside the darkness. It was undulating, throbbing. It heaved and shrank, as though its entire mass were drawing breath.

U-ri raised her voice again. "What are you? If you have a name, I would hear it!"

When the thing responded, she heard its voice not with her ears but with another organ—it seemed to speak directly to her heart.

I am an envoy of the King in Yellow.

Michiru grabbed U-ri's sleeve from behind. *I wonder if she heard it too?* Atop U-ri's shoulder, Aju's whiskers trembled, tickling her cheek. Sky still stood behind her, arms spread wide.

You are the allcaste?

U-ri glared back at the darkness.

Don't make me laugh, the voice continued. *Why must it always be children who know not even the true value of the mark upon their heads who seek to bring balance to the Circle?*

The darkness was quivering. *It's laughing at me.* It began to undulate faster now. Something circular was spinning in the very center of its mass. Like a giant beach ball—no, larger than that. U-ri's eyes were glued to the thing.

"Lady U-ri," Sky said, "do not let it draw you in."

U-ri took a quick breath and vigorously shook her head. She peered sidelong at Sky to protect herself. The writhing darkness was not reflected in his deep purple eyes.

"If you are an envoy, you have come on some errand," Sky called out. "You are indeed before the *allcaste*, creature of the King in Yellow. Why have you come? Why has your king sent you?"

The spinning in the center of the darkness stopped.

"Or has the king tired of its freedom already and wishes to return to the Hall of All Books?"

Then the thing roared at them with a sound like the rumbling of thunder, and the circular shape in its center opened. *It's an eye!* It was a giant eyeball. Where it should have been white, it glowed a dull gold, and the pupil was narrow and pointed like a cat's. It glared at Sky.

You are nothing but a crude figure, shaped of the dust of this Circle, yet you dare call upon my master?

A huge vibration issued forth from the giant eyeball. The very air shook. A wave of force hit the party, and U-ri staggered. Behind her, Michiru was thrown back through the air. She collided with the library door and crumpled to the floor.

Then the darkness disappeared—swallowed by the golden eyeball that now hung suspended in the air. In the space of a breath, the eyeball receded to the back of the corridor, from where it released another wave of energy. U-ri lowered her head and braced herself, dropping to one knee as the wave hit. Behind her, Sky still stood with his arms open wide.

"Lady U-ri! You must escape into the library and take the Lady Michiru with you!"

U-ri looked down the hallway to see something else emerging from the eye—a swarm of tentacles. The tips of the tentacles gleamed like jet-black spears as they cut through the air straight toward Sky.

"Look out!" U-ri threw herself at Sky a moment too late. The tentacles whipped around him, and in an instant lifted him off the ground. Sky struggled in their grip, his shaven head only inches below the fluorescent lights on the ceiling.

The tentacles retracted at the same time that the golden eyeball came barreling down the hallway toward U-ri. The tentacles constricted then loosened, wrapping around him, then unraveling. The eyeball came so close to him she thought they might touch.

Then U-ri noticed that the golden eyeball was coated in some milky white mucus-like substance that came dripping down to splatter on the floor next to U-ri's hand where she lay. There was a sizzling sound, and the floor melted beneath the drops, leaving holes in the tiles. U-ri's eyes went wide. *Acid!*

She jerked back her hand and shot to her feet. Another drop of the mucus fell, right where her head had been only seconds before.

Above her, the tentacles had completely wrapped around Sky. By now she could only see his head and the tips of his fingers.

Ahh...came a startled sound from the eyeball. *You are a very interesting little dust puppet, aren't you?*

Groaning with pain, Sky struggled to turn away from the eyeball's gaze. The tentacles lifted him up and lowered him down, bringing his face closer to the eyeball. It blinked, causing a thick flow of mucus to drip onto the tops of the tentacles. The eyeball was examining Sky, with all the interest of a boy looking at a freshly captured bug through a magnifying glass. *You are the gate?* it shouted, its voice high with excitement.

Aju chirped, jumping from the top of U-ri's head. He managed to reach one of the tentacles with his forepaws and began to climb up it at an incredible speed, biting with sharp teeth as he went. "Let go of him, you big eyeball freak! You don't even have proper arms and legs!" he shouted.

Though completely dwarfed by the size of the eyeball, Aju made good progress at first. He reached the spot where Sky's head emerged from the writhing mass, but then another tentacle whipped around from behind the eyeball and casually batted the mouse off into the air. Aju fell like a stone.

"Aju! Sky!"

U-ri didn't even have time to stand. She felt like her heart would beat right out of her chest. Her mind was a blank. *What do I do? What can I do? How can I even begin to fight this thing?* She could only gasp for breath.

What did the other allcastes *do?*

Suddenly, U-ri heard a whistling noise in her ears. *Another tentacle! Where's this one coming from?*

She tensed, ready to move, when something small flew in through one of the windows. Moving faster than her eye could follow, it severed several of the tentacles. The eyeball howled with rage, flattening out sideways as though it was squinting against the pain.

The next attack came directly after the first. This time, U-ri saw it happen. It flew in an arc through the window. *A boomerang!* The steel boomerang flew clear around the golden eyeball, slicing off the tentacles it happened upon along its orbit. The ones clutching Sky loosened. The devout kicked hard at the eyeball, then plummeted headfirst toward the ground.

Wh-who's there? the eyeball sputtered in her mind. It drifted up toward the ceiling, shedding tentacle after tentacle. The severed ends writhed on the floor, steaming in pools of their own acidic blood.

U-ri saw a black-gloved hand grip the window frame. Then the owner of the hand swooped in, like a giant raven alighting in the hallway.

U-ri lunged toward the unconscious Sky, picked him up in her arms, and turned to face the raven. She found herself looking up at him—he was a man in fact, not a bird, but his countenance was bizarre. She had thought him old for a moment on account of his long white hair—so long it reached the middle of his back, bound in a long braid. It was as though a bucket of ash had been poured on his head. The jet-black robes that swirled around him were also covered with ash—*no, dust.* A thick collar protected his neck, and there were additional pads on his shoulders. His cloak, ripped and torn in places, was long enough to sweep along the floor.

The man walked forward, taking long strides, his thick-soled boots making a metallic clang. He walked forward and casually stomped on the still-writhing tentacles in front of U-ri before kicking them off to the side. The floor sagged ominously around the puddles of acid left by the eyeball.

His black-gloved hands moved quickly, replacing the steel boomerang that came arcing back to him inside the fold of his cloak. When his hands next emerged, they held blades—a pair of swords. Their hilts were wrought silver, and the blades themselves shone with a translucent light, like glass. They were each longer than U-ri's forearm.

The man held the swords up to either side of his face and let them fall to the side, lowering his shoulders. He turned to the giant eyeball.

"Not someone so important that I feel the need to announce myself," he said in a calm, deep voice. It was different than any grown-up's voice U-ri had heard before. "In that respect we are the same, underling," he addressed the eyeball, a teasing tone in his voice.

The golden eyeball howled with rage. The sound was like the grinding of gears in some half-broken machine—a sound to curdle souls. *You dare mock an envoy of the king!*

Then U-ri saw a line form across the center of the eye. She thought for a moment that the eye was rotating in midair, but then the line opened and spread, creating a huge gash of a mouth, one bearing countless sharp fangs.

U-ri screamed. The nightmarish mouth bore down on her. But the man leapt into action, his every move as graceful as a dancer's, dual blades slashing through the air. The first cut set the eyeball spinning, and the second slashed into its backside, sending it howling off a wall and back up to the ceiling.

U-ri looked up. She felt tiny fragments of something dusting her forehead and cheeks. *The fangs. The severed fangs are raining down on me.*

The giant mouth closed once and the whole thing trembled—then it began to rain fangs like countless arrows. The man dodged the blast, his cape swirling behind him. His feet shifted beneath him and he deftly changed direction, taking another stab at the envoy. The giant mouth dodged to one side at the last minute, but the inertia sent it spinning down the hallway, its maw hanging half open. The man chased it, but it had been a ruse—the eyeball lurched around, and a bright red tongue emerged from between the fangs and whipped itself around the man's right wrist. Without a moment's hesitation, the man slashed it in half with the sword in his left hand. Black blood sprayed out of the wound, making the floor slick beneath it.

With a murky gurgling scream—*like a hundred drunks voiding the contents of their stomachs at once*—the massive sphere of fangs and flesh began to spin rapidly. It shot up, ricocheting off the ceiling, the walls, the floor, the windows. Everything smelled of the creature's blood. The stench was unbearable. *Make that a thousand drunks.* The envoy whirled and slammed into the walls, spraying fluids and gradually growing smaller and smaller.

Youuuurrrgh!

The great mouth snapped shut, and the creature was an eyeball once again. It stopped in a corner of the ceiling and blinked. The white of the eye was now blood red.

The man in the cape bounded lightly over to U-ri. With his teeth, he pulled the glove off his right hand and swung it around toward U-ri. Before she knew it, his hand was on her forehead. He released her almost immediately, then turned back to the bright red eyeball, his hand up—the same hand that had touched U-ri's face—raised.

A single band of light erupted from the man's hand, striking the giant eyeball dead center. The eyeball screamed, then dropped down to the floor like a fly hit by a blast of insecticide. It morphed back into a nasty lump of toothy flesh on the way down, shooting out its fangs in a last desperate attempt. U-ri hardly saw the man move at all. His swords were a blur, and his cape swished, knocking every last fang out of the air. In one smooth motion he ran over to the fallen eyeball, knelt, and thrust his swords into it. This time, the envoy didn't even scream. There was just a faint hissing sound, like the air escaping a punctured tire.

And then it was quiet.

The giant eyeball creature slowly collapsed—like a time-lapse movie of a sand castle eroding in the rain. Soon there was nothing but black dust on the floor where it had been; then there was nothing, leaving the man kneeling there with his swords in the shape of a V, stabbing the empty hallway.

The man withdrew his swords and stood. He turned, his black cloak billowing. U-ri was sitting where she had fallen on the floor, hugging the still-unconscious Sky. Behind them, Michiru lay flat by the library doors.

The man turned to look down at U-ri. Their eyes met, and U-ri unconsciously flinched.

The man looked much younger from the front. He was in his mid-thirties, his early forties at most. He had a long face with a dramatically pointed nose and chin, as if his features were carved from wood.

His brows were bushy over his eyes, black hair streaked with white. His eyes were black, and his lids were half closed, almost like he was sleepy. One of his ears had been pierced, and a silver chain hung from it down to his jaw.

Everything beneath his cloak was black too. His shirt with a raised collar was black. And on top of that he wore something like a vest made out of several overlapping layers of black leather. He wore a thick belt wrapped twice around his waist and loose-fitting black pants beneath that with ragged holes in them where something had burned through. U-ri noticed that his boots had straps at the top that wrapped tightly around his legs, like the sandals she had seen in history books.

He was still holding his swords, but when U-ri's eyes went to them he seemed to notice, and spinning them around once, he sheathed them in two scabbards at his belt.

U-ri took a deep breath. Something was creeping up her back. She jumped, picturing a tentacle snaking out of the floor. It was Aju.

"You okay, U-ri?" Aju looked slightly flattened, like he had been thrown down one too many times, but otherwise he was none the worse for wear. She nodded, and he breathed a sigh of relief—stopping short when he noticed the man in black. "Uh, who's that?"

The man smiled with half of his mouth. His skin was brown and had the look of tanned leather. "I am afraid I have not yet introduced myself."

He lifted his thick-soled boots and took two strides toward them. U-ri shrank back, though she hadn't intended to. Her eyes were transfixed by the man's angular chiseled face.

He knelt on one knee before her and extended the index finger of his right hand, pointing it squarely at U-ri's forehead. "You saw how I used it just now on the envoy?"

He's talking about the glyph.

"I'm guessing you're new at this, Lady *Allcaste*," he added, smiling again with half his mouth. "Are you injured?" His voice was surprisingly gentle.

"I don't think so," she replied—though she wasn't so sure about Sky.

"And this nameless devout and…rat are with you?" The man peered at Aju and frowned. "You're a dictionary, aren't you? If you were going to transform into something, why not pick something a little more useful?"

Aju's whiskers trembled. "How rude! I'll have you know that U-ri gave me this form!"

"I see. How like a girl." The man sighed and U-ri thought she heard him mutter, "Why'd it have to be a girl?"

U-ri's mouth curled into a frown. Apparently, he didn't think she was good enough.

"There something wrong with being a girl?"

The man ignored her question. "I think it's past time you revived your servant, there."

U-ri blinked, suddenly embarrassed. "H-how do I do that?"

The man placed his bare right hand on his forehead. When U-ri didn't react, he sighed again, took her right hand and put it on her forehead for her.

"Like I just did. The power of the glyph goes into your hand, see?"

He's right! A faint circle was glowing on her palm—it was the exact same pattern as her glyph.

"Now place that on your servant's forehead."

U-ri did so, and Sky moaned softly. He opened his eyes. A second later, he jumped to his feet, almost butting heads with U-ri on the way up.

"Lady U-ri! Lady U-ri, are you all right?"

Seeing him pop up like a jack-in-the-box made U-ri smile despite herself. "I'm fine, Sky."

U-ri then turned to do the same to Michiru, but the man in black grabbed her wrist.

"The girl is not your servant, is she?"

"No, but—"

"Then let her sleep awhile. Until we are through talking, at least, for we have much to discuss." The man's eyes went to the door. "I sense books. That's a library?"

"Yes."

"Excellent. That should provide a perfect place for us."

Without waiting for U-ri to respond, the man scooped Michiru into his arms, cradling her gently. U-ri stood and opened the door.

Once they were inside the library, the man in black laid Michiru down on the book checkout counter.

"What if someone comes—"

"There's no danger of that. The field formed when that creature arrived still stands. The people in this region will not be able to see us or hear us."

Now that he mentioned it, U-ri noticed that no one had come out of the classrooms to see what was going on, even with all the ruckus.

The man walked toward the back of the library. Around him, the books began to whisper to one another. "A wolf! A wolf has come!"

The man paid them no attention. Grabbing the back of a nearby chair, he carried it over to U-ri. "Have a seat, Lady *Allcaste*."

U-ri remained standing. "You're a wolf?"

The man put a hand to his waist and bowed slightly.

"*Allcaste! Allcaste!*" The leader of the books in the library—that female from before—called to Uri in a trembling voice, though she seemed more excited than fearful. "He is a wolf, a famous one. They call him the Man of Ash."

The man in black smiled faintly, then turned to address the books. "You know much for children."

"We may be young, yet we still possess knowledge," the female voice responded.

"Yes. Your network of friends is quite valuable."

"Didn't you know who he was?" U-ri whispered to Aju on her shoulder. But before he could respond, the man in black turned to her. "Books that have few dealings with people know little of this world, Lady *Allcaste*. Your dictionary companion there spent a long time stored away somewhere, I would imagine."

Aju bristled at that. "How rude!" he squeaked, but very quietly.

"Not to mention he bears the Yellow Sign—though it's rather faded."

He could tell that just by looking at him?

"The majority of books lose themselves when exposed to the power of the King in Yellow. They forget who they are. Perhaps that is why your wee one knows so little. He has lost both wisdom and knowledge to the King."

Aju didn't even squeak this time. He crawled up to the nape of U-ri's neck where he curled into a tiny ball.

"Don't be too hard on yourself, little one. You'll remember everything in due time," the man said, though his tone was more explanatory than consoling. U-ri petted Aju with the tip of one finger.

Then the man in black, the Man of Ash, straddled a chair and sat. U-ri stayed standing. Sky walked up shakily, leaning on the back of her chair, then hurriedly stood back when he saw that U-ri wasn't sitting.

"It's okay, Sky. You should rest."

The devout's eyes were still slightly unfocused. U-ri took him by the hand and pushed down on his shoulder, forcing him to sit. "Don't laugh at us," she said with a sidelong glance at the Man of Ash. "We're new to this, like you said."

The Man of Ash didn't even smile. "I'm not concerned, and neither should you be. It is this way for all *allcastes* in the beginning."

U-ri felt herself relax slightly. Though the man looked frightening, it seemed he wasn't as darkly cynical as he had appeared at first.

"Thank you...for saving us."

"You're welcome."

"How did you come here? How did you know we were here, I mean."

"We wolves have a nose for this sort of thing, *allcaste*. If we didn't, we'd be out of a job."

U-ri took a long look at the man. He lifted a half-shut eyelid.

"Not good enough for you?"

"No."

The Man of Ash sighed deeply and looked away. It was a while before he returned his gaze to U-ri. "I have been chasing the Book of Elem since it first appeared in this region."

U-ri closed her lips tightly and nodded.

"Yet I was unable to find and claim it before the last vessel was filled. I was too late."

What the man did next was entirely unexpected. He apologized.

"Because of my failure, there were casualties. I'm sorry."

"The vessel...my brother is the last vessel." Aju tickled U-ri's neck to console her as she spoke.

The man raised an eyebrow. "Your brother? Odd. I thought for sure it was one of your parents."

"Why's that?"

"Because, Lady *Allcaste*, only those who are related by blood to the vessel may receive the glyph—and only children."

"My name is U-ri," U-ri said then, as coolly as she could muster. "Do not call me *'allcaste'* until I am worthy of the title. In fact, don't even call me 'Lady.' Just U-ri is fine."

The books around them began to whisper to one another again, so U-ri turned to them and apologized. Now that the fright of her encounter with the envoy had passed, she found herself blushing with shame. She had put everyone there in danger and been entirely unable to help. She had panicked like a little child. And she was upset that the Man of Ash told her not to worry about it.

"Very well," the man replied, staring at her.

"Will you tell me your name? I'm guessing that 'Man of Ash' isn't the one you were born with."

"You can call me whatever you like—"

"Ash-head," Aju suggested, cutting in.

"That's hard to say," U-ri said with a chuckle. "Are you named that because of your hair?"

The man gave his long braid a shake. "Quite so."

U-ri thought a moment, then said, "I'll call you Ash, then." That was the name of the main character in a comic book she liked, and as the Man of Ash looked so much like a comic book character himself, it fit.

Aju wrinkled his nose. "I dunno. That's not all that different from what you call me."

"Well, you'll just have to deal with it. Don't worry, there's no danger of me mixing the two of you up. And," she looked at Ash, "this is my servant, Sky."

Sky was rubbing his head, a pained expression on his face. He was about to bow, but Ash shook his head, cutting him off.

"I know who you are, nameless devout. You need not introduce yourself. I would hear what has happened before you met me. Have you found anything out about your brother, U-ri?"

U-ri explained everything as best as she could. Aju, done moping for the time being, pitched in now and then with additional information to round out the story.

Ash listened, his eyes half closed the entire time. It made U-ri uneasy. It was hard to tell what he was thinking, and U-ri risked losing the thread of her own story several times. If Aju hadn't been there to help, she was sure she never would've made it through the whole thing.

Finally she got up to where they had met Michiru in that very library, and when she was finished, she felt like a student at a music recital, waiting for the teacher to give her a grade.

Ash stroked his pointed chin with his fingers, and his half-lidded eyes slowly turned to U-ri. "Best not to give that girl Michiru a false sense of hope. There is no guarantee we can bring Hiroki back."

U-ri felt her hackles rise. "What do you mean we can't bring him back?"

"Maybe not in the way that Michiru hopes, at least. He has become the vessel, after all."

It sounded like he was declaring that Hiroki Morisaki would never again return to his old life. U-ri swallowed the cold fear she felt rising in her throat. "So we can't even find him?"

"That I do not know. It's mostly up to you."

"How do you know that?"

"Because I've been around." Ash turned to Sky. "You there." His tone was cold, accusatory. Sky tensed. "Why did you accompany U-ri?"

U-ri stepped between Ash and the devout. She felt like she had to protect her servant, though she wasn't sure why. "Look, when the Hero broke free of its prison the Hollow Book was damaged." U-ri quickly began to explain all that had happened in the Dome of Convocation—mixing her own thoughts with what the Archdevout had told her. Ash listened without blinking. It was less like he was actually listening and more like he was simply letting U-ri explain herself into exhaustion. When she paused, he looked again at Sky.

"I asked you, not her," he said. "I want to know what *you* think."

U-ri glanced sidelong at Sky. He looked confused. When he began to speak, he did so shakily.

"I am...a nameless devout. I waited in the nameless land for Lady U-ri to arrive. I...wanted to see the world beyond. I wanted to join her. That is why I was cast from the nameless land—"

"That's enough," Ash grunted, cutting him off.

U-ri gritted her teeth. "He's just answering your question! Why do you have to be so mean to him?"

"Be mean? To a nameless devout? Now there's an interesting concept." Ash pointed at Sky. "He is nothing, you understand, and nothing else. Whatever you think he might feel or might think is all illusion."

"Then why did you ask him what he thought?"

"I merely wished to know what the illusion contained," Ash said. "And what he told me was pretty much what I expected. I don't need to hear any more of this."

Now U-ri was really getting angry. *I take back what I thought before. His heart is as black as his robes.* "Sky is my servant! I'd have you treat him with the respect he deserves!"

"Respect?" Ash lifted an eyelid and leaned toward her, fixing her with his gaze. "Did you just say 'respect'? Very unusual."

U-ri stammered, taken aback. "B-but I'm an *allcaste*."

"And that's something special? Is that what the Sage and the nameless devout told you?" Ash pointed his chiseled nose toward the ceiling of the library and laughed out loud. "Newly forged, and yet you strut with the best of them. You don't even know why *allcastes* exist!"

U-ri recalled how the man had dispatched the eyeball creature in the hallway. How he had sighed when he saw her.

"I didn't mean to be prideful," U-ri said at last, restraining her desire to shout at him. "Just, I don't think you should call Sky 'nothing.'"

"Why not?" came Ash's immediate retort.

"Because he's standing right here. He's not 'nothing.'"

"Lady U-ri," Sky whispered, touching his fingers to her arm. "It's all right. I am indeed fashioned of nothing."

"You're just going to let him call you that?"

Sky shrank away from her. Ash bent his thin legs and sat again, shaking his head. "So quick to get all excited. This is why I don't like dealing with girls."

U-ri's eyes blazed. "There you go again!"

"Learn to walk the walk if you choose to talk the talk, child," Ash advised her, raising one of his bushy white-streaked eyebrows. "Standing there with your pet and your servant. How very like a child you are."

Unconsciously, U-ri took a step away from Sky.

"And as far as Sky is concerned, I believe you were far more frightened in the hallway than he was. I'm surprised you haven't given up chasing the Hero yet and gone home."

She thought he was teasing her, but then he pointed at her forehead. "You should go to the Sage who gave you that glyph and have him take it off. You'll be free of all this then."

U-ri stepped back, ashamed of the fear she felt. "B-but then you'd be in trouble, without me."

"Not particularly. Not at all, really. It would just make my job a little bit more difficult. First I'd have to find another *allcaste*."

U-ri was as shocked as she would have been had he slapped her cheek. "A-another *allcaste*?" she stammered.

"Another *allcaste*, yes. Or did you think you were the only one in the entire Circle? No wonder you thought you were so special. Technically speaking, there can be as many *allcastes* as there are vessels. More, even, since they only need be related to the vessels, and most people have more than one relative."

"Well maybe we'll just find ourselves another wolf," Aju squeaked, baring his teeth. "There's lots of them around. We'll just find one who's nicer, and kinder, and more respectful of U-ri."

Ash didn't seem concerned. "You could. Though I don't think that's your best option. Know why?" The man touched a large hand to his chest. "I know the Book of Elem inside out. I don't know how many hairs are on my head, or how many in my eyebrows. But I know that copy well. I know exactly what's written inside it. I know the number of words, the number of lines. I know how many times a particular word appears in a particular chapter. And I know all the names it contains. I even know the words that appear in it only once. Were it not taboo, I could recite its contents entirely from memory for you here right now. I've recited them to myself many times. Thankfully no one was nearby to hear. That's why you should join me. Either that, or you'll waste time wandering—"

The man stopped in the middle of his monologue. His mouth opened then snapped shut like a word had escaped unspoken.

He lowered his eyes and lightly shook his head in the direction of the checkout desk where Michiru lay.

"The more time you waste," he said quietly, "the more the sadness will spread around you. The more little worlds will end, one after another." He looked at U-ri, his voice gentle again. "You don't *like* conflict, do you?"

U-ri was still thinking about what he had said—about little worlds ending.

That's exactly right. Each of us lives in our own little world. In Michiru's, there was a Hiroki Morisaki who fought for her, who saved her. But now he was gone. Michiru's world was crumbling apart.

"You..." Sky joined in, speaking softly. He was looking at Ash. "You have seen much sadness like this, haven't you?"

Ash did not respond. He seemed to be ignoring the devout, as though Sky weren't even in the room.

"In other words," Ash went on, lightly tapping the back of his chair. "Whether we like it or not, we must join forces."

"Well I don't like it." Aju bristled. "Let's find someone else, U-ri. I'm sure there are other wolves out there who know the Book of Elem as well as this one does."

In her heart, U-ri could hear the sound of tiny worlds breaking, crumbling into countless fragments of sorrow.

"A wolf needs an *allcaste*," Ash said to her, ignoring the mouse. "In order to defeat the King in Yellow, I require that glyph on your forehead. Though a wolf might be able to thwart the King on occasion, I cannot bend it to my will, nor return it to the Hollow Book." He chuckled. "We have to work together. You might say we share a fate. Should the King in Yellow defeat you, then I'm done for."

U-ri looked up. "You'd join me even though I'm just a girl?"

"I'll take a chance."

U-ri smiled. She knew better than to think Ash had decided to trust in her. *All he wants is the power of the glyph.* U-ri was just the glyph's means of transportation.

But who cares? U-ri felt a kind of resolve growing inside her. "Fine," she said. "But mark my words, I'm going to make you glad you had a girl for your *allcaste* by the time we're through."

Ash laughed out loud. "A sore loser, I see. That's good." He stood. "Let's be off."

"To where? Do you know where to go?"

"Of course I do. I told you I knew the Book of Elem, didn't I? We are going to my region—which happens to be the place where the Book of Elem came from."

"Where is that? Another country? Europe, maybe?"

Ash had been walking toward the exit, but now he stopped and looked around at her. "Wait—you mean to say you don't even know the difference between the Circle and a region?"

"No, I—"

Ash rolled his eyes skyward. "Look, it's simple. The Circle is everything. Speaking in terms you can understand, it's everything out to the ends of the universe. That's the Circle."

"I know that."

"Well then, regions are worlds that exist within those boundaries. There are many. A countless number, in fact. This reality you live in is but one region. And Europe but an area within that region—part of the same place. My region is something entirely different from this world."

"Then where is it?"

"The Haetlands," he said, though his answer did her little good. "To be precise, my region is called *The Haetlands Chronicle*."

U-ri looked at Aju, giving his sleek fur a pat.

The little mouse's tail shivered. "Well, I wasn't expecting that," he squeaked. "U-ri, he means he's a character in a book called *The Haetlands Chronicle*. He's not a human. He exists in a story, U-ri!"

U-ri's eyes went wide. Something the Sage had said about stories creating their own regions flashed across her mind. *Every book is its own region...*

"As the mouse says, I am what you would call a 'fictional character.' The weaver who wrote *The Haetlands Chronicle* created me."

U-ri pointed at Ash. "But you're not fictional. You're here right now, talking to me!"

"Something wrong with that? Didn't the Sage who gave you your glyph tell you anything?"

"Weavers create stories," Sky breathed.

"Yes. The weaver that made me died a long time ago. Yet I still live. I'm immortal. At least, until someone writes a sequel to *The Haetlands Chronicle* and kills me off. Or I am devoured by the King in Yellow." He sighed. "Roughly half of all wolves are like me. The other half are humans such as yourself. It does much credit to the human wolves, really. Their lives, like those of most weavers, are limited, after all."

"Most weavers?" U-ri echoed. "You mean some weavers were created like you?"

"Very good. I do believe you're catching on."

"Ah! Because authors write stories with authors in them sometimes, right? But don't the characters they create end when the story ends? How can they do things that aren't in the story, or become wolves like you, or weavers, making their own stories?"

U-ri felt herself growing confused even as she spoke.

"What makes you think they can't?" Ash asked, turning to face her. "I see. You think that the weavers write only what they wish to write, and set down their pen, and that is all. But it's not. The region they have created is there. It continues to exist. It lives, even if all within it are fictional. That's why," Ash said, a gleam in his eye, "the weaving of stories is a frightening thing indeed. They are creating worlds, creating countries, creating history, creating lives. Even should their creator go away, the stories remain. Until they are returned to the nameless land, that is."

He paused. "Actually, I said something wrong just now. We fictional characters are not immortal. Our entire region vanishes the moment that the story containing it is returned to the Great Wheels."

He fixed his eyes on her. "U-ri, from here on out, until I say so—"

"Until you say what?"

"Until I say it, do not ask me what something is, or what it isn't. In fact, ask nothing at all. You waste our time."

U-ri nodded glumly.

Ash turned back toward the exit. "The field is collapsing. You'd best wake Michiru."

U-ri spoke with Michiru alone. When Sky tried to join her, Ash violently pushed him away, ordering him to "leave that to the womenfolk."

U-ri didn't ask why, since she had only just now promised not to. Besides, Michiru couldn't see Sky anyway. Though she couldn't imagine what the problem was, she resisted the urge to protest.

U-ri couldn't tell her that Morisaki wouldn't be coming home. She just said they didn't know how long it would take. Michiru would have to keep herself well until then.

"You should go home now. Get some rest."

The girl was in a daze. Ash had warned U-ri that though she could use the power of her glyph to bring humans back to consciousness and mend their wounds they would suffer some memory loss as a result. It hadn't been a lie. When Michiru came to, she had trouble recollecting who U-ri was at first.

"I want you to try coming to school again. I'm sure your friends in class and the teachers won't let the teasing happen again."

"All right," Michiru said, though she sounded doubtful.

"And...try to cheer up. Morisaki would be sad if he saw you like this."

Michiru nodded again and left. U-ri stood in the library window and watched her walk out along the edge of the schoolyard and out the front gate onto the street beyond.

Ash announced that the envoy's field was down, and sure enough when the bell rang again, the hall quickly filled with students. U-ri and the others walked through their midst, unheard and unseen, till they reached the middle of the schoolyard. Ash had insisted they come here.

"So these are the people Hiroki lived with." Ash squinted, looking up at the school building.

Students poked their heads out the window, calling to friends in the yard below. A teacher in a short-sleeve shirt walked out of the building, heading for the gym. He held a clipboard with an attendance list on it over his head for a bit of shade from the warm sun.

"It's quiet," Aju said, sounding a bit irritated. "When you think about what happened to Hiroki—" The mouse's pink nose trembled with anger.

"And they don't know anything about it! Even if they do, they're not taking responsibility or being properly punished."

Ash said nothing. The nameless devout stood still, staring up at the blue skies.

A shout went up from the school building, coming from a window on the second floor. Some of the boys were laughing and playing by the window. One stuck his arm out the window. He was holding a notebook.

"Come and get it! C'mon!"

He waved the notebook in the air outside the window, calling to someone in one of the classrooms. Not calling, *teasing*. The boys laughing around him were probably the bully's friends. U-ri heard someone egging him on: "Drop it out the window! Drop it!"

Directly beneath the window was a small pond. U-ri heard another voice—a thin voice, crying for the notebook back.

"Lady U-ri," Sky whispered, walking over to her. He blinked. "I agree with Aju. It makes me angry too."

U-ri had no way of knowing whether the boys up there had anything to do with what had happened to Hiroki. But watching them still made her feel sick.

The teacher was returning now from the gym. He didn't even look up at the shouting boys. He just calmly walked across the yard and back inside the school building. The boys hadn't noticed him either.

Now U-ri caught a glimpse of a smaller boy—the owner of the notebook. His face was pale with fear. He tried to grab at the book, but someone pushed him. He fell back, out of sight.

"Wait here for me, guys," U-ri said, running toward a stand of trees at the edge of the schoolyard. They were cherry trees, and rather large ones at that. They were more than large enough to conceal U-ri.

U-ri transformed, borrowing the shape of Officer Kashimura, the policewoman she had met at the station. She remembered the uniform and those round eyes of hers. The only thing she felt like she shouldn't copy was the name badge on her chest—she didn't want word of this getting back to anyone at the station.

In truth, Officer Kashimura had been a bit too motherly for U-ri's purposes. She would have preferred someone more frightening. But all she really needed right now was the uniform. It belatedly occurred to her that she could have gone for one of the policemen she'd seen on patrol in the area—but there was no time for that now.

U-ri stepped out from behind the cherry trees and strode purposefully across the schoolyard. Looking up, she put her hands on her hips and scanned the second-story windows. The boys were still at it—though they had replaced the notebook with the notebook's owner. Now it was the boy hanging half out the window. The color had drained from his face, and he was struggling to get back inside, but several arms pushed at him, keeping him hanging over the windowsill. The shouts of encouragement from the other boys were only growing louder.

U-ri spotted a laughing face over the boy's shoulder. It was the boy who had been holding the notebook hostage. He had the boy in the window by his shirt collar and was busily peeling the boy's fingers off the edge of the window.

"Time to fly! C'mon, you can do it! Hey, someone grab his legs!"

U-ri took a deep breath and shouted, "Stop that at once!"

All motion in the second-story window ceased. Several pairs of eyes turned to look down at the schoolyard, where U-ri stood in full policewoman regalia. A few new faces appeared at the window, looking out to see what was up.

"Uh-oh, it's a cop!"

U-ri wasn't sure who had spoken. Whoever it was, they didn't sound all that concerned. U-ri's anger went from a simmer to a full boil.

Still in her uniform, she touched one hand to the concealed glyph. Then she thrust her hand toward the source of her rage. Every boy except the one hanging half out the window was instantly knocked back. A breath later, there came the sound of tables and chairs crashing together from inside the classroom, and girls screaming.

"Teacher! Teacher!"

Someone was crying. *So now they call the teacher.* U-ri clenched her hand into a fist. The boy clinging to the window was staring at her, his mouth wide open.

U-ri undid the transformation. The policewoman vanished.

For moment, U-ri thought that a cloud had passed over the sun—then she looked up to see Ash towering behind her.

"Hardly actions befitting a lady *allcaste*," he said, though there was a hint of mirth in his voice and a sparkle in his eyes as he looked up at the school building. "Were they involved with Hiroki?"

"I have no idea. I couldn't let them to do that."

The teacher had arrived on the scene. The boy clinging to the windowsill turned to look back toward the classroom. He flinched—the teacher was scolding him.

"It looks like he thinks it was all the boy's fault. What are you going to do now?"

U-ri didn't want to believe that the teacher could be so clueless—but there he was, roughly dragging the boy the others had been picking on away from the window. A man was shouting. U-ri gritted her teeth. *I don't believe this!*

"Time for round two?" Ash said quietly, drawing his right-hand sword. He spun it in his hand, muttered something quickly, then pointed the sword tip directly at the window.

A wave of force shot through the air. Not just the boy's window, but all the windows around it rattled loudly. The teacher, his hand on the boy's neck, was flung back out of sight while the boy at the window was tossed backward into the classroom.

Teachers were nervously looking out the windows on all three floors now, a strange line of bobbing heads. U-ri watched them for moment, then turned to Ash. "Hardly actions befitting a wolf."

"Oh? I merely thought you'd like to see my mageblade in action." He had already sheathed his sword. The wolf smiled. "And it appears you're making progress in understanding the use of your glyph."

"It's embarrassing," U-ri said. "The people in my region aren't all like this, you know."

Ash thrust his hands into his pockets and nodded. "I know that quite well. I've been around, you know. There is evil everywhere. Sometimes big, sometimes small."

U-ri heard a commotion from the school building. Now the fire alarm was ringing.

"To the Haetlands," Ash said.

U-ri turned away from the school and began to walk.

CHAPTER NINE

The Land of Fear and Loathing

Ash was able to jump from region to region at will. According to him, it was a skill every wolf possessed. "It's basic glyph magic. No one can become a wolf without the ability to use it. You need to be able to travel between regions for the chase, after all. But it only works for me."

With their current numbers, they would have to travel a different way. It was decided that they would first go to Minochi's cottage. From there, they could use the magic circle on the reading room floor to travel together wherever they liked.

U-ri felt a slight dizziness during the teleportation—that always seemed to be the case when she was moving through Yuriko Morisaki's reality. Sky gripped her hand tightly.

"Ah, you have returned!"

Even before U-ri had found her footing on the reading room floor, the low voice of the Sage welcomed them. The reading room was as dim, dusty, and quiet as always. Even though it was brimming with the presence of so many ancient books, there was a sense of calm to the place. U-ri noticed it all the more, having come directly from the noise and brightness of the outside world.

U-ri was about to say something when Ash stepped outside the magic circle, looked up toward where the Sage sat, and announced himself.

"It has been too long."

"I see it is you," said the Sage to the wolf.

"Yes. The chase happens within my domain, you might say."

Quite suddenly the Sage and Ash were engaged in a deep conversation of which U-ri understood only fragments. Aju and Sky looked equally confused. The three of them stood staring, watching the wolf and the Sage talk. They spoke rapidly, Ash occasionally nodding, occasionally shooting quick glances at U-ri and Sky. The wolf and the book were using so many unfamiliar words, U-ri felt completely out of her depth. On her shoulder, Aju squeaked irritably.

Then Ash turned to U-ri, took a half step back, and bowed. With a nod, he indicated that she should speak.

"We went to my brother's school," she began, looking up at the Sage.

"Yes, I have heard what happened. It must have been most difficult for you." The Sage spoke gently, twinkling a soft, deep green as he spoke. "And you will next go to the Haetlands, whence comes the Man of Ash," he continued. "You have found a strong ally."

"You knew that Ash would find us, didn't you?"

"We have known each other for quite some time," Ash interjected. He pointed at the magic circle beneath their feet. "Yet it seems I am not the only one who has come. Observe—someone has touched up your glyph here."

Indeed, the unskilled, erratic lines of the first circle that U-ri had drawn were bolder now, thicker, and more distinct upon the floor.

"Another wolf?"

"Indubitably, yes."

"Wolves can draw magic circles too?"

"With ease. Who was it?" He looked up at the Sage. "Voont?"

"Carnacki, actually," the Sage said, a happy ring to his voice. "Him I had not seen for an even longer time than you. He went right back after I told him you had already arrived, however. Said he'd leave things to you. He left a message saying that if we should require his services, he could be found hunting beastmen in the Barren Mountains of Dukaschy."

"The old man's still doing well, it sounds like."

"He's hardly older than yourself," the Sage chuckled. Once again, U-ri and her companions were left out of the conversation. "Incidentally, while he was here, he put up a void-hedge around the cottage."

"That'll be a help. For you as well as us."

"Okay, what's all this then?" Aju interjected, unable to contain himself any longer. "Do you think you guys could talk in a way that we can understand? What the heck is this void-hedgey thing?"

"Sage in Green," Ash said, ignoring the mouse. "Why did you choose such an unseasoned dictionary? Was this intentional?"

"Perhaps it is better to say that it was not I but the Yellow Sign that chose him. You of all people should understand this."

"Indeed. But the mark on him is already quite faded. Perhaps because of his proximity to U-ri's glyph?" Ash turned around to face U-ri. "Will you not choose another dictionary to bring with you?"

U-ri shook her head so vigorously she could hear her hair swish through the air. "Aju's coming with us."

"Thanks, U-ri," Aju squeaked in a tiny voice.

Ash rolled his eyes and nodded. "That's decided then. Incidentally, the void-hedge is a device that works to conceal this cottage from the eyes of people in the world outside. In addition, it will make it difficult for those who already know about the cottage—U-ri's relatives specifically—to recollect the cottage and its location."

"And what's this about hunting beastmen?" U-ri asked. The unfamiliar word had piqued her interest.

"There is a book," Ash said, moving his hands as though he were flipping pages, "that turns all who read it into beastmen. It's one of the copies. Carnacki has been chasing it now for over five years."

"Oh," was all U-ri could say to that.

"Do not worry. This copy is not in your region."

"Can the beastmen ever be returned to their original form?" Sky asked.

Ash fixed the devout with an icy stare. "No. Nor will they ever regain their former intellect. Leave them to roam, and they attack other men and eat them. They are simple beasts—twisted creatures. The most charitable thing one can do is kill them."

Sky's gaze dropped to the floor.

"That's horrible," U-ri said. The dark side of the Hero's power worked in frightening ways.

Then a thought crossed U-ri's mind, like a cold draft through the door. *What if something like that has happened to Hiroki? Maybe he hasn't only been possessed; maybe he's been altered in some irreversible way.*

Ash stepped into the center of the magic circle, his tattered cape billowing around him. "If stories like that are enough to scare you, we are in trouble. The Haetlands is a far more terrifying place than that."

U-ri looked up at his face, then over at the green light of the Sage. "But that's where the Book of Elem came from, isn't it?"

"Indeed it is."

"Then I'll go. I'll go anywhere I have to."

Sky nodded and moved over to stand by U-ri's side. "Let us be off."

The magic circle on the floor began to glow with a pale light.

🌱

"Waachoo!"

The instant U-ri arrived, before her feet even touched firm ground, she sneezed loudly.

It was cold. The kind of cold that went straight to your bones. *What is this place? Am I on a mountaintop? In the middle of a glacier? No—this is inside.*

The floor beneath U-ri's feet was wooden. The walls were made out of some kind of hardened clay. Rafters hung low above her head. There was a window. Strips of ragged cloth hung from the warped frame—a haphazard attempt at a curtain, she surmised. The cloth was fluttering. That was where the cold wind was coming from.

Something in the room was creaking rhythmically.

U-ri looked down at her feet. There was a magic circle—a glyph—here too. This one was slightly smaller than the one in the reading room. It hadn't been drawn on the floor, but physically carved into the wood with a knife of some sort. The wood floor was damaged in other areas as well.

They seemed to be in a shack of some sort. There were signs of habitation. A bed stood against one wall, and next to it a crude wooden hanger for clothes. There was a table, a chair, and a desk. Here and there stood bookshelves, each stuffed with books—overflowing in fact. Books sat on the floor, on the chair, and in stacks by the bed.

"Welcome to my humble abode," Ash said as he stepped outside the magic circle with the ease of someone returning home. He took off his black cloak and threw it over the nearby chair. Then he removed his boots and tossed them onto the floor. Walking across the small room, he went to the window with the ragged cloth curtains and began tugging on something like a handle, trying to close it.

U-ri gaped. She had never been in a home so cluttered, so rough, and so bone-chillingly cold.

The desk was covered in books and bound scrolls. A pen holder lay on its side at one edge, and several pens were scattered across the top. The front side of the desk was plastered with documents and scraps of paper, attached with pins, so dense that the papers looked like strips of bark growing on the side of a stubby tree.

U-ri spotted some bottles atop the table.

There was also something like a chemistry set, complete with test tubes, and some items that were unmistakably weapons: swords, knives, and something like a bow. All of them seemed sturdy, their edges sharp. She stared at a larger roll of paper—maybe a map. Next to that stood a sphere in a holder.

"Is that a globe?"

U-ri stepped hesitantly toward the desk. On the other side of the room, Ash had finally managed to shut the window. The chill wind ceased, though it was still cold.

"Have to get that fixed one of these days," he grumbled, walking back to the table and throwing himself down in a chair. Before he sat, he kicked aside a pile of stuff, clearing a spot on the floor. "Sit where you like."

It seemed safest to sit directly on the floor, so that was what U-ri did.

"What's the deal with the cold here?" Aju screeched angrily from U-ri's collar. "Don't you have a heater? Or a fireplace or a stove, or anything?"

"I've got a fireplace, sure. I just don't know whether it's usable."

He pointed over to where a brick mantelpiece poked out from behind a mountain of books. Sky offered to take a look and gingerly walked over to examine it.

"That's a globe, right?" U-ri asked again, pointing at the sphere on top of the table.

Ash raised his hand and gave it a spin. "Of this region, yes."

That explained why none of the continents looked right from where she was sitting. "Are the directions the same? I mean, is up still north?"

"It is."

"Where are the Haetlands?"

Ash extended a long finger and stopped the slowly rotating globe. He spun it a bit to the right. Then he pointed at a spot near the top of the sphere. "Here. We're as far north as you can go."

"Is it a big country? How large is it?"

Ash did not answer. He stared meaningfully at the spot where his finger touched the globe.

"You mean, it's so small you can cover it with one finger?"

"That's right."

Creak, creak. U-ri heard the sound again. It seemed to be coming from somewhere above them, but she could feel vibrations in the floor beneath her at the same time.

"What's that sound?"

Ash pointed up. "There is a windmill up there. This village uses windmills for power."

There was no electricity here, in other words. U-ri noted a few lamps sitting here and there, and a few candle sconces hanging from the ceiling.

"It is a cold, poor, and small country—and this village lies at its farthest northern reaches."

The village's name was Kanal. The locals supported themselves by hunting and farming.

"Take a look out the window if you like."

U-ri walked over to the window, startled to see her breath white before her face. She noticed tiny icicles hanging down around the edge of the window.

Even though it was incredibly cold inside, the window was fogged with condensation. She wiped at it with one hand and discovered that it wasn't just condensation—the window was incredibly filthy. Ash wasn't a fan of housecleaning, apparently.

"It's snowing..." Large flakes drifted down outside the window.

"It's still early winter, actually."

Aju hopped up to the top of her head and stuck his nose to the glass. No sooner had he done so than he began to sneeze uncontrollably.

U-ri noticed something else about the glass. Underneath the fog and the dirt, it wasn't all that transparent to begin with. Like a very old window— *maybe they don't have the technology to make good ones yet,* she thought, the realization dawning on her. The Haetlands weren't like Japan and America and Europe in the twenty-first century. This wasn't that kind of world. She was in the world of "a long time ago."

U-ri boosted herself up as high as she could and peered outside. Beyond the drifting flakes, she saw a world encased in glittering white ice. She spotted rooftops, angled sharply at the top, and several of them had small windmill towers extending even higher. The houses were made of wood and bricks, with wooden planks running between larger rafters. Everything man-made was drab. Apparently there was no paint in this world. A few trees stood between the houses, but they were all bare—ice sculptures with pointy branches. There was no grass, not even the strange colorless grass she had seen in the nameless land, nor any flowers.

A small path wound between the houses, muddy and half frozen.

She heard a dog howling somewhere. *At least they have dogs here.* She had been beginning to wonder if anything lived here at all.

"There is much land around here that is too hard for hoeing, even in summer." At some point Ash had walked up to stand beside her at the window. "Still, there is a wheat field to the south of the village. Harvest time has long since come and gone. From now until winter's end, we hunt."

The men would venture out into the frozen woods and mountains, hunting animals for meat and hides. Back in the village, the women would work the hides and flesh, first making what clothing and food the village needed to survive, then selling the rest. There would be no green vegetables or fruit until spring, but roots and tubers could be stored in cellars. That would be their main sustenance through the winter.

"Most of the wheat is taken to pay taxes, in any case. Bread's a luxury item here. For the most part, we eat potatoes. Is your stomach strong, U-ri?"

"I think so," she said. *But I think I'll use magic to keep me full for the time being.*

The cold air leaking in through the window made her eyes water. "There doesn't seem to be anyone outside."

"The women and children are all in their homes. It's too early in the day yet for the men to come down from the mountains."

She would've expected to see lights in the windows then. Even though it seemed like noontime outside, the weather was so gloomy, U-ri would have wanted light. *Lamp oil's probably a luxury item too.*

"We're pretty high up here, aren't we?"

U-ri couldn't look down very well, standing on her toes, but the clouds seemed close above them. Ash stepped behind her and lifted her up so she could see better. Her toes found a beam sticking out of the wall to take some of her weight.

"My house stands on top of the hill. The Hill of the Dead."

U-ri trembled. "Why's it called that?"

"The land around us is a graveyard. You'll see it immediately if you care to walk outside."

"And why do you live here again?"

"Because I am close to the dead."

"There, that's flint—I think," she heard Aju say from behind her. He must have jumped off her when Ash approached. U-ri looked around and saw that

Sky had finished excavating the fireplace, stacked some logs inside, and was now attempting to start a fire. Aju was perched atop his head.

A small tongue of flame licked up the side of the logs. Sky grinned. "There we go."

The firewood began to burn. U-ri saw the dancing flames reflected on Sky's bald scalp.

"There is an oven down those stairs," Ash said to Sky, indicating a corner of the room where wooden steps led down from a hole in the floor. "Make a fire and boil some water. I'm sure U-ri would like something warm to eat."

Sky nodded and quickly headed down the stairs. His hard footfalls echoed as he left.

"I'll help," U-ri said, standing.

"Leave it to him. You sit."

"But Sky isn't some errand boy," U-ri protested.

"He's your servant, no?" Ash asked without a trace of humor in his face. "And besides, now is a good time for your precious *whys*. You'll regret it after if you don't take this opportunity to ask, and I won't answer them later anyway."

"You don't seem to like Sky very much, do you, Ash? It's like you don't trust him."

"I merely understand that the nameless devout have a role to fulfill, and that is all."

U-ri was silent. Ash began picking up the bottles sitting on the table one at a time, giving them a little shake to ascertain their contents.

"I think I'm going to go see if we're really surrounded by a graveyard."

Without waiting for the wolf's approval, U-ri ran down the stairs, Aju clinging to the back of her collar.

The ground floor was as cold and as derelict as the floor above. The ceiling was lower here and covered with wattled mud, making it feel like the burrow of some subterranean creature.

Sky was busily preparing the oven. She assumed this was the kitchen, since the oven was here, but there was no sign of any food stores or spices.

When Sky saw her, he smiled. "There is tea, Lady U-ri. And the water in the kettle is fresh. I believe Master Ash has someone to look after his place while he's absent."

Too bad he doesn't have them clean the place up while they're at it.

U-ri announced she was going to take a look outside, and she headed for what appeared to be the exit. It was a rough door, made of logs bound together with iron. She found it surprisingly heavy.

She pushed, managing to open it several inches, and the snow came swirling in. Her face froze in the cold wind. U-ri squinted against the blast, pulled up the hood of her vestments of protection, and stepped outside into a world of whites and grays, the color of frozen ground. A few steps led down from the shack, with a railing on one side. She walked down carefully, holding tightly onto the railing to keep from slipping. Her black robes were soon white from the snow that seemed to fall ever harder.

Ash had been telling the truth. The shack stood at the very top of a gently sloping hill, covered in every direction by evenly spaced gravestones.

The graves were simple—rectangular stones jutting up from the ground with no adornments—and too numerous for her to count. There were slight differences in coloration between the stones, which she attributed to differences in age and exposure to the elements.

U-ri exhaled a long white stream of breath. "Wow."

"Yeah," Aju said from beneath her collar.

"I've never seen this many graves in one place."

It was like the graves had wandered here from some other place to gather around Ash's hut.

"That's got to be the whole village under those stones," Aju said. He meant it as a joke, but somehow it didn't come out sounding like one. "I mean this town ain't that big. There's got to be more graves than residents."

U-ri walked between the stones, careful not to step too close to any. Her feet trod the frozen ground, occasionally crushing frozen chunks of snow. The gravestones really did look like they had gathered there—she wasn't imagining things. All of the stones, carved with letters she couldn't read, were facing toward the shack at the top of the hill, looking up at the second-story window where Ash made his home.

U-ri looked down toward the bottom of the hill where a large fence of stone and iron circled the entire graveyard, enclosing the hill and the two-story shack with its creaking windmill at the summit. There was only one gap in the fence with a gate of solid-looking iron. The gate was leaning off its hinges, as though they were not strong enough to support its weight. The side that opened had been wrapped with a chain, from which hung a sturdy padlock. To U-ri it seemed less like Ash was taking care to lock the door and more like someone on the outside wanted to keep him and whatever was under those gravestones from getting out.

U-ri went back up the steps to the shack, brushing off the snow before she entered. The fire was burning in the oven. Sky turned as she walked in.

"I think I'm getting used to the cold," U-ri said, smiling at him. "Probably thanks to these vestments."

"I would think so," the devout said. He sounded concerned. "Just a moment, I'll bring you some tea."

U-ri went up the stairs. Ash was sitting with his legs up on the table, slouching against the back of his chair.

"Satisfied?"

She walked into the middle of the room, then sat down, opening her vestments and hugging her knees to her chest for warmth. "Did the people without magical robes like mine all freeze to death here?"

Ash raised both eyebrows and snorted.

"Or was there a plague? Or a war? How many years' worth of graves is that out there? They didn't all die at the same time, did they?" She stared at the wolf. "What are *you* doing here, Ash?"

Finally the smirk faded from Ash's face. "You've not read *The Haetlands Chronicle*, I gather."

"Nope. I hadn't even heard of it until you told me."

"No, I suppose you wouldn't have. It's not the kind of book a girl your age goes out of her way to read. I'm not even sure it's been translated into a language you *can* read." Ash removed his feet from the table and sat up straight with a rustling of clothes. "This country has been an independent country for one thousand years. *The Haetlands Chronicle* is its history."

U-ri nodded for him to go on.

"As I showed you before, on the globe, the Haetlands is so small as to be easily covered by one fingertip. Yet war rages here incessantly. Other countries invade, or we invade them. There have been civil wars too. We have been entangled in such a war for the last one hundred and fifty years."

"Don't you have a government?"

"We do. There is a royal house, and a parliament beneath made up of nobles and those from the privileged classes. We are in essence a kingdom. But there are several bloodlines within the royal house. And they love to feud amongst themselves. That is what leads to our internal strife."

"But it's such a small country!"

"Perhaps they fight so viciously *because* the stakes are so small." Ash leaned forward. "If your grip were to extend just far enough, you could seize this entire kingdom for your own—so do men suffer greed and delusions of grandeur."

Sky came up from downstairs carrying a heavy-looking tray in both hands. The tray held a large silver pot and some polished silver cups. U-ri hadn't expected anything fancy, and for a moment all she could do was stare.

"There's no plastic or vinyl in this world," Ash said with a chuckle at U-ri's surprised expression.

"I knew that, I guess. Just...that's a very beautiful pot."

"Silver is strong. And good against poisons," he explained casually.

Good against poisons?

"As there is little point in wasting our time with a lengthy history lecture, I'll merely touch upon the major points. We don't need to go back the whole one thousand years. What concerns us most is the last century and a half."

Taking a silver cup from the tray, Ash continued. "The civil war that began one hundred fifty years ago and continues to this day is, simply put, a feud between two brothers in the royal house. Half brothers, to be precise. They never did get along, even as children. When they became adults, they gathered loyal retainers around them, raised armies, and took their struggle to the field of battle."

The first round of fighting had gone on for ten years and left most of the country devastated. Then, fearing that the Haetlands would be utterly destroyed, the nobles intervened and compelled the brothers to come to an agreement. Kings would be chosen from both of their lineages, alternating every generation.

"Yet when it came to their grandchildren's generation—though only thirty years had passed since the accord—both camps began to eye each other with envy. They struggled for rank and territory, found fault with one another and with the terms of their treaty, each trying to claim the right of secession for their bloodline alone. With both sides equally engaged in such foolishness, there was little hope of stopping it."

It took another few generations—about fifty years, Ash explained—for their struggles to once again spread to the general populace. When the conflict had been confined within the bounds of the royal city and palace, the Haetlands had gradually recovered its strength. Fields once burned grew green, cities were rebuilt, and trade with their neighbors had increased.

"This village of Kanal was founded just in the last fifty years. Man did not live in places like this before. The villagers here now are the grandchildren of the original settlers."

But, as abundance returned to the land, the struggles of the royal house grew fiercer. The richer the lands one side held, the more eagerly the other side fought to claim them.

"Fifty-seven years ago, in the ninth month of the 877th year of our Holy Calendar, there was a great upheaval in the capital city. That was the start of the current round of fighting." Ash tapped his chest lightly. "The weaver who made me wrote most vividly about those events."

That's right, U-ri remembered, *this is all a story. A story of war.*

"At the time, the elder son's lineage had just claimed the throne, as decreed by the treaty of one hundred years before. The 17th Holy King of the Haetlands, Cadasque the Third. Incidentally, it was also one of the elder son's lineage who started the war—the new king's cousin, a noble yet impoverished lad by the name of Kirrick."

Cadasque the Third was a boy-king, only eight years old. His father who had been king two generations prior had died of an illness at the age of thirty, and his successor—the current king's uncle—died in an accident only two years after taking the throne. He had fallen from his horse during a mock battle held to honor the king's birthday.

"Rumors of assassination surrounded both royal deaths. Tempers flared, and the arguments began to spread outside the bounds of the palace."

At only eight years of age, the king could do little by himself. He did what his relatives, his steward, and his ministers advised him to do.

"Once again, turmoil spread through the land. Feudal lords and members of the privileged classes who thought of nothing but fattening their own bellies began to devour themselves from the inside out."

Some of the nobles and landed gentry had begun dealings with one of the Haetlands' neighbors across a long-disputed border. Together they hatched a plan to install a puppet government in exchange for privileged positions in the new regime.

"You know what we call their kind?" Ash asked, smiling crookedly beneath sleepy half-lidded eyes. "Traitors." He looked at U-ri. "I'm guessing you've never seen a traitor yourself. They don't have fangs, or two faces, despite what you may have heard. They look like regular folk. It's their roots that are rotten."

U-ri nodded. "And this boy Kirrick rose up against them?"

"That's right. He started a rebellion—a successful rebellion at that."

There had been several sporadic uprisings before Kirrick came on the scene. But all had been crushed by royal forces before they could spread, or undid themselves before they could pose a real threat.

"The royal army has always held the greatest portion of power in the land," Ash went on. "There are many in this land who wish to join the army."

"Why? I can't believe that anyone in the royal house would have so many devoted admirers, what with the history of this place."

Ash lifted a long finger. "For one, there is the deeply ingrained concept of 'southern progression'—more of a desire than a concept, actually. The people of this land have long wanted to spread to the warmer territories in the south. In order to do that, we must invade another country, and for that, we must have a strong army. As I said, we have fought many wars to expand our borders—though few were successful. Next"—he lifted a second finger—"the Haetlands are a northern country. We spend more than a third of each year encased in ice. We are thin, with little land worth tilling. It is difficult for us to live off the bounty of the land alone. Hunting and livestock help, for certain, but it's not enough."

However, the Haetlands were rich under the soil. Iron, copper, gold, silver, and coal could all be found in large amounts. The mines had produced precious gems as well—diamonds and emeralds by the bucket.

"Trace the family lines back, and you'll find most of our nobility were once in the mining business. As the landed nobles struggled with one another for access to the richest veins, the lords and their followers joined in alliances, eventually forming the kingdom as we know it today."

Merchants, endowed with the right to trade under the watchful eyes of the nobles, soon gained power, creating another class of the wealthy and privileged. They were joined by the larger land owners, who controlled a large portion of the sparse farmland in the Haetlands.

"Though the land is poor, we are rich. At least, in certain places. There is a great disparity in wealth, which means that those with the gold require military strength to protect their privileged positions. Luckily for them, their coffers are overflowing, and they can well afford to maintain a sizable active army."

In the Haetlands, the military also took on the task of preserving order—effectively becoming a kind of well-armed police force.

"Were I the second son of a poor farmer, my choice would be clear: I would join the army. It is more than just secure employment. To a certain extent, soldiers and keepers of the peace are given authority."

U-ri thought about what he meant for moment. "So they go from being poor, overworked, and in danger of arrest to being well-fed and the ones doing the arresting."

It wasn't about loyalty to the royal house. It was about choosing sides. Did they want to be counted among the ones with wealth and power, or the ones without?

"A farmer with a single plot of land will never escape poverty, not in a lifetime. Working the mines earns better pay than farming, but the danger is commensurate. There is no guarantee you'll keep your job, either."

"What about merchants? Are they free to do business as they like?"

Ash explained that in order to become a merchant, royal decree stipulated that one had to join a merchant guild, for which one needed a considerable amount of collateral and the backing of a merchant already in the guild.

"Must be a whole lot of bribery going on," Aju squeaked from U-ri's collar, where he had been pretending to sleep since she came upstairs. "I bet it's all over the place."

"Enough for even a young dictionary who knows little of the world to sniff out, yes," Ash said with a grin. "It is as you say, Aju. One cannot simply become a merchant. Some try to become officials of the state, but that requires this." He tapped his head. "And the proper lineage. So that's not easy, either."

U-ri sighed. "So it's all about where you're born."

"Not if you join the army. There, it's possible to get ahead in the world through your deeds. It's not entirely unreasonable to imagine a boy from a nobody family in a nobody village becoming a great soldier, even a general. Thus are new nobles born."

Once systems like these became established, it was hard to overturn them, Ash explained. "The young ones who joined the army know the poor life of the farmer and the unbearable working conditions that the miner must endure. But once your own lot is steady and secure, it's hard to get all that enthusiastic about changing the way things are."

Which was why all of the uprisings before Kirrick had begun among the disenfranchised, the small-time farmers and mine workers. They rebelled against overtaxation or stood up in rage when mine cave-ins or pestilence claimed the lives of their friends. The people who rose up were the ones who could sink no lower.

And the ones who put them back in their places were the soldiers of the royal army.

"And none of the soldiers take the side of the people?"

"What reason would they have? Without ideals or righteous indignation, it's hard to imagine them wanting to lift a finger to help. And even if they did have these things, they wouldn't last three days." Ash spoke plainly. "Even in the midst of injustice, if one's own position is not endangered, it is only human to defend the status quo."

"Well then," U-ri said shrugging her shoulders, "why doesn't everyone just join the army? Leave the mountains and their fields to rot. That would get the king and those nobles where it hurts."

"U-ri, U-ri," Aju squeaked, petting her cheek with the tip of his long tail. "The farmers and miners are tied to the land. It always works like that. They have laws to keep them where they are, under the watchful eye of their lord. They couldn't leave if they wanted to. They don't have freedom. If they tried to just run away, they'd be punished. I mean, isn't that obvious? Haven't you ever read a history book?"

U-ri looked at Ash. "It appears I left something out of my explanation," he said. "You see, in order to join the army or become an official, one needs the permission of the local minister of the land. Aju is correct. The common people are not permitted to move freely."

Many youths joined the army, but only when the land could spare them. The system took all excess labor force from localities across the kingdom, absorbing them into the government via the army, Ash explained.

"What about girls? Can they join the army too?" U-ri asked, the thought suddenly occurring to her. "Are there many female soldiers?"

Ash blinked slowly. "There are some. Mostly from the more prominent military houses whose ancestors were generals for many generations."

"What about village girls?"

"They go to the mining towns or the farming towns to become wives and mothers, and give birth to the next generation of laborers. All while working themselves, of course," Ash told her. "They have no freedom, either."

"Don't they ever rebel?"

Ash guffawed, as though he had never heard such a thing. "That...would be difficult. In places where there has been a disaster or famine, and they can no longer live there, the village girls go to the towns—" Ash's smile vanished and U-ri thought a look of pity came into his eyes. "In order to survive, many sell themselves. Even girls your age. Without a family or proper papers, there's little hope of finding decent work, even in the larger towns."

"I get it, I get it," Aju squeaked, switching his tail and climbing on top of U-ri's shoulder. His tail stung a bit where it slapped the back of her neck. "I get what kind of place the Haetlands is. So tell me why you say Kirrick's rebellion worked. There is still civil war, isn't there?"

Ash crossed his legs and grunted at the mouse. "I was getting to that— perhaps I took a little too much time with the preamble."

The tea in U-ri's silver cup had gone completely cold.

"Kirrick's rebellion succeeded—at first." Ash's eyes dropped to the floor-boards beneath his feet. "Cadasque the Third was imprisoned, and his family and those stewards, retainers, and officers who didn't bow to Kirrick were apprehended and sentenced. Kirrick was made king.

"He was of the royal bloodline, after all, so he had a claim to the throne. That was another thing that set Kirrick's rebellion apart from all that had come before. But," Ash added, lifting a finger, "there was another problem. The rebellions before had come about at the hands of common folk, who used nothing but their hoes and mining picks for weapons. Up against a trained, properly armed military, their weapons might as well have been made of wax. They were crushed with ease. Not so Kirrick's army. He led neither starving farmers nor angry miners."

"You mean he had his own army? I thought he was poor," Aju said.

"No army at first," Ash explained, shaking his head. "But he built one. An immortal army."

U-ri's eyes went wide. "Soldiers that can't die? How's that work?"

"They could not die because they were dead to begin with," Ash told them. "Kirrick led an army of the walking dead—"

He was interrupted by Sky, who had been sitting a short distance away by the window. "Someone comes," the devout said.

U-ri ran over to him. Getting her footing on the crossbeam, she grabbed the windowsill and lifted herself up so she could see the terrain. Below, a small child wrapped in rags was dashing through the gravestones, occasion-ally jumping over them, making for the entrance to the hut.

"Dmitri!" she heard him shout. "Dmitri, are you home?"

It's a boy. U-ri peered through the snow and noticed with a start that the ironbound gate at the bottom of the hill was still closed, the padlock securely attached. *How did he get inside?*

"Who's Dmitri?" Aju asked.

"Me," Ash replied and went down the stairs.

U-ri quickly followed him as quickly and as quietly as she could—though she knew the vestments of protection hid her from both sight and sound.

The heavy door to the hut opened with a loud slam.

"Dmitri!" The boy's eyes found Ash immediately, and a smile spread across his face. Then he shot across the room like a cannonball. "I'm so glad you're back!"

The boy jumped and Ash—or Dmitri, rather—caught him in midair with a practiced ease.

"Why didn't you tell me you were back?" The boy hung on to Ash's neck with one arm, and playfully hit Ash's shoulder with a tightly clenched fist.

"I've only just returned," Ash explained, a gentle curve to his sleepy eyes. "How did you know?"

"The smoke from your chimney," the boy said with a triumphant chortle. He then sprang away from Ash as lightly as he had jumped to him. It was like watching a tiny acrobat at work. He didn't just leap down, he did a backflip before landing on the floor.

U-ri stared at him. *Who is this boy? Is he from a circus?*

"You bring me a present?" the boy asked as he jumped about the room like an organ grinder's monkey, snooping for hidden treasures.

"I see you're as energetic as ever, Udsu," Ash said, taking a seat at a crude wooden table. "How's your mother doing?"

For the first time since she had spotted him through the window, the acrobatic boy stopped. From this close, she could see that his clothes were little more than ragged strips of cloth wrapped tightly around him. Loose threads hung from the hem like spaghetti. At the wolf's question, a cloud came over the boy's small face. The boy's eyes were sharp, but his cheeks were pale. His body was thin—almost emaciated. U-ri wondered how old he was. *Maybe seven or eight?*

"Not so good. She's been getting a fever at night."

"I see."

"She's taking the medicine you gave me, though, Dmitri."

"Perhaps I should adjust the formula. I'll give you a new batch soon. You have to wait for your present until then. I haven't even begun to unpack."

"I'll help you!"

"Now, you know that won't do. If they find you're here, the village elders won't be pleased."

Udsu stuck out his lower lip in a pout. It seemed that even in a region as different from U-ri's as this, kids were the same.

"I don't care. The elder doesn't scare me."

"Rules are rules, child. If you want to break them, at least have the wit not to flout them openly."

Udsu frowned, his arms dropping to his sides. The sleeves of his ragged robes swept the floor.

"Fine. I'll be waiting at home, then."

"That's a good boy."

"You'll come soon, right? My mom'll be waiting."

Ash assured the boy he understood, guiding him back to the door. Ash opened the door and called after him, "Be careful, all right?"

"Me? I'll be fine!" the boy shouted, dashing out at breakneck speed. U-ri watched him leave, jumping over gravestones and swerving between them like a slalom racer. Two mysteries were solved—one, why Ash had told the boy to be careful, and two, how Udsu had been able to get over the fence.

It was simple really. He had jumped it. On the way out, he did a forward flip over the high iron bars, waving back to Ash as he landed on the far side.

"That kid human?" Aju asked, standing up on his hind legs. He was clearly impressed.

"He's human," Ash replied, shutting the door firmly. "Though he has 'springfoot.' It's a kind of, well—" he paused, searching for the right word.

"It's a kind of disease."

"A disease that makes you stronger? I didn't know there was such a thing." To U-ri's eyes, the boy had looked like a star athlete. How could that be an illness?

"You saw how he runs?"

"Yes. His legs are amazingly strong."

"Indeed—but he cannot run in a straight line."

Now that he said it, she realized it was true. There was a proper path from the gate up to the little shack, but the boy hadn't used it at all, choosing (she'd thought) instead to weave through the gravestones.

"Springfeet have superhuman strength in their legs. But they can't control it. That's why he can't sit still, not even for moment. His legs keep moving of their own accord."

The boy couldn't go to school nor work in the fields, Ash explained.

"Are all the people in this village like that?"

"No," Ash replied, indicating the stairs with a jerk of his head. "Let us continue our previous discussion while I brew that medicine for Udsu's mother. What I was telling you about is related to this, after a fashion."

Unbelievably, it looked like he intended to make the medicine on that incredibly cluttered table with the high school chemistry set. Ash opened a small drawer next to the table and began to pull out what looked like the roots of plants, leaves, and a sandlike powder he kept in a small flask. Then he sat and began to work.

"Kirrick raised the dead and made soldiers of them." He handed an empty flask to Sky, asking him to fill it with water. With a small knife the size of U-ri's pinky, Ash began cutting the roots.

"In a poor country ravaged by war, the one thing in abundance is the dead. If you could raise them and make them your own, you'd have a very powerful army on your side."

"Yeah, but can you raise the dead?"

Ash's hands stopped in mid-cut, and he glanced at U-ri. His expression told her everything she needed to know.

"You can…" she whispered. Suddenly her throat felt dry. "Did he use the Book of Elem?"

"Very good," Ash grunted.

"Wait. Just wait a second—" U-ri began dashing around the cluttered room like the boy had below. She found she couldn't sit still. "I've heard something like this before. In Mr. Minochi's reading room, from the Sage—the Sage in Green told me. He said that Mr. Minochi collected all those books because he was trying to find a way to raise someone from the dead."

Ash nodded slowly.

"But the Sage in Green said that was impossible! He said he tried to convince Mr. Minochi of that over and over, and he never listened."

"Why would he? Minochi had the Book of Elem, after all."

"You mean Mr. Minochi did it? He succeeded in raising someone?"

"No. He did not."

"Huh? Why not?" U-ri stomped across the room, shaking her fists in the air. "If Kirrick could do it, why couldn't he? None of this is making sense!"

Aju squeaked, "U-ri, sit."

"But, Aju!"

"Just sit down."

Frowning, U-ri found a spot on the floor. The mouse leaned over from her shoulder and gave her a whack on the nose with his tiny paw. "The *allcaste* has to keep her cool at all times, U-ri."

"I'm sorry. I just got excited."

Ash lit a small alcohol burner on the table and placed a beaker full of water on a stand over it. The stand's legs were long and wobbly. The whole apparatus looked dangerously unstable.

Sky returned with the water and stood by the table, ready for his next task.

"Let me first tell you of how the Book of Elem was created," Ash continued once they were quiet. "It began as a history, a chronicle of the great deeds of one hero. You could call it a legend."

The hero's name was Altius.

"They called him King Altius the victor."

He had led the armies of the Haetlands five hundred years ago, triumphantly repelling an invasion by one of the Haetlands' more powerful neighbors.

"At the time, war raged all over the continent—not just up here. It was the same everywhere you went. One country would invade another, absorb its armies, then launch another invasion. Kings rose victorious only to fall a week later, and maps that attempted to draw political boundaries were rendered useless in the span of a year. It was an age of continental warfare."

Surrounded by enemies, and small as the Haetlands were, invasion followed upon invasion. As soon as they drove off one would-be conqueror, another would take its place, leaving them barely enough time to catch their breath before they'd be strapping on their armor again.

"You'd run out of soldiers at that rate," Aju observed. "Small countries have small populations."

"True enough," Ash said, nodding. "Which is why King Altius decided he needed something stronger—powerful, forbidden magic. Magic to raise his fallen soldiers and create an immortal army."

"Magic," U-ri whispered. Of course it was possible here. The Haetlands were in a story, after all—an imaginary world. Magic could be anywhere, as long as the weaver who had created the Haetlands wrote about it.

Anything was possible.

"Thanks to this magic, the Haetlands fought on successfully throughout the duration of the continental war, maintaining their independence." Stories of a forbidden magic with the power to raise the dead had been told in legends since the Haetlands first came together as a country, Ash told them. "But even back five hundred years, knowledge of this magic was fragmented at best, and it had been much embellished with legend, making it useless as it was. It was a military mage in the service of the king who performed experiment after experiment, refining the magic until it worked. The mage's name was Elem—a woman, incidentally," Ash added, much to U-ri's surprise.

"A female mage?"

"That's right. I recall you were asking about girls who made a difference? Well, she was one."

That's not quite how I meant it, U-ri thought glumly. The power to raise the dead seemed frightful. Though it had saved Elem's country, U-ri wasn't sure that made it right.

"It's ironic," Ash muttered. "Only a woman can truly create life. Perhaps it requires a woman to raise the dead, as well."

After the victory, both King Altius and the mage Elem were revered by their people.

"But Elem, she did not consider it an honor in the least. She left the palace. While the Haetlands enjoyed prosperity such as it had never known before—after its victory it was far better off than most of the other countries on the war-weary continent—Elem chose to find an abandoned corner of the country and there live in solitude."

"Why?" U-ri asked though she expected the answer was forthcoming.

"Because she understood. She knew why the magic to raise the dead had been forbidden. When she first completed the spell, she went to the king and told him it would only invite more conflict. The magic would create an invincible army, but not one that would benefit the people. She asked if the king still approved—and King Altius did. 'What troubles you, Elem?' he asked of his mage. 'Is it not to defend our land that we drive back the invaders at our gates? How does this not benefit our people?' With Elem's magic, it was possible to completely revive someone who had died. This wasn't hedge magic, like animating zombies. It was a full person returned to the living, soul intact."

"But didn't that make people happy?" U-ri asked. "I would think they'd be overjoyed to have their sons and husbands return from the dead—and to know they'd never lose them again?"

"The continental wars ended," Ash continued in a low voice, ignoring her question. The liquid in the beaker he had placed over the burner had begun to boil. U-ri watched as the liquid turned a deep red. "In the end, the Haetlands boasted an army of immortal soldiers twelve thousand strong. They would never die, they would never fall. They were perfect warriors. And in a world at peace, there was nothing for them to do." Ash adjusted the flame. "Some put their sturdy bodies to good use, working the mines and the fields. Most of them had begun there before becoming soldiers—they simply returned to their roots, so to speak. But many were career soldiers, or had grown used to military life and to being treated like heroes. They did not want to dirty their hands in the soil again. They could not go back to their regular lives."

Ash gave U-ri a long look. "Think about it," he said at length. "You're immortal. You cannot die. What do you do? What do you become?"

You wouldn't fear danger. You wouldn't fear anyone.

"I'd think there wouldn't be much that could stop them from doing whatever they wanted."

Ash bowed his head, his face grave. "Not a decade had passed since the end of the continental wars when the Haetlands devolved into a nest of bandits and murderers. They had won the war, and it ruined them—just as the mage Elem had warned."

Still, for the space of seven years, the victor King Altius struggled to maintain peace. He knew there would be more fighting on the continent before long. The Haetlands needed their immortal army.

"Yet there was a limit, and it came quickly. While they draw breath, people change. Those women who rejoiced at seeing their sons and lovers returned to life watched them turn into something inhuman before their eyes, creatures of magic, made to do an insufferable amount of work, and they could not stand it.

"In desperation, King Altius sent scouts out across the Haetlands in search of Elem's whereabouts. But she came to the palace of her own accord. 'What must I do to undo the spell?' the king asked, and she answered, 'You must end my life.' For you see, the arcane magic Elem had used was tied to its creator's life. Were she to die, the men she had raised would in that very moment turn to ash."

So it was that Elem had been sentenced to death by hanging in the palace courtyard. The immortal soldiers turned to ash, as she said they would. The ash rose into the air, becoming a dark cloud that, it was said, blotted out the sun over the Haetlands for ten full days.

"Soon after, every book wherein had been written Elem's magic and the history of her immortal army, and the many victories of King Altius, were torn to shreds and burned."

"What!" Aju shouted, leaping up to his hindlegs. "So the Book of Elem was lost?"

"The original was, yes," Ash explained. "But there was another mage who had secretly copied parts of Elem's work, preserving them in a scroll."

The scroll had then been lost to the depths of the history.

"...until it reappeared suddenly, fifty-seven years ago, in the hands of an impoverished noble of royal lineage named Kirrick."

Kirrick had taken up arms to save his countrymen from the suffering he saw around him. He was no fool. His aims were noble, his eyes clear, and his heart burned with righteous indignation.

"That is why he did not seek to duplicate Elem's magic in whole. He went to a teacher of his who was knowledgeable in the ways of sorcery."

It turned out that in Kirrick's lineage, on his mother's side, there had been many royal mages. Magic ran in his blood.

"Kirrick was able to fill the gaps in the imperfect copy of Elem's spell."

Thinking that the problems had arisen when men had been restored to their former humanity—and only requiring soldiers, in any case—he sought not to return men to the world of the living, but to create fighting machines to do his bidding. He would simply raise their bodies, but leave their hearts to rot. His soldiers would not think or desire anything for themselves. They would exist to follow orders and hunt their prey like well-trained hounds to attack Kirrick's enemies.

"When his rebellion was over, all he would need do would be round them up and dispatch them."

"That's horrible," U-ri whispered.

"And foolish," Ash declared, placing his boiling blood-red liquid in a decanter. "He didn't stop to think why, five hundred years before him, Elem had raised men whole, souls intact. She had a reason to do so, you see."

Dead men forced to walk again without a soul were mere cases of flesh, with gaping holes where their hearts belonged. "And into those holes, darkness crept. The spirits of the earth, the destructive forces that fly unseen through the air, and the evil thoughts of the living began to accumulate within Kirrick's undead. He led them in a rebellion for his people, and the cheers of those he freed from oppression were many. Yet even as his victories mounted, his army was slowly corrupted."

Kirrick's rebellion ended quickly, and he was made king. Peace was restored to the Haetlands, and governance for the people was about to begin. "But the darkness quickly filled the shells of the men he had raised, and it changed them from inside, making them something other than men. Having no other recourse, Kirrick forced his undead soldiers into a great dungeon beneath the royal palace, there to remain until he was ready to dispose of them for good. But then creatures fell and horrid began to appear from that dungeon. The guards were their first victims. You see," Ash added, his expression cold, "these creatures ate human flesh. They were cannibals, of a sort, because they had begun their afterlives as men."

"Ewwww," Aju groaned before U-ri had even finished processing what she was hearing.

"With great urgency, Kirrick assembled the royal mages and led them against the very creatures he had created, beneath the halls of his own home. His version of Elem's magic should have enabled him to turn his raised army back into corpses. But the darkness inside them had taken the shape of souls, giving them a new life, and his magic did nothing."

The fiends broke from their dungeon prison, ransacked the palace, and spilled out into the capital and the countryside beyond.

Ash closed his eyes, either recollecting the scene of mayhem, or trying to keep an imagined scene from escaping his head. "Among the survivors of the royal house that Kirrick had destroyed were those who sought to use this opportunity to defeat him. Instead of attempting to quell the new threat, they worked more magic on the fiends to bend them to their own will."

But that had only made matters worse.

"The conflicting magic cast upon the creatures made them huge and violent, transforming them in unpredictable ways. Of all the resulting monstrosities, the worst were those that developed the ability to reproduce."

"You mean the creatures had children?"

"Not like that. There were some that, if you cut off their arm, another whole creature would grow from the severed limb. Cut off their head, and another creature would grow from that."

U-ri, Aju, and Sky were all speechless. It made U-ri sick to her stomach just imagining it. A chill ran down her spine, and not on account of the cold wind blowing in through the cracks in the walls.

"Were they able to drive them back?" Aju asked, hoping beyond all hope for a happy ending to the story.

Ash nodded. "Yes, but it took much effort. They had to kill them one at a time."

"How did they do it?"

"Most of them they burned. It was no pleasant task, I assure you."

In the ensuing fight against the creatures, Kirrick lost his life. He had been on the throne for only sixty days.

"Some historians call him the King of Two Months."

Something about the way Ash talked of these events tugged at U-ri's mind.

"So there you have it," Ash said, his voice hoarse from the telling. "All of these events are written in the Book of Elem, which showed up in the years afterward. There are some who call the book the Chronicles of Kirrick, but only those who stayed with him throughout the chaos. Few use that name now."

"And that book was sitting in Minochi's reading room," Aju whispered, gnashing his teeth.

"Not the original. That was a copy of a copy of a copy. Books deteriorate over time. If only their contents deteriorated as well."

Ash had finished brewing his medicine. He stood, taking a vial small enough to fit in the palm of his hand out of the drawer by the table along with a piece of white paper that had been cut into a square.

"Ash," she said. "Were you there?"

Ash stopped what he was doing.

"The weaver who wrote you wrote about Kirrick's war too. Where did you fit into the story?"

Ash smiled then, much to U-ri's surprise. "You remembered about the weaver."

U-ri felt her palms begin to sweat. "I couldn't help but get the feeling that you knew Kirrick when you talked about him."

His smile widened. "You have good instincts."

Next to them, Sky gasped, startled.

"Kirrick's family was poor, but being nobles, they had territory. It was nothing much: a cold village deep in the mountains called Danae. Kirrick's father had been a caring lord to his people, rare for the time. He had even waived taxes in years when crops fell short. No doubt contributing to his family's relative poverty."

Kirrick had been an only son, and his mother had died soon after giving birth to him.

"He was raised by a nursemaid. The nursemaid had a child of her own, newly born. That child was me." A distant look came into Ash's eyes. "We studied the ways of magic together. In those days, an old hermit lived in Danae Village who had once been chief among the palace mages. His name was Master Brann. He had been a powerful mage in his day—extremely powerful—but he had grown weary of palace politics and infighting. Thanks to him, Kirrick and I were able to learn much magic from an early age. Even things they did not teach in the royal academy."

It was Master Brann who had helped Kirrick find the scroll that contained the partial Book of Elem, and it was he who helped him complete his own version in later years.

"When Kirrick began his rebellion, I intended to go with him. But he asked me instead to stay in Danae. He wanted me to look after the village and Master Brann."

"They will surely need your protection should my rebellion fail."

"Throughout the struggle, I never had cause to go to the capital. It was not long between the time when the rebellion ended in success and the fiends reached the mountains of my village."

By the time they managed to drive off the creatures, the village had lost more than half of its population.

"Word of Kirrick's death came soon after. Master Brann took his own life. I think he planned on doing that from the start. He'd made a special poison for the occasion."

But Master Brann had left Ash with his knowledge—including knowledge of the nameless land and of the King in Yellow.

"It wasn't Kirrick who had been possessed by the King in Yellow. It was Master Brann. He thought that by lending his power to that clear-eyed lad, he could bring eternal peace to the Haetlands and fortune to its people. Master Brann's heart wished this, and it called out to the Hero...which brings us to now."

Ash spread his hands, as if to show he had given all he had to offer. Silence fell on the room. U-ri didn't know what to say next. Aju was curled up in a ball on the floor.

"What of the graves?" It was Sky's voice that broke the silence. "What of all the graves surrounding this house, and the child Udsu's extraordinary strength and agility? You said these things were related to your tale."

U-ri turned her eyes to Ash. "So I did, nameless devout," Ash said. His gaze was cold. "And here I thought your head was empty."

"Would you quit talking to him like that?" U-ri interrupted. "Sky is my servant, but he's also my friend."

Ash turned away, looking out through the clouded window. "Remember what I said about the creatures eating humans? They would always start with the head, and not stop until every last bit was consumed. But sometimes, rarely, a person so attacked would be saved with only injuries. These people, the survivors, developed strange abilities in the following months and years."

They grew incredibly strong. They could see in the middle of the night as though it were day. Their hearing improved to the point that they could hear someone talking on the other side of a mountain.

"The venom of the creatures flowed into their bodies, and in time, it changed them."

"And they all became supermen?" U-ri asked hopefully. "That doesn't sound bad at all."

Ash shook his head. "It didn't last long. Those affected would die in two or three years after their powers manifested themselves."

"Oh. That does sound bad."

"Most sane people avoided touching the bodies of the affected. They didn't want to burn them either, because that would be treating them no better than they had treated the creatures. It is our custom here in the Haetlands to bury our dead whole. Gradually, a business started up of collecting the corpses. That was my work here. Dmitri the undertaker, they called me."

"But this all happened fifty-seven years ago, didn't it? How could those people still be around if the transformation killed them?"

"They are still among us. You saw Udsu yourself."

Udsu's great-grandfather had been bitten as a young boy, but his powers did not manifest for years. He took a wife and had children. These children grew, married, and had children of their own—and all of them were affected.

"So..." U-ri began in a timid voice. "It's hereditary?"

"Yes. That's why it does not end."

Yet those who manifested their powers were dwindling in number by the year. It was rare for children as young as Udsu to manifest powers so early. Most only learned they were affected by the time they were grown with children of their own.

"I believe the creatures' venom is acting to preserve itself—to keep replicating itself down through the bloodline."

That makes it sound like the venom has a will of its own!

"Udsu is shunned here in Kanal. The other villagers fear him. He lives with his mother in a small shack outside the village."

"So you're his only friend, then."

She expected him to brush the comment off, but what he said surprised everyone. "And Dmitri has no friends save Udsu."

There was silence again. Aju hopped off of U-ri's shoulder, snuck down through her robes up to the other side of her head, and stuck his nose in her ear. "Hey, U-ri," he whispered. "You know, I've been thinking, maybe this Ash guy isn't so bad after all."

U-ri put a hand over her mouth and smiled. Ash was too busy putting medicine in the pouch he'd fashioned from the small square of paper to notice. U-ri smiled at Sky—then froze.

Sky was standing stiff as a board, a dark look on his face. U-ri wondered if what Ash had said before about his head being empty had offended him. *Or maybe he's frozen solid.* It was still terribly cold in the room.

"We leave for the capital tomorrow," Ash said, his fingers busily working. "Rest well tonight. It will be a hard road."

"Why don't we just jump there," Aju suggested, pointing to the glyph on the floor.

"U-ri cannot take us all there by her power alone. And I have business along the way, besides."

U-ri thought to ask him what but decided he probably wouldn't tell her anyway. She was tired, besides, and wanted to rest.

"Okay," she said, and that was that.

CHAPTER TEN

In Search of Clues

U-ri woke up early, the sunlight bright in her eyes.

She had slept through the night remarkably well considering that she was lying on the hard floor by the fireplace and was wrapped in a scratchy old blanket. When she opened her eyes, the first thing she saw was a square of blue sky. There was a small skylight in the ceiling above her head that she hadn't even noticed in the gloom of the day before.

The cold seemed to have subsided somewhat, though she wasn't sure whether it was because the weather had turned or because of the vestments of protection. U-ri sprang to her feet and ran over to the window to look outside. The village, dismal in the cold falling snow the day before, now looked bright and tranquil, almost beautiful. On the houses around their hill, thin blankets of snow were spread across the rooftops down to the eaves like elegant lace. From the smoke rising from several chimneys, she saw that the day had already begun in Kanal. Here and there windows and storehouse doors hung open.

She heard a noise downstairs and skipped down the steps. Sky was standing next to the stove, in which a merry fire burned.

"Lady U-ri. You're awake."

She wondered if Sky had slept at all. He looked pale.

"Morning, U-ri," Aju squeaked from atop one of the kitchen shelves where he sat nibbling on a leaf he held in his tiny fingers. "You sleep well?"

"Quite well, actually."

The door opened, and Ash came in with a small bundle of firewood under one arm. Ash was fully dressed for the day, but his hair was loose and disheveled. Its halo made him look even taller and skinnier than usual, like a beanpole topped by a scarecrow's wig.

"You're up early."

"It's so bright outside today. And the sky's so pretty. I had no idea." U-ri smiled at the devout. "You know I named Sky here after the blue skies in my region—he seemed to like them so much. But I'm afraid my region's got nothing on the sky in this village." She turned to the devout. "Have you been outside?"

Sky smiled weakly. "No, that's all right. It was enough for me to look out the window."

"It's unusual for the sky to be this clear during the winter—a noteworthy event," Ash said. "Thanks to you, no doubt."

U-ri lifted an eyebrow. "Me?"

"That glyph on your forehead has worked to drive back the evil clinging to this land."

U-ri put her palm to her forehead and stared at him.

"Go down to the river and wash your face. Watch your step, the path is very slippery."

At the small river, U-ri noticed that the water was crystal clear, but she could see no fish. *Maybe it's too clear for them?*

She caught a glimpse of some of the villagers. A line of men was leaving the village, heading up toward the mountains—hunters, most likely. They carried bows on their backs and something like rifles across their shoulders. Their thick boots trod heavily on the hard-frozen ground.

She saw women too. They wore long, brightly colored skirts, and stoles across their shoulders to keep away the cold. Some used brooms to sweep up around the houses, while others led horses from their stalls to brush their coats, or walked down to the pens to feed the livestock, or carried large buckets of water back to their homes for cooking. She heard animal noises coming from the stalls that sounded just like the pigs and cows of her world. *If they have horses, the other livestock here is probably the same as ours too,* she reasoned. Though there was magic and monsters and royalty, and no electricity, the Haetlands seemed to have the same sort of people and animals as U-ri's region. *Which means that the weaver who made the Haetlands was familiar with horses and cows and pigs. Maybe they were even from my region.*

The sound of laughter drifted up from one of the stalls at the bottom of the hill. Two women were standing outside and talking across a hedgerow. Even at a distance, she could see the smiles on their faces. *Looks like the weather has everyone in a good mood.*

For the first time, U-ri actually felt proud of the mark on her forehead. The words of the creature she had met in the library at Hiroki's school crossed her mind.

"Why must it always be children who know not even the true value of the mark upon their heads who seek to bring balance to the Circle?"

Is this what it meant by value?

She touched a finger to her forehead.

Her mark had been able to damage the envoy of the King in Yellow. It had revived the unconscious girl Michiru Inui. And here, it had pushed back the evil clinging to the land, bringing a rare spell of good weather.

Ash had said that wolves need the *allcaste*'s power. They needed the power of the glyph—her mark. That was her mark's purpose. Yet what the creature had said made her think there was more to it than just that.

Crouching by the small river, U-ri looked at her own reflection in the water and thought. *Value...*

"Lady U-ri?"

U-ri looked up to see Sky coming down the path rapidly, his black robes swept back behind him.

U-ri stood and waved. "Come look, the water's beautiful. And the air here's so fresh."

She took a deep breath. Sky's pace slowed as he came nearer. He was looking around, wide-eyed.

"Look up at the sky! Isn't it gorgeous?"

The devout hesitated at first, then finally looked up. He didn't blink once—even though he was staring right at the sun.

"Doesn't it just make you feel alive to be here?"

What's wrong, Sky? He hadn't said a word. His face was still grim. *He was so impressed with the sky in my smoggy region—surely the sky here is ten times as impressive.*

"Do you not like the Haetlands, Sky?"

She could understand why he might not, after their history lesson the night before.

"Lady U-ri, this region exists within a story. It's an imaginary world."

"I know that. But for the people who live here, it's real enough. What if my region had been made by some weaver? It would certainly feel real to me."

"I understand how you might think that, but you are mistaken," Sky said, no trace of humor on his face. "The place from which you come is the only reality, the Circle, in which all other regions exist. It is different from other places," the devout quietly explained, his voice only just audible over the burbling of the brook and the twittering of small birds from the forest around the village.

"That and the nameless land, right? That's a real place too, isn't it?"

Sky turned his gaze from the sun finally. A wave of indecision crossed his features.

"Sky?"

"Lady U-ri," Sky began, slowly—frightfully slowly—turning his face to look at her. "Lady U-ri, I..."

Their eyes met. The devout's eyes caught the morning sun and glimmered a bright purple, the color of violets in early spring. "I—" he began again. He swallowed. "No, it is nothing."

That was certainly not *nothing. What were you going to say, Sky? Are you hiding something?*

"Let us return. Master Ash seemed in a hurry to be off."

Sky turned and practically fled back up the hill. U-ri had to run to keep up with him. She wanted to ask what it was he had been about to say, but she was too out of breath even to call out.

Aju recommended the leaves he had been nibbling on, so U-ri sat down to share in a "typical village breakfast" with Ash. Even though the vestments of protection kept her stomach full, she was still curious—a curiosity she soon regretted.

"You're accustomed to richer foods than this, I see," Ash commented with a smirk.

"I guess you're right," U-ri said, still gagging on the gruel. "I always thought what I ate was pretty normal."

They cleared the bowls, then Ash spread out a large scroll on the table. It was a map of the Haetlands. There were mountains and rivers, towns and villages. The borders of the country looked like a slightly warped oval, and near the southern edge had been drawn the large picture of a castle.

"The capital, Elemsgard," Ash announced, jabbing a finger at it.

"Does that have something to do with the Book of Elem?"

"Very good. It used to have a different name, but it was changed after Kirrick's rebellion."

In the old language of the Haetlands, the name meant "the grave where Elem is buried," Ash explained.

"But aren't capitals usually in the middle of the country? And why call a city a 'grave'?"

"Because that is where the mage Elem is buried, and where the Book of Elem that Kirrick possessed was kept under careful guard."

"Is that so?" Aju asked, giving the castle a light smack of his tail. "Too bad the Book of Elem isn't still there."

"That's right. Someone took it from its place of safekeeping, and it passed from hand to hand, until it reached the library of Ichiro Minochi."

"Who took it?"

"I do not know, nor does it matter now. Probably some greedy minister, or a warrior-mage charged with the book's protection. As we cannot turn back time to prevent the book from being stolen in the first place, there is little point in finding out who it was now."

Ash was evidently a realist, first and foremost.

"Still, I'm surprised," Aju squeaked. "This mage Elem was the source of so much evil, yet they still gave her a proper burial?"

"To be more precise, the capital is where the severed head of Elem was brought after the success of Kirrick's rebellion. It was not buried so much as put on display that others might take a lesson from it. A powerful spell of binding was placed on the gravestone," Ash explained.

"What about King Altius?" U-ri asked. "Did they do the same to him? Yesterday you said that they threw out all the records of his time, but they still called him the victor-king, right?"

Ash turned his half-lidded eyes toward U-ri. "The king's grave remained where it was. There are few willing to disturb the remains of royalty."

"So Elem got to shoulder all the blame, then." Aju had called Elem the "source of so much evil," but that seemed a bit harsh to U-ri. She had only researched the spell she used in the first place to protect the Haetlands, and she had given the king fair warning before using it. *If anyone were to blame, it would be King Altius.*

If he had only been a bit more cautious, or the situation his country faced a bit less perilous, Elem might have gone down in history as a revered contributor to their victory in the continental wars. Certainly not put on display five hundred years after being put to death of her own free will. She would have been nothing but brittle bones by then. Yet they dug her up, carried her to the capital, and shamed her memory.

A realization pricked at the back of U-ri's mind like a needle. *She had been a hero, before she was stricken down. Almost like Hiroki.* Mr. Hata, his teacher, had pointed out the boy's "heroic" aspirations. *"Hiroki has to learn his place,"* he had said.

But were what Elem did and what Hiroki did really the same? Were there similarities between their stories? Elem had raised the dead and made an army—what was an unthinkable act for the average person. Hiroki had saved Michiru from being picked on by her classmates, which was certainly brave, but not epic by any means.

But that's not all that happened, was it?

Hiroki didn't just turn against the bullies. He turned against their teachers as well—a rebellion, of sorts. Meanwhile, Elem had gone against the very cycle of life and death, breaking the boundary between the two. It was hard to think of two acts more different in scale. But you could say that both of them acted to overturn the orders governing their respective worlds.

That was why they had both been hailed as heroes at first, only to be reviled later.

There it was—the two sides of the same coin. The Hero and the King in Yellow.

"U-ri? Something wrong?" Aju asked from atop her shoulder.

U-ri shook her head. "It's nothing. So—when are we heading for the capital? Will there be something there to help me find my brother?"

"It's a possibility," Ash said, his eyes fixed on U-ri's expression.

Maybe he always looks sleepy so people won't notice that keen gaze. His eyes looked like they could see through to the back of her skull.

"And there may be clues at the place I plan to stop at along the way. That's why I came to find you, *allcaste*. To take you with me."

Suddenly, their goal was coming into focus. U-ri straightened her back. "Really?"

"Right here." Ash pointed a long finger at a spot on the map. There was a mark like a wall on top of one of the mountains, next to which was written a word in tiny letters that looked more like someone's scribble than a proper caption. U-ri found that she was able to read them.

"The 'Katarhar Abbey Ruins'? Is that what that says?"

"That's right."

The state religion of the Haetlands was monotheistic. They revered the royal bloodline as having descended from one creator god. However, there were several other religions scattered across the countryside. Some of them had roots that went back even before the founding of the kingdom. These were tribal religions, tied deeply to the land where they thrived.

"When the current royal family unified the Haetlands under one rule, these minority regional beliefs were discouraged at the point of a sword. Orders were dissolved, sacred scriptures destroyed, churches and monasteries reduced to rubble. Now, the local beliefs exist only in the form of traditions kept alive within the communities." Even still, Ash explained, the more meaningful holy sites were still properly respected by the locals. The royal family chose to ignore this practice. It was a waste of time to further destroy buildings already in ruins, and most of these were so remote that leaving them alone seemed the most harmless choice. "Katarhar Abbey is one such place," Ash continued. "Though publicly it is considered deserted, in secret there are still monks there, protecting the ruins."

"What kind of clues are we going to find in a place like that?" Aju snorted, wrinkling his tiny pink nose. It had become a habit of his to openly dispute Ash's statements whenever possible.

"There are clues. There is a person—" Ash said, pausing slightly. "An *individual* with information." He seemed to be having difficulty defining just who this contact of his was.

"You mean a monk? Like Sky?"

Next to Aju, Sky nodded, both of them staring at Ash. But the wolf did not seem to notice them.

"Look at this map well, burn its features into your mind. There is a glyph in the central courtyard of this abbey. For us to go there, you must grasp both distance and direction, U-ri."

"What the heck's a glyph doing in a place like that?"

"Because I carved one there, you irritating little rat." Ash picked up Aju with swift fingers, then dropped him onto the map. "Stop chittering away and try helping U-ri for a change."

That said, Aju wasn't sure how he could help her, and U-ri had no idea where to begin. All she could do was stare at the map. The Katarhar Abbey ruins were much closer than the capital. All they had to do was cross the mountains to the southwest, and they'd get to what was either a lake or a very large swamp. A large river flowed there, but they weren't to cross it. They would follow it southward, and once they hit the forest, they would turn east.

"Hey, I can see the buildings—" Aju chirped suddenly. He sounded like a sparrow twittering with joy. "That's what you meant by helping her." Aju had one paw on the picture of the Katarhar Abbey ruins on the map. "It's okay, U-ri, I can guide us there. I can see the buildings in my mind."

Behind them, Sky turned to Ash. "Master Ash," he called out softly, "will we be leaving soon?"

"Is there some reason we shouldn't?"

"I was wondering if we shouldn't say farewell to the boy who visited here yesterday."

Udsu, the springfoot. U-ri looked up from the map. "That's right. Didn't you make medicine for his mother?"

"That I delivered last night," Ash told him, standing up from his chair. "He won't care if we leave without telling him. Once he sees the smoke gone from the chimney, he'll know I've left."

Sky bowed curtly. "Then I will see to putting out the fire in the stove down below. I daresay there's no need for you to lock up?"

Above their heads, the blades of the windmill turned with a slow creaking that sent shivers through the crude shack's floor. U-ri was thinking about this as she stepped inside the magic circle, but soon she forgot everything as the room went black around them, and the wind whistled in her ears. Then U-ri flew up into the sky and away, and they were gone.

U-ri tried pinching her nose. She could feel her fingers, but she could see nothing. It was pitch black, except that after a while, brief flourishes of color would flash in the darkness, sometimes beneath her feet, other times to one side or over her head—bits of landscape suddenly appeared and disappeared like a magician's painted scarves. She caught a glimpse of mountains, forests, towns, and villages.

"That's right, U-ri, that's it," Aju navigated from atop her head. "Wait— you're going a little far south. Come back, back!"

Sky held her hand tightly. Ash apparently didn't need to physically hold on to her to travel. From the moment they had departed, she hadn't seen or sensed his presence at all.

She felt her spirit ease as they rushed through the darkness. She was one with the darkness, and at the same time, she was a wind cutting across the void. She was free of gravity, free of time, free of all material bonds. Even Aju's squeaking sounded like it came from impossibly far away. But it didn't matter. Aju was at the helm, and U-ri was the ship. She left the navigation to him, and let herself soar.

This feels great! None of her previous jumps had felt even remotely the same. *Had they been too short?* Or maybe it was the difference between traveling within a region and going from one region to another—or to the nameless land as she had on her first jump from Minochi's cottage.

U-ri closed her eyes and relaxed. She lost sense of everything, even the boundaries of her own body. She was the wind—

Yet she could still feel the warmth of Sky's hand in her own.

Sky's a gentle soul. A warm feeling grew inside her as her heart drifted out into the darkness. He had been so concerned about Udsu after only meeting the boy once. *I never would have thought to say goodbye to him.*

It was strange. She wondered who Sky was—who he had been. Up until now, she never had the time, nor any particular need, to think about it. Not that she had a need now, but here in this darkness, in this wind, flying freely, the only person she felt any connection to at all was the nameless devout. She felt it like she felt his warmth. At that moment, he was everything to her.

Why?

Maybe it's this darkness. Maybe it's because the darkness resembles him.

Because Sky doesn't exist. Because he is empty, hollow. Like Ash said—he is nothing.

But that wasn't right. Sky wasn't nothing. *He just hides who he is beneath those black robes—he hides his warmth, his kindness. I know. I can feel who he is when he's near me.*

"Yet, like the darkness, you will never know his true form."

Who said that? Whose thoughts were those? U-ri tried to look around in the rushing darkness.

"Stay away!"

Someone was screaming, making the darkness around her shudder. Then U-ri found her way blocked. Like a bird flying into a window, U-ri hit a wall in the darkness, hard. Sparks flew behind her eyes.

"Stay away! You must not come any closer!"

The voice rose like the howl of a wounded beast, trembling with rage at first then fading, choked with fear. No, it wasn't fading. The voice still repeated its warning to stay away—it was U-ri's consciousness that was fading—she slipped and fell—

"U-ri!"

It was Ash. A long arm reached out, grabbed U-ri by the collar, stopped her fall. But U-ri's arms flew up over her head and she slipped easily out of the vestments of protection.

"Lady U-ri!" Sky's anguished cry receded into the distance. U-ri was falling, falling, falling—down and down into the darkness.

It seemed she would never hit the bottom. *If this darkness even has a—*

Then she broke free, out of the bottom of the darkness into the light. Color returned to her eyes as the world took shape around her. And she was still falling.

"Waaaugh!" U-ri screamed. *No—that's not me, it's Aju.* The little mouse was clinging desperately to her hair. Every hair on his body stood straight on end, and his tail whipped through the air above them. "Fly, U-ri, fly!"

"Fly? How?"

They were up in the air, at about the level of the clouds. They passed through the cotton candy swirl of one cloud, falling ever downward.

"Wave your arms like you're swimming!" Aju squealed. He began rapidly reciting a spell. It was a silly-sounding spell, with lots of *da*'s and *pa*'s—but he chanted it with an intensity she had never seen in him before.

"—*handanaranipa, ujrawitika, nadapamun-dpamurupa!*"

It sounded so comical, U-ri found herself laughing. *How can I laugh at a time like this? I'm falling to my—*

But she wasn't falling now. U-ri was floating through the air. She was soaring, flapping her arms like a bird. She passed through a ragged cloud. *Yipes, that's cold!*

"Whew, we made it." Aju breathed a sigh of relief, still clinging with all four paws to U-ri's hair. His own fur seemed to have settled down. "We'll just fly like this for a bit, nice and slow. We'll have to pick an inconspicuous place to make our landing."

Beneath them was a town, one of those beautiful, European-style places she had only seen on television and on postcards. The houses were white, with red triangular or slanted blue roofs. Glittering towers rose from stonework manses. There were wide parks with bubbling fountains. Cobblestone streets ran between the buildings, and here and there stood small copses of trees. A large river flowed nearby, quietly reflecting the blue sky. A bridge traced an elegant arc over the water, and she spied a horse and carriage crossing it.

"We came out way too soon," Aju was muttering. "Look over there. That's the mountain with the Katarhar Abbey ruins."

He yanked at her bangs, directing her eyes off to the left. Sure enough, rising from the beautiful pastoral scenery below was a dark, clouded mountain. It was not much taller than the foothills surrounding it, but its sides were covered thickly with trees, so thick they seemed to jostle for the sunlight. They looked like pines, with pointed tops and dark foliage, lending the mountain a shadowy, jagged aspect. Here and there, bare cliff faces stood out from the forest, as though some giant beast had taken its claws to the mountainside to leave gaping scars where no trees grew.

She spotted a narrow road that wound up the mountain toward the peak. At the end of the road, she thought she saw something like a gray wall. U-ri flailed her arms, trying to get closer, but it seemed her powers of flight were not on par with a bird's after all. The more she thrashed, the more altitude they lost.

She could make out details in the town below now. Flower boxes outside of windows in which red and yellow blossoms bloomed. There were people in the streets. And shops. Carts carrying goods rattled to and fro, and the sound of music rose up from somewhere. It resembled a church organ—and there were children singing in a chorus. *Maybe there's a school nearby?*

"This is a much bigger place than Kanal. Richer too by the looks of it."

"Yeah, I can smell a confectionery," Aju said, his nose twitching at a sweet scent on the air.

"What a different place. There are flowers everywhere."

"We have to take care who sees us. Let's land over in the forest, U-ri."

With Aju's guidance, U-ri shifted her body just so, avoiding the trees as they landed.

She could tell immediately they weren't out in the wilderness. Tiny paths crisscrossed through the trees, and there were guideposts at some of the intersections. U-ri went up to one, but she couldn't read the writing at all.

"U-ri!" Aju hissed, "don't stand out in the open like that."

U-ri quickly ducked beneath some shrubs off to the side of the path.

"Without your vestments of protection, you just look like a Japanese schoolgirl."

U-ri heard someone talking beyond a nearby tree. U-ri pressed herself down beneath the bushes. Footsteps approached. It was two women, each carrying a basket, walking slowly along. They wore aprons over long skirts and blouses with puffy sleeves. Their hair was bound on top of their heads and wrapped in white lace. The women smiled as they talked.

Well, they look happy, but I can't understand the slightest bit of what they're saying.

Without her vestments of protection, she couldn't read or understand the local speech.

"This is bad, Aju," she whispered to the little mouse, feeling a panic come over her. *This is no time for gazing at scenery and taking leisurely walks in the woods!*

"Just calm down. Leave it to me."

Aju hopped onto the ground by her feet and began to whisper a spell. The words of enchantment sounded like the rustling of leaves.

U-ri felt a cold wind sweep around her, and when she looked down, she found that she was wearing the same clothes as the two women. Even her hair looked the same. The only differences were that instead of an apron, she wore a vest, and where the women had worn leather sandals, she wore boots.

A small purse hung down over one shoulder. It was cute. "I'll give you marks for fashion sense, Aju."

Aju grinned triumphantly, pink nose in the air. "Not bad if I dare say so myself." He looked proud, U-ri decided, *even though with him on the ground like that, I could very well step on him by accident.*

"You fit in now."

"But what about the language?"

"Just talk normally. They'll think you're a foreigner or some such. You can use gestures—show them you were traveling with your parents, but you got separated. Wave your arms around a bit and they'll see you're lost."

U-ri frowned. "You sure that's going to work?"

"'Course it will. Some kind person will show you the way to Katarhar

Abbey, no problem."

"I'm not sure I'd be able to follow directions even if they did tell me."

"But I'll understand, and I can interpret for you. As long as you look the part, everything will be fine."

U-ri nodded, then quickly shook her head. "No, Aju, wait. I've got a better idea. Why don't we just fly again?"

Aju chirped irritably, beating his little paws on the ground. "Come on, have you no idea why we're in this fix to begin with? No? U-ri?"

"I remember we were flying—and then we fell."

"Because we hit a magical barrier, U-ri. It canceled out the power of your glyph and knocked us out of the air. Someone at Katarhar Abbey doesn't fancy you dropping in on them."

U-ri remembered the voice shouting for her to stay away. *"You must not come any closer!"* the voice had said.

"Or maybe it wasn't you but your glyph they didn't want getting any closer. In any case, we won't be able to use magic to get any nearer to Katarhar Abbey than we are now. If you don't believe me, just try. We'll be knocked out of the sky as sure as the sun rises in the morning."

U-ri decided she would give that one a pass. She didn't fancy slamming into any more invisible walls anytime soon.

"But what about Ash and Sky? Did they fall somewhere too?"

"No idea," Aju squeaked, his face looking as stern as a field mouse's could. "We might've been wrong to trust him as much as we have."

"You mean Ash?"

The mouse nodded, his beady red eyes glowing brightly.

Maybe he's mad.

"I wonder what he's after."

"What he's after? Isn't he a wolf?"

"Just because he's a wolf doesn't mean we can trust him, U-ri. He might be working for the enemy. He could be a spy!"

A spy! U-ri hadn't even thought of that. She almost laughed, then stopped herself. Aju was dead serious.

"But, you know, I think Ash tried to save me when we hit that barrier. Didn't you notice, Aju?"

Aju frowned, and it wasn't hard for her to read his expression. He *had* noticed it.

"Besides, if he was planning something, why mention Katarhar Abbey to us at all? I'm sure he's right. There's a clue there that will help me find my brother."

"How do you know? He could've been lying."

"Well, obviously someone, or *something*, wants us to stay away. We know that for a fact."

Whoever had erected that barrier had their reasons for doing so. Finding out who that was could be the key. Or they were holding the key, at the very least. "Anyway, wherever those two landed, I'm sure they'll be heading for the abbey ruins just like us. Let's go. I'll play the lost child as you suggested, Aju."

U-ri sprang lightly to her feet, inspected her new garments, then stepped out onto the path, a smile on her face.

"U-ri!" Aju squeaked. He was still on the ground, stretching to stand as tall as he could. "You know, it might've been Hiroki who stopped you back there."

The smile vanished from U-ri's lips. She felt it go. "What do you mean by that?"

"I'm not sure. It's just a guess. But it occurred to me that Hiroki *might not want you to find him.*"

Who knows what had happened to U-ri's brother after he became the last vessel. *He might not even be human by now.* The thought crept up on her once again, sending shivers down her spine.

"Of course I'll still help you try to find him, if you want to."

U-ri wasn't sure whether to thank him or get angry. Either way, she ended up with an expression on her face not unlike that of a young girl frightened at losing her parents in a strange land—saving her the effort of trying to act the part.

Mouse on her shoulder, she walked alone, the purse over her shoulder her only luggage. The two women were long gone by now, so she walked toward town, looking around cluelessly like the lost child she was. Thankfully, it seemed that the people of this town were not without heart. She had only just left the forest when someone called out to her. When they found out she couldn't understand them, they became even kinder, and more people gathered.

Before half an hour had passed, U-ri was sitting inside a greengrocers, drinking sweet tea. Large wooden crates lined the shop, each filled with fresh vegetables and fruit. Price tags hung on the front of each crate. The proprietors were a couple, each as round as the other, with ruddy faces and boisterously loud voices.

"They seem like good people," Aju whispered from U-ri's shoulder. He had relaxed considerably since the time of their landing. "The big woman's name is Aisa. The customers call her 'Old Lady Aisa.' She takes care of them, and they of her. Looks like they're all regulars."

She was something like a village elder then.

"Are they going to take us to the police? Are there any police here?"

"I would think so, in a town this size. Her husband just sped out the door—maybe he went to fetch one of them."

"What was she saying when she kept pointing at you a few minutes ago?"

"She was worried I'd nibble on her vegetables. Wanted to know if I was tame or not. If I had manners."

Aisa came in from greeting customers outside her shop and began to talk to U-ri. From her expression and gestures, U-ri realized the woman was asking if she was cold. U-ri shook her head, then let her eyes fall to the floor. The woman put both hands to her waist and smiled nervously as if to say, "Now what are we going to do with you?"

"Aisa wants to know where you and your parents were headed."

U-ri set down her tea and stood. Taking the woman Aisa's hand, she led her out to the cobblestone street in front of the shop. The woman's hand was calloused and dry against her skin.

With the woman watching, U-ri pointed to the darkly clouded mountain rising in the distance.

"Katarhar," she tried saying. "Ka-tar-har."

That word seemed to do the trick. Aisa's round features grew suddenly stern. She pulled back her chin, fixed her eyes on U-ri, and began to speak very rapidly.

"She wants to know what business your parents had going to a place like that."

U-ri couldn't exactly admit the mouse was interpreting for her, nor could she communicate outside of body language, but somehow she was going to have to get this woman to show her how to get to the Katarhar Abbey ruins.

U-ri shrugged and attempted a weak smile. The woman gave an exaggerated sigh.

"She says it's tough, you not being able to understand her."

"She's telling me," U-ri muttered.

Clasping her hands in front of her, U-ri made a motion like she was begging the woman. She pointed toward the mountain again. Then she repeated her gestures. *Please understand; I have to go to Katarhar Abbey.*

Aisa put a hand to her forehead.

"Your father and mother have gone the wrong way."

What does she mean by that?

"You cannot go up that mountain from this village. There is a mage-hedge blocking the path, and besides it is forbidden."

U-ri opened her eyes wide, still pretending not to understand, and the old woman tried crossing her arms out in front of her face, as if to communicate to her that the way was barred.

A customer arrived, and the woman stopped to help her, motioning for U-ri to wait where she was.

"What do you think she means by a 'mage-hedge'?"

"I think she's talking about something like that barrier we ran into. There is a wall of magic around this town. I can smell it."

"But we got in?"

"It's not a wall to keep out people, U-ri. It keeps out, well, other things."

U-ri recalled the story Ash had told her about the risen soldiers who turned into horrible creatures and the strange and fatal powers their poisoned victims developed.

"Maybe that has something to do with why this place seems so rich compared to Kanal." Towns this pretty were rare even in U-ri's world. It felt like a theme park.

"Well, I think your sampling isn't so great. Ash's village is probably one of the poorest around," Aju squeaked quietly. "Might be because of the graveyard. I wouldn't be surprised if towns with graves like that were kept apart from those without."

That didn't seem very fair.

The woman returned from speaking with her customer—the two had been glancing in U-ri's direction the whole while—and spoke.

"She said that the town guard would be coming soon to take you to the local garrison."

The woman looked up toward the clouded mountain. But she didn't point—almost as though she were afraid the mountain might see.

"She says if you talk with the guard, they might let you approach the abbey. She hopes your parents got there ahead of you okay."

The woman motioned for her to have a seat, but U-ri simply lowered her head and remained standing in front of the shop. She wanted to watch the people go by, living their peaceful lives, protected by the mage-hedge around the village. From all she had heard from Ash, the Haetlands did not sound like a particularly beautiful or peaceful place. But clearly there was room for beauty and happiness here, if only in selected locales. Places where the relics of the Haetlands' troubled past were there to remind people of what had gone before.

"It's all the same, you know," Aju whispered. "There are bad places in the region where you live, U-ri. You might've been lucky and never seen war or starvation, but it's there all right."

"You're right, I know," U-ri whispered back.

They were interrupted by the sounds of rushing feet and loud voices. A large number of people were running right toward them, from the street to the right. There was shouting. U-ri couldn't understand a word, but it was clear from the tone of the voices that something had gone terribly wrong.

Aju pricked up his ears and stood up on his hind legs on top of U-ri's head. Then came the sound of several explosions, one quickly after the other, like gunshots. A scream rang through the streets. Now more people were shouting.

Aisa came dashing out of the back of the shop. A young woman came around the corner and ran to Aisa as soon as she saw her. Her face was pale and streaked with tears, and she was wailing and pointing back in the direction from which she had come.

"She says one of the town guardsmen was trying to apprehend a bandit!"

The guard's carriage had been crossing the street, Aju explained, when the soldier spotted a man threatening someone with a knife, and tried to apprehend him.

"That was probably the guardsman coming to meet me!" U-ri shouted. "Let's go, Aju!" She took off. Behind her, Aisa was shouting something—no doubt trying to get her to stop.

"Go and do what, U-ri?"

"I don't know—I'll think of something!"

As U-ri dashed down the cobblestone street, she heard more screaming and more gunfire. Everyone on the street was running toward her—only U-ri went against the tide. A well-dressed gentleman reached out as he passed, grabbing for her arm. *"Don't go—you'll be in danger!"*

She didn't have to go far—through an intersection and right at the next corner—before she reached the scene of the commotion. A circle of people stood in the road in front of her. *Spectators, come to see what's going on!* It seemed people's reactions to crime were the same in every region.

Some distance beyond the crowd stood a uniformed town guardsman with his pistol drawn. He was crouched low, taking aim as he carefully crept across the cobblestones. His horse and carriage sat off to the side of the street, half up on what passed for the sidewalk. A flag the same color as the crest on the guardsman's shoulder fluttered over the carriage.

Another man stood further down the street, in the direction the guardsman's gun was pointing. He wore a white shirt, open in front, and pants that only went down to the tops of his knees. He was barefoot, his hair cropped close to his head. He looked remarkably pale and very skinny.

His right arm hung loosely down by his side; in his hand he held a sword the length of U-ri's arm. She wondered what he had intended to use it for. The blade had two edges and came to a fine point at the end.

Blood was spattered on the man's face and body. There was a particularly large stain on one of his knees. *His blood maybe.* He walked with a lurching tilt, dragging the leg as though it were injured. The man glared at the guardsman, and the guardsman glared back at him, like two beasts circling.

"U-ri!" Aju squeaked in a sharp voice. "I know what's going on! He's been possessed by an *unattached*!"

"An unattached what?"

"No, U-ri, an *unattached*—those stories I was telling you about that just sort of drift through the Circle without ever getting written down in a book. See that stuff like thin smoke in the air around his head?"

She looked and indeed, she could see something like a pink wisp of smoke coiled like a serpent around the man's head. "That's an *unattached* story?"

"You bet. It's got him good—the thing has a hold on his heart for sure."

Suddenly the man let out a war cry, and lowering his blade, he charged toward the guardsman. The guardsman fired. The bullet grazed the man's left shoulder, and blood sprayed into the air. There was the stench of gun powder. Howling, the man went down on one knee. As one, the spectators took a step back.

"Throw down your weapon!" the guardsman shouted.

"Those unattached stories can just possess people?"

"Yeah. They don't have forms themselves, so they yearn for any they can get their hands on."

The guardsman stood and made to walk over to the possessed man just as he began to howl where he lay on the cobblestones. Sitting up, he began flailing the sword about. His eyes shone as bright as the steel of his blade, a warping, jagged light that reflected this way and that.

"Whoa," Aju whispered. "I think it's devoured that poor fellow's mind."

"Shoot him, shoot him!" one of the spectators shouted. The wounded man howled in the direction of the voice.

"Wait—if it's a story that's possessing him, can't I do something? Can't I use my mark?"

Aju hesitated and said, "Well, you can—but are you sure you want to?"

"I can't just do nothing! He's going to die!"

U-ri burst through the ring of onlookers, almost tripping in her hurry to reach the man before it was too late. The guardsman whipped around to see who was approaching. When he saw U-ri, his eyes almost popped out of his head with surprise.

U-ri stood up straight, pressing one hand to her forehead. "Here! Look here!" she shouted, knowing that the guardsman, the spectators, and the man with the sword probably couldn't understand a word she said. *I'll just have to communicate by sheer willpower.* The man looked up at her. His glimmering eyes met hers.

The guardsman sprinted toward U-ri, but she held up her other hand, stopping him. "It's all right! Stay back!"

The guardsman blinked, uncertain of what was going on. Beads of sweat dripped down his face.

Then the man with the sword lunged toward U-ri. He knocked her flat on her back and had her by the collar before she knew what was happening. The man's blade swung up into the air.

Instinctively, U-ri took her hand from her forehead and placed it on the man's face. She could feel the bony ridge of his nose beneath her palm, the hollow curve of his cheek. "Leave this man at once, traveler without a home! You do not belong here!" she shouted.

The man froze, the point of his sword pointing straight up toward the sky.

"Be still, traveler," she repeated, gripping the man's forehead tightly.

She could hear words in her head. *They're coming from the glyph!* It was telling her the words of the spell she needed to recite. All she had to do was repeat after the voice.

"Pitiful wanderer in eternity, you have lost your way. You do not belong in this place; this man is no fit vessel for you."

The possessed man's head dropped, and he began to groan. Spittle mixed with blood dripped in a viscous line from his mouth, staining the cobblestones below.

"State your name, traveler. Tell me your name."

The man shivered beneath her hand. More saliva poured from his mouth. His cracked lips opened.

Behind her, the guardsman and all the spectators stood frozen. There was complete silence on the street.

"I...have no name."

"Tell me your name."

"We are many...we are unattached...we have no name."

Large tears began to fall from the man's eyes. His hand fell, the sword clattering to the ground. He crouched and U-ri sat up, moving her hand from the man's face to the top of his head. She tried stroking his hair. She could sense the mark on her hand glowing. She could feel its warmth.

"Nameless traveler. Hear the echoing of the Great Wheels. Hear the voice summoning you back to that land removed from the tides of time."

Your father is the vast darkness, your mother the eternal light.

"There you must return. The Great Wheels call to you. To their circling you must return. Leave!" U-ri shouted the last word, removing her hand from the man's head and pointing straight upward.

As though following her finger, the pink haze around the man's head began to drift upward. Pulled by her will, it lifted into the air, until the man was entirely free of it. It twisted like a snake swimming through the air, going straighter the higher up it went, until it became a sharp line, like a spear, shooting straight up into the heavens.

The crouching man fell heavily on his side. He was unconscious.

There was a moment's silence. Then everyone began to shout at once. There were cheers mingled with screaming. A few brave souls stepped toward U-ri, while others sought to flee.

The guardsman lowered his pistol and walked over to her. He looked down at U-ri with a hard expression on his face. "Who are you?" Aju interpreted from the back of her collar. She didn't have to answer him though. The guardsman stuck his pistol in his belt and turned to the spectators. "This girl here's a mage!"

A ripple went through the crowd. Some of the ones who had been trying to run away slowed their pace and came back.

"You're not from this town, are you? You traveling? By yourself?" the man asked, reaching out to offer his hand to U-ri and help her to her feet. U-ri shook her head several times to indicate she couldn't understand him.

"She's the one, she's the one!" one of the spectators—an older woman—shouted, pointing at U-ri. "She's the lost child from Aisa's!"

The guardsman's eyes went wide and the little mustache beneath his nose crinkled as he smiled. "Is that so!" he exclaimed. "Well, you've just saved me some trouble then."

The spectators stepped aside as another town guard carriage came swiftly down the street, a little late for the action. The guard with the mustache called out to the new arrivals. "You take care of him," he called out, indicating the fallen man. "I'll handle the lady."

A few minutes later, U-ri was climbing into the guardsman's carriage, not in the back, but up front, next to him in the driver's seat. The step was too high for her to climb, so the mustached guardsman had helped lift her up.

U-ri caught a glimpse of Aisa among the milling spectators. She waved and nodded her head to the woman. Aisa simply stared back, not even acknowledging her.

Maybe mages aren't all that welcome in this town. It had certainly caused a commotion amongst the spectators when the guard announced her in the street—but she had attributed that to mages being a relatively rare thing. Some of the town children ran after her carriage as they took off. Everyone wanted to catch a glimpse of the new mage.

The garrison of the town guard was a solid-looking stone structure two stories tall, with some carefully trimmed trees in the front yard. U-ri stepped out of the carriage by the front door, and the mustached guardsman let her inside. The ceiling was high and though the light was dim, the place had a lively feel with people running this way and that, some in uniform, others in civilian clothes.

She was taken to a small room with a window overlooking the front garden and told to wait. As she sat patiently, she spotted one or two of the children that had chased after her carriage hiding behind the trees outside the window. U-ri waved, and the children began whispering furiously to one another. Then U-ri jabbed her finger straight at them, and they scattered like cockroaches in the light.

"It's not nice to tease the children, Lady *Allcaste*," Aju said, chuckling with her. "And I noticed you were able to communicate with your glyph by yourself. Congratulations."

"Is that what happened in the street?"

"Yes. You recited all the proper words without me having to tell them to you."

I'm getting used to this, slowly.

A moment later, a guardsman with an impressive-looking crest on his shoulder came into the room, together with a man dressed all in black and wearing eyeglasses. U-ri thought they might be the mustached guard's commanding officer and some sort of local official, but as Aju interpreted for her, she discovered that the man in black was a priest in the Church of the Haetlands. U-ri began waving her arms and making gestures again, occasionally saying the word "Katarhar."

"A mage that can't use magic of tongues? That's inconvenient," the officer said, rubbing his rather large belly through his uniform.

The priest smiled. "She is still young. Yet, if one skilled in the ways of magic wishes to go to the Katarhar Abbey ruins, it falls to us to do everything we can to aid her. Besides, we must reunite her with her parents."

It was decided they would take her there by carriage. She was made to wait a little longer, during which time they brought her some bread and soup. It was delicious—another stark difference between this town and the village of Kanal.

Once again, U-ri found herself riding in a carriage. This one was slightly smaller than the one before. She sat in the back, where there were only two seats. Yet two horses pulled in front, instead of the usual one. *Probably to get us up the mountain road,* U-ri decided.

The priest and yet another guard she had not seen before sat in the driver's seat in front, leaving U-ri alone in the back where she could speak freely with Aju.

"Looks like we have to head in the opposite direction first," Aju commented as the carriage raced out of the town, onto a broad thoroughfare heading north. U-ri worried that they might be going to a different place entirely, but the road soon curved several times. Soon, they were making straight for the dark mountain.

"I wonder what the people of this town think of the abbey?" U-ri wondered out loud, thinking about what the priest had said about them doing everything they could to help her get there.

"I doubt they think about it much at all. It's probably a gathering place for mages or students of magic these days—hardly their concern," Aju conjectured from his place in U-ri's hands, where he curled about himself sleepily. He did not sound overly concerned.

"Even though the place is a ruin?"

Aju shrugged. "Didn't Ash say people still went there?"

Neither of the two in the front so much as glanced back at U-ri while the carriage sped along. They stopped once to rest the horses a short while after entering the hilly forest at the foot of the mountain. U-ri got out of the carriage to stretch her legs, and the priest offered her a canteen of water. The priest said something, but Aju was back in the carriage sleeping. U-ri said she was sorry and looked as apologetic as she could. Then the priest put one hand to his chest and drew the shape of a cross on his forehead with the other. It was a slightly different cross than the Christian one, with two vertical lines and two horizontal lines. U-ri couldn't tell whether he was giving her his blessing or warding himself against some evil on the road ahead.

The carriage began to climb the mountain road, bumping as it went. The vibrations woke Aju immediately, but they could hardly speak to another. U-ri was afraid she'd bite her own tongue if she tried to talk, so violently the carriage swayed. The road angled upwards steeply and was very narrow. Rocks littered the ground. The two in the driver's seat ahead were rigid, clinging to railings on the sides for dear life. U-ri hit the back of her head on the carriage window several times.

The forest covering the mountainside was thick, though individually, the trees seemed very thin. Dry clumps of leaves clung to broken branches.

Fallen leaves followed their carriage, drawn into the road by the wind of their passage. Several came fluttering in through the window. The leaves were a pale green color, and they crinkled and disintegrated when U-ri grabbed them and squeezed them between her fingers.

The higher they went, the narrower and darker the road became. The priest lit the lantern hanging off to one side of the driver's platform. Up in front, the horses whinnied with exertion.

When they suddenly broke free from the dense forest into a flat clearing, it felt like they were emerging from a long, dark tunnel. U-ri turned around, grabbing the railing with both hands to look out.

U-ri had never seen ruins before, and she wasn't entirely sure she was seeing then now. About the only thing standing was a tall stone wall about U-ri's height that circled the site of the abbey proper.

The most remarkable features of the mountaintop were the giant, jagged rocks lying about everywhere. All of them were the same smoky gray color, with occasional blotches of darker sandstone here and there, all different shapes and sizes.

"I'll bet all of those were one rock once," Aju whispered. "It's like a giant boulder fell right on top of the abbey, hitting it so hard the rock itself broke into pieces."

U-ri looked around, eyes wide, and she had to agree with the mouse. Next to where the carriage had stopped was a fallen pillar of some sort with a lantern on it. It made something like an arched entranceway where it leaned against another pillar, leaving a gap through which a person could pass.

Someone came out just then, a man dressed in black. He stooped under the arch and blinked in the sunlight beyond. His clothes looked very similar to those of the nameless monks, though his head wasn't shaven. Also, where the nameless devout wore no jewelry or accoutrements of any kind, this man had a rosary-like ring of beads around his neck.

The guard stepped off the carriage and began to talk with the man in black. The priest turned and helped U-ri down.

"We've arrived," the priest announced brightly, though he was clearly wary of his surroundings. His eyes darted back and forth. "I hope your parents are here somewhere. Though, even if you've missed each other, your magic should work here in order to contact them. I'm sure your parents are capable of such a feat if they found it within their abilities to teach one as young as you."

The negotiations between the man in black and the guard completed, she was now in the man's keeping. He extended a hand to her, and pulling her close, he whispered in her ear. "Your companions have been waiting for you."

I understood him. He speaks my language!

The guard and the priest exchanged a few brief words with the man again; then they jumped back onto the carriage, gave the reins a tug, and headed back down the mountain road so fast they could have been fleeing.

"I am a caretaker of this abbey," the man said by way of introduction. "My name is Saulo. It is an honor to have you here, Lady *Allcaste*." Saulo bowed reverently. His hair was white, and his face was weathered and jagged, but his eyes were gentle, his voice warm.

U-ri spotted the vestments of protection draped over his arm.

She sighed with relief. "Ash must have hung on to them!"

Saulo held up the vestments for her, and U-ri hurriedly slipped her arms through the sleeves.

"We are glad you made it."

As soon as she had on the vestments, a wave of relief passed over U-ri. She was impressed she had made it to the abbey on her own.

"Ash told me you would be fine on your own. Your servant, however, was very worried, I'm afraid."

"Why should he have been? I was with her the whole time," Aju squeaked, sticking out his nose.

Saulo did not seem startled by the talking mouse in the least. "And you must be the dictionary."

"Do you know Ash?"

Saulo smiled and nodded. "There will be time to talk of that in a bit. Please, come into our hall."

Leading U-ri by the hand, the man walked across the rubble. Though the ruins seemed almost impassable at first glance, when she looked closer, U-ri spotted the signs of wear that come with frequent human passage. They were on a proper path. Even still, they had to duck under fallen pillars and clamber over crumbled sections of wall, and nowhere could she get a view of the ruins as a whole.

Saulo walked ahead of her now; then suddenly the path dipped downward and the man turned briefly to warn U-ri to watch her step. U-ri had assumed they were going down into a cellar of some sort, except nothing about the passage looked man-made at all. There were no steps, nor a ladder, to be seen. From the feel of the rock beneath her feet, she guessed they were heading into some sort of naturally formed cavern.

Keeping one hand on the wall for balance, U-ri walked quickly so as not to fall too far behind. The tunnel twisted from side to side, always going down. While at first the way had been so narrow that U-ri could reach out her hands and touch the walls on either side, the tunnel became wider as she descended. Soon side passages started appearing, as did chairs that had been carved out of the rock walls here and there, next to tiny ledges upon which candles burned. The light of their flickering flames glimmered off of the smooth walls of the tunnel. Saulo stopped and waved for U-ri to join him. She walked up until she stood by his side.

"Wow…" U-ri breathed as she always did when truly amazed. Her voice was almost reluctant to leave her mouth.

She stood on the cusp of a giant, naturally formed hall, with a floor like an inverted ziggurat, descending into a sea of darkness marked by countless pinpoints of candlelight. The hall looked big enough to hold U-ri's entire elementary school and then some. The path they were on went around it in a descending spiral so deep U-ri couldn't see the bottom from where she stood.

Bridges wide enough for a man to pass crossed the hall in both directions, shortcuts linking side passages that opened in the cavern walls. A line of men dressed just like Saulo—in black with beads around their necks—was crossing one of those bridges. Some of them carried weighty tomes, others carried bottles. One stopped midway across the bridge, holding up a light to look in their direction. U-ri brought her hands together and lowered her head.

"This cavern was mostly unused while the Katarhar Abbey still stood," Saulo explained. He peered down into the depths of the cavern. His voice sounded weak, drawn off into the empty space. There were no echoes here. "When the abbey was destroyed, many monks fled to here, and thus were their lives spared. Scriptures, books, and valuable pieces of art from the abbey were carried here as well. More than half were saved from destruction, confiscation, and theft in this way."

That had all been thirty years ago, Saulo explained.

"The Church of the Haetlands has cracked down on sects such as ours several times throughout history, yet Katarhar Abbey's remote location meant it was spared for a longer time than most. The round of cleansing where it finally met destruction was a particularly vigorous one for the church."

"I noticed burn marks among the rubble," Aju whispered from atop U-ri's head. "Was there a fire?"

Saulo nodded. "The head abbot was taken and executed together with the more prominent monks from the abbey. In exchange, the many other monks who had been left with no place to go were allowed to dwell here in the abbey ruins—that agreement was the result of a secret contract forged between the church's inquisitors and our order. Of course, our order still had to pay the church heavily for the right to live on their old property."

"Does the church still suppress religions like yours?" U-ri asked.

"No. There is an inspection once a year, but it is only a formality."

The abbey ruins had ceased to be primarily a place of worship and now were largely used as a place to house the sick and the poor and others who had been forced to leave their land due to bad crops or other difficulties. Acknowledging this, the state church largely left the monks alone.

"However, they do not permit free passage between here and the surrounding towns and villages."

"Yes—they said some sort of barrier had been erected around the town in the foothills where I came looking for a way up the mountain."

"Ah yes, the mage-hedge." Saulo smiled. "That barrier was raised by the members of the inquisition, and our magic cannot touch it. You must be an *allcaste* to have noticed it."

"Actually," U-ri said, pointing up at her head, "it was the mouse who noticed it. I was impressed with how peaceful it seemed in the town below—they seemed very well-off there."

"We know peace here too, Lady *Allcaste*. Partially because we employ our own spells to hide the full extent of these caverns from the inspectors."

"So you don't believe in the royal lineage coming from one creator god, is that right?" U-ri asked as Saulo urged her onto the descending spiral path. The moment she set foot upon it, she found she could hear other people talking in the cavern. The scents of daily life in a village floated in the air. Steam rose from here and there in the hall. Apparently, there was quite a large number of people living here underground.

"The gods we worship are the gods of the natural world. All that is holy, all that is magic, even all that is darkness comes from nature. Thus, there are many gods whom we worship, and our gods are everywhere. There are gods even in the pebbles you might find by the roadside."

That did seem incompatible with what U-ri had heard of the Church of the Haetlands' beliefs. Though as a concept it wasn't all that unfamiliar to her.

"We have the same sort of belief in the land where I come from," she explained. "There are lots of gods, in everything, and they watch over us."

"I am glad to hear that," Saulo replied.

Atop her head, Aju squeaked. "I think I hear a familiar voice."

"The mouse has keen ears," Saulo remarked, leading them down a side tunnel that left the spiral path about a third of the way down the cavern wall. This new path was as wide as the one they left, and it divided again. They took the branch leading toward a collection of small domed buildings within another cavern ahead. There were no doors at the opening where the tunnel widened into a larger space beyond, and U-ri could see faces looking at them. Women and small children mostly. She saw crude furniture and other signs of daily life. Children were playing around the houses, and laundry hung outside the windows.

"The one you seek is there, in the room closest to the intersection," Saulo said, pointing ahead. U-ri broke into a run. Surprised people stuck their heads out of the little stone windows of the cells to watch her speed by.

"Ash! Sky!"

U-ri left the tunnel, emerging into a space much larger than she had anticipated. She ran into the house so fast she barely had room to stop herself before hitting a large wooden table. Ash was sitting at the table across from a man in black robes. The wolf was leaning on one elbow, talking. When U-ri entered, he only lifted his eyes. "—and this tomboy here is the Lady *Allcaste* who accompanies me," he finished saying.

The man in black across from Ash looked in her direction. U-ri's mouth hung open. He was incredibly handsome.

He smiled, stood from his chair, and bowed.

"I welcome you, *allcaste*."

CHAPTER ELEVEN

Confessions

U-ri blushed bright red. She could feel the color rise in her cheeks.

"What are you staring at?" Ash asked with a smirk.

She ignored him. U-ri had eyes only for the handsome man in black sitting in front of her. She bent one knee slightly, gathered up the hem of her skirts, and curtsied like a ballerina.

"M-my name's U-ri."

"And I am Latore. I am the doctor here in the abbey."

She guessed that the handsome doctor was slightly younger than Ash. He was tall, with clear eyes that looked out from beneath thick black hair.

"Please, be seated," he said, pulling out a chair for her. "I'm glad you made it here all right. We were worried."

U-ri sat down in as ladylike a manner as she could manage.

"We didn't have to worry. Aju was with her," Ash grumbled. He didn't seem to be in the best of moods, but U-ri found she didn't particularly care. "You pull your own weight out there, rat?"

Aju stuck his nose out from U-ri's collar and bared his tiny teeth. "If you'd held on to me a little harder we wouldn't have gotten separated in the first place!"

They started to argue, but U-ri didn't hear a word. *I've never seen anyone this handsome. And not just handsome, but smart, and kind, and strong...*

Unconsciously, U-ri leaned forward, which was when she noticed Dr. Latore had purple eyes—though much lighter than Sky's. She remembered how Sky's had looked that one time, like violets blooming in the springtime sun. That was how the doctor's eyes looked right now.

"I heard you came from Tato. They are not fond of strangers in that town. Nor do they get many travelers coming through. I hope your welcome there was not too unpleasant."

U-ri shook her head dreamily, only lowering her eyes when she noticed the doctor beginning to blush.

"W-we were fine," she squeaked, her voice as high as Aju's.

"I've never heard of an *allcaste* who was this much trouble."

Ignoring Ash's remark, U-ri straightened out her skirts, lowered her eyes, and rested her hands on her knees. "A kind person informed the town guardsmen, and as soon as they heard where it was I was heading, they arranged for a carriage—"

"That wasn't kindness," Ash cut in. "The people in Tato want nothing to do with the mountain or anyone associated with it."

"Not that the mountain was all that welcoming either," Aju squeaked back. "You felt it too, didn't you? We hit a mage-barrier on our way in. Knocked us right out of the sky, it did. And someone was shouting at us, telling us to stay away. Who was that?"

The wolf and the doctor exchanged glances. The kind smile faded from the doctor's face. "Perhaps I should arrange a meeting," the doctor said to Ash.

"If time and circumstances allow," Ash replied.

"Very well," Dr. Latore said, standing. "We should go quickly, then. If warding magic's been used, there might be some…difficulties."

"We are ready," Ash said.

Dr. Latore bid them farewell and quickly left. U-ri followed him with her eyes. She had wanted to speak with the doctor longer. Actually, she didn't need to talk. She would be happy just staring at him. "What are you talking about, and what's the big rush?" she asked, turning to Ash.

"I'll explain when the time is right."

"Why not now?"

"This is why I don't like working with girls," Ash growled, not bothering to mask his displeasure at all now that they were alone. "Try thinking about my position for a change, instead of pining over that physician."

"But he was so nice…" U-ri said with a sigh. She liked seeing Ash so visibly annoyed. *Maybe he's more human than I thought.* U-ri grinned inwardly. She decided to change the subject. "With a doctor and all, this is really a proper town, isn't it? How many live here? One hundred? More?"

"I'm not sure exactly. They're not eager for anyone to know. I do know that the monks alone number eighty in all—" Ash frowned at U-ri. "You seem unreasonably taken with this cave, so let me be frank. This is not a happy place or even a pleasant one. The people here—"

"Are poor, or sick, or homeless," U-ri said, cutting him off. "Saulo told us on the way in. I saw children too."

"Orphans, for the most part."

"You seem to know a lot about this place, Ash. And Dr. Latore…"

Ash furrowed his brow, his mood still as dark as the low ceiling above them. "There are people here like Udsu, the springfoot you met in Kanal. No other place will take them in. They are driven out, chased, hunted, until they find this place. And here they die. Down in this cave far below the ground." Ash shook his head. "And when they die, they need to be buried. That's where I come in."

U-ri nodded, understanding entirely. Udsu was going to die. The flush left her cheeks.

"There is a graveyard on the very bottom level of this cavern. I am the undertaker there as well."

"I see—" U-ri began, when she heard a voice calling quietly, "Lady Allcaste."

She looked around and saw two bookshelves standing in a corner of the room. She seemed to be in a sort of living room. There were paintings on the walls and flowers—probably dried, given that they were far from any sunlight—in a vase on the table.

"I'll go say hi," Aju offered. He hopped from U-ri's shoulder and quickly scampered up the bookshelf. The books with their old, cracked bindings tittered as the mouse's tail brushed their spines. U-ri smiled in their direction and bowed curtly in greeting.

"That reminds me," she said, turning to the wolf. "Where's Sky? He was with you, wasn't he?" U-ri felt a sudden chill run down her spine. What if Sky had fallen someplace else, apart from all of them?

"He's been down in the infirmary, playing nurse," Ash told her, his tone as cold as it always was whenever he spoke of the nameless devout.

Why does he have to be so mean to him all the time?

"He said he couldn't sit still, he was so worried about you. At first he was determined to go searching for you himself. Saulo had to stop him. Your servant gave the man no end of trouble."

"I'm sure Sky was very concerned! He's supposed to be, you know." U-ri stood. "I'm going to look for him. Where is this infirmary?"

"Leave him be. We don't have time for—"

"I'll be right back, promise!" U-ri shouted, dashing out the door. *What's his problem?* She wanted to see Sky as soon as she could. She couldn't imagine how distraught the poor fellow must've been this whole time, separated from the person he was supposed to protect. She ran down the spiral path, her vestments billowing out behind her.

The further down she went, the more people she saw. With their sunken eyes and thin faces, the residents of the subterranean abbey couldn't have been more different from the people U-ri had encountered on the streets of Tato. The only ones walking with any pep at all were the black-robed monks. They were the only ones who weren't startled to see her. Everyone else froze, eyes wide, sometimes even backing away from her, fear plain in their eyes.

There were two infirmaries in the complex, one on either side of the large passage in which she now stood. She looked in one room, but Sky was nowhere to be seen. Instead, she found a boy sitting in a bed, crying. A monk with a vial of medicine was stroking the child's hair, muttering something in a low, soothing voice. The child's mother was there too, crying along with her boy. There were some others in the room—all women and children, lying on wooden pallets jammed in so close together that the monks had to walk sideways like crabs to get between them.

The scent of blood and something worse hung in the air. She started to walk out when someone grabbed her wrist. U-ri shook herself free and whirled around to see an old woman lying on a bed by the door. The woman drew her hand back as though U-ri had bit it, and shrank from her.

"I-I'm sorry," U-ri stammered. "I didn't hurt you, did I?" U-ri knelt down by the woman, her nostrils filling with the smell of medicine and the old woman's own stench. She was terribly frail, and going bald. What little hair she had left was of the purest white. One of her eyelids was closed, and a membrane the color of curdled milk obscured her other eye.

"Please help me," the old woman said, her tongue thick in her mouth. She had lost most of her teeth, and her lips were cracked and blistered.

Swallowing the fear she felt, U-ri took the old woman's hand in her own. "Please, don't get excited, you need to stay calm. You'll be all right. A doctor will be with you soon." U-ri fled.

Outside, she leaned up against the corridor wall, putting a hand over her racing heart to keep it from beating out of her chest. U-ri gasped. The glyph on her forehead was warm—hot, even. She hurriedly touched it and felt its heat slowly fade beneath her palm.

Something has awakened it.

U-ri lowered her palm in front of her face and stared at it. She wondered if it could heal disease like it had healed the man possessed by the unattached back in Tato.

Can you?

She pressed her hand to her forehead again. There was no reaction from the glyph this time.

Guess not. Or maybe I can, but I shouldn't. Is that why you're being quiet, glyph?

"Lady U-ri!" The voice was Sky's. U-ri whirled around so fast she almost lost her balance. Sky was standing in the entrance of the small dwelling just behind her. His eyes and mouth were open wide. Sky spread his arms in greeting, and U-ri ran into them, shouting his name over and over. Sky received her standing stiff as a board, completely unprepared for her enthusiasm.

U-ri barreled into him, and they both toppled over with a loud crash on the floor. The sleeves of their black robes tangled. When she realized what she had done, U-ri shrieked and extricated herself. She scrambled to her feet, mortified. "Sky! What are you doing?"

Sky sat on the ground, dazed.

"Are you all right?"

"Lady U-ri—" The devout's eyes regained their focus and he picked himself up, but he did not stand. Instead he crouched down on his knees and began to bow. "I beg your forgiveness. I could not be with you. I have endangered the *allcaste*."

The devout's bald head rubbed against the floor. U-ri stood there, flustered. People further down the corridor had stopped to stare at them. Behind her one of the black-robed monks had come out of the infirmary to see what was the matter.

"Never mind that, just get up. You don't have to bow to me like that, especially not here." She grabbed Sky's arm and managed to drag him to his knees. He seemed unwilling to stand, so she crouched down to his level and stared him in the eye. "As you can see, I'm fine. Aju was with me the whole time. We had a bit of an adventure, actually. I'm glad we fell where we did. We were in a town called Tato. Oh, Sky, it was so beautiful—"

U-ri snapped her mouth shut. The devout's eyes were filled with tears.

"You were worried, weren't you? I'm sorry."

"No, it is I who should apologize. I have failed you," Sky said. He touched a finger to his wet cheek and hurriedly turned away.

He's crying. This empty "nothing" is crying. It's because he's not empty. He's not a nameless devout anymore. He has a name, and that's Sky. I'm not just imagining this.

U-ri took Sky's hand. Then she realized something. Something so big, she nearly yelped when it hit her. "Sky! When I was down in Tato, you were here looking after these people, right? They told me you wanted to go look for me, but they stopped you."

Sky nodded, his head hanging in shame.

U-ri pointed at herself. "That means that you had a form, Sky, even though I wasn't nearby. You had a body. You could walk around and do things just like normal people, couldn't you? And everyone around you could see you! I'm right, aren't I?"

Sky's purple eyes went wide, and his mouth gaped open again. U-ri's mouth was open too, and the two stared at each other like that for some time.

"Right?"

"You...are right." In a daze, the devout touched his own body as though to make sure he was really there.

"See? You are not hollow anymore! You're a person again!" U-ri declared loudly. Sky's experiences while separated from U-ri had to be proof of that.

"B-but, Lady U-ri. You might not have been here, but the vestments were. Perhaps their power lent me form."

"What? No way! The vestments of protection are just tattered old rags if you take *me* out of them. Don't even think that!" U-ri slapped Sky on his thin shoulder. The noise of the blow echoed down the hall. The devout winced.

Maybe I hit him a little too hard. That bit about the vestments being tattered old rags might have been overdoing it too.

"Ack, sorry! Sorry, Sky."

More than all that, though, U-ri was glad to be back with her friend again. And she was glad that Sky was still Sky. Her face was warm with excitement and embarrassment all mingled together. She thought she might cry.

"I think we're going to see the person Ash was telling us about, the one who might have information on how to find my brother." U-ri took Sky by the hand. "Let's get back to the others!"

For the first time, she noticed a pleasant scent hovering around him. It smelled like incense. She looked up and noticed that it wasn't just Sky who smelled good. Thin blue smoke was drifting from the dwelling behind him—the one he had just stepped out of.

"Wait. Weren't you helping in the infirmary, Sky?"

"No, actually, I—"

U-ri stepped past him and into the entranceway. The place was dimly lit, with only a few candles burning low in sconces on the walls. "This isn't an infirmary."

U-ri walked all the way in. It was a small room, carved out of the cavern wall. The walls and ceiling were all bare rock, hung with several paintings. Some of the larger ones had been too big to hang, so they sat leaning up against the walls. U-ri saw the smoke rising from a tall, round table in the center of the room. *That's where the incense is burning. But what is this place? An art gallery?*

"What were you doing in here, Sky?" U-ri asked as she slowly walked over to the table. The devout hesitated a moment at the entrance, then followed her inside.

"I was going to go back up to the others, when I lost my way—"

Lost your way? But this is right next door. U-ri was about to bring that up when another discovery pushed such thoughts out of her mind. She had gotten close enough to see the paintings in the dim light, and she realized that they were all portraits. U-ri walked up to the largest of them, the one sitting directly across from the entrance. It showed a man in silver armor with a long crimson cape flowing from his shoulders.

He's another handsome one. He was a little younger than Dr. Latore; a young warrior in his prime. And not quite the same type. Dr. Latore was what you thought of when you thought of a man—a paragon of handsomeness, maybe—but this warrior was beauty itself. Abstract, genderless, perfect beauty in human form.

U-ri guessed his age at about twenty. He had a prominent forehead and angled nose. His eyes glittered ebon black. Thick black hair fell in gentle curls down to his neck. The man's cheeks were as fresh as a baby's, adding to his youthful demeanor—marred only by a streak of silver in the hair over his right temple, like the painter had accidentally marked the portrait there with his brush.

His right hand rested on the hilt of a sword at his belt. His left hand was half-concealed beneath his cloak, but she could see a large ring on one of his fingers. The crest engraved into the ring was the same as the ones that adorned his shoulders where the cloak attached. U-ri carefully removed a candle from one of the wall sconces and brought it closer to his face.

"It *is* the same crest."

Behind her, Sky spoke. "It is the sigil of House Dijkstra."

"Who are they?"

Sky stepped up to stand next to her in front of the oversized portrait. "Kirrick's birth family."

U-ri's eyes opened wider, and the candle in her hand tilted. A drip of melted wax fell on the ground by her feet. "You mean—"

"This is a portrait of Kirrick Roth, twelfth count of the House Dijkstra, painted on the occasion of his first battle at the age of nineteen."

U-ri blinked. So this was he. Leader of the rebellion, commander of an army of the dead, and Ash's half brother. The cursed hero.

"It is said that the rightful heir of House Dijkstra is always born with a streak of silver hair over his right temple. This is the proof of their legitimacy."

U-ri stared unblinking at the portrait. After a short while, she took a few slow steps backward to glance at the others. There was one of a newborn baby, wrapped in white swaddling clothes. And another of a young boy standing with a dog beneath a tree. A strong boy, with ruddy cheeks—

"All of the paintings here are of Kirrick. This gallery is a record of his growth from infant to man."

"But why keep them? Didn't Kirrick's rebellion end in tragedy?"

Sky replaced the candle in the sconce. "On account of his undead army, Kirrick lost favor in the capital as quickly as he had won it. Those who blamed him most loudly were the nobles and members of parliament loyal to the old royal line, those who had clung to their riches and authority before Kirrick brought them down. Under pressure from them to act, Kirrick led a small force down to deal with the creatures spawned from his army—and they never returned."

Though he had no choice in the matter, when he left the palace, Kirrick had gone from being the new king to being a traitor of the state. His enemies in the capital made it so. And those who dragged him from his throne in the end had plenty of justifications for what they did, what with Kirrick so newly arrived to a power he had gained by means dark and questionable. A few whispered words in the right ears, and Kirrick went from being a hero to being the source of all the kingdom's woes in the space of a fortnight.

Kirrick was forced to flee before he could bring the creatures under control, and eventually his enemies killed him.

"But his change of fate in the eleventh hour was the doing of highly placed supporters of the royal family in the capital. The populace still loved and supported Kirrick throughout. He had begun his rebellion to free them from oppression, after all, and though the king who replaced him branded him a traitor and hunted him down throughout the land, there were those who aided and harbored him before he met his end."

U-ri walked quietly in front of the five portraits, looking carefully at each. "So the Katarhar Abbey was on his side, then."

"That is correct. Even today, they revere him as a hero of the people, as a king who would have brought peace were it not for the tragedy that befell him. This is Kirrick's room, Lady U-ri."

U-ri imagined the monks carrying the portraits here during the wave of religious suppression thirty years ago. Why would they have bothered, if they didn't still revere Kirrick's memory?

"It seems like they could have put his portraits up in a more appropriate place. Why here, across from the infirmary?"

Sky smiled. "I believe it is because Kirrick always stood on the side of the weak, and who is weaker than the very old and the very ill?"

U-ri smiled back at him. She felt sorrow for Kirrick, an almost physical pain in her chest, though seeing the portraits hung here did much to ease that. "Let's go." U-ri turned to the portrait one last time and curtsied before leaving the room. She returned with Sky to the living room above where she had first met the doctor. Ash was standing in the back, facing the bookshelves. When they came in, he turned, a sour look on his face. "Where were you?"

"I'm sorry. I got lost."

Aju was up on top of one of the shelves. "The books here say they want to talk to you, U-ri. We have a little time, don't we? Please, Ash?"

That's not like Aju to ask permission. I wonder what's up?

U-ri walked over to the shelves, and the tightly packed books began to wink and glimmer at her.

"Protector of the Circle, great Tuner of the Chords. Young Bearer of the Glyph, Apostle of the Good Light. You who bear the Providence of the Seal. Lady *Allcaste*—" a chorus of voices called out in greeting. All of them were glimmering more brightly now, the light illuminating U-ri's face. "Welcome to the Haetlands. Welcome to Katarhar."

"Thank you," U-ri curtsied, a little taken aback. *What was all that they just said? Something about bearing providence?* She wasn't sure she had caught the meaning of everything—she only knew she had never heard anyone greet her quite so formally before.

"Lady *Allcaste*." The chorus had now become a single voice, that of an old woman. "We of the Katarhar Abbey are linked to the Hero's escape through ties that go back many centuries. Ties as thick as living blood and as deep as the abyss at the Circle's end. Lady *Allcaste*, we would lend you our wisdom, through your sage, Aju, if you would have it. Please use it as you see fit."

Aju's nose twitched proudly. "They taught me lots, U-ri. Learned some new spells too."

"That's...that's great, Aju."

Ash had left the bookshelves and was leaning up against the rock wall by the entranceway, his arms crossed. His face was stern, his gaze almost painfully sharp.

"Th-this is my servant, Sky."

Sky turned to the bookshelves and bowed curtly. The glimmering of the books faded, their winking becoming more sporadic—like someone frowning at an unfamiliar sight.

Sky's expression was hard. For some reason, though the light from the shelves fell on them the same, in it his cheeks looked pale, his skin tightly drawn across the bones of his face, casting strange, hollow shadows.

"We were about to—" U-ri began, when the old woman's voice interrupted her.

"We know where you go, Lady *Allcaste*."

U-ri thought she sensed the books shiver, as a person does when saying something they are reluctant to admit.

"Be strong, Lady *Allcaste*. You must be strong. And patient."

"Huh?"

What's that supposed to mean? And why is Aju nervously scratching at his nose?

"What connection does Katarhar Abbey have with the Hero's escape? You said there were old ties, from a long time ago. What did you mean?"

Just then she heard the sound of hurried footsteps on the path outside. It was Dr. Latore.

"Are we all met?" the doctor asked, striding into the room. He turned to Ash. "He's calmer now. Says he won't try to run and hide, now that the time's come."

"How generous of him," Ash said, standing up from the wall. "We are off, U-ri. Time for your audience," he said.

Ash was brimming with energy. By comparison, Dr. Latore looked positively dejected. He stood with his shoulders slumped, staring blankly toward the back of the room.

"Am I going to meet the person with information about my brother?"

"That's right. Try to keep up for once," the wolf growled as he strode toward the doorway.

U-ri stepped away from the bookshelves, trying to figure out what was going on. Why was everything so mysterious all of a sudden? Why wasn't anyone telling her anything?

"Do I know everything I need to know?" she asked the room. "If there's something else, you think you could tell me now? Please?" U-ri ran her fingers along the spines of the books on the shelf.

Aju hopped lightly on her shoulder. "Don't worry, U-ri. They told me everything we'll need. Let's just get going."

"You know what's going on too, don't you! Tell me!"

"You'll see for yourself soon enough. I think that's better than me telling you, anyway."

The more she heard, the more confused she became. And afraid.

I'm afraid. I'm really afraid!

260

Ash strode across the room, grabbed U-ri by the arm and pulled. "Enough of this!"

"No, Master Ash. Stop," Sky said, moving to step between them.

"You stay out of this!" Ash roared. He violently shouldered the devout out of the way.

"Hey, don't do that to Sky!" U-ri shouted, her anger rising. U-ri thrust forward with her arms, pushing Ash away from her. Still not satisfied, she lifted her hands and charged. *I'm going to hit him, or scratch him, or bite him, or I don't know what—*

"U-ri!" Aju squealed from her shoulder.

U-ri swung her hands down at Ash, but they stopped inches away from the wolf's face. Ash's hands gripped her tightly by the wrists. She couldn't move either arm.

"If you are an *allcaste*, why don't you start acting like one? Miserable child," Ash growled in a low voice. He flung her away, sending U-ri staggering into the arms of the nameless devout. The two stared at each other across the room.

"Lady *Allcaste*," the old woman's voice said tearfully, "please, you must follow the wolf for now. You must go to meet the one who waits for you in the depths of Katarhar."

U-ri spoke to the voice, though her eyes stayed fixed on Ash. "I noticed you books went dim when Sky bowed to you. You don't like him either, do you? Maybe you know why Ash seems so bent on making Sky's life miserable. He's been like this from the start! All high and mighty, and cruel to Sky—and now he's keeping important things from me!"

"It's all right, Lady U-ri," Sky said from behind her. "It's all right. I—"

"No it's *not* all right! Not until I say it is. You be quiet, Sky."

"U-ri," said a quiet voice. Someone grabbed her by the elbow and gently pulled her away. It was Dr. Latore. She hadn't even noticed him come into the room. "We must go. There is little time."

U-ri stood there with her mouth in a pout, ready to retort even though she had no idea what she might say, but the doctor's eyes fixed on her. "It will not be in the proper state for you to speak with it for much longer."

"It?" U-ri gasped. *What's this now? I thought we were going to see a person, not an it!*

U-ri swallowed her outburst and let herself be led from the room. Dr. Latore turned to Sky. "You will stay here. Please. For U-ri's sake."

U-ri didn't see how Sky could be any better informed than she was about all this, but he simply nodded and withdrew. In fact, he stepped back so fast, he hit the bookshelves behind him. The books blinked and glimmered like fireflies caught by a sudden rain.

Ash walked silently ahead. The three had gone a ways down the path when U-ri turned to Dr. Latore. "I'm sorry. I won't act that way again."

The doctor smiled at her. But it wasn't the kind of smile that had charmed her the first time they'd met. There was sorrow in his eyes now, and U-ri could see it.

Ash walked swiftly, apparently familiar with the twists and turns of the cavern's many paths. Dr. Latore walked behind U-ri, who occasionally had to jog a little to keep up with the wolf.

The three of them were alone. Aju had protested loudly when Ash said he couldn't go either. The wolf had scooped him up and for a moment it looked like he was going to toss the little mouse against the wall. U-ri had run to stop him, but for some reason, it was Sky who talked her down. Aju would remain with him and the books. It was better that way.

Now that she was actually walking down to the bottom of the catacombs, it seemed far more distant than she had imagined it would be from the top. As they passed down the levels, the candles along the walls that lit their way were replaced by torches. And they were fewer and farther between—though U-ri didn't notice that so much as she noticed the increasingly large pools of darkness around them. A railing ran down the path along the inside edge, and when she peered over it, all she could see were flickering torches burning below. There were few monks down this far, and fewer residents.

"In the lowest levels, there are solitary chambers for the gravely ill. That's where we're headed now," Dr. Latore informed her.

"Solitary chambers?"

"Dmitri has told you of the creatures that rose from Kirrick's undead army, and the venom they carry?"

U-ri nodded, slowing her pace. They had been walking so quickly she had to catch her breath.

"Once the poisoning makes itself known, the victims do not live long. Yet, in their remaining days, they often become quite violent. It falls to us to protect the other patients, and the victims themselves, from harm. Thus the solitary chambers. We might say that their maladies are the side effects of the magic used to raise the dead."

U-ri blinked, surprised to hear the doctor use the same kind of medical language doctors in her world used.

"Because the venom is magical in nature, medicine is of little use in its treatment. We must rely on magical means ourselves."

"Has any progress been made in countering the venom's effects?"

The doctor shook his head. "Once men have set their hearts on a path, they can be very passionate about making progress—but should their direction change, or the need arise to backtrack, they find themselves far less prepared than they were before."

U-ri thought she understood what he meant.

"Even if they did find a way to cure the venom's effects now, it would be of little benefit to the royal house or the nobles. I'm sure things work the same in your world, lady U-ri. There are few who would devote their time and efforts to something that bears no reward of riches or power."

Though his tone remained gentle, U-ri realized that Dr. Latore was criticizing the mages of the Haetlands, and harshly.

Finally the three arrived at the lowest level. A large pair of torches stood at the bottom of the descending spiral path. All above them was dark. Sparks flew up from the torches, ascending along with the smoke into the blackness over their heads.

Once again, U-ri felt herself growing afraid. It occurred to her that if for some reason she never made it out of this place, she would never again see the light of day. She tried to banish the thought from her head, but could not.

"The cavern sides do not fall straight down," Ash said, wiping a lock of sweaty hair off his forehead. "The entire cavern slants gently, you see. Perhaps you noticed it on the way down?"

She hadn't. U-ri shook her head.

"To use a metaphor you might understand, think of it as an ant colony."

That did seem to fit with what she had seen—the countless side passages and innumerable rooms. It was a bit like a giant ant colony. She had seen a picture of one in her biology class.

"We should show our respect to the monks of Katarhar that made this place livable for men. No matter how dark it was, or how stifling the air, these caves are homes now thanks to their work. We may be underground, but this is no underworld. For many people, this is the only place they can live a free life. The only place they are safe. So don't look so glum," Ash concluded. "You do a disservice to the glyph upon your forehead."

Ash smiled wryly, and U-ri understood he was trying to cheer her up in his own way. She lightly touched her fingers to her mark. For a brief moment, it flashed white in the darkness. She felt a faint warmth beneath her fingertips. It was a vote of confidence. The glyph was urging her onward.

"In the place where we now go, you may see and hear things that surprise you, even terrify you. But you must not despair. You understand?"

"Remember that the people who live here have come here of their own free will, Lady U-ri."

U-ri nodded, and Dr. Latore stepped forward, removing a large ring of keys from beneath his cloak. The ring was silver, and the keys on it too numerous for her to count. It looked heavy.

"This way."

He walked toward a wide opening in one of the rock walls. A tunnel led from there, its entrance barred by an iron gate. Dr. Latore turned his key in the large lock, and a small section of bars opened outward. "Please watch your step."

There were no side passages in this tunnel. Holes in the wall opened directly onto small rooms. Each of the openings was barred by an iron gate similar to the one at the entrance. The torches from the cavern outside were gone—the main source of light here came from candles stuck directly onto bent nails that protruded from the rock face. Tears of wax ran down the walls beneath each of them, all the way down to the floor of the passage where they formed white misshapen lumps. It was cold down here. A layer of chill air drifted along by her feet.

All the rooms they passed were empty, save for some crude wooden sleeping pallets. There were no occupants.

"We have our hands full with one special guest at the moment. All the other patients have been moved to higher levels." Keys in hand, Dr. Latore took the lead. They walked a bit farther, until they came to another iron gate blocking the passage ahead. He opened it. Beyond that was another gate.

So that's why he needs all those keys. But I wonder why they need all these gates?

U-ri felt herself tense. Her feet were moving more slowly now. Fear made her breath come in shallow gulps. She wished Sky had come. She wished Aju was there to make wisecracks and cheer her up.

"Do not be afraid," Dr. Latore said, looking over his shoulder at U-ri. "There is no one here you need fear, Lady U-ri."

Just then, a heavy creaking sound came from farther inside the cavern. It was the kind of sound you might hear when pushing open an old door with broken rust-covered hinges. Or the sound a coffin lid might make when opened for the first time in a hundred years.

The three stopped in their tracks. U-ri shivered as a sudden realization hit her. *That's not a sound. It's a voice.*

A chill ran down her spine. U-ri turned and fled. *I can't take it. I need to get out of this place! I can't stay here, not for another moment!*

She slammed into the iron portcullis behind them with her entire body, fumbling clumsily for the handle to the smaller door. Her knees buckled, cold sweat streaked down her back, her eyes filled with tears.

"Lady U-ri!" Dr. Latore was calling to her.

U-ri didn't care. *Nothing I need to fear, my foot!*

Again the voice drifted from the cavern ahead. This time it was louder. She could make it out more clearly. It sounded like someone, or really, *something*, groaning.

U-ri finally managed to open the small doorway in the gate. She crouched down, yet still managed to hit her head as she stumbled through to the other side, when she heard the voice groan a third time, the sound echoing off the ceiling and walls of the narrow tunnel, chasing after her.

"Yur...U-ri."

U-ri froze.

"U-ri."

That rasping voice in the depths of the cave was calling out to *her*. Gripping the bars of the gate, U-ri looked up. She could easily imagine how she must look: like a ghost, all the color drained from her features. *If a real ghost saw me, I'd probably scare it to death. Again.*

"I'm sorry...U-ri."

U-ri stopped breathing, her mouth open. The chill air of the cavern stabbed at her throat. She began to cough, doubling over with the exertion. Dr. Latore walked back to her and patted her gently on the back.

"He wants to meet you. No, he has to meet you—he's been steeling himself for this just as you have," Ash said. "He's even apologized for knocking us out of the sky with that barrier."

U-ri clung to him, standing up with his support. A tear streaked down her cheek. "You mean he's the one that told me to stay away?"

Ash nodded. Dr. Latore kept patting her on the back, trying to rub out the chills.

Is it my brother?

A strange mixture of hope and fear froze the question in her throat before she could even form it, but Ash seemed to understand all the same.

"No," the wolf said calmly. "It is not your brother."

Dr. Latore shook his head. The lump in U-ri's throat unfroze, and she felt like she could move again.

"This is just a clue to guide you along your path, U-ri. He is not Hiroki Morisaki, nor his remains. I've said this many times. You—" Ash's voice dropped lower and became even more stern. "You need to learn how to listen better to others. As you are now, you hear nothing and think less. You are drowning in your own emotions; they toss you this way and that, like a leaf in the wind."

It would have been an unfair criticism of an elementary school girl. But U-ri wasn't a little girl anymore. She lowered her head and let him speak.

"I'm sorry."

U-ri passed back through the gate and returned to stand next to the wolf, her head hanging.

Dr. Latore's large, warm hand touched U-ri's shoulder. The voice moaned her name again, louder than before. She could make out the word more clearly this time.

It's crying, she thought. *Whatever it is—imprisoned here in this cavern of its own free will—it's crying.*

U-ri strained her eyes and looked through the darkness there beneath the earth, the treacherously flickering candle her only source of light.

The voice was still crying in short, wet sobs. U-ri felt another emotion enter her now—along the same pathway, now thawed, that had kept her from asking her question aloud by the gate. It was an emotion she could not name, or well express, even as it filled her chest and stabbed at her heart.

I pity you.

U-ri walked deeper into the cavern. Dr. Latore lifted an eyebrow, then followed after her. They came to another gate, and he stepped ahead, unlocking a padlock the size of a child's fist to open it. "This is the last lock I will open. There is one more gate beyond, but it remains closed."

U-ri went to the gate.

A bent nail protruded from the rock face directly in front of her, on which was stuck the remains of a single candle, still burning, but so weakly it looked like it might flicker out at any moment.

All of the candles up until now had been affixed to the side walls. This was the first one she had seen straight ahead.

This is the end. The deepest part of the depths.

She turned her head slowly to look off to the right, where the cavern seemed to extend further. Her feet shifted beneath her until she was facing a final set of bars hanging in the gloom, just at the edge of the tiny circle of light cast by the candle. Utter darkness swallowed everything outside that. The sobbing she heard coming from beyond the bars stopped. The cavern was silent, save for U-ri's own quick, ragged breaths. Even those she heard not with her ears, but internally. The sound seemed contained within her body. Outside her body, everything was quiet and dark, dark, dark.

Then there was a rustling of cloth. Dr. Latore came in through the gate behind her. U-ri was surprised to notice Ash standing next to her on the other side. She hadn't even seen him come through, and he made no sound. He was like an image with no physical presence, a hologram.

"Gulg," Ash called through the bars in front of them. "I've brought her."

Did the darkness just shift, or am I seeing things?

Ash chuckled. "Actually, I take that back. She came here by herself. She came here to see you. She wants to know where her brother's gone. So stop making things difficult and talk to her."

Now she was sure the darkness was moving. U-ri squinted and was able to make out a vague outline. Whatever it was, it was huge.

"*Gulg!*" Ash called out again. He sighed. "Weep here for another century if you like. Nothing will be resolved, and nothing new will begin. This is your best chance to atone for what you've done. Miss this moment, and you will never be saved, not for an eternity. You know that."

From someplace near the floor came the sound of something wet sliding across stone. A memory rose in U-ri's mind, jarringly out of place. Her mother was washing the whole family's blankets. She did it once every year, using a special detergent for wool and lots of fabric softener. U-ri had helped her. It was hard keeping the blankets from falling on the ground. It had taken both of them just to pull the things out of the washing machine—

"Master Gulg," Dr. Latore joined Ash. "Please."

"Perhaps he objects to his new name," Ash remarked, a sharpness to his voice. "We could call you by your original name, Ichiro Minochi."

U-ri's eyes went wide. She took a step back. Behind her, the candle on the wall sizzled, sending up a plume of inky smoke.

"Ichiro Minochi?" *My great-uncle? The one who owned the cottage in the mountains? The eccentric, rich hermit who traveled the world in search of ancient books is here?*

U-ri knew him only by his name. She had never seen his face. Up until the previous year, she hadn't even known he existed. Of course she knew more about Ichiro Minochi now than she had ever wanted to. About how he had been trying to raise the dead, and how he had obtained the Book of Elem.

A face loomed up, pale and white behind the bars. It appeared so quickly, and so low to the ground—about the height of U-ri's knees—that U-ri gasped and practically jumped out of her skin.

She could see his face clearly from the hairline down.

It was that of an old man—Japanese, with streaks of white in his eyebrows. His cheeks were sunken, the skin dry, and the flesh below his drooping eyes and around his mouth was torn and scarred.

But his eyes were the bright eyes of a boy in his tenth summer looking up at a cotton candy cloud scudding through a blue sky. Red veins ran through the bloodshot whites—it was his pupils that were islands of youth, floating amidst an aged face. Tears began to streak down his thin cheeks, leaving his skin red and sore where they passed.

"Great-uncle?" U-ri called out, and the old man's face fell even closer to the floor, his eyes cast downward in shame.

"You're really Ichiro Minochi?" U-ri said. "I'm Yuriko, your brother's granddaughter."

U-ri took a step forward, then hunched over to get nearer to the face. She reached out a hand and her fingers touched the bars in front of her. She grabbed one. Then she knelt even lower. She had to in order to look Minochi in the eye.

"I'd heard that you were dead. They said you died in France—but you left our region and came here, to the Haetlands. Why? I've been to the cottage, and your reading room. They're just as you left them."

Minochi receded into the cavern. The darkness swallowed his face. There came another sound like something heavy and wet scraping across the floor, and the tiny choking sound of a man holding back sobs.

U-ri pressed her forehead to the bars. "I know that you had the Book of Elem. After you disappeared, my family visited your cottage in the mountains, and we found the reading room. That's where my brother found the book. The Hero got him, Mr. Minochi. My brother became the last vessel."

U-ri heard more weeping from the darkness, coming from a spot just above the floor. The sound seemed to creep along the bottom of the cavern, wrapping itself around her ankles, traveling up her legs, then her entire body to her ears.

"I'm looking for my brother. Ash said you might have information that would help me find him. That's why I'm here. Please," U-ri said, lowering herself so she was now lying on the floor. "Please. If you know anything about where my brother might be, tell me. You know a lot about the Book of Elem, don't you? You know what happens to people who are taken by the Hero? You know how I can find my brother? What am I supposed to do? Where do I go—"

Without a word, Ash grabbed U-ri by the shoulder and pulled her away from the bars.

The pale face of the old man reappeared from the darkness. He had given up trying to hold back the tears and wept openly now. His eyelids were red and swollen.

"I'm sorry."

The dry lips opened and he spoke. His face floated closer to U-ri, then quickly drew away. U-ri smelled something in the air, a musty, raw stench. *What is that? His breath?* It smelled like the old fishing net wrapped around a rotting post at the corner of a dock she had discovered on a trip with her parents to the aquarium the summer before. It had been so dirty and smelly that even when her father told her what it was, she didn't dare go near it. She had been convinced the abandoned net was a sea monster, up from the depths of the ocean to sneak onto shore for a bit of sun.

"Forgive me," Minochi was saying, bowing his head over and over. U-ri caught a glimpse of something above the face.

What was that?

It looked like hair growing out in a bundle from the top of his head. It was jet black, a stark contrast to the peppered eyebrows on his face. Then it seemed to her that the dark clump was too thick to be hair. It was more like a large rubber hose—*or maybe I'm seeing things.*

"It is all my fault. I brought the Book of Elem into our region. I deciphered it and called forth that which slept within its pages."

Though the man's voice was almost entirely strangled with his sobbing, she could make out the words quite clearly. It reached her ears unfiltered by the vestments of protection. He was speaking Japanese.

"I was punished," Minochi continued, tears dripping from his eyes. "The severity of my punishment was such that I could no longer remain in my own region, and so I fled here. I wanted to forget my transgression, cast away my responsibilities. I left my cottage and all my books and I ran."

U-ri's heart had begun to strain against her. It wanted to leave. Soon her entire body joined in the rebellion. It wanted to flee. Every bone in her body wanted to be as far away from this place as possible. U-ri had to grab onto the bars tighter to keep herself from running away.

"Are you talking about how you tried to raise the dead? That is why you sought magical power, isn't it?"

The weathered, pale face nodded.

"And that's why you wanted a record of Kirrick's life? Because of the clues it might contain to the spells he used?"

Minochi's face, still twisted in grief, shifted from one side of his enclosure to the other. U-ri watched it move but couldn't comprehend what was happening. His face slid about six feet to the left, maintaining an even height of a foot or so off the floor. She couldn't see how someone could move like that, even crouched on the floor or lying on their side.

Warning bells went off in U-ri's head. *This is too much*, her body was screaming. *It's not natural! I can't stay here any longer. Something's wrong. Something's terribly wrong!* U-ri gripped the bars so tightly her joints ached all up and down her arms.

"U-ri," the thing said in a thick voice that rumbled in its throat. "That is your name here, is it not?" Minochi's eyes looked at her. His head lifted until it was even with her shoulders. "It is my fault for bringing the Book of Elem to your brother, my fault that he became the last vessel. I cannot apologize to you enough. You have the right to blame me, to take my very life for what I have done to your family."

U-ri was speechless. Even in the weak candlelight that seemed so ineffectual against the concentrated darkness of the cavern, her eyes were beginning to adjust. She was starting to see more beyond the bars—whether she wanted to or not.

The outline of Ichiro Minochi's body came into view on the other side of the gate. U-ri didn't even have to strain to see it now.

He was enormous. Large enough to fill the entirety of his solitary cell. And he wasn't human.

"That's enough of your maudlin prattle," Ash said from somewhere above U-ri's head. His tone was even and devoid of emotion. "If you want to die so badly, take your own life."

Ash grabbed U-ri by the arm then, lifted her to her feet, and pulled her away from Minochi. But U-ri's fingers still clung to the bars. They were frozen, hooked around the metal like claws.

She had never felt so terrified before. *I can't even move.*

"Just tell us one thing before you die," Ash was saying. "Where is the Hero? You of all people should know, after the power you drew from the Book of Elem."

Ichiro Minochi's pale face looked down at the floor. She could see him even more clearly now. The thick strands growing from the top of his head weren't hair. They looked like tubes of rubber, shining darkly, with many jointed segments along their length. When the tubes bent they made a faint rattling noise, like a beetle walking across a crisp sheet of paper.

"If the Hero used the Book of Elem as its key to escape—" Minochi was talking. U-ri now realized that what had sounded at first like a rasp or a tremble in his voice was just noise resulting from an inhuman physiology. Her great-uncle's voice wasn't coming from a throat as she knew it but from some other organ entirely.

The rattling sound grew louder. Ichiro Minochi's face swayed from side to side, as if a breeze rocked the bundle of cords that stretched down from the ceiling.

The heavy, wet sliding sound drifted up again from the floor.

"It will seek Kirrick's flesh."

"You mean Kirrick's body?" Ash asked sharply.

"Indeed." The pale visage nodded. "After his death, Kirrick's body was divided into eight pieces, each placed in magically sealed coffins and buried in the earth. The Hero will try to retrieve those coffins, revive Kirrick's flesh, and inhabit it."

U-ri heard the sound of someone breathing quietly. It was Dr. Latore. He had come up close behind her and was now reaching around her on both sides, his hands touching hers where they clutched at the iron bars. Gently, he began removing her fingers from the bars, peeling them off one by one.

He began with the thumb on her right hand. Then her index finger. She could hear him breathing by her ear.

"There is no talk of what you say in any of the legends or records," Ash protested. "What the legends do say is that Kirrick died in battle. His remains were tossed together with those of a hundred other soldiers. He doesn't even have a grave!"

For the first time, Ichiro Minochi laughed. "Yet what I have told you I had from Kirrick himself! His spirit still resides in the Book of Elem, you know. It spoke to me."

The fingers on U-ri's right hand were now completely free of the bars. Dr. Latore began working on the left. One hand free, U-ri began to tremble like a dry leaf in the wind.

"Tell me where the graves are, then. All eight of them."

Minochi's face drifted to one side. "Tell you? No, knowledge is not to be dispensed, but seized by one's own hands. Only then is it truly useful."

"I'll show you useful, you fiend," Ash said, raising his voice.

U-ri's left hand slipped from the bars, and Dr. Latore dragged her quickly backward just as Minochi's face came lunging forward. With a loud clang, his forehead smacked against the iron bars.

He was laughing loudly, his mouth a gaping hole bordered by sunken cheeks in that pale face. His eyes burned with a wild black flame.

U-ri clung to the doctor. He wrapped the sleeves of his robes around her.

"Gulg! Remember who you once were. Remember Ichiro Minochi the human, the one they called a sage. This little one is of your blood!"

He can't hear. He can't hear a single thing we're saying. He's gone completely mad. The realization filled her with enough fear to freeze the blood solid in her veins. Her great-uncle was no longer human. He was no longer sane. His mind had become unhinged.

"In order to employ magic powerful enough to raise the dead," Minochi said, grinning evilly, "the spell-weaver must surrender his own body as a reagent. It is the mage's body that acts as a battery, gathering up the life energies that flow through the Circle, bringing them together, storing them.

"Life energies are the energies of chaos," he continued, beginning to ramble. "It is the raw primal force. The more one gathers, the greater the pressure one must face—only those who can control it, who can fight it and win, can pass that energy on to the dead."

Minochi giggled. "I was successful. But still a far cry from what Kirrick was able to accomplish—"

"Why?" U-ri asked, though she found that she didn't particularly want to know the answer. "What did you lack?"

"I...I gathered the life energies, and—"

"We've heard enough, Ash!" Dr. Latore said. "We need to leave now."

Dr. Latore began to move back toward the gate, still clutching U-ri in his arms. U-ri dug her heels into the cavern floor, resisting. She couldn't take her eyes off her great-uncle. She couldn't escape the burning black flame of his gaze.

"No! What happened after that?"

"U-ri!"

Ichiro Minochi's mouth opened wide. A black tongue snaked out. U-ri noticed that all of his teeth had fallen out.

"My body could not withstand the energy, no, no—I did not lose. I merely changed into a form better suited to contain the energies I sought!" Minochi's eyes flared then, and his laughter was full of pride. The light from his eyes grew until all darkness was abolished from the cavern. U-ri could see the entire chamber now, from corner to corner. On the other side of the bars, Ichiro Minochi's shape was revealed.

"Witness, young *allcaste*. This is my true form. This is my true power!"

He looked like a black lump of foulness, a heap of putrescent mud piled high into a mound. His skin was black and wet; it glistened in the light and was stacked in layers, here retracting, there bulging out. It was impossible to tell which parts had originally been arms and which legs. He looked like a collection of rubber hoses tangled in a mass of rotten seaweed.

Then the mass moved, and she spotted tentacles rising from it. One, two, three rose from the black mound, snaking out into the cavern. Each tentacle was covered with countless suckers, like an octopus's legs. The suckers opened and closed with every twitch of the mound. They were hungry, thirsty, lusting for nourishment, lusting for everything.

And Ichiro Minochi's gaunt face hung from the end of one of those tentacles, like someone's devilish idea of a lantern.

U-ri screamed. She didn't make any words, just screamed, and screamed, and screamed some more. Dr. Latore carried her from the cavern in his arms. With her head hanging back, she screamed the entire way.

Dr. Latore sped like the wind through gate after gate, gently holding U-ri's head to him with one hand. She buried her face in his chest, her screams eventually becoming one repeated, frantic demand: *Get me out! Get me out of here! Get me out!*

Her last gargled scream trailed off, and U-ri slumped in the doctor's arms, her breath exhausted. U-ri's eyes closed and she lost consciousness, slipping from the darkness of the cavern bottom into a darkness even more total and silent.

"Hiroki?"

U-ri stood in a darkness so pitch black, she felt like she had lost the power of sight completely.

"Hiroki, are you there?"

Then, in the distance, she saw her brother's face. He was pale, frail, and thin—but it was him. It was Hiroki Morisaki. He was smiling. He lifted an arm and waved to her.

Goodbye.

"Wait! Don't go!"

U-ri wanted to chase him. *If I run really fast, I can still catch him.* But her feet wouldn't move. Though her mind willed them to race ahead, she took not one step.

Hiroki's pale face receded even further into the distance.

"Hiroki!"

U-ri noticed that something was wrong with his hands. They had turned into black tentacles. U-ri flinched, then looked at her own hands as they reached out for him.

They were transforming into something longer, something sleeker—glistening black.

"No!" U-ri shouted, leaping from her dream back into reality. She was sitting up in bed, a blanket falling from her. In front of her stood not Hiroki, but Sky. His purple eyes met hers.

U-ri's entire body was tense, and cold sweat ran in rivulets down her skin. She noticed her bed felt unusually hard. She looked again, and found that she was amongst the rubble of the Katarhar Abbey ruins. She had been lying not on a bed, but on the top of a fallen square pillar.

"Lady U-ri—" Sky stood from where he had been squatting next to the pillar and reached out a hand to support her. U-ri shrank away. Sky stepped back in surprise, his open arms hanging stupidly in the air for a moment before he thought to cross them at his chest.

U-ri felt something cool on her cheek. It was wet. *I've been crying. It's so cold here.*

The blue sky stretched above U-ri's head. White clouds drifted off to somewhere along the horizon, their bellies pink with the late afternoon sun.

U-ri took a deep breath. The cool, clear air filled her lungs. The rhythm of her swiftly beating heart began to slow. She took another breath, deeper this time. She coughed, but with every inhale, her breath came easier to her.

"U-ri, it's us."

That's Aju's voice. Where are you?

She spotted him on Sky's shoulder. He crinkled his nose and shook his whiskers in the air. "You mind if I come over? You aren't going to flinch and knock me off, right?"

Aju's ears and the tip of his nose were red in the chill air. Sky hugged his arms to his shoulders against the cold.

"Both of you come here. You too, Sky."

U-ri reached out her arms. Aju jumped to her and she slipped him inside her collar. She took Sky by the hand and pulled him close, hugging him.

"I'm sorry. I'm so sorry. I'm all right now." U-ri began to cry.

She cried and cried, while her friends watched and waited. When she was done, U-ri wiped her face with a handkerchief and caught her breath. Someone appeared at the cavern entrance in the rubble—Dr. Latore in his black robes. He was carrying a large copper cup from which a plume of steam was rising.

"You're awake. That's good. You should drink this."

The drink had a sweet fragrance to it. U-ri took a sip, and her throat sang with relief.

"Try touching the glyph on your forehead," Dr. Latore said, tapping his own forehead with one finger. "It should be able to cure you as well as it does your allies. Hopefully it will be able to mend what damage your vestments could not protect you from."

U-ri did as instructed and immediately felt a warmth coming from the mark. The warmth traveled through her body, filling her limbs and making her skin glow down to every last pore. She felt the strength return in her as the warmth faded.

"You see? The Lady *Allcaste* has no need of a doctor." Dr. Latore smiled. U-ri smiled back, then turned to her friends.

"Ash is going to chew me out again for being a crybaby."

"Ash?" Dr. Latore asked, lifting an eyebrow. "Oh, you mean Dmitri."

The doctor swept back his robes and sat down at U-ri's feet. The sun had begun to dip toward the horizon, but it was still bright outside. Even out here, in the light of day, Dr. Latore proved remarkably handsome.

"Please do not be angry with him for bringing you to meet Gulg—the creature who was once Ichiro Minochi."

U-ri nodded, gripping her cup tightly in both hands.

"Or with me for not stopping him," he added quietly.

"No problem, Doctor."

"I'm afraid Ash needed you to open your eyes, so he used the most direct way possible."

U-ri nodded again, silently.

"He wanted you to understand that, even should you find your brother and be reunited, that your finding him might not make your brother happy."

U-ri felt Aju's furry body rubbing her neck beneath her collar.

"I understand, I think. That is, I thought I understood before, but now I really get it."

A chill breeze stirred, ruffling the doctor's thick hair. "Ash has gone in search of Kirrick's whereabouts. There are many records of Kirrick's life and rumors about him, even more regarding his death, and yet very little truth. I fear it will take him some time to find anything of value."

"The history books of the Haetlands aren't any help?"

"Not really. Most were rewritten by those who wanted Kirrick dead. Such as it always is with history."

U-ri wondered if the weaver who created the Haetlands wanted it that way. Wouldn't the weaver be on Kirrick's side? Would she want the true account of his life told?

Or was the Haetlands already out of its weaver's reach, its own entity, existing without a creator. Which meant that weavers could only create worlds, not control them. *How useless is that?*

Dr. Latore looked kindly at Sky where he stood by U-ri, acting as a human shield against the wind. "You came from the nameless land, did you not?"

Sky's purple eyes flashed, then he looked down like a nervous schoolgirl. He hadn't expected the doctor to address him directly.

"Sky is a nameless devout," U-ri offered. "You know of the nameless land, Doctor?"

"Ash told me of it. He knows much." U-ri noticed the doctor's voice had a certain reverence in it when he spoke of the wolf. "This is how I know that the world in which I live is a created one—how do you feel?"

U-ri removed her hand from her forehead. She felt infinitely more settled now, and her pulse was steady. It seemed that not only her physical strength but the vitality of her spirit too had been restored.

"Though," the doctor continued, "I sometimes wish that our weaver had made the Haetlands a slightly more peaceful and livable place." Dr. Latore squinted up at the clouds above them. "Yet I am still thankful that I have been given a life here."

That, despite the Haetlands' dark history.

"U-ri. Have you ever wondered if the world in which you live was not created by someone?"

"Yes, but our world—"

"The source and center of the Circle, yes, I have heard. But might there be not one weaver as with my world, but many weavers, that at this very moment continue to spin their countless stories, continuing the creation of your world?"

U-ri blinked. "Oh, you mean they're maintaining the Circle by creating new stories?"

"Yes. For better or for worse. You—" Latore placed a hand on U-ri's shoulder. "You are one of those weavers, U-ri. You may not be an author or historian, nor an artist. Yet these are merely differences in role and standing. Simply by living, we all create our own story."

"Even me?"

"Yes." Dr. Latore nodded deeply, then turned again to Sky. "It is why it is not only the weavers who bear sin. Nor just the nameless devout. We are all sinners of a kind. By simply living we sin, for we have no other means to live."

The doctor stared directly at Sky, and the devout averted his eyes. Aju squeaked lightly, as though he were about to say something to change the topic and lighten the mood—but in the end he said nothing.

"Sky. It seems to me that yours alone is a far purer existence than the rest of ours," Latore said.

"That is ridiculous!" Sky said, breaking his silence at last. "I am inculpated. And furthermore, I was cast out from the nameless land! I am a sinner among sinners."

"No, I do not believe that to be the truth of it," Dr. Latore continued, a look of kindness, empathy, and deep understanding on his face.

Empathy? Suddenly, U-ri became uneasy. She could feel her body reacting to the doctor's words. *Why? Why is he telling all this to Sky?*

"You are free," Dr. Latore continued, heedless of U-ri's consternation. "The burden you once bore has been lifted."

"What do you mean by his burden?" U-ri asked, standing quickly and stepping between the two of them, effectively shaking the doctor's hand from her shoulder as she stood.

"I was told that Sky became a nameless devout because he had committed a sin—the sin of living a story. Is that what you mean by his burden? What's the truth? I don't understand what you're saying."

"U-ri, easy now," Aju squeaked from her collar, batting her jaw with a tiny paw. The tone of his voice reminded her of how he had sounded before he had become a mouse and she an *allcaste*—when he had been a book, all-knowing, and harsh.

"It's all right, Aju," Dr. Latore said, his eyes still fixed on Sky. "You understand my words, don't you? No, rather, I see that you are beginning to understand them. *You must do this*, devout. It is not something from which you can turn."

U-ri turned to look in Sky's direction, and he lifted his eyes to meet hers. His eyes were bloodshot and wet with tears.

U-ri swallowed. *What is it, Sky? Do you really understand what he's saying? Is there some deep meaning here that everyone but me can see?*

"I am inculpated," Sky repeated, his voice cracking. He struggled to stand and his robes wrapped around his legs, making him stumble. Still, he stood and began to run toward the cavern entrance.

"Sky!" U-ri ran after him, but Aju hopped to the top of her head, squeaking, "No, U-ri! Stop! Let him be by himself."

U-ri stopped, feeling dizzy with shock. "What, don't tell me you understand what he's saying, Aju? If you do, you better tell me. What was Sky's sin? What's his burden? What does the doctor mean that it's lifted?"

"Man, don't you know when to shut up?" Aju jumped in the air, landing with a smack back on her head. "Can't you act like an adult, like an *allcaste*, just this once? Stop yelping and squealing like a little girl all the time!"

U-ri's body trembled with shame and rage. "I can't help it. No one tells me the truth! No one tells me what's going on."

"Look, I—" Aju began, suddenly withered. His tail went slack against her hair. "There's lots of things I don't know either. I'm just a little dictionary after all. A youngster. Sorry," Aju added, sounding like he might cry. "That said, I'm starting to put things together. But, Doctor—" Aju's nose twitched in the direction of Dr. Latore. "I'm not sure I like this."

Dr. Latore nodded. "I understand."

"The books here told me some things."

"They possess much knowledge."

"Yeah, well, I wish they had given me some of that knowledge back when this whole thing started."

The conversation was going over her head again, but U-ri managed to keep ahold of her temper this time. To the contrary, she felt her chest grow cold. Aju might not be making much sense, but she could tell he was frightfully serious and more than a little afraid. She had never seen him like this.

"Even if you had known back then, you would not have been able to put what you knew to use," Dr. Latore was saying. "Were you to tell your story, you would not have been believed. You would have been forced to wait in silence until such a time as you *could* be believed." The doctor fell silent for moment, then added in a quiet voice, "Just as Ash does now."

Aju scrunched up, becoming nothing more than a fuzzy white ball, then sprang from U-ri's head and dashed between two pieces of rubble and out of sight.

It was a while before U-ri found her voice. "Doctor, is Aju—"

"Wipe your eyes, U-ri."

U-ri put a finger to her face. It was streaked with tears. Hurriedly, she rubbed at her eyes with the back of her hand. "I'm sorry. I'm so confused."

The doctor shook his head, frowning. "No, I was careless. I have said too much and I apologize."

The wind picked up, ruffling their black robes. The bangs lifted from U-ri's forehead, revealing her glyph.

"Something happened while I was asleep, didn't it?" U-ri asked, growing more convinced she was right even as her lips formed the question.

Dr. Latore, his face still strained, managed a smile. "No, no. Nothing really happened."

He's lying.

"You're the one who brought me up from below, right? I remember half of our trip. I remember going through several of the gates, up to the part where we reached the hall at the lowest level of the cavern." *I remember screaming the whole way.* "Something happened then, didn't it? That's why Sky and Aju were all worked up, and you were trying to calm them down just now."

U-ri wanted to fall to the ground right there and beg him to tell her what had happened. She wanted him to reach out and yank the veil from her eyes. What made all this so maddening was that even though everything was wrapped in mysteries, she had caught glimpses of the truth, and she wanted to see more. She felt like if she just tried a little harder, if she could just take that first step, she would be able to unravel everything. The answer was right there in front of her if only she could see it.

"U-ri."

"I know you aren't telling me out of kindness, Doctor. You don't have Ash's cruel streak."

So tell me. What happened? U-ri put her hand on the doctor's black sleeve, tightening her fingers around his wrist, when she heard a loud *thunk* and her feet seemed to lift beneath her.

An earthquake? U-ri jumped. Dr. Latore braced himself, putting his arms protectively around her.

Another tremor passed through the ground. Dust drifted up from the rubble. Part of one of the fallen pillars split away and fell to the ground right beside U-ri and Dr. Latore.

Together, they looked up at the sky.

CHAPTER TWELVE

The Labyrinth

The sky was peacefully making its transition to dusk. The tilting sun scorched the edges of the clouds. No, it was more like the clouds had put rouge on their cheeks. They drifted lazily, save in one corner of the sky where a group of them had clustered to form a red-painted thundercloud.

Then lightning flashed across the sky, a brilliant bolt with three arms. It split the sky into pieces once, then twice.

A shadow came over the sun. To U-ri's eyes it looked like the sun had slipped into a lightning-rent crack in the sky. But when the lightning flashed a third time, she saw that the sun still hung in the sky—except where it had been a golden orb before, now it shone pitch black.

Thunder rumbled so loudly it seemed like the world might split in two. With each shattering roar, the sky fragmented further, until U-ri thought it might fall down from the firmament above onto her head, and she instinctively lifted her arms to protect herself. Dr. Latore stood on unsteady legs and took one or two steps away from the pillar upon which they had been sitting. His eyes were fixed on the far horizon. He took another several steps forward, as though drawn by some invisible force.

"What is the meaning of this?" U-ri heard him mutter.

She stood as well, joining him in staring into the distance. But then she took a step back. Her body tensed, ready to flee.

Far in the distance, in a gap between two hills, she could see the western horizon—the very spot where the sun should be setting beautifully in an hour or two. But what she saw there now defied U-ri's attempts at comprehension.

At first she thought it was a tornado, but realized that, were it a tornado, it would have to be impossibly huge to appear so large from a distance, and it lacked that familiar sand-pouring-through-the-hourglass shape. So what was it, then? It seemed clear that it was some movement of the wind. It writhed and churned upon the ground, sucking up everything beneath it, tossing all it encountered into the air, tearing everything to pieces.

It's a giant pair of hands. That was the only way she could describe it. She could even see the fingers, the bend of the knuckles. A giant pair of hands had grown from the western horizon and begun wreaking havoc on the earth. As she watched, the right hand lifted into a fist and smashed something on the ground. Then the left hand picked up whatever it was and tossed it high into the air.

U-ri crouched behind a fallen pillar, using it as a barricade against the gale force winds blowing over her head. "What is it, Doctor?" She had to shout just to be heard, and the doctor was standing only a few feet away. The wind had been blowing toward the north only moments before, but now it shifted to a westerly. It was blowing from the direction of those giant hands. It was hard for U-ri to even keep her eyes open. The gale became a blast as the winds increased in ferocity, whipping up a cloud of sand and small stones off the ground. The debris felt like needles against her skin.

U-ri held up her fingers to protect her face and called out to the doctor again. The giant hands lifted from the horizon, and U-ri spotted recognizable shapes in the detritus falling from them: steeples, such as one might find on a church or a castle. The wind quickly whipped them about, reducing them to dust.

"That is the direction of the capital," Dr. Latore called back to her.

"Those buildings—are the hands destroying Elemsgard?" U-ri called back at the top of her lungs. Dr. Latore had his head down, braced against the wind, but the wind gusted and he lost his balance. It tossed him back, slamming him into a mountain of exterior wall fragments. The wind pressed him against its rough surface, pinning his arms and legs as though he were nailed to the stone.

"U-ri!" he shouted, his voice barely audible above the roaring wind. "Into the cavern, now!"

I have to help him. I have to go get help. U-ri began to crawl across the ground toward the entrance, when she heard the doctor scream, "No!"

U-ri stood. A breath later, something supple yet strong wrapped around U-ri so tightly that she couldn't breathe.

Then she was flying through the air. She thought it was the wind tossing her, but she was still right-side up. Her hands were free.

She wasn't caught up in some tempest—Dr. Latore was holding her again. He had his left arm around her, and with his right he was clinging to the pile of rubble, slowly crawling upward. He found a grip, pulled, then found another grip higher. Each time he lifted, they swayed in the wind.

Dr. Latore's arms were no longer those of a human. His skin was brown, the bones black and bulging out like the roots of a withered tree. His hands had grown so that his palms alone were twice the size of U-ri's face. His fingers were long, bare and delicate, and they slashed through the air like hooks, clinging tightly to the mound of rubble when they found purchase.

Incongruously, U-ri was reminded of the artificial monkey mountain she had seen once at the zoo. She had watched a mother monkey holding her child in one arm as she made her way across a tree branch.

Dr. Latore climbed with her to the summit of the mountain of rubble that was the Katarhar Abbey ruins. U-ri could see much farther from up here. She looked west and saw a black wave advancing in a line along the ground from the western horizon, making straight for the abbey.

It was as if the giant hands had clapped together, summoning up a great wall of wind. U-ri screwed her eyes shut. Gripping her tightly, Dr. Latore pushed off from the mountain of rubble. Then they were hurtling through the air, while below them the black wind-wall smashed into the ruins.

U-ri watched as the wind tossed up the pillars that had lain on their sides for years, breaking them into pieces until they fell back down to the ground to smash against the rocks. U-ri thought they should make a tremendous noise, yet it did not reach her ears. She was flying through the air. Dr. Latore's robes fluttered almost elegantly in the evening sunlight. They were high up now—well above the rushing wall of wind.

The doctor swung one of his strangely shaped arms, and it clawed at the air like a black wing, creating an updraft strong enough to briefly reverse their slow fall and lift them up into the air once again.

"U-ri, your glyph!" the doctor shouted.

In a daze, U-ri touched her hand to her forehead. She didn't know what spell to cast. Aju certainly hadn't taught her anything. She thought with her own words: *Please, please, please, please! Protect us! Return us safely to the ground!*

The glyph flared brightly twice. She looked and saw that she and the doctor were enveloped in a ring of white light. The speed of their descent lessened. The doctor flapped his arm again, and the ring of white light shifted around them, until U-ri felt like she rode in comfort upon an invisible chair. They drifted slowly downward, the doctor steering them with occasional shifts of his arm.

The wind-wall had passed. U-ri watched it recede into the distance. It had decimated what was left of Katarhar Abbey, yet that hadn't slowed it down. It was like a giant black scythe, reaping the mountain beneath the abbey, sending trees flying into the sky, cutting down all in its path. An avalanche of stones covered the narrow road up the mountain. Trees, branches, and leaves swirled into the sky like dust in the wind.

Dr. Latore's feet hit ground first, followed quickly by U-ri's, and the ring of light faded. The doctor stood firmly, bracing himself, but U-ri's knees buckled beneath her.

The rubble left on the mountaintop was as finely minced as if a giant had gnashed the whole of it between his teeth and spit out all he couldn't swallow. Whereas before it had been possible to make out pillars and the remnants of walls amongst the wreckage, some internal decorations and fragments of furniture, now there was nothing but undifferentiated dust.

U-ri shook some of that dust off her robes and looked west. The giant hands had utterly disappeared. A natural wind blew across the mountaintop, gently sweeping the dust away. The sun and the sky had both seemingly returned to normal.

"Those giant hands became the very black blade of wind that swept over this mountain," the doctor said. "I wonder how far they will go, destroying all in their path, before finding their final destination."

U-ri glanced at the doctor, then looked away. With a start, he put his arms behind his back, but not before U-ri noticed that his skin was returning to its regular color. His hands, once giant, were now shrinking back to their regular size.

Once both of his hands were safely hidden within the sleeves of his black robes, he looked again at U-ri. "I too carry the venom within me."

U-ri nodded. She had figured this out some time ago.

"I am sorry if I startled you. And I apologize for concealing it until now."

U-ri decided not to say anything. Then she sneezed. Fine dust drifted up from her vestments of protection. The doctor patted her shoulder, brushing off some extra dust.

Then, much to her surprise, U-ri sobbed out loud. "Doctor Latore...will you die soon?"

Dr. Latore's eyes softened, and his mouth, twisted grimly with the knowledge of the curse he bore, lifted into a smile. "You have a gentle heart, U-ri."

She felt like she might cry again, even as she marveled at her own capacity to feel sorry for this one man's fate when she had just witnessed the utter destruction of Katarhar Abbey and quite possibly that of the Haetlands' capital city as well.

"I do not know how much longer I have on this earth. That is why I have come here. I thought to spend what time remains to me helping others who must be suffering as I suffer."

Dust still rose from the ruins of Katarhar Abbey. Dr. Latore reached out again and brushed off U-ri's shoulder. There was no distinguishing either of his hands from those of a regular person's now.

"I discovered my condition three years ago. At first, there was no discernible difference in my physiology. I had merely become stronger than the average person, able to lift remarkable weights with ease."

His transformation had soon progressed. What had begun as a gradual change turned into a rapid chain reaction of symptoms.

"Now, when I use my strength, my hands change shape as you saw. I have no doubt that my legs will soon follow."

U-ri recalled how he had leapt from the mountain as the wave of wind descended upon them.

The doctor nodded, reading her expression. "Even the king of beasts would envy my legs, it's true."

"There's a boy in Ash's village named Udsu," U-ri began.

"Yes, I know of him. We have even met. So he lives there still? I have no doubt that he and his mother will have to leave before long. When the transformations become more apparent, it becomes increasingly difficult for the affected to live amongst the general populace—and they come to rely on a greater variety of medicines."

And in the end, Ash will bury them.

"Does the transformation...hurt when it happens?"

"Not in the slightest," Dr. Latore replied, rubbing his hands together and stretching his fingers. "Though you do *feel* different. Wilder, you might say. Remember that I told you those infected with the venom become violent as they near the end of their lives. It is like that. I'm only glad that it is still within my control."

The dust finally settled. The air around them had begun to clear, until now there was no sign of the wind's passage—as long as you didn't look down.

"There is no proper name for the transformations I and Udsu and others like us suffer. There are nicknames, like 'springfoot' of course, but no proper medical terms. That is because it is officially forbidden to talk about us or to mention us in the chronicles. Such attention would only serve to highlight the questionable pasts of our leaders. U-ri, if something is not given a name, not spoken of, and not recognized, then it does not exist. One could explain us away, saying that people like Udsu or myself are rare mutations, with no relation to the Haetlands' history. Why name or recognize something so insignificant? In time we will all be gone anyway."

U-ri bit her lip.

Dr. Latore continued, his tone even, like a teacher giving a lecture he had given a hundred times before. "We did not wish for our disease. We received our afflictions by sheer chance of fate. How it angered me before. How full of rage I was. But something happened to change my thinking. My body and short lifespan were not laid upon me because of some wrongdoing of my own, you see. They are merely the spoils of ill fortune. Yet in this world, there are those who have fallen prey to bitter fate through no other fault but their own."

U-ri whispered, "You mean like Gulg?"

Dr. Latore nodded deeply. "Yes. Though I and Udsu might feel sorrow, pain, rage, even self-pity, we never need blame ourselves for what we have done. For we have done nothing to bring our afflictions upon us. Not so with Gulg. What he suffers now is his own doing. He knows better than any of us what his actions have wrought. No matter how much sorrow he feels, how much pain, how much rage, it all comes back to him in the end."

Thus, Dr. Latore explained, true pity and forgiveness must be reserved for those like Gulg. Not those like him and Udsu. "The same can be said of your brother. Only you, who truly love him, can truly forgive. You seek him now for this purpose alone: to forgive and to release him. This will bring you no satisfaction or consolation, yet still you must do it, for you are the only one who can."

While the doctor spoke, U-ri had unconsciously been rubbing the glyph on her forehead. Dr. Latore smiled, and gently taking her fingers, removed them from it. "I do not speak to you in this way because you are an *allcaste*. I'm talking to you because you are a little girl who cares for her brother. You understand?"

U-ri gripped the doctor's fingers back. She realized with a start that they were holding hands—and she realized that she could have sat with him for hours without ever feeling the cold.

There was a loud crash from behind, and part of the mound of rubble behind them crumbled as a single panel of wood was jettisoned down the slope, leaving a small hole where it had been. Ash's silver hair poked out of the hole. "Everyone still alive?"

Dr. Latore and U-ri laughed. Ash's head disappeared again, then his entire body burst from the mound. "What are you two doing, anyway?"

"Is everybody below all right?"

"Aye, that cavern is nice and solid," the wolf replied, hands at his waist. His eyes went wide, surveying the damage around him.

"Yes, I had hoped it would hold," the doctor said. Then, "Where is that mouse Aju?"

U-ri gasped. She had completely forgotten about Aju.

"Here, I'm here," Aju squeaked from Ash's collar. "What are you doing down there with the doctor, U-ri?"

"What are you doing up there in Ash's collar? And where's Sky?"

"He's down below, calming some of the children. The cavern might have held, but the noise was something else!"

Aju left Ash's shoulder, walked down his arm, then hopped onto the ground, tossing his nose in the air. "I escaped by a whisker, myself. When I saw that wind coming in, you can bet I made for the cavern entrance as quick as I could."

"Leaving U-ri to her fate," Ash noted.

Aju's ears pricked up. "H-hey, that's not fair. I mean, I would've been blown clear off the mountain—"

"Come here, Aju," U-ri said, extending a hand. "Don't you pay attention to what the cranky old man with the gray hair says."

"I used a mage-glass to watch what was happening above ground," Ash said, turning to look at the western horizon. The red setting sun was large between the hills. "It was in the capital, yes?"

Dr. Latore nodded.

"I'm sure many of the towns and villages along the high road were not spared either."

"And Tato?"

"No idea," Ash said softly. "Either way, there's nothing we can do about that now. We're not in the business of tending to survivors. We must leave for the capital at once."

"Did you find out anything about Kirrick?" U-ri asked.

"No, that's why we're going to the capital. Besides, I'd like to see what's become of the place. That plan unsuitable for you?"

Dr. Latore gently pulled on U-ri's sleeve and whispered, "Don't mind him. He's irritated, and understandably so."

The two stood and walked toward Ash. "I have heard," the doctor said as they walked, "that some of Kirrick's personal goods—armor and weapons and the like—were buried by Elem's gravesite in the capital."

"That story is accurate as far as I can tell. What's more, it's likely that more was buried there than just rusting metal."

"Does this explain the attack?"

"It might."

"You know, I've been wondering something," U-ri cut in. "Remember how Minochi was saying that Kirrick's body had been divided into eight pieces? Well, I was wondering how the body was divided. I mean, there is the head, two hands and two legs, and the rest of his body. But that only makes six. What about the other two?"

"Well, it ain't pretty," Aju squeaked, once again secure atop U-ri's shoulder, "but my guess would be his eyes and his heart."

"But that's three pieces, Aju," U-ri protested, swallowing her nausea at the thought of taking out someone's parts like that.

"The pair of eyes are very small, so traditionally they only count as one," Aju explained.

"To borrow Gulg's words," Ash said, "the Book of Elem was the key to the Hero's escape. From this we can infer that the Hero possesses Kirrick's memory—Kirrick's mind forms the core of the Hero. And the energy of the vessels filling it are what gives it form."

"Yet in order for the Hero to fully resurrect as Kirrick, it will require Kirrick's corporeal body," the doctor concluded. "It is the body in which Kirrick's mind, and his fury, still reside."

It again occurred to U-ri that when they talked about this Kirrick as though he were some distant legendary figure, they were talking about Ash's half brother. Thus she was startled by what the wolf said next.

"Were I Kirrick," Ash began, turning to stare with a stern face at the western horizon, "what would I want back first? What part of myself?"

U-ri and Dr. Latore both looked at their own bodies—their hands, feet, and their chests with hearts beating within.

Ash shook his head violently. "No, I'm a fool. There's no point in playing guessing games, we'll find out for ourselves soon enough."

"I would want my eyes first," said a voice. It was Sky, standing by the ragged hole that led down to the cavern.

"I would want to look upon the Haetlands as she is today with Kirrick's eyes," Sky said softly.

U-ri realized she was holding her breath. Everyone was.

Ash swiveled to face Sky. "Look upon it, then destroy it?"

"You would have to speak with him to find out what he intends. You should know that better than any of us, Master Ash."

Sky stood straight as an arrow, his eyes fixed on the wolf's. Gone was the meek, subservient devout. He put a hand to his own chest. "Let us go to the capital."

For a moment, Ash did not reply. The two looked at each other in silence, and a feeling of dread rose inside U-ri. Inwardly, she frowned at herself. *This is a moment for action, not for cowering!*

The mark on U-ri's forehead glimmered. Then she knew in her heart what she had to do—the glyph had told her, though not in words or images.

"We fly to the capital," U-ri said, giving voice to the glyph's message. Then, letting it guide her, she knelt upon the ground and took her palm from her forehead, lowering it to the rock below.

Where her palm pressed into the gravel, the rock began to glow. Lines of light spread from her fingers, brilliant bands, dividing and spreading as they formed a giant image of the mark she wore.

"The glyph will guide us truly."

U-ri stood and motioned to Sky. He hesitated a moment, then ran to her, taking her hand.

"Dr. Latore?" U-ri called out.

"Yes?"

"I bid you well. Please await my return here."

The doctor knelt amongst the stones and fragments of architecture scattered across the ground. He bowed his head and intoned, "May the protection of the Circle be with you."

Ash stepped inside the magic circle's ring to stand behind U-ri. "No falling off this time, rat."

"Same to you!" Aju shot back, bearing his tiny teeth.

U-ri took a deep breath and closed her eyes, feeling the energy stream from the glyph up through her entire body.

❦

They were flying once again in darkness. There were no glimpses of scenery such as they had seen on their first attempted trip to the Katarhar Abbey ruins. Just plain, uniform darkness rushing past.

Yet there was a presence in the darkness, filling it. Some giant creature was there with them—and U-ri could hear the breathing of a thousand people, maybe more. And whispering and shouting, but much to her irritation it was all too distant for her to make anything out.

She wondered why the trip was so different this time. *Is it because the*

Hero's strength is growing? The great creature's presence was such that it drowned out all others. The darkness became thicker, more dense, until U-ri felt like a tiny fish pushing its way through a deep-sea current, the glyph upon her forehead her only guiding light.

If this darkness truly does spring from the Hero, then it can't be all evil. The Hero has a good side, after all.

The Hero was true and just. A positive force in balance with the darkness of the King in Yellow—the other side of the coin. So there was no need to categorically fear the darkness, she realized. She would simply have to look through it until she found the light.

And there was another thing she shouldn't forget. Hiroki Morisaki was somewhere out there in this darkness. No matter how enamored he had become of the King in Yellow, no matter how unlucky his fate as the last vessel, U-ri was sure that his heart still yearned for the good side of the Hero.

Maybe if I call to him...Hiroki!

Again and again, she called out to him in her heart, as she had called him so many times before, when their lives had been more peaceful and happy.

Whenever she called him, Hiroki would answer. Sometimes grumpily, with a "Now what?" or a "Not again!" But sometimes with true concern. "What's wrong, Yuriko?" And sometimes they would laugh together. Other times, he would get angry on her behalf. They thought through problems together and worried together. They lived together, brother and sister. Why should things be any different now?

I'll find you soon, I promise!

U-ri opened her eyes and came out of the darkness, onto the ground.

"Whoaaa!" Aju squealed, clinging to her hair. "Where the heck are we? Why are we so high up?"

He was right. It seemed they had landed on top of a rickety wooden frame of some sort, a good thirty feet off the ground.

"We're at a checkpoint," Ash said, landing lightly on the structure beside them and looking down. "There are several along the high road to the capital. This is the watchtower at the first checkpoint from the city gates. We're standing atop it."

U-ri spotted a wide, dusty thoroughfare beneath them. It went past the tower, winding off into the distance through brown hills. There were scores of people on the road. Some had stopped, their carts standing still, their horses stomping at the ground, looking up at them.

"Which way to the capital?"

She couldn't see any palace. The road was full of people, though in places the clouds of dust hid them and the twilit sky from sight.

"You think they're refugees?"

Everyone on the road was heading in the same direction. Some people seemed to have run from their homes with only what they had on and their children, while others led carts piled high with belongings. They *were* refugees. She had only seen them in movies before now, but these were definitely the real thing. U-ri felt the strength go out of her legs.

Ash leaned from the edge of the watchtower and called out to the people on the road below, "What happened to the palace?"

An old man shifed the weight of a large sack upon his back to look up. "Where'd you come from?"

"The ruins of Katarhar Abbey. That wind passed through and turned the trees to sticks."

The old man's face was black with soot. Even from their height, U-ri could see that not only his face, but his entire body, was covered in grime.

The rest of the people had begun to move again. No one had time to wonder about groups of strange travelers suddenly appearing on watchtowers. The old man backtracked against the tide until he reached the foot of the tower.

"Nothing good's come to the palace," the old man said. "That's for sure. It's like another war's started."

"Was the palace destroyed?"

"Can't say. Can't say at all. There was a lot of dust, and a lot of smoke. Took my cart with it, it did." The man trembled so violently that his bag slipped off his back. He staggered.

"It disappeared, that's what it did! Just up and disappeared!" a young woman pushing a baby before her in a cart called out in a shrill, high voice. Her face was pale beneath the grime, her eyebrows raised in fear.

"What, the palace?"

"That's right. It's gone. Gone! Only thing left's a big hole in the ground."

The top of the watchtower had begun to creak ominously and sway to one side. Ash leapt lightly down to the ground below. The tower continued to tilt, so U-ri and Sky jumped as well—the vestments protected her from the fall, and Sky seemed to be able to handle it on his own. In a breath they were swallowed up by the crowd of travelers, jostled this way and that, until Ash reappeared, leading two horses behind him.

"Where'd you get those?"

"Don't ask," Ash replied. He snatched up U-ri and threw her up into one of the saddles, then handed the reins to Sky. "Ride or walk, I don't care, just follow. We're leaving!" Ash straddled the other horse and gave its flank a kick with the heel of his boot.

"R-right," Sky replied, his lips pale. Getting one foot in the stirrup, he managed to mount U-ri's horse behind her. "Hold on tight, Lady U-ri."

"You sure you know how to ride one of these things, Sky?" Aju squeaked from U-ri's collar.

"I am sure I do not, but I will try."

"Try?" U-ri and Aju shouted together, but Sky had already reached around her and grabbed the reins. "Hyup!" he barked, and the horse sped forward.

The tide of refugees heading in the opposite direction only seemed to swell as they made their way toward whatever was left of the capital. Travelers spilled over the edges of the road, forming lines along the sides. Here and there, a cart had stalled, and men stood around it, arguing. Once, right before U-ri's eyes, a magnificent dappled black horse reared, threw off its rider, and ran off into the fields. She had caught only a glimpse of the horse's eyes as it reared, but it had been enough to see the fear in them.

Thanks to the general confusion, Sky's horse was able to weave its way against the flow of the crowd, maintaining an even distance behind Ash's lead. Up ahead, Ash stopped frequently, occasionally to whisper something into his horse's ear.

"Ash, is something wrong?" U-ri called out.

He turned and looked back at her through a cloud of dust. "You can't hear it?"

Without waiting for her response, he turned and pointed in the direction the palace should have been—there was nothing but blue sky there now. Just then, a passing man stopped by Ash and tugged upon his cloak.

"Hey, you're an undertaker, aren't you?" the man asked. He was slightly overweight and wore a heavy coat.

"I am close to the dead," Ash replied with a nod.

"Then if you go to the capital, go around to the west gate. The guards there are looking for help."

"What of the palace? Is it true that it has disappeared?"

The man nodded and wiped at the grime on his face. "Looked to me like it was just sucked straight into the ground. Weren't destroyed, nor did it collapse—just went straight down, with all the people in it."

"And the capital guard? What has become of them?"

"Scattered to the four winds, I suspect. I haven't seen even a one of them myself," the man said.

"Then they probably went down with the palace," Ash muttered. "Why did you stop me, goodman? By your coat, you are a doctor, no?"

"I am. Just a local physician from the Midwall Quarter. I was out in front of the victory gate on a call when the palace went down. Saw it from there. The guards on patrol just on the other side of the gate, they turned the moment the palace and the grounds got swallowed."

"Turned?"

"Aye. Into demons. That'd be you undertakers' department, right? I heard those guards at the west gate putting out a call for every undertaker in the kingdom."

"What do they expect us to do?"

"Put together a search party, er, a vanquishing party to go down under the ground and deal with whatever's there." The man glanced at the refugees flowing around them. "That's why they're all leaving. They figure that if they hang out around the capital, either they'll become demons themselves, or they'll be volunteered to go fight the ones who did."

The doctor was right. When they reached the west gate of Elemsgard, there were the same throngs of people on the road, but here there was at least a semblance of the order that had been lacking by the watchtower. Furthermore, it seemed as though the number of people going through the gates toward the town center was greater than those going out.

The guards set to watch the gate were easy to find. They wore light breastplates and greaves strapped to their legs. All bore swords, and a few had quivers slung across their backs. Large ballistae had been placed inside the walls of the city.

A guard by one of the gate columns shouted his voice hoarse, his face a grimace as he barked orders to passersby. They left their horses outside the gate, and Ash went straight to the guard, thrusting his papers in the man's face, and they were let inside.

"So Elemsgard is a walled city!" Aju squeaked from atop U-ri's head. "Look at those stones, U-ri!"

The stone walls encircling the city rose to a height of at least ten stories.

"The city is arranged on three concentric circles, with the palace in the center," Ash explained, his eyes watching the people on the road around them. "Outwall, Midwall, and Heartwall, the sections are called. Each is divided by a moat with a single drawbridge crossing it, and everything in the central circle is the property of the royal palace."

U-ri wondered what the palace had looked like before today. Looking at the blue sky that hung above the city now felt like looking at a stage after the play had finished and the scenery carried away.

"There, that tent," Ash said, pointing toward a canvas tent off to the right of the road. U-ri got Sky's attention and followed after him.

There were several tents here, some filled with doctors and their patients, others piled high with supplies or filled with off-duty guardsmen. One seemed to be serving as a local guard post. Several horses were hitched outside.

This area of the city—Outwall—seemed to be mostly storefronts. *It's like a shopping mall!*

There were still people around, and some of the shops were open (though most of their goods had already been confiscated by the city guard, it seemed). Other shops had their doors shuttered.

U-ri spotted one family piling their belongings onto a cart outside of the house, faces drawn tight with worry and fear.

The tent Ash was heading for was a busy one, with a constant stream of people entering and leaving. Some of them were soldiers, but for the most part, they were all dressed exactly like Ash.

"What are we doing here?" Aju chirped nervously.

"We have to go underground, to where the palace disappeared, if we're ever going to find out anything," Ash replied, matter-of-factly. "And if we're going underground, we'll need to check in here first."

"We're going?"

"If you don't want to go, you're welcome to stay," Ash grumbled, his hand lifting the tent flap. Just then, a large man with a scraggly beard came bursting out of the tent. He nearly ran straight into Ash, and his eyes opened wider than they already were.

"What's this? The Man of Ash? When did you get back? I thought you were off in Culuque hunting goblins."

"Don't play the fool, fatty," Ash said, giving the bearded man a loud slap on his sizable belly. "I don't believe that the biggest ears on this continent haven't heard about the escape yet. What I want to know is what *you've* been up to."

The big man thrust his belly out even further and laughed loudly. "That would be a trade secret, that. Same as you, friend. Oh, if you're here to sign up, you'd best be quick about it. Most of the soldiers here are of a mind to give up looking for survivors altogether and just fill up that gaping hole in the middle of—"

The man broke off in midsentence, his eyes finding U-ri behind the wolf. He squinted. "Well, well, well, I see you've been busy. That girl is marked."

"Rude as always, I see," Ash grumbled, looking back over his shoulder at U-ri. "This is Morgan; he's in the same line of work as I. He's a bit of a filthy old lard ball, but I suspect underneath all that is a good man. Or two."

"Couldn't ask for a finer introduction," Morgan said with a frown. "Don't you listen to him none, missie with the mark. I'm just one good man who happens to like a hearty meal now and then."

U-ri took a step forward and bowed her head. "You, I take it, are a wolf as well?"

Morgan put a finger to his lips and leaned in close to her. "That's a secret, that. I'm no warrior like your friend here. Wouldn't want word getting out and people getting the wrong idea, eh?"

Ash announced he would sign U-ri and Sky up and disappeared inside the tent. The two men who came out as he entered were carrying lengths of rope and long, spearlike poles. One of them turned as he exited the tent, the butt of his spear accidentally brushing the hem of U-ri's vestments.

"Whoa there," Morgan said, quickly sliding his arms around the girl and lifting her briefly before setting her down a short distance away. "Busy spot, here. No place to be swinging around such long implements of destruction like that."

"Who're you?" Aju squeaked, sticking his head out from the neck of U-ri's robes. His nose twitched with suspicion. "And what're you doing picking U-ri up?"

Morgan didn't seem particularly startled by the mouse's sudden appearance, nor the fact that it could talk. He smiled broadly. "Do you mind?" he asked U-ri, then he reached down and picked Aju up by the scruff of his neck.

"Hey! What's the big idea? Lemme go!"

"Isn't this interesting! This little one your friend, missie?"

"He's only a mouse because I wasn't very good at magic."

"I think not," Morgan said, dangling Aju in the air. "This one was *little* to begin with." He lifted Aju higher, inspecting the mouse's belly. Aju squeaked with rage.

"A dictionary, I see—an *aunkaui* dictionary, no less. Been a while since I've seen one of these."

Aju's fur bristled. "You take that back!"

Seeing U-ri's confused look, Morgan leaned down and whispered in her ear. "An *aunkaui* dictionary is another way of saying a false dictionary. Lots of misleading passages and blanks, hardly of use to anyone—unless you know how to use it, of course."

"That is so not true!" Aju squeaked loud enough to draw glances from surprised passersby.

U-ri took Aju back from Morgan's hand, and the little mouse quickly dashed back inside the folds of her vestments. "Well, I don't know what that means, but Aju is a fine friend of mine."

"I'm sure he is," Morgan said, nodding. "Understand, I'm not belittling your little friend. It is the power of the glyph that determines the value of one's servants, in any case."

Suddenly, the man's smiling face became tense. He was looking over U-ri's shoulder at the road behind her. U-ri turned around and saw Sky standing on the other side of the bustling street. He was looking off into the sky, as if he might see the vanished palace, his back to the closed front doors of a shop. Even when a passing soldier collided with him, he merely stumbled and went immediately back to looking up into the sky.

Morgan gave the nameless devout a long and disapproving look and slowly swallowed, his Adam's apple moving up and down. Sky didn't even seem to have noticed him.

"Is...*that* your servant as well, missie?"

"If by 'that' you mean Sky, then yes, he is."

"What? It has a name? Oh, you must have given it one. That's a nameless devout, that."

The man's friendly nature had put U-ri at ease for a moment, but now anger rose inside her. "Yes, he is my servant. He's taken very good care of me, I'll have you know. So stop calling him 'that'! Sky is a person."

Morgan's eyebrows—as bristly as his beard—rose, and he frowned. "Now then, no need to get so angry," he said, shrinking back and wringing his hands together. "I take it the Man of Ash—or simply Ash as you seem to prefer—knows about that, er, the nameless devout?"

"Of course he does. He's been with us the whole time."

Morgan lowered his voice. "And he didn't say anything? Well, no, I suppose he wouldn't." Morgan nodded, muttering to himself. "And, er, no other people you've met on your little excursion had anything strange to say about your servant?"

Now it was U-ri's turn to be tightlipped. People had said things, lots of things, but she wasn't sure what it all meant, and she certainly didn't want to tell anything to this man whom she found herself liking less and less—but he could already see the truth in her eyes.

"I see you've been wondering about it yourself, then," he said, a surprising gentleness in his voice that stopped U-ri's heart for a beat.

"Ash is always cold to Sky, when he bothers to talk to him at all. And he keeps telling me to not worry about Sky so much." She glared at the large man's face. "What about you, Morgan? Are you going to write him off just because he's a nameless devout?"

"Write him off? Hardly. He's a holy man."

U-ri's eyes went wide. "Holy?"

"That's right. His is a far purer, far higher existence than ours, and something this world desperately needs. Far more than it needs the Hero, that's for sure."

Morgan was dead serious. *He's not joking.* And U-ri thought she detected something else in his eyes: a hint of sadness.

"But he should not be a servant, let alone yours. He should not be anywhere but the nameless land."

"I know, but Sky was cast out—"

Behind him, Ash emerged from the tent. Morgan left U-ri standing there and jogged over to him, pulling him aside by his cloak. Ash lifted an eyebrow, a bemused expression on his face.

"What do you think you're doing? She doesn't know anything, does she?" Morgan whispered, probably intending for U-ri not to hear, but he was so excited and his voice so reverberant, she caught every word.

"What do I think I'm doing about what? What are you talking about?"

"I'm talking about that nameless devout!"

Ash and Morgan both turned to look at Sky who was still standing across the road, oblivious to everything around him. U-ri walked over to the two men purposefully.

"What's so wrong about Sky?" she demanded.

For a moment, Ash's brow twitched with anger. Morgan covered his eyes with a large hand.

"What's wrong with him?" Ash replied coolly. "I have no idea what you mean. Is he feeling unwell? Looks to me like he's just standing there like some kind of scarecrow."

"Don't pretend you don't know what I'm talking about!" U-ri raged.

"Give it up, missie," Morgan cut in. "Asking questions won't get you anywhere with this one. He's being willfully obtuse." Morgan clapped a hand on Ash's broad shoulder. "Look, let me be frank. If you insist on going below, the nameless devout stays here. He can't go with you."

"If I wanted your advice, I'd have asked for it," Ash said coldly. He turned to U-ri. "It appears that the palace has become something of an underground labyrinth. There's only one entrance. Some soldiers have gone down looking for survivors, but all they've found are demons and worse, and not a single survivor rescued. In other words, it's dangerous." Ash fixed her with his gaze. "Will you go, Lady *Allcaste*?"

"Are you going?" U-ri asked back.

"Of course I'm going. I'm sure that this is where the Hero has come in search of Kirrick's remains."

U-ri was tense with anger and fear, but she swallowed both. "How can I not go? What could you accomplish without me there with you?"

Ash grinned. "You've still got your spirit, I see. You there, Aju?"

The mouse poked his nose out from U-ri's collar. "What do you want?"

"We're going to get ourselves some weapons. I want you to find something U-ri can use, a mace, perhaps. Something with *malfonde* silver in it—even a little is okay. I trust you can tell the difference?"

Aju reluctantly emerged, and Ash grabbed him with a gloved hand and walked in the direction of yet another tent. "If you want to know about Sky, talk to him yourself," Ash said over his shoulder to U-ri as he walked away. "If he wants to go down below, we'll take him. If he doesn't, he can stay here. Don't listen to the fat man's ramblings. And don't dawdle, we leave immediately."

Next to her, Morgan was wringing his fingers together again. "I know my advice is not always welcome—"

"Do you know something I don't?"

Morgan shook his head, then responded with a question of his own. "The vessel, he was a relative of yours, missie?"

"Yes, my brother."

"Oh, I see. Didn't know that. I'm sorry for you. Being an *allcaste* is always a sorry thing. 'Specially with you being children and all." Morgan put his hand on U-ri's shoulder and pushed her in Sky's direction. "Go have a talk with your friend, then. If you've made it this far, I don't see why you shouldn't keep on keeping on the way you've been going. Yes, Ash has the right of it. He so often does."

U-ri sensed that the big man was genuinely concerned for her and Sky. So concerned, U-ri started to get scared again. "Morgan, I..."

"Don't you worry about me, missie. I'll be disappearing soon enough. Don't have what it takes to go down below, myself. Just one last word of advice, if you don't mind?" Morgan stooped down, bringing his eyes on a level with hers. "No matter what happens down there, remember it's none of your doing, missie. None of your brother's either. Neither of you have done anything bad. It's not your fault. It's just fate. The people who live in this region of the Circle are stuck in their story as it goes to and from the nameless land—they can't get out." He straightened up again. "So, you can cry if you like, but don't despair."

U-ri thought she felt the man lightly tap her shoulder, but Morgan was suddenly nowhere to be seen. He was so huge, and yet he had vanished in an instant like some kind of fairy.

When he said he was going to disappear, he meant it literally.

U-ri thought about what she knew of the wolves. It was true there seemed to be more than just one type, with more than just one role to play in their struggle.

U-ri held closed the collar of her vestments against the wind sweeping down the street as she hurriedly weaved through the passersby to join Sky. The devout's eyes were as wide as ever, but he wasn't looking at anything. He was just staring vacantly. *It's almost as if he's hollow.*

For a moment, U-ri couldn't help but wonder if there really was nothing under those robes of his. She looked at them fluttering in the wind. *Of course there's something there. What am I thinking? How many times have I held Sky's hand?*

And yet—

"Sky?"

There was no response. She grabbed his hand, shook him again and again, and still his eyes stared out into space. All he did was sway back and forth.

"Sky? Sky! What's wrong? Wake up!"

U-ri's nose wrinkled, and her voice cracked. From beyond the tents— probably around where the palace had once stood—she heard a crowd of people shouting, though she couldn't tell whether it was in fear or anger.

Sky blinked and seemed to notice U-ri standing there for the first time. His purple eyes were dry, and dust from the street clung to his lashes. "Lady U-ri?" he said, and the old Sky was back. He blinked again, and his eyes began to water.

U-ri's knees went weak as relief washed through her, though it was not enough to completely lift her unease. "We've come to a really scary place. And to be honest, I'm getting more than a little frightened. No, I'm downright scared."

Sky wobbled again, his arms hanging down by his sides.

"We're going down there," U-ri said, grabbing his hand. "We're going down to where the palace fell. Will you come with us?"

Sky did not answer immediately. He wobbled again, shifted his feet, then turned to look at the doors he had been leaning against this whole time. They were double doors, built strong, with narrow weatherboarding covering the front.

"This...appears to have been a greengrocer's," he said.

The windows on the front side of the shop had been smashed, and U-ri noticed that though the doors were closed, they were slightly askew and hanging from loose hinges. It looked like there had been an awning, but that too had been destroyed, leaving only a bent frame above the door. U-ri looked around but could see no shop sign announcing the name of the place. If there had been a sign once, it was long gone now.

"When we first came through the gate, I saw the owner of this store closing up. He'd put all he had for sale into boxes and was carrying them away," Sky whispered to her. "As he worked, he prayed. He prayed again and again for protection. He prayed for the favor of the gods."

Sky put a hand on the door. "I knew his prayer. I had heard it before."

U-ri stepped up beside him then, and she too placed a hand upon the door. She thought that maybe if she did what he did, she would feel the same things he had.

Sky slowly turned around, looking at U-ri. "Lady U-ri. I know this town. I know Elemsgard. I remember her streets. I remember how the people live here. I remember what the palace—here until just this very morning—looked like, towering over the rooftops. *I remembered—*"

The wind blew against Sky's black robes, thick with dust and smelling of charred wood, pressing them against his emaciated body. U-ri wondered anew at how thin the devout looked. Yet there were his shoulders, and his chest, and his legs. Sky was right in front of her, so why did it feel like he was growing more and more distant? The real Sky was escaping her, little by little. It was a strange, illogical feeling, and yet it made her tremble all over.

What, Sky? What did you remember?

"Maybe," U-ri managed to say in a tiny voice, "maybe before you became a nameless devout, you lived here, in the Haetlands. Here in the capital. Maybe that's why you remember it." *That has to be it.* Sky wasn't a nameless devout anymore. He was gradually regaining his former individuality as a human being. Slowly but surely, it was happening. Hadn't Dr. Latore said as much back on the mountaintop? He had talked about Sky's burden having been lifted. Yet the weight on U-ri's chest felt heavier and darker by the day. Sky getting his memories back should have been a wonderful thing. She should be jumping with joy, so why was she so anxious? *It's Morgan's fault for filling my head with questions again. And Sky's fault for looking so scared.*

"Sky," she said, hoping to get it off her chest once and for all, "you're becoming human again."

"Because I became your servant?" Sky muttered, his head hanging, his eyes blank circles.

"Yes—because you stayed with me and protected me."

"I have done nothing," he said weakly, his shoulders sinking.

"That's not true at all. You've done lots. I know. I remember." U-ri held a hand out. "Let's go. Or aren't you coming with us?"

Sky looked up at U-ri's hand. His arms still hung limply by his sides. He slowly raised his eyes further until he was looking at her face. "Lady U-ri, I am frightened."

"Why? What's there to be frightened of?" U-ri said as bravely as she could, though it felt like the wind whipping down the street blew right into her heart. It gusted past U-ri and Sky, pulling them away from each other.

No, I won't let it.

"I'm with you, Sky. I am the *allcaste*. You have nothing to fear," U-ri declared loudly. She grabbed his hand. It was startlingly cold. U-ri could feel the numbness spread from his skin to hers. Doubt, bewilderment, mysteries sinking into her flesh, stabbing into her bones. *Why did Morgan say that? Why can't Sky go below with us? Why did he pull Ash aside and chew him out like he did? Where did he get off acting like that?*

U-ri heard a pair of heavy boots hit the ground. She looked around and saw Ash, Aju on his shoulder. He had a dirty cloth sack on his back and was holding what looked like a tarnished silvery club in his hand. What appeared to be weapons and various tools protruded from the top of the bag on his back.

"Here, your mace," Ash announced, thrusting the silver club in front of U-ri's face. It was a simple thing—basically a stick with a round bulge at one end. U-ri accepted it without thinking and found it surprisingly heavy.

"Bless it with your glyph," Ash told her.

U-ri put a hand to her forehead, then used the same hand to grip the silver club. From the spot where she gripped it, the metal's color shifted from silver to platinum. White light spread to both ends of the mace. At the same time, the weight of the thing seemed to evaporate, until it was lighter than a feather in her hand. U-ri gave it a swing. She wouldn't even need to use both hands to wield it. She spun the mace around and brought it in front of her eyes. The orb at the top sparkled with light.

Ash, his face straight, turned to Sky. The nameless devout let go of U-ri's hand. His purple eyes still looked empty, yet there was a new resolve in his expression as he looked up at Ash.

"Will you join us?"

Sky's lips trembled almost imperceptibly.

"If you come with us below, you'll get your answer—the answer to that question that only now has begun to take shape inside you."

If you know all that, why not tell him the answer now, right here? U-ri was about to shout when Aju hopped onto her head and squeaked, "Let's stop chatting and get going!" He began furiously tugging on U-ri's hair and pounding on her scalp with his tiny feet.

"Ouch! Aju! Just wait a minute! I want to know—"

"If you're going to sit here and blab all day, we're leaving you behind, U-ri!"

U-ri was about to retort when she noticed the sadness in Aju's voice. She felt something tiny and wet fall on her head—the tears of a mouse.

"Let us go," Sky said firmly, stepping up to Ash. "Take me with you. I will go. I must go." He turned back to U-ri and smiled. "Perhaps it is as you say, Lady U-ri. Perhaps I once lived here in the Haetlands, and by being with you I have slowly regained some of my past, some of my humanity. If this is true, how could I stand by and do nothing? How can I stop now?"

Sky's smile and that look in his eyes reminded U-ri of a little boy who, after falling from his bicycle, stands up, brushes himself off, and shouts to his mother that he's fine. U-ri knew she was supposed to smile back. *That's right, you're fine.*

"The way down is this way," Ash said, swiftly turning to walk in the direction from which they had seen several soldiers and other men leave. U-ri's confidence wavered, and it took her a moment to take that first, hesitant step. Sky was already ahead of her, following after Ash. His eyes were cast downward, one hand clenched in a fist, the other holding his black robes close to his chest.

"Why are you sad, Aju?" U-ri asked as she walked, more swiftly now, putting up a hand to stroke him where he sat clinging to the hair on the top of her head. "If you don't want to tell me, it's okay. I won't ask. Just, don't cry, okay?"

"S-sorry," Aju squeaked after a moment. "I'm not sad, U-ri. I'm...I'm ashamed. I'm ashamed of what I am—a false dictionary. I'm a fake, U-ri—"

"You know, I heard Morgan say that, but I have no idea what it means, so I don't really care, Aju."

They passed between the thickly clustered tents toward the middle of town until they emerged onto a brick-lined street that must have once been a broad city thoroughfare, but the scene that awaited them was enough to make U-ri pinch her own cheek, just to make sure she wasn't dreaming.

It *was* very much like something you'd see in a dream, or maybe a nightmare. U-ri just stared.

There, no more than thirty feet ahead of where they stood, the town simply ceased to exist. Whatever had been there before was gone, sunk into the ground along a fault line so straight and clean it was as if the giant hands of some god had reached down and carefully folded the city center into the ground, creasing the edge with a massive thumb. Everything was gone: the palace, the roads, all the buildings, leaving nothing but the blue sky stretching overhead.

"Come look, Lady U-ri," Sky said, stopping and pointing. "There, where the road was severed. Look at the colors."

She saw it immediately. It was like a thin screen, floating up from the edge, rippling with a rainbow of light.

"That is where the roads were pushed underground," Ash told them, walking forward. "I heard one of the patrolmen talking about it. There's no fear of further collapse. The entire palace and its surroundings are below here now."

U-ri shook her head, and realizing her mouth was hanging open, she snapped it shut and steadied her breath. "How did it happen like this?"

"I'm sure we'll find out."

When they approached the rainbow screen, U-ri realized they wouldn't need ropes or ladders to go below. Though the line of the edge was straight, the road did not drop straight down, but instead sloped down in steps. Where the road had been straight before, now it traced a gentle spiral, like the path along the edge of the cavern beneath the abbey ruins. It was as if the palm that had pushed the city down had slowly twisted at the same time. Here and there she spotted guards on watch duty or lying injured on the ground, or huddled together in fear.

At the bottom of the spiral lay the darkness that had swallowed the palace whole—a giant rent in the earth. She could see strata of earth along its ragged edge. And there was something else—

"That's Kirrick's family crest!" U-ri exclaimed.

It seemed to have formed naturally from pieces of rubble along the rock wall where she could see the layers of sediment—the same crest she had seen in the portraits under the ruins of Katarhar Abbey.

U-ri walked toward the opening. Aju stood up on her shoulder. "The crest of House Dijkstra?"

"Yeah, that's it. I'm sure of it."

As she said it, the mace in her hand flashed brightly. Then the crest of House Dijkstra hanging over the crevice began to glow in response. A moment later, the glyph on U-ri's own forehead began to glow as well.

The strange three-part chorus of lights was over in a few seconds, each light winking out at precisely the same moment.

U-ri heard a voice. It was distant, coming from an indeterminate direction, but there was no mistaking it.

"Yuriko!"

U-ri's eyes and mouth opened wide. She wanted to shout, to cheer, to scream, but nothing came out. Emotion filled her chest to bursting.

It's Hiroki. He's calling for me!

"Hiroki!"

Finally, she found her voice. U-ri ran to the entrance of the underground labyrinth, but before she could reach it, strong hands grabbed the collar of her vestments, and her feet were treading air.

"Let me go! Let me go!"

Hiroki's calling for me! He's waiting for me!

"Don't listen to it." It was Ash. He tossed her back behind him, away from the entrance. Sky caught her before she could fall.

"If that's all it takes to get to you," Ash said, "you can't be allowed to go any further."

U-ri pushed Sky away and stood catching her breath; then she launched herself at Ash, flinging her fists at him, kicking, screaming and spitting, her teeth bared.

"Get out of my way! Out! Who are you to say where I belong or don't belong? What do you know?"

Ash said nothing. He did not block her blows nor try to stop her. But when she pushed past him, he again grabbed her by the collar and tossed her back. In a rage, U-ri attacked again, only to have Ash grab her and toss her back once more. Over and over they repeated this until U-ri was completely out of breath. Dizzy, she collapsed into Sky's arms.

"I've been hearing that voice for some time now," Ash said calmly, standing between her and the way down. He was less like an impenetrable wall and more like a drawn blade: barring the path, slicing into U-ri's heart. U-ri felt the blood rise to her head, and she glared at him, never seeing the darkness in his eyes.

"You mean you heard it back up on the road?" Aju asked. He had somehow managed to cling to U-ri through all that charging and being thrown around. "You did hear it. But it didn't sound like Hiroki to you, did it? To you, it must've sounded like—"

Like Kirrick's voice.

U-ri slowly came to her senses. Catching her breath, she let Sky help her to her feet. She recalled how Ash had stopped on their way into the city, as though he were listening to something. *He heard Kirrick calling to him all the way back there?*

"It means nothing, no matter who you hear or how many times you hear it," Ash said, straightening his bag on his back and turning to face the entrance to the labyrinth. "It's merely an illusion, a figment of your imagination. A trap, set by the King in Yellow to divert those who would pursue it from their path."

"But it was my brother's voice!" U-ri protested, trembling.

Facing away from her, Ash laughed. "See? You hear nothing, learn nothing. How childish you sound, how unreliable. How weak." Ash swiftly turned back toward U-ri. "That's what it wants you to think. What's the best way to turn a glyph-wielding *allcaste* back into a powerless little girl? Make her think she's got her big brother back. That's what the King in Yellow will try to do.

"Cover your ears. Close your eyes. Put a lid on your very heart. Believe only in the power of that mark upon your forehead. That's what I've learned through years of trial and error. That's why I get to tell you what to do, little miss *allcaste*."

His words were overbearing, yet his voice was filled with pain. "With my ears, I have heard Kirrick calling to me dozens, hundreds of times. I have heard him calling for help, and I have searched and searched and found nothing. I know that he is not where the voice leads me. He is no more. *And neither is your brother.* Time's arrow flies forward only, never in reverse. No one can undo what has been done. There is no going back, U-ri."

U-ri stared back unblinkingly into Ash's eyes, noticing with a start that for the first time Ash had called her by her new name, her *allcaste* name.

"It is the power of stories that makes us think we can turn back time to bring back what was lost. That is the logic of the Circle. It is something beautiful and warm, and sometimes it can touch the truth in our hearts. But it is not truth itself. That is why we say those weavers who spin the Circle's stories are sinners. You cannot bring back the dead," Ash said, resting a hand on the hilt of his sword at his belt.

"Where we go, we will not find Kirrick. Nor will we find your brother. The vessel has been used and spent, its life ended. Only phantasms remain. If you cannot prepare yourself to fulfill your role as *allcaste*, to stare at those phantasms and see them for what they are, then you should leave now. The glyph will not stop you."

The mark on U-ri's forehead glimmered once then, as though to agree with the Man of Ash. Her skin prickled beneath the glyph. She touched it gingerly with her fingers and found that the lines of the glyph were raised on her forehead, like a boil. It was as though the glyph were saying *"If you wish it, I will leave you this instant and fly away."*

Tensing her fingers, U-ri pushed the glyph on her forehead back down. The glowing stopped. Her forehead was as smooth as before.

Then she heard the voice again in her ears, calling directly to her heart, it seemed. *Yuriko.* U-ri straightened herself and gritted her teeth.

"I won't turn back. I'm an *allcaste*, and I'm going to meet the Hero."

U-ri stepped forward, her vestments of protection billowing up behind her.

CHAPTER THIRTEEN

Reunion

"Get ready. The world is about to change."

Ash's piercing warning came as they stepped through the rift. U-ri found herself unable to walk through the rift with her eyes open, so she had closed them, but she soon discovered the meaning of Ash's words for herself.

What is this? Are we really below ground? No way! This isn't underground, this is—

"Are we inside the palace?"

They were standing in the center of a large octagonal hall, stone walls on all sides. U-ri spun around, looking in every direction, but nowhere could she find the rift they had just come through. Corridors led from the hall in four directions, and in the corner directly before them stood a raised, semicircular platform with a railing that ran along its length. U-ri assumed the platform was flat on top, like a stage, but it was so high up—at least as high as a five-story building—that she could only guess. Stairs climbed to the top on either side of the platform.

The ceiling of the hall was even higher above their heads. She had to tilt her head back a full ninety degrees to see it. The ceiling was also octagonal in shape, with a mosaic of gold, silver, and some black stone—obsidian, U-ri guessed—adorning its center.

"The crest of the current king, Harvein the Second," Ash said, looking up. His breath was white in the air. For the first time, U-ri noticed the freezing cold.

"You may recall the story I told you of the Haetlands royal family's long history of sibling rivalry? That is why our kingdom has more than one royal crest, in case you were wondering."

Countless candles had been set in holders along the walls, so high up it made U-ri dizzy to think of how anyone managed to change them. The weak flames flickered, yet managed to light the entire vastness of the hall. A pair of much larger sconces stood before the central stage, illuminating the relief on the wall behind it—and something else.

"Someone's there!"

Ash had his foot on the first step of one of the staircases. "If my memory is correct, this room is the king's audience chamber."

The metal studs on his boots rang against the stone steps. U-ri hurriedly followed after him, and taking Sky's hand, she began to climb.

"Odd that we should first enter here—directly into what was once the very heart of the palace." A great stone throne sat atop the platform, its back to a large painted relief on the wall. A thick cloak hung over the back of the throne.

"Who's there?"

A knight in silver armor sat slumped against the railing of the platform, facing the throne. A large double-edged sword lay on the ground next to his leg. An arm that had once been the knight's was attached to the sword, but no longer to him. In the dim light, the blood that had spilled from his shoulder looked black as tar. The blood had clearly been drying for some time, though the nearest candles reflected wetly off its surface.

"He's one of the rescue party." Ash knelt by the fallen knight. "Good sir," he said, "if you still draw breath, tell me what happened to the occupants of the palace."

U-ri stepped closer, noticing the delicate ornamentation on the knight's armor. The grip of his sword was similarly decorated. He must have been a man of some stature.

"All dead," the knight whispered. Merely drawing breath seemed painful for him. Not only his arm, but his face too had been savaged terribly. It was not the kind of wound such as a sword or spear might make. The deep gouges in his armor and in the side of his face suggested giant fangs and wicked talons.

The knight spoke again, his voice growing weaker with every word, "—or they were swallowed by the darkness as they lived. They became...started to become—"

"Don't talk, you'll wear yourself out," U-ri said as she and Sky tried to help the man lie down on his side. He resisted, feebly batting at them with his remaining arm. U-ri noticed he was missing an eye as well.

"The palace is as you see it," he continued, his voice somewhat stronger. "It was an evil magic that did this...twisted the very fabric of the place. Rooms in place of other rooms, nothing where it should be. I know these halls well enough to walk them blindfolded, and still I despaired of finding the way out."

The knight's breath came in pained, ragged gulps as he turned his face to look toward the throne. "The king is over there. If you can, please take him outside."

U-ri jumped back in surprise. She had thought what lay over the throne was only a cloak.

Ash walked over and almost reverently lifted a corner of the cloak. The cloth was covered with fine embroidery, and the hem lined with jewels. Yet it was marred with dark splotches of blood and torn clean through in places.

A man's arm swung out from beneath the cloak, but it was gravity that moved it, not life. And the arm wasn't so much an arm as the bony remains of one, hung with tattered strips of dried skin.

His face a blank mask, Ash swept the cloak away, revealing the body. A delicate lace collar still hung around the corpse's neck. All the hair on U-ri's body was standing straight on end.

"It attacked the king's chambers first."

Ash acknowledged the knight's pained whisper with a nod.

The knight continued, "By the time we arrived, the king was already as you see him now."

"I see no crown."

"It was stolen."

Ash nodded again, then asked, "You are one of his personal guard?"

"I was in the third...squadron. Perhaps my captain is...yes, he must still be alive. You, if you should meet my captain..."

Ash turned to the dying man. "First tell me something. A part of Kirrick's remains was buried somewhere inside this palace. A knight of the personal guard should know where that is. I'm sure a guard was posted."

At the sound of Kirrick's name, a look of violent disgust passed over the knight's bloodied face. "What's this now? Kirrick? So Kirrick has come back to claim what was his?"

"The thing that attacked the king, what did it look like?"

The knight's remaining eye swam with fear. "It...had no shape. It flew in like a fell wind. A dark shadow...bearing the stench of blood."

"Did it say anything?"

The knight barely managed to shake his head. "There were...no words."

Ash turned again to the body of Harvein the Second and casually tossed the cloak back over it. "Perhaps only the king knew the location of the remains. That is why Kirrick went for him first, to drink of his knowledge and memory." Ash straightened and said, "Looks like there's no way to go but further in."

U-ri blinked with surprise. "You're just going to leave him there? Wasn't he your king?"

"And now he's just a corpse. There's no saving him," Ash grumbled as he headed back toward the stairs. "Nor do I think that knight there would look kindly upon me touching the corpse. Lowly undertaker that I am."

U-ri had her hand on the knight's armored shoulder, and she felt him tremble violently at Ash's words.

"What?" he gasped, his bloodshot eye looking like it might pop out of his skull. "An undertaker? Your hands are stained with the demons' blood! You touched the king!"

The knight struggled to stand, and U-ri hurriedly held him down, placing one hand on his forehead, thinking to heal him. But the knight pushed her away with a growl. "You're only a child! What are you doing in this place?"

"Just sit still a moment."

"You are friends with that cursed man? If so—" the knight's mouth twisted with rage. "Stay...stay away from the king, you foul creature!"

"U-ri, something's coming!" Aju squeaked from her collar. U-ri looked up. Next to her, Sky braced himself. The two were scanning the chamber when something stung U-ri's cheek.

"The ceiling!" Aju screamed.

"Hurry!" Ash shouted up from the bottom of the stairs. "Get low!"

U-ri crouched by the railing and looked up.

Far above their heads, the royal crest was starting to break apart. First the silver and gold parts, then the black gems broke away and fell down in streams of dust. The streams narrowed, twisting like cyclones, bending through the air of the cavern, tangling with other streams, then breaking back into showers of dust—

Then the streams began to take shape.

From the black dust grew a pair of wings, and soon from the swirls of debris emerged a bird of dust. A bird as large as U-ri. Its long beak snapped shut with a loud clap that reverberated through the chamber. Soon another bird-thing formed, then another, and another, their numbers increasing as she watched.

The gold and silver streams of dust became gold and silver snakes, but snakes with arms as long again as their bodies. Three claws formed at the tip of each arm, each as sharp as a blade. The snakes' arms tangled together in the air, their claws sparking like flint where they met.

Ash lifted a two-handed sword above his head and ran for the staircase. As though they had been waiting for that signal, the creatures of gold, silver, and black rushed down from the ceiling as one, howling as they descended toward him.

"Sky, watch the knight!" U-ri shouted as she hefted her mace. Aju dived under the collar of her vestments and began chanting furiously.

"Swing your mace, U-ri!"

She did so, and a translucent disc appeared, shining as it hovered in the air before her.

"That's a shield! Grab it!"

Mace in her right hand, shield in her left, U-ri met the creatures as they slid down through the air. The orb at the tip of her mace flashed brilliantly, its light enough to send the creatures spinning and writhing away from her. She actually struck a blow, shattering the claw of the snake that reached for her like it was an exploding chandelier. Its body cracked down the middle, the severed halves crumbling back to inanimate dust before Uri's eyes.

Aju jumped atop her head. "Don't let me fall off, U-ri!"

Standing on his hind legs, the mouse began to spin, singing the words of a spell. As he spun, tiny orbs of light sprayed forth from the tip of his long tail. Each orb was no larger than a pea, yet when they hit, the creatures roared with rage and pain.

Ash stood his ground in the middle of the hall, swinging his mighty blade, hewing down like a farmer cuts wheat any creature foolish enough to have been lured away from the throne. The dust from their remains billowed like clouds, until U-ri could barely see him through the haze.

"Ack, I'm getting dizzy!" Aju squeaked. He tumbled down onto U-ri's shoulder. One of the black winged creatures darted toward them, and U-ri met it with her mace. Close up, the thing was even more repugnant than she had imagined. It had no eyes, nor anything you could call a face. Its beak looked like a metallic pyramid emerging from its body. The tip of the pyramid opened, swallowing the head of her mace, and the creature exploded from the inside.

"Now that's just disgusting!" Aju leapt from U-ri's shoulder through the air onto Sky's head, spitting out dust particles from the creature as he flew. Sky huddled over the wounded knight, a human shield for the fallen man.

"U-ri!" Aju squeaked. "Swing your mace this way a bit! Sky, grab that shield and fight!"

Sky reached out and grabbed the translucent shield, holding it out in front of himself with both arms. The knight was sprawled on the floor, grasping for the hilt of his sword. A gold and silver snake darted toward them and slammed into Sky's shield, then screeched as it was repulsed and sent tumbling against the throne.

"Sword...my sword."

The knight had just managed to get his fingers around the hilt when a pair of black wings hurtled through the air, directly toward the knight's back.

"Look out!" Sky let go of the shield and threw himself over the knight.

"Sky!"

It all happened so fast, U-ri could do nothing. She had only just lifted her mace when the creature's gleaming beak slammed into the nameless devout.

U-ri screamed and kept screaming. But nothing happened to Sky. The creature passed right through him and vanished. It was as if his body had simply absorbed the monster.

U-ri's head wobbled, the shock silencing her.

Sky looked up at her. His eyes were blank.

"Will you pick up the shield, Sky!" Aju shrieked. "Pick it up now! Quickly, quickly! Do it!"

Hand still on his sword, the one-armed knight twisted his head to look at Sky. His one good eye opened wide. "What are you?" he said, and then in a whisper, he added, "...cursed thing," just loud enough for U-ri to hear.

She couldn't believe it. Though he could barely move, the knight was pushing himself away from Sky. With all the strength that remained in his damaged body, he sat up and pointed the tip of his sword directly at the nameless devout.

"Who are you? All of you!" The knight's face was twisted with fear and rage. His voice cracked, and spittle flew from his lips. "Who are you? You're friends of the thing that did this, aren't you!"

As she hammered at another one of the creatures, U-ri shouted back, "We are most definitely not cursed!"

As she said it, the tip of U-ri's mace glowed brightly, flooding the entire top of the dais with light. The white orb of light grew larger and larger, swallowing up U-ri, Aju, and Sky. Then it expanded further still, flooding over the steps until it reached down as far as where Ash was standing in the hall below.

Smoke began to rise from the leather pads on the wolf's shoulders. He held up a hand to shield his face from the light and roared, "U-ri, close your eyes! Everyone down!" Ash ran back toward the throne platform.

The circle of white light filled every last corner of the octagonal hall and quickly swelled toward the vaulted ceiling. It wrapped everything in its brilliant energy, briefly illuminating the shapes of people and creatures before swallowing them whole.

The light reached the ruins of the crest at the top of the ceiling, and the crest responded by glowing from within. A moment later, the crest exploded. Every last one of the creatures dancing in the air shattered, losing their forms in the light.

The force of the explosion knocked U-ri to the floor. She had taken Ash's warning to heart, and her eyes were still tightly closed. Above her head, the creatures screamed. Oddly enough, with her eyes closed they sounded different than they had before. *They sound almost human.* She heard the voices of men weeping in pain and sadness, screaming with rage and terror.

"They're not monsters, they're people!" U-ri heard herself shout, and she opened her eyes. The world around her was made of white light. Then Ash was beside her, slapping a gloved hand over her eyes and pulling her under the flap of his cloak. There was another explosion. The floor of the hall shook. The screams rose in pitch and intensity.

🌱

U-ri came to. It seemed she had been unconscious for a short while. She was lying on the hard stone floor. Ash knelt behind her, propping her head up. His hand was no longer over her eyes.

Ash breathed a long sigh. "Good work," he said, giving U-ri a pat on the head.

Silence had returned to the hall. Half of the candles in the sconces set around the hall had gone out, and something like white ash covered entire sections of the walls. The floor was littered with burnt torch holders.

U-ri looked up at the ceiling. The royal crest was gone, and the ceiling had fallen, revealing the utter darkness beyond. Still, within the hall it was light. It took U-ri a moment to realize that the main source of the light was herself, more specifically, her forehead. The glyph was shining more brightly than it ever had before. Not like a candle or torch or even a searchlight. It was like a warm light that illuminated everything in the room evenly from all directions, yet it all came from her.

"You okay, U-ri?" Aju poked his head out of Ash's pocket. U-ri wondered when he'd slipped in there. "How about you, Sky? Can you stand?"

Sky was lying on the floor behind U-ri, curled up like a sleeping child. The knight's sword lay on the ground next to him. But the arm that had been gripping it and the knight that arm belonged to were gone.

"This place has been purified," Ash said softly. "Look. Harvein the Second is gone as well."

Only the tattered cloak hung over the throne.

"Sky, are you okay? Did you get hurt? Let me see!"

U-ri stood and reached for him, but when her hand touched the devout's shoulder, something like sparks shot up from his body, giving her a shock. U-ri stepped back, her eyes wide. Sky crawled away from her and pressed his back against the stone wall at the far end of the dais. His purple eyes were filled with a terror so intense U-ri found herself unable to speak.

"Did I do something?"

Nothing.

"What's wrong, Sky?"

The devout's terror was catching. U-ri's throat was dry. Ash stood, throwing back his cloak and stepping up beside her.

Sky was still in the throes of fear, his eyes wide and his lips trembling. "What am—"

"What are you?" Ash completed the devout's question, his voice as sharp as his sword. "What did you see just now in the light?"

Though he did not blink, something in Sky's eyes was turning. His eyes shone with light, then went dark. There was something reflected in them, not from the outside world, but from his heart. Whatever it was, it was too small for U-ri to see clearly.

Sky clenched one hand into a fist and began to beat his own chest. His expression did not change, yet he kept striking himself, meting out punishment. With each strike, his head jerked backward, striking the wall behind him, while he stammered, "I-I..."

U-ri dashed forward and grabbed Sky's hands. There were no sparks this time. His skin felt icy cold against hers.

"It's nothing," Sky whispered, though he sounded on the verge of tears. Delicately, he removed U-ri's fingers, gingerly nudging her hand away as though it were some fragile object.

He looked up at Ash. "We are going further in, yes? Let us be off."

Ash nodded and turned. Behind him, Sky stood, bracing himself against the wall for balance. He put a hand to his chest and rubbed it where he had been hitting himself only moments before.

With the exception of Ash, none of them were familiar with the palace in the least—which was now an advantage it seemed, since they would not be misled by memories twisted into distractions by the incredible changes that had been wrought to the geography of the place.

Not only was nothing where it was supposed to be, but rooms were connected to rooms in the most haphazard and unconventional ways, as though the giant hands had reached in and scrambled the palace interior heedless of left and right or up and down.

There were stairs stuck in odd places, and corridors that wrapped back around on themselves. The one thing they could count on was the threat of dust-creatures around nearly every corner. U-ri quickly got used to the weight of the mace swinging in her hands, and with each encounter felt an increasing awareness of the extent of her glyph's power.

They saw some people, but far less frequently than monsters, and only a handful of the people they found still drew breath. Most were knights in shredded armor, though occasionally they found a minister in courtly robes, or a woman in a long dress.

On one occasion they found a man lying on the ground, still breathing, though only faintly. He did not stir when they called to him. When U-ri tried using her glyph, Ash stopped her, saying it was too late for that. Again and again this happened. They would find a new room, defeat what creatures lay in wait by the entrance or that came storming up from a dark corner, and then U-ri, Ash, and Sky would look around inside at the scattered corpses in the vain hope of finding a survivor.

"Why would Kirrick do something like this?" U-ri asked, her breath short—not due to the constant exertions of battle, but with frustration. "What possible meaning could any of this have? Killing people, then mutating them into monsters just so that his pursuers can finish them off?"

"It's all conflict, isn't it?" Ash said. He was in front, but spoke without glancing back. "Furthermore, this is not Kirrick's fault. This is the work of the King in Yellow."

"But isn't Kirrick at the King in Yellow's heart?" U-ri insisted.

"He is. Together with your brother."

"Say," Aju cut in in a high squeaky voice, "I thought a search party came through here before us. Funny we haven't run into them. Maybe they're just up ahead?"

"Which way would that be?" U-ri wondered out loud, voicing the thought in everyone's mind.

They reached yet another dead end. The ceiling in this chamber was high, though nothing on the scale of the throne room. Smooth, cold walls surrounded them on four sides, and the floor was littered with the bodies of various creatures. There was only the door through which they had entered and a small slit high up on the wall to the right-hand side, with no visible means for reaching it. The search party must have fought here, been victorious, and continued on—but which way?

"Looks like we go back." U-ri sighed. Then she heard someone calling out in a weak voice. The four of them turned, looking to see where it might have come from.

"Is someone there?"

The voice is coming from that slit in the wall!

"One of the search party," Ash said. He looked up and raised his voice: "There is a wall between us—we cannot get through. How did you get where you are?"

There was no immediate answer. U-ri imagined a man wounded, lying on the other side. *We have to get to him! Quickly!*

"The wall..." came the voice again. "It is enchanted."

Ash lightly rapped the wall with one fist, then turned to U-ri. "Knock it all down!"

U-ri put a hand to the glyph on her forehead, then turned it toward the wall, and in that instant, the giant gray slab of rock stretching up in front of her vanished like a mirage, opening up an entire vista beyond. Aju clung tightly to the back of U-ri's neck. Even Ash seemed startled. For a moment, U-ri thought they had somehow returned to the Katarhar Abbey ruins. They were staring at a giant mountain of rubble. The room containing it all was enormous, with another high ceiling and chunks of stone and plaster piled high to the very top.

U-ri looked up and spotted something glimmering there. They all saw it.

"The crown," Ash said. "It's Harvein the Second's crown."

The owner of the weak voice they had heard was sitting at the foot of the mountain of rubble, his legs splayed out in front of him. He was not a knight. He wore clothes similar to Ash's, with black hair falling over a young face. His cloak had been badly torn, and part of his chest seemed oddly crumpled inward, like a dented sheet of metal. He was bleeding.

U-ri ran up to him, and the young man attempted a smile. "You a wizard, little girl? Good on you. My partner couldn't even make a scratch on that damned wall."

"Try to sit still. I'll fix you up."

She knelt down, noticing that one of the man's legs had been torn apart, leaving little flesh by the knee.

"Did you see what did this to you?" Ash asked over U-ri's shoulder while she sat there, trying to decide where to start in mending the man.

"I did not, for it was invisible. It went down there," the man said, pointing toward the rubble with a trembling finger. "This wreckage is what's left after it devoured the palace. This here's the leavings the thing spat out."

Ash walked across the room, examining the rubble as he went. "Interesting."

He tapped a pile of stones with the pommel of his sword. "There appears to be more room beneath this one, as though it were hollow. Here. It's a way down."

U-ri applied the light of her glyph to the man over and over, but the bleeding would not stop. She would just manage to mend one wound only to have a fresh one open beside it.

"Give it up, little one. It's too late for me."

"You be quiet. It's not too late!"

"You're an undertaker too, I see," the man said to Ash. The wolf nodded.

"My partner—Narg's his name—he's a wizard. Couldn't handle that wall you just took out, though. He went down the hole by himself, thought he might find a way out that way." The man attempted another smile. "If you're really going down there, you'll save him for me, won't you?"

"That we shall," Ash said quickly. "Did any others descend deeper?"

"Some knights," the man rasped, then he began to cough violently, each spasm leaving blood-flecked spittle on his lips. "The first patrol. We were in the second. But no one's come back."

"Ash, stop making him talk!" U-ri protested, but the man took her hand in his own and gently pushed it down. Two of his fingers were broken, the nails ripped clean off. The young man stared at Ash.

"Be careful," he whispered. "Its voice...I heard it. It has no shape, but it can speak." He coughed. "It spoke with the voice of a child—a boy."

U-ri froze.

"A boy no older than this little one here," the man added, his eyes losing their focus as he spoke. His head slumped to one side as he continued his tale, more weakly now. "Reminded me of my little brother, it did."

Ash stepped up beside him, then knelt on one knee. "What did this boy say to you?"

The man turned to Ash, summoning the very last of his strength to do so. His lips parted and a trickle of blood spilled from them.

"He was laughing...he was happy. He said...he said he was going to make the world beautiful. Get rid of all the filth that's messing it up. And..." He paused, catching his breath. "And he said no one's going to stop him."

The man's head slumped forward. U-ri looked at his still-open eyes and realized that the life had fled them. Her own eyes were stinging with tears. *What can I do? What is there to do?* U-ri trembled and could not stop for some time.

"It was my brother," U-ri said, the taste of iron on her lips. *My own heart is bruised and bleeding. Pretty soon, it'll break, and I'll be coughing up blood just like this poor dead man.* "The King in Yellow is using my brother's voice!"

U-ri swayed and nearly fell, catching herself on the floor with both hands at the last moment. Her body convulsed like she was vomiting, and a sob came from her mouth.

"No crying, U-ri!" Aju squeaked in a high voice from the top of her head. "No crying! Stand up!"

The little mouse yanked on her hair as hard as he could, but U-ri felt no pain. She wiped her tears, sat up, slapped her face several times with her hands, and lifted her eyes at a world blurred by sorrow.

But she could see them—Ash standing there like a hungry ghost. And Sky, all in black, even thinner than the wolf.

Up until now, whenever U-ri had broken down, it had always been Sky who ran to her first. Now he shrank away, frightened, clutching his black robes tightly to his chest and staring at her. Their eyes met for only an instant before he quickly looked away. Ash set down the grimy sack he carried, pulled out a coil of rope, and asked, "Ever rappelled down something?"

"Why would I have done something like that?" U-ri snorted.

Ash lifted an eyebrow and told her, "It's a lot easier going down than it is going up." Then softly, "You can close his eyes now."

❧

Stairs led down the mountain of rubble, the steps crafted from seemingly random collections of rock and sand—as if whatever exterior force had pounded the earth here had caused it to fracture just so, creating descending ledges. Several of the "steps" were taller even than U-ri herself, so she had to clamber down, sometimes with Sky's help. It was very dark. Ash and Sky had both discarded their torches as they needed their hands free to navigate the steps. Only the light of U-ri's glyph lit their way, like a spelunker's headlamp. The light it cast cut a perfect circle out of the gloom, so that whichever direction U-ri wasn't facing was plunged in utter darkness.

U-ri had been under so much tension for so long that now her tears had completely dried. She was even beginning to think, as she listened to her own ragged breath, that her chest was heaving only with the exertion of their descent and not the pain she felt in her heart.

Yet the wound in her heart still ached and bled. Partly because of her brother's voice, and partly because of Sky's increasingly odd behavior.

He had always been there right by her side, before. Now she had to turn around to find him, somewhere back in the darkness behind her. She had always been able to sense him before too, even when he did not speak, but now it felt like Sky was intentionally trying to disappear—out of sight and out of mind.

"What did you see in the light?"

Ash's question to Sky. He hadn't answered. He had hit himself, like he was punishing himself for something. Then he urged the party on, as though nothing had changed.

What did you see in the light of my glyph, Sky? Did what you see do this? Did it draw you further away from me?

What was it?

The questions spun around inside her head, and U-ri had to screw her mouth shut tightly to keep them from spilling out. Going down the rough-hewn steps felt less like a descent and more like sinking into the depths.

They met no more creatures on their dishearteningly long and dangerous way down. When they had reached what appeared to be the bottom, U-ri noticed that the ground was hard and level in a way that none of the many steps above them had been.

The walls, illuminated by Uri's glyph, had clearly been man-made.

"We seem to be in some kind of underground complex," Ash said. "I'm sure in the past there were proper paths down here from the palace. But the force that did this damage chose none of those paths, instead preferring to simply open a hole in the ground."

From U-ri's shoulder Aju squeaked, "I think that room up top with all the rubble was a prayer hall of some sort. I spotted an altar and some fragments of religious-looking paintings."

"That would make it the royal family's private chapel. Makes sense. It would want to destroy that first," Ash said, unwilling to call "it" by its proper name.

Behind him was an impassable wall of wreckage. *No way to go but forward.* U-ri fixed her grip on her mace. They began walking by the light of the glyph, and small bits of plaster rained down on their heads from the darkness above. Ash extended an arm, barring U-ri's path. "Walk carefully. The impact that destroyed the palace has left its mark here."

U-ri nodded, swinging her head to give them a better view of their surroundings. She found a crack in one wall, a fallen sconce, and some broken candles. *So this place was once lit like the rooms above.*

The corridor was flat and wide enough for two to walk abreast, yet it turned frequently, always at a right angle, and following a pattern: they would come to a right turn, which led to an intersection where they went straight, only to come to a left turn. This happened over and over.

"It's a labyrinth," U-ri muttered.

"An inverted swastika, actually," Aju chirped, his voice filled with an unusual confidence. "A *manji* to you, U-ri. Isn't that right, Ash?"

"It is. Not bad for an *aunkaui* dictionary."

"Thanks," Aju replied coolly.

"But you're both right. It's a labyrinth made up of *manji*, the ancient symbol for eternity and cosmic balance. Not a labyrinth in the sense of a maze so much as a labyrinth in the sense of a spiritual path," said Ash.

"What's that mean?"

"Like the path one walks to visit a grave," Ash explained, a sense of urgency in his voice. "And I am sure that, at its terminus in the center of the labyrinth, we will find the grave of the mage Elem, whose symbol the *manji* is." After a pause, he added, "Or, to be more precise, it was the symbol of those who worshipped her."

Though Elem did not take on a single disciple during her life, there were many in the Haetlands whom she had saved with her power and knowledge. It was only a matter of time before some began to worship her as an apostle of the creator. Though not on a large enough scale to be considered a proper sect, her followers gathered to her, assisted in her research, and joined her on her many travels.

"The followers of Elem bore the mark of the *manji* upon the palms of their hands."

"That's all very fine and well," U-ri said, "but why did they have to go and make this whole labyrinth?"

"Probably to keep Elem from leaving easily," Aju suggested. "This is how the royal family of the Haetlands held Elem here beneath the palace. Only they would've known the proper path for winding their way through."

They turned, walked, went straight for a while, then turned again. As they went, the walls around them gradually began to change. They were whiter here, and brighter, adorned with murals faded and crumbling from the walls but with parts that were still visible. Most of the paintings depicted people. There were young and old, men and women, standing in orderly lines. All of them wore hooded white robes, their heads bowed reverently, with both hands held up by their chests. U-ri could make out the inverted swastikas on several of them.

"And images of her followers were placed along the walls of the labyrinth to quell Elem's restless spirit," Ash said with a sneer, quickening his pace. "We're nearing the center, where we'll find Elem—and something of Kirrick's buried with her, be it a possession or a body part."

Though they lived at different times, both mages were guilty of the same sin. Elem had planted the roots of it, and Kirrick had caused the sin to bloom like an evil flower.

"In other words, we're heading right where *it* went," Ash said.

They soon came upon the bodies of many other fallen knights, their vacant stares underscoring Ash's words. Some had their armor stripped from them and rent to pieces. U-ri was saddened, but she did not slow her pace.

"I wonder if the mage friend of that man we saw at the top of the stairs made it any further?" U-ri asked. No sooner had she said that than a bloodcurdling scream split the darkness ahead. Ash ran forward without a moment's hesitation, while U-ri stood rooted to the spot for a breath before following after. But then she stopped again—and this time it was of her own volition.

"Sky?"

Sky was hugging the wall, terrified by the scream. He slid to the ground before her.

"You're not going? Will you wait here?"

Forehead to the wall, Sky slumped, then shook his head. "No. No...I will go."

"Let's go then," U-ri held out a hand.

Sky looked away. "I will go, but you must stay here, Lady U-ri. Please wait here."

"What? Don't be ridiculous! I can't stay here!"

U-ri had just about had it. *Whatever. Do what you like!* She dashed off down the corridor, feet stomping on the ground. She was just around the next corner when something sleek slid through the air, and she reflexively swatted at it with her mace.

The corridor had grown suddenly wider. The darkness was less complete. *We're getting close.*

U-ri blinked and saw that most of the open space she had come to was filled with one particularly large creature.

In form, it greatly resembled the thing that had appeared outside the library at Hiroki's school. But this one had legs, two of them, each with sharp claws. Above them hung a misshapen lump of a body from which tentacles grew in every direction, making it impossible to tell which way the thing was facing.

If it even has a face.

U-ri recalled the creature whom she had met deep beneath the Katarhar Abbey ruins, the one that had once been Ichiro Minochi.

The creature was bleeding green blood. Ash had already severed several of its tentacles with his two-handed sword. Still, it was clinging to something—a man, his arms and legs hanging limp, his head flopping on the end of his bent neck. The monster held it aloft with many of its remaining tentacles, holding the body high over the ground and not letting go. From the robe he wore, U-ri guessed this was the mage.

"Let him go!"

At U-ri's shout, the creature shifted perceptibly. It stamped on the ground with its two legs.

"I said let him go, you fiend!"

Whatever it was, it seemed to understand her words. The creature complied, flinging the mage toward her. U-ri and Ash dodged aside, a spray green and red blood splattering their cheeks.

The creature lashed out with another tentacle. Ash leapt between it and U-ri, while U-ri readied her mace and took a deep breath. She placed her left hand to the glyph on her forehead, and the glyph began to shine.

Lifting the glow in her hand, U-ri roared, "Unclean gatekeeper, open the way to us!"

Platinum light streaked from her hand across the room. Aju squeaked, shutting his eyes against the glare, and even Ash raised his arms to shield his eyes. U-ri stood, head up, unfaltering.

In the space of a breath, the creature was gone. Even the severed tentacles that had been leaking green blood on the floor evaporated.

"Where did you learn those words?"

U-ri lowered her mace and answered, "The glyph told me."

"I see." Ash sighed. "It *was* a gatekeeper."

The gatekeeper to the graveyard, watcher over Kirrick—

U-ri and Ash walked abreast into the space the creature had left behind.

They were in a large, circular hall, from the very center of which rose a circular dais, topped by a pair of crosses laid across one another. They were crosses like the ones in U-ri's region, but she had never seen crosses arranged like this at home. The crosses she knew would have been driven into the ground like stakes.

"The grave of the mage Elem," Ash said in a hushed voice.

"Look at the walls," Aju squeaked.

Images of Elem's followers had been drawn here too. They surrounded the graves, each with the mark of the *manji* on their hands.

"Why is it so light in here?"

There were holders for torches and sconces scattered around, but none of them were lit. U-ri tried covering the glyph on her forehead with her hand, but the light in the hall did not lessen. It wasn't her glyph that was lighting it—there must have been another source.

Then she saw that a faint light, a thin, golden mist shimmering like the air sometimes does in the summer, was coming from behind the crosses.

And then the mist *sat up.*

That was the only way she could describe it. Even though the mist wasn't shaped like a person or an animal, it moved like one. U-ri realized that Ash was holding his breath.

"Who are you?" he asked, finally, his voice even and composed. "No, let me rephrase that. Who are you *here* and *now*?"

U-ri still had her hand over her glyph. Light spilled out from between her fingers—and not a warm glow like before, but sharp rays of radiance that stabbed like blades at the golden mist beyond the crosses.

Several of the rays pierced the mist. With each ray that penetrated it, the mist began to coalesce, its outline taking shape. U-ri stood watching it, her mouth hanging open.

The golden mist was transforming into the shape of a person. U-ri saw that it wore long robes flowing elegantly from its shoulders, like those of a person of noble stature. The figure was facing her.

"U-ri!" Aju whimpered, his tiny body shivering where he hid in the collar of her vestments. "Don't be scared, U-ri! It can't do anything to you! It can't touch you!"

U-ri wasn't frightened by the sight, though. She was entranced. She understood how this figure could steal men's hearts. How all who faced it fell under its spell.

Just like my brother had.

It was *the Hero*.

This was the source of that wild energy that had broken from its prison and descended upon the Circle, a subject of devotion and adoration wrapped in tremendous brilliance.

Then the shining Hero reached forward with one hand, clutched one of the crosses upon the dais and gently slid it off. It lifted the cross lightly above its own head, then tossed it over its back.

Ash raised his sword and charged. But the Hero simply lifted one hand, and Ash was knocked back as if struck by some invisible whip. He flew through the air and landed at U-ri's feet.

Ash was up on his own feet again before she could help him. U-ri stood, transfixed. She remembered what she had seen on that summer night so long ago: her brother bowing his head before a figure in a long cape.

"U-ri, U-ri!" Aju swatted U-ri's cheek with a tiny paw and thrust his cold nose into her ear. "Snap out of it, U-ri!"

U-ri felt the strength leave her limbs. Her hands fell limp by her sides. The mace had almost slipped out of her grasp when she realized it and lifted it again to defend herself.

Ash charged once more, and the Hero knocked him away. It was playing with him. While it tossed Ash around with the slightest motions of his fingers, the Hero lightly lifted up the other cross and tossed it against the wall. The shattered pieces fell with a racket.

"Kirrick—" Ash groaned, falling to one knee. "You are Kirrick. Remember! Remember the man you were! Remember how you once raised your sword to defend the oppressed!"

Even though the shining outline in front of them had no face, U-ri was sure that the Hero was smiling.

I have no name!

Its voice was neither that of a man or a woman. It was neither old, nor young. It was unlike any voice she had heard before, and yet it tugged at her memory, the forgotten whisper of a story she had heard as a child.

I am no one and no thing.

Did that mean it was nothing? Was that even possible? How could *nothing* possess such oppressive power? How could *nothing* shine with such radiant beauty?

"Then let me change the question," Ash shouted, spitting blood. "Why are you here?"

The Hero lifted its hands in front of its face.

All happens according to the will of the Circle, it replied in a weighty voice. Then clapping its hands together, it thrust its arms into the dais where the two crosses had lain.

White light suffused the chamber, and the ground shook like something deep below the surface was awakening, rushing up toward the Hero.

And the Hero was waiting for it.

Then the tremor that had begun deep underground reached the surface, and the glowing outline of the Hero began to swell. Maintaining its human shape, it expanded to giant proportions. The ground trembled violently, cracks appearing in the rock beneath their feet, and pieces of the ceiling and walls began to break free and fall to the floor of the labyrinth.

"Kirrick, stop this!" Ash shouted, but he could not move. Neither of them could take so much as a step toward the Hero. A circle of incredible energy had surrounded it and was beginning to expand. U-ri had fallen to the ground when it shook, and now she found herself pushed backward across the rattling stones, as though driven by a powerful wind back toward the entrance. Ash too was steadily being driven back from the grave.

"Sky! Where are you?" U-ri shouted, her voice almost a scream, but there was no answer. The force pushed her further back. Her vestments of protection fluttered around her violently, whipping in the wind. She was afraid the buttons would snap off. This was no wind, no natural flow of air. This was an incredible energy erupting from the ground, clearing the gravesite, pushing away all the clutter, including U-ri and Ash.

"Can't hold on! Auuuuugh!" Aju squealed as the force pulled him away from U-ri's collar and sent him spinning into the air. U-ri reached out a hand to grab him, but the force pushed down on her with an incredible weight, pinning her to the floor. She would have been swept away herself if Ash's hand hadn't caught her ankle. He had managed to hold his ground, clutching the grip of a short sword he had thrust into the hard-packed floor with his other hand.

"Grab on!" He extended his empty hand. U-ri couldn't reach.

Then everything was still. The flow of power ceased. The rumbling in the earth quieted. The light spilling from the grave began to recede.

U-ri lifted her head. Ash gave his own head a shake and sat up.

Then they saw it.

The Hero had grown until its head reached the ceiling over the grave. It appeared even more human now. Its face, perfectly smooth before, now had two eyes. There were no pupils, no distinction between the whites and the center of those eyes. They were just open pools of inky darkness in the shape of eyes. Though they were dark, they seemed to shine with even more strength and pride than the rest of the Hero. A new power roiled in their depths.

"So that's what you left here, Kirrick," Ash said, his voice a rasping lament. "Your eyes."

And the Hero had retrieved them. Now the Hero looked out on the Haetlands through Kirrick's eyes, once again able to see the breadth of the Circle it so desired to fill.

U-ri stood in a daze, entranced once again by the Hero's sheer presence. *I wonder what those black shining eyes see?* she thought. *I wonder what the Circle looks like to it?*

Little thing. Seed of my being. That was another voice, one not her own, in her head.

There you are, the Hero said.

U-ri blinked, coming to her senses. *What is it saying? Who is it calling to? Not me or Ash.*

It was Sky.

He was there, walking past Ash and stepping over U-ri who was still lying where she had fallen on the ground. Sky's robes gently swayed as he approached the Hero. They had fallen loose, revealing one emaciated shoulder.

Sky walked as though intoxicated. He took a step, and one of his legs bent, but instead of straightening himself he merely toppled over. Still, the devout did not stop. The Hero was drawing him in.

"No, Sky, don't go to it! You must stop!" U-ri shouted, but Sky did not so much as glance in her direction. Standing shakily, he stepped inside the light that surrounded the Hero in a glimmering aura.

There he fell to his knees and bowed to the ground.

The Hero's light washed over the devout's thin body.

U-ri held her breath. Even her heart stood still. Everything stopped.

No. This can't be happening. I don't believe it!

Enveloped in the Hero's aura, Sky was ceasing to be. His black robes melted in the light. Then a bright glow swallowed his shaven head. The last glimpse of him U-ri caught were his leather sandals worn from the long journey and those knobby ankle bones. And then Sky was completely gone.

Lying on the ground in his place was Hiroki Morisaki.

U-ri's brother. Yuriko's brother.

U-ri put a hand to her mouth.

Hiroki Morisaki lifted his head. She recognized him, everything about him. The arch of his back. His legs. The back of his neck.

He was wearing his school uniform. The soles of his favorite sneakers were coated with...*blood. The blood of the classmates who bullied him. He stepped in their blood as he fled.*

Don't look around, U-ri shouted in her heart. *Don't let me see your face.*

Hiroki turned. Tears streaked his cheeks. His lips trembled. "Yuriko—"

Then the ground shuddered and a laugh erupted, shaking the walls and ceiling of the burial chamber.

The Hero was laughing. The King in Yellow was laughing.

The dregs of my vessel. You may have it, if you wish!

The laughter grew louder, and louder still. The Hero was shining ever more brightly, boiling with light like a sun going nova.

"Nooooo!" U-ri screamed, and Hiroki stood.

For a second, U-ri thought he would come to her, that he might run to her side. But he did not. He only looked at her with his tear-streaked face—a look that lasted for only the space of a breath.

"I'm sorry," she heard her brother say. It was definitely her brother's voice. His words. "Goodbye."

He waved. His fingers were caked with blood.

Then Hiroki turned, ran to the Hero, and dove headfirst into its light. The light swallowed him and he evaporated. The Hero gave a last triumphant laugh, and the burial chamber began to collapse.

"No! Hiroki! No! No! No!"

U-ri made to dash after him, but Ash grabbed her and held her tight. The ground heaved and cracked, sending them flying into the air, while around them the walls began to crumble.

The Hero rose, levitating over the burial chamber. Its light and power spread, swallowing them.

"Use your glyph!" Ash shouted, but U-ri, still crying out for her brother, could not hear him. Ash forcibly grabbed U-ri's hand, putting it to her forehead.

The Hero took flight. At that moment, the ceiling of the burial chamber fragmented and fell—and the two tiny shapes left behind vanished.

Darkness swallowed U-ri. It felt like they had resisted an incredible gravitational pull at the last moment, and now she and Ash were hurtling through the void. She could feel the power receding from them—its beauty, its brilliance.

The Hero left them, trailing a wake of light through the darkness after it. It was like everything she had ever wanted—her brother—had jumped onto a comet and sped off into space, leaving her behind.

Images of her brother flickered through U-ri's mind as she flew. One after the other, like photographs in an album. All pictures of his face: smiling, scolding, angry, worried.

Goodbye.

How could he say that, her only brother? After all she had been through to find him? After all her searching.

And he had been with her the whole way. How had she not noticed? Why hadn't she been able to recognize him?

A shock ran through her body. Ash's arms around her, U-ri was ejected from the void onto solid ground.

They were back in the nameless land. She was sprawled in the same spot where she had arrived when she traveled here from the magic circle in Ichiro Minochi's reading room.

U-ri managed to get her arms beneath her, and lifting herself up, she stood. Giving her head a shake, she turned to where the lights of the Hall of All Books flickered in the distance.

There! There he is! Ahead of them, a single nameless devout in black robes was running toward the hall, occasionally tripping and falling to his knees, only to stand again and continue running.

"Hiroki! Sky!"

U-ri broke into a run. Her vestments were practically coming off now, and where they wrapped around her limbs they only seemed to get in the way. She slipped and fell, banging her knees on the ground, shouting all the while, chasing after the devout.

The nameless devout never looked back at her. He simply ran and ran, running away from her.

He's not Hiroki anymore.

He's not Sky anymore.

"Wait! Wait!"

No matter how fast U-ri ran, she couldn't catch up. Ahead of her, the nameless devout disappeared inside the outer wall of the Hall of All Books.

Still U-ri ran. *I'll search the whole place, and I'll find him! I'll drag him out of there, I swear it! And then we'll go home, together.*

But U-ri's exhausted legs would no longer listen to her. She staggered, tripped and fell, then stood up only to fall again. She was clutching the grass, trying to stand again, when she felt Ash's hand on her shoulder.

"It's no use. Give him up."

U-ri looked toward the hall, gritting her teeth. She felt that if she didn't keep her mouth shut, she'd bite out Ash's throat, so full of anger she was. So full of hatred.

"He is once again a nameless devout. He does not remember you. He does not retain even a fragment of the individual known as Hiroki Morisaki."

He had become no one, nowhere.

"It's better that way. It's better."

U-ri's hand lashed out on its own, slapping Ash's cheek. The wolf didn't even blink.

"You knew," U-ri said. "You knew and you didn't tell me."

That's why he was always so cold to Sky.

"Why didn't you tell me?"

"If I had, would you have believed me? Would that have satisfied you?" Ash slowly shook his head. "Neither you nor he would have believed it. Until you both faced the truth with your own eyes, my words would have had no more meaning to you than the wind that blows across this nameless land."

He's right, U-ri thought. Though it vexed her to no end, Ash was always right. U-ri thought to slap him again, but the strength had left her hand.

Tears welled in her eyes. *How many times have I cried already?* How many times had Ash laughed at her for being a crybaby? But she had never cried like this—cried tears that seemed to scorch her own cheeks.

"The nameless devout you named Sky was *incomplete*," Ash said, kneeling on one knee beside the weeping U-ri. His hair was disheveled, his chiseled face as white as his ashen hair. "And an incomplete devout is a danger both to the nameless land and to the Circle. That is why we could not leave him to his own devices. Someone had to purify him," Ash explained. "That was the reason for your glyph. That was the reason for your journey."

Ash extended a hand to her. "Stand up. Let us go to the Hall of All Books. In the Dome of Convocation you may see with your own eyes all that you have accomplished."

CHAPTER FOURTEEN

The Truth

The Dome of Convocation lay silent in the deep night of the nameless land. The whole place seemed much darker than it had during U-ri's last visit. Even the torches seemed to burn in shadow.

The Archdevout was waiting in the middle of the circular dais that U-ri had, on the occasion of her first visit, thought looked like a sumo *dohyo* of some sort. The casket containing the Book of Heroes—the Hollow Book—was there as well. Next to it, four nameless devout stood at attention.

When they saw that U-ri had arrived, all of the devout swept aside their black robes and knelt on the floor. A little unsteadily, U-ri made her way to the center of the dais. She approached the casket, its surface carved with innumerable symbols. Her eyes could see them all, and her feet could feel the solid floor beneath her, but U-ri felt nothing. She had no sense of anything—even distances seemed fluid and changing to her now.

Ash touched U-ri's shoulder, indicating that they should stop. She brought her feet together, steadied her breath for a moment, then announced to the nameless devout, "I'm back."

The Archdevout lifted his face. First he nodded to Ash, then his eyes went to U-ri. "We have been waiting for you."

The eyes in that wrinkled face were dry and told U-ri nothing—though surely he must have noticed her tears. There was no consolation in them, nor any regret that U-ri could see. His eyes were black and deep as the darkness outside.

Next to U-ri, Ash spoke. "*Allcaste,* go to the casket."

U-ri did not move. Her body felt like a giant sandbag with a small rip at the bottom through which sand streamed, leaving her to empty out on the floor.

"Your glyph has served its purpose and now returns to its rightful place. This ritual is necessary to close the Hollow Book. Step forward," Ash said again. His voice was gentle. His words a request, not a demand.

U-ri took a hesitant step forward. The Archdevout righted himself, then shuffled up to the casket on his knees and bowed again. Moving as one, the four nameless devout went to the corners of the casket, inserted metal poles in the rings, and opened the lid.

Reverently, the Archdevout lifted the Hollow Book from its resting place. Then he shuffled away from the casket, still on his knees, and held the book out before U-ri.

"Look upon it."

U-ri blinked. The cover of the Hollow Book bore a glyph. Though faint, U-ri could see it was the same as the mark on her forehead. The image was worn almost to the point of illegibility. The lines of the design were broken in places, like someone had tried to scratch it on with a pen that was running out of ink.

"Take it in your hands."

U-ri did as she was told, picking up the Hollow Book in both hands. Her fingers were dirty from the hill soil and there was black mud beneath her torn fingernails.

The book felt incredibly light in her hands—almost weightless, like it wasn't really there. The glyph on U-ri's forehead began to give off a white light. U-ri started and tilted her head back away from it, but the Archdevout commanded, "Stay as you are. The glyph will now leave you."

The glow from the glyph on her forehead grew stronger until the circle of light it cast enveloped her hands and the book. Then the faded glyph on the book's cover began to absorb the light, its own glow increasing. First the outside arc, then the details grew more pronounced, the lines thickening with brilliant light.

My glyph's returning to where it came from.

U-ri's eyes grew wider as she sensed the transfer of power in the light that streamed from her into the Hollow Book. Though the light was bright, it was not harshly so, nor was there any heat. It was simply pure light.

When the glyph upon the book was finally complete, the one on U-ri's forehead dimmed and went dark. Only at that moment did the Hollow Book suddenly feel heavy in her hands and faintly warm to the touch.

Now the glyph on the book was beginning to fade as its power was integrated into the book itself, filling its pages with its power and light. When the glyph had entirely disappeared from the cover, the only light inside the Dome of Convocation came from the flickering torches set around it.

The Archdevout gently lifted the Hollow Book from U-ri's hands and solemnly returned it to the casket.

Then the four nameless devout replaced the lid of the casket, bowed in unison, then passed their metal poles through the rings at the four corners and lifted the casket to their shoulders. They walked out of the dome, their black robes soundlessly sweeping the floor.

"Where will they put it?" U-ri asked, her voice clear even though the proceedings had rendered her mute for some time and before that she had been screaming and crying herself hoarse.

"Deep within the Hall of All Books," the Archdevout replied. "We will guard it until such time it can be sealed once again."

Ash stepped up and bowed his head. The Archdevout bowed back twice as deeply.

U-ri touched her forehead with her hand. It was smooth. No white light shone upon her fingers. The glyph was gone.

"So, what do you want to know first?" Ash asked. He straightened from his bow and turned to U-ri. The steel tacks on the soles of his boots clicked on the stone floor.

The Archdevout stepped back to stand by the wolf's side.

"What...?" U-ri muttered, feeling dizzy. The sandbag that was her body was nearly empty now. "I don't understand anything. I don't even know where to begin."

The only thing she did know was that Sky was gone. And that Sky had been her brother.

And how stupid I was for not realizing it.

The bell tolled, and Ash suddenly looked up toward the ceiling of the dome. The Archdevout joined him.

It rang once, rested, then rang twice before resting again. This pattern repeated three times before the bell was still, though the sound echoed through the dome for some time.

U-ri had her first question. "What was that bell for?"

"That was the Third Bell," Ash said, his eyes cast downward, his head cocked, listening to the fading echoes. "It tells us that the gate has closed."

"The gate to the Hall of All Books?"

Ash opened his eyes and slowly shook his head. "No, this 'gate' has a different meaning."

Something about the word tugged at the back of U-ri's mind. She had heard it used before in some unusual way, but where?

Ash was staring into U-ri's eyes. It occurred to her that the reason he always seemed to know what she was wondering was that he knew things she didn't and hid them from her. *That's why he's always one step ahead. Of course, with that intense gaze of his, maybe he really is reading my thoughts.*

"I've heard of this gate before, I think."

"You have. I remember it myself," Ash said, nodding, and a smile flashed across his face—but whether it was the cold smile of an uncaring heart or a wry smile of regret, U-ri could not tell.

"When you asked me what it meant before, it took me some effort to make up something I could tell you."

When was that? U-ri thought back, picking through her memories, but she soon gave up. She was exhausted.

"Let me explain it to you from the beginning then," the wolf offered. "This will take some time. You might want to sit."

U-ri slumped down on the spot, hugging her knees. She would have been perfectly happy to sit there for an eternity and never move again.

Then the Archdevout walked over and sat silently down beside her—like a kindly grandfather come to console a distraught grandchild after she'd received a scolding from her parents for some trifling infraction. It was a gesture filled with gentleness and warmth.

The only difference between that kindly grandfather and the Archdevout was the way he sat, with his black robes tucked neatly beneath his knees.

"You must be angry," he said. Though his eyes were still dry, there were tears in the Archdevout's voice. "I will not ask for your forgiveness. We sent you forth knowing full well what awaited you. We set you on this path, your bags packed with nothing but lies and subterfuge, while we kept the truth to ourselves."

U-ri marveled at how calm she felt. She had been so furious just a short while ago, but now she wanted only to bury her face in the Archdevout's robes and cry.

"In order for the Hero to break free, a person must serve as the last vessel," Ash began, turning his face slightly toward U-ri's. "In order to return the Hero to the flow of stories, thus bringing it back to this land where it can be bound, it is necessary to drain the power from the last vessel who resides within the Hero. Only the *allcaste*, in whose veins flows the same blood as that of the last vessel, can hope to accomplish this. Why? Because only the *allcaste*'s voice may reach the last vessel, and if that voice cannot be heard, neither will the Hero know the power of the glyph.

"Thus does the *allcaste* join the hunt for the Hero, for the King in Yellow. This is when the Book of Heroes becomes marked with the same glyph that marks the *allcaste*'s forehead. If the *allcaste* should be successful in finding the Hero and the last vessel is released, then when the *allcaste* returns to this place, the mark upon their forehead and the glyph upon the book become one, and the Hollow Book is once again filled."

Ash looked directly at U-ri. "All of this is true, and all of this you were told before you began your journey, more or less." The wolf spread his hands, looking for her acknowledgment.

U-ri nodded. "That is what I expected my journey to bring, more or less."

Next to her, the Archdevout's face was lowered.

"Yet, rarely—extremely rarely—things do not go according to plan." Ash paused, then asked her, "What do you think becomes of the vessels?"

"Aren't they absorbed by the Hero? Used as energy or something?"

"That's right. They fuse with the Hero, becoming a part of it. The Hero only takes them in the first place because they fulfill all the requirements: they possess great anger and an equally great desire to express that anger. This desire calls out to the Hero. Yet, once it has absorbed these vessels, nothing is left. Not even the anger which drove them in the first place." Ash licked his lips before continuing. "There is one exception, however: the last vessel. For the last vessel serves as both vessel and Summoner. The Summoner is the one who calls the Hero, the one who gives form to the Hero. You might call them a conspirator—and conspiring with the Hero is a sin. Thus, even if the vessel loses their human form, the sin they committed remains. Now, U-ri, what shape do you think that sin takes?"

U-ri didn't have to think long. Even as the details refused to come into clear focus in her mind, she knew the answer to the question her heart had been asking since her journey had begun.

"A nameless devout."

Ash nodded deeply. "All last vessels, without exception, become nameless devout. And here, in this land, they do penance for their sin."

All that remained of them *was* sin. They retained none of their individual hearts, forms, or thoughts. That was why all of the nameless devout were identical in appearance—they were literally without selves. They existed only as manifestations of their sin. The nameless devout were one and they were many. They were many and they were one. That was their truth.

"However," Ash added, shifting his feet so that he now faced away from U-ri, "As I said, in very rare circumstances, something happens to the last vessel. Things, well, they do not go according to plan. I, and others, believe that this is because only the last vessel has the opportunity to face the Hero not just as a vessel, but as the Summoner, before being banished to the nameless land.

"In that instant—and it may last no more than an instant—the last vessel has access to the entirety of the Hero's memory and the full extent of the Hero's strength. In this, they reach a state of being that no other vessel, nor even a wolf, could hope to attain. It is there that they touch the mystery that lies at the heart of the Circle and gain the power of true sight.

"Should that moment give birth to regrets within the last vessel, it can result in an *incomplete* nameless devout," Ash explained. "Though an incomplete devout is still a nameless devout, still lacking individual memory and appearance, their deficits are only temporary. They have only forgotten who they were, not lost it completely."

"And that's what my brother, what Sky was?" U-ri asked, her voice more shrill then she had intended. "Is that what you were talking about up on the hill?"

Ash turned, looking U-ri straight in the eyes. He nodded.

"But that doesn't make sense!" U-ri said, her voice rising. "That's not what Sky said at all! He told me that he had been waiting for me to arrive. That when he heard the First Bell ring, it moved him."

Sky had been nothing, but in that moment, something was born inside him. He wasn't just "remembering" something he already had—or was he?

"The ringing of the First Bell did not give him a heart, if that's what you're thinking. It awakened the fragments of the heart he once had. But the fragments were incomplete, and their number few."

U-ri had to put a hand on her chest to steady her own breathing. "And he didn't realize anything until then? He didn't know he had a heart? He didn't know that he was different from the others? I mean, if he knew when he had come to the nameless land, then—" U-ri drew a sharp breath.

There is no time in the nameless land.

"He did not realize the truth," the wolf stated bluntly. "He merely acted out of instinct. He had forgotten who he once was, yet when you came here, he knew he must join you on your journey. He wished it of his own accord. I believe it was Sky trying to make right for what he had done as your brother, whether he knew it or not."

Ash sighed. "An incomplete devout is dangerous. They have touched the Hero, they have touched the King in Yellow. While they hold on to the fragments of who they once were as the last vessel, they maintain a tenuous connection to the terrible power of the Hero."

Then the Archdevout, silent until now, spoke in a low, calm voice. "You might think of him as being a nameless devout who bears the Yellow Sign."

U-ri stared long and hard at the Archdevout. He made sense. In fact, it was probably the best way he could have explained it to her at that time, she realized.

"You mean, he had to purify himself."

That's why Sky became my servant. That's why the Archdevout cast him out of the nameless land. That's why he told me to take Sky with me.

"So if he was near the glyph, that would purify him? Like with Aju!"

Ash shook his head. "It does not work for an incomplete devout as it does for a book. Mere proximity to the glyph is not enough to remove the Yellow Sign."

As in the moment when the Summoner enables the Hero to escape, all must be brought together: Summoner, the Hero, and King in Yellow. Only then would the last vessel return to its former shape, Ash explained. "And when the last vessel has regained its self, it must once again throw itself to the Hero."

This, Ash explained, was because the incomplete devout, with its tenuous connection to the Hero, was more like a reflection of the Hero than anything. Until it returned to its master and became whole, there would be no destroying it, nor purifying it.

"That is why they are so dangerous. The incomplete devout is none other than a bad seed that the Hero has planted in both the Circle and in the nameless land. Through that seed, the Hero can exert a direct influence on the world. To purify the last vessel and thereby make the nameless devout complete is the *allcaste*'s true mission."

Ash fixed his gaze on her then. "You have completed your mission, U-ri. That was the very goal of your journey from its beginning. Or rather, when Sky appeared, your goal changed from the recapture of the Hero to purifying the nameless devout."

And no one told me the truth.

"The culling of such bad seeds is as important and as vital as sapping the Hero of its strength and returning it to this land. It had to be you who purified Sky, and thereby Hiroki Morisaki."

"You lied to me so I'd do it." U-ri realized she had been gritting her teeth. Her hands were clenched into fists. "No one told me the truth. You deceived me!"

The Archdevout swayed under the barrage of U-ri's voice. Ash stepped closer to her, kneeling between them as if to protect the ancient man. "Do not blame the Archdevout. Until he saw the sign, he too was unaware that an incomplete devout had been created."

"The sign?"

The Archdevout looked up, blinked slowly, and said, "When we opened the casket, withdrew the Hollow Book, and saw that the glyph of the *allcaste* was not upon its cover, that was the sign."

"That's why you were so surprised!"

The state of the book had been a shock to the Archdevout, even more so the arrival of Sky—a nameless devout like them, but younger, different. The nameless devout who was not complete.

"He wasn't just surprised by the turn of events, U-ri. The Archdevout was sad for you! He was sad because he realized you no longer journeyed to imprison the Hero."

"But why?" U-ri shouted. She clutched the Archdevout's robes, pulled his frail body toward her, and glared sidelong up at Ash's stern face. "Why didn't any of you tell me then? If I'd only known—"

"What would you have done?"

"I would've thought of a different way to do things!"

"What different way? You didn't have any choice in the matter."

"What if I had? What if I could've found one?" She turned to the wolf, grabbing his coat collar and shaking him. "I could've taken him back home! I could've taken my brother home!"

"Sky was not your brother. He didn't even look like him."

"But he used to be my brother!"

Why drag him to the Hero to purify him? He wasn't some bad seed to be culled! He was my brother!

"Didn't my brother become an incomplete devout because he regretted what he had done? Didn't he regret getting sucked in by the Book of Elem? I would have forgiven him!"

Of course I would have. He's my only brother.

"U-ri." Ash shook his head, and his white bangs fell down across his forehead, making him look suddenly older. *Or maybe just tired.*

"Didn't I just tell you that an incomplete devout is a dangerous thing? Were you to bring him back to the Circle, it would mean calamity."

"How do you know that? If I brought him home and he met Mom and Dad again, if he could have returned to his old life, I bet all his memories would have come back. Maybe even his old form!"

"They would not," the Archdevout said quietly. "They can never come back, Lady U-ri. Once a part of the Hero, always a part, unchanging until the day they are purified."

"The bad seed is also sometimes called the 'gate.'"

U-ri's eyes went wide at Ash's words.

"It is a gate through which the Hero may exercise its power. It is an entrance. You said you had heard someone use the word before? Do you remember where? It was when that giant creature appeared at Hiroki's school and took Sky in its tentacles."

"Little dust puppet...you are the gate?"

"In their original forms, the Hero and the King in Yellow are nothing more than stories, invisible to the eye. Though they may reside in men's hearts and guide their actions, they cannot manifest physically within the Circle."

"But the Hero took Kirrick's form back in the capital!" U-ri retorted. "That was because it took his eyes, wasn't it? Not because of some gate!"

Ash smiled mysteriously. "This is because the Haetlands is itself a story. It is an imaginary place. Had you forgotten?"

U-ri put a hand to her mouth. "So stories like the Hero and the King in Yellow can take shape in regions woven of stories?"

"Yes, but this is a parlor trick, ineffective in the Circle. And yet, that creature appeared quite readily by the library in your brother's school. Do you know why? It is because Sky was there. That giant eyeball manifested itself through Sky. That is what is meant by the 'gate.' Were you to bring Sky back home with you, you would be giving such creatures free access to the Circle. They would boil forth and destroy all within their reach. And the people would rise up to drive them back, weapons in hand. There would be war.

"I am sure you do not need me to tell you what war entails. It is nothing less than a most terrible sign of the coming of both the Hero and the King in Yellow to the Circle," Ash said, his voice growing stronger. "What happened in Elemsgard could happen in the Circle, in your region, your country, your town, your school. The ones you love would be devoured by monsters, transformed into horrible things. Lamenting, they would bury the bodies of their loved ones and drift through the wreckage of their world, forced to hunt down and destroy former lovers, friends, brothers, and sisters who had become something other than human. Do you really want your hometown turned into Elemsgard?"

U-ri had forgotten even to breathe, had forgotten that Ash and the Archdevout stood before her. She had retreated entirely inside herself. Visions of the bodies she had seen strewn about the wreckage of the palace filled her mind. The terrible, deformed creatures that seemed to bubble forth from the ground, no matter how many they slew—

That could happen in my world.

If she hadn't seen what she had seen, her choice would've been simple. If the Archdevout had turned to her and told her the truth the moment he took the book from the casket and saw the sign, U-ri would have taken Sky by the hand and brought him directly back to Ichiro Minochi's reading room. Then they would have gone home. No matter how much they might have pleaded with her, U-ri's desire to save Sky—to save her brother—would have been stronger, pushing all such concern aside.

"So you did it to convince me, then," U-ri whispered, and a tear rolled down one cheek. She didn't even remember having wept it. "You hid the truth and sent me on my journey so that I would see it for myself."

"And for that we are sorry," the Archdevout apologized as he prostrated himself before her. U-ri looked down at him and sniffled. Her next tear fell from her chin onto the nape of the Archdevout's neck.

"During your journey, did Sky not begin to recover fragmented memories of Kirrick and the Haetlands?"

So Ash had noticed too.

"He did remember, and it made him worry."

"The Book of Elem was the key to the Hero's escape. That is why Hiroki Morisaki, as the last vessel, possessed a dim recollection of Kirrick. That is what Sky remembered."

"And Morgan, the wolf we met in Elemsgard?"

Ash nodded.

"He said you were doing something terrible. He knew what was going on, didn't he?"

Ash cast his eyes aside, as though he were ashamed to meet her gaze.

"He thought it was wrong to bring Sky along with me."

"He has a good heart, that Morgan."

"But he lacks wisdom," U-ri said, startled that Ash's wry smile from before seemed to have made its way to her own lips. "I had to go. There was no two ways about it."

"Do not judge him so harshly," Ash said. "It was only right for Morgan to censure me. And right for him to want to better your lot. Anyone with a heart would do the same."

What was that Morgan said to me, there in the chaos of the broken city, with the mob thronging around us?

"...You can cry if you like, but don't despair."

Good advice, thought U-ri. She let her tears fall.

"Did Doctor Latore know the truth too?"

Ash nodded.

So that's why he stopped Sky from going with me to the bottom of the cavern to meet my great-uncle.

"And Aju?"

There was no immediate response, so U-ri looked up at Ash. His face was drawn in a scowl.

Then U-ri remembered something terribly important. "Back in Katarhar Abbey, after we met Mr. Minochi, I passed out—" *And when I awoke everyone was acting so strange.* "Is that when Aju discovered the truth?"

Ash sighed, his face still dark. "When you saw Minochi's true form, you screamed, did you not?"

"Yes."

"Sky heard that scream and came running down there, all the way to the bottom. He ran without thought, concerned only for you, wanting to save you, pushing aside all who tried to stop him. Yet he never reached Minochi's cell. I barred his path.

"I do not believe that Sky fully understood why at the time, though he must have thought it odd, and perhaps even guessed at the truth—but Minochi knew. As soon as Sky came close, he sensed it, I think. It was to prevent this that I stopped him. But I was too late."

Ash shook his head. "Minochi began to call out. With his power—the very power that twisted him into the form you saw—Ichiro Minochi could peer through Sky's mask to see the remnants of Hiroki Morisaki within. He called Hiroki by name. His madness took him, and he howled with laughter, screaming 'Hiroki' over and over."

Minochi had laughed and babbled words of apology that made no sense, then began to chant the jumbled words of a curse. Minochi had completely lost his mind.

Thankfully, none of his words reached Sky. But, Ash explained, Aju was not so fortunate.

"The *aunkaui* dictionary knew deep shame then. While you slept, we discussed it together. Aju spoke with the books in the abbey, asking for their advice."

It had been Ash's suggestion that Aju leave as soon as it was possible.

"But Aju swore he would stay by you to the last. He wanted to be there when you learned the truth."

Warm tears streamed down U-ri's cheek. "Where is he now?"

The last time she had seen him was in Elem's burial chamber, when the Hero's power had literally blown them all away. "I didn't even get a chance to say goodbye."

"Do not worry. I'll find him and return him to his original form. Books cannot die," Ash added, a genuine smile on his face for the first time in a long while.

"Archdevout," U-ri asked, wiping her face with the sleeve of her vestments and turning to the ancient man. "If the nameless devout were all last vessels, that means you too were once a last vessel, yes?"

The Archdevout sat with his hands on his knees and nodded slowly. "Though I have no way of counting the time that has passed in this land where time stands still, I believe my own transformation happened in another age, far in the distant past."

"I remember, before I left here the first time, when I asked you what bad the nameless devout had done, you told me that you were guilty of the sin of trying to live a story—trying to live a lie, to make the lie real. What does that mean? How could that be worse than allowing the Hero to escape?"

The Archdevout did not reply, but quietly raised his eyes and looked in Ash's direction.

The response came from Ash, in the form of a question. "What is a story, U-ri?"

"Something a weaver makes, I suppose. A lie."

"Not only weavers make stories. All people make stories simply by living out their lives."

Doctor Latore had said something similar. He had told her that there was no other way for men to live.

"As people walk through their lives, they leave stories behind them, like footprints in the sand. Yet sometimes we place stories in front of us, choosing the brightest from those that hang in the firmament of the Circle to guide us—and when we try to live those stories, we fall prey to foolishness. For we are attempting to imitate the story as we think it should be, not as it is.

"These stories we follow have many names. Sometimes they're called 'justice.' Other times 'victory' or even 'conquest.' Sometimes they are simply called 'success.' We charge forward, following a vision invisible to those around us. That is the sin of trying to live a story. In our pride, we place the ideal before the deed, and this brings only misfortune. The sin of living a story is great indeed. So great that the last vessel becomes a nameless devout sent here to atone for that sin over an eternity.

"But let me be clear," Ash continued, "the sin lies not with the story. Yet the weavers know that sometimes stories can mislead our hearts. They know this, yet they continue their weaving. That is a conscious act that invites karmic retribution—still they are allowed to continue in their work because they also bring hope, goodness, beauty, warmth, and the joy of life to men.

"As the Hero and the King in Yellow are two sides of one coin, so are the nameless devout who turn the Great Wheels of Inculpation here and the weavers who remain in the Circle. The cycling of stories is also the cycling of human deeds," Ash said, his tone that of the philosopher expounding on a well-known truth to one of his students.

"My brother was guilty of such a great sin?" U-ri asked, her voice faltering, her body swaying. "He did something so bad?"

"He tried to become the Hero," Ash replied, "the very embodiment of heroic justice. And he did not wisely choose his means to that end. Your brother took the life of one of his classmates. Without a moment's hesitation, he sullied his hands with the blood of another child of the Circle."

All for justice, for victory.

U-ri shouted, "But the kids he was dealing with were really bad! They attacked him first! You mean you're not allowed to strike back?"

"Does that make it all right to commit *murder*? Was it all right for him to be their sole judge and executioner?" Ash shook his head. "When a child anywhere in the Circle takes up a weapon in order to remove those who do not see as he does, this leads to war—a war great enough to destroy the entire Circle. It is not an isolated event. Surely you understand that now."

A world in which a child may take the life of another is the same world in which ten thousand soldiers may kill ten thousand more. One is many, and many are one.

U-ri realized that "ten thousand" wasn't just a number—it referred to the idea of everything, everything inside the Circle.

"So who gets to judge evil, then? Are we not allowed to accuse people who do wrong?" U-ri asked, her voice almost a scream.

Ash waited for the echoes to fade before he replied, calm as ever, "That is why men created the story we call 'law.' Even as we walk on through an eternity, leaving repeated mistakes and endless sacrifices as we cross rivers of tears, we have found a story that attempts to put things right. The story of law is written in the language of our footsteps. Because of this, it is not without faults. Yet should we forget the law and make stories as we wish for us or others to live, that is a sin."

U-ri hugged herself and cried. Then another thought occurred to her.

"But the people he fought—that teacher and the bullies in his class—they all did the same thing. How was their 'justice' any better than Hiroki's?"

"It was not. They are sinners too. Inculpated, and rightly so," Ash said, his voice expressing nothing but sadness. "Yet they did not find the Book of Elem. They did not meet the Hero. Thus are they judged only within the Circle and not here in the nameless land."

"But that's not fair!"

In that instant, U-ri understood why Ichiro Minochi roared in the dungeon beneath the Katarhar Abbey ruins. She understood his thirst to put things right by his own hands, to make just the unfairness that had taken his one hope, his one consolation away.

That's why he wanted to raise the dead.

U-ri whimpered. "My brother might have wanted what the Hero had to offer the moment he picked up that knife, but that was the only time. Just one moment out of so many. Why should he have to give up the rest of his life to atone for that?"

The Archdevout laid his hand on U-ri's back. "There is no time in the nameless land."

So does that mean there's no suffering? No weariness?

Something thing Morgan had said flashed through U-ri's mind. *Hadn't he called the nameless devout holy men?*

Holy men. Carrying the weight of man's sins.

"Your brother is not here in the nameless land," the Archdevout said then. "All that is here are nameless devout."

Ash nodded. "And the nameless devout are nothing. Your brother's soul rests in the great flow of stories until such a time as it will reenter the Circle inside another life. You see? He waits for rebirth. He feels no pain. You ensured that when you purified him."

But the wolf's words did not reach U-ri's heart, and all she had to offer in response was more tears.

"What will I tell my mom, my dad? They're still hoping, still worried, waiting for Hiroki to come home."

"Leave that to stories, for facing grief is one time when stories can help most. And pray with them. Weave a new story with your prayers. That the peace your brother has found might someday enter the hearts of your parents as well. Now stand," Ash instructed. "It is time for you to return to the Circle. Remove your vestments and return them to the Archdevout."

For a moment, U-ri didn't understand what he was saying. And when she did, her body went rigid, and she clutched the vestments to her, doubling over where she stood.

"I won't! I can't go home!"

On the floor, she began to crawl away from Ash and the Archdevout. "I'll stop the Hero! I'll avenge Hiroki! I'm the only one who can do it, right?"

And the Hero is still free.

"I am the one who bears the mark!"

. Eyes closed, Ash shook his head. "Not any longer. The glyph has left you. Your role here has ended. Remember just now when the glyph was absorbed into the Hollow Book? The glyph you bore had no further purpose after you purified Sky. You are no longer the *allcaste*, nor will you ever be again."

"Why not? Why can't I be?"

"Don't you wish to return home?" Ash asked, a hint of his old mocking tone returning to his voice.

"Well, what will you do now then, Ash? How are you going to bind the Hero without an *allcaste* to help you?"

"There are other *allcastes*, U-ri. I merely need to find them. In fact, you might say that the tides have shifted in my favor. The Hero used the Book of Elem to create a material form. It becomes more and more like Kirrick every day. An enemy that imitates my brother is an enemy I know well."

So all Ash would have to do was find someone, an *allcaste*, whose voice could reach Kirrick.

"U-ri," Ash called her name, his voice more gentle than she had ever heard it before. "The nameless devout were once last vessels, yes? How many nameless devout do you think are here in this land?"

U-ri thought about it a moment, and her mouth opened wide.

"That's right. More than any of us can count. This, more than anything else, is proof that the Hero has escaped many times before, and been caught just as many times. In fact, the times when the Hero is *not* in the Circle are fewer than the times when it is. The Hero's imprisonment is the exception. He is imprisoned only for brief intervals between long stretches of time during which he roams freely," Ash explained. "It is a testament to how much men desire the Hero. They desire it, even when they know the dangers of the King in Yellow. It is in our nature."

Ash smiled. "So do not worry. You're still young. Return to your world and live out your life. Live, and be happy. I will handle things on this side. That is why we wolves exist—why we are allowed to live."

Ash extended his hand from his tattered robes. U-ri took it and stood. Beside her, the Archdevout stood as well.

"Just be careful. The Hero is in the Circle. A time of conflict is at hand," Ash warned her, squeezing her hand tightly in his own. "You're one of few in the Circle to return there, knowing the ways of this forsaken land. When conflict rages and men look up to the Hero, their eyes deceived by the lure of the King in Yellow, you will know what to say. Do not lose your voice. Your eyes can see what is right, and what must be. Do not close them. Your courage led you here and to the successful completion of your duties as *allcaste*. It will not fail you.

"If today, one child should learn how to sheathe a blade, then tomorrow the armies will halt their march."

One leads to many, to all.

"Master Ash," the Archdevout called out to the wolf. "You have forgotten something very important." The Archdevout smiled at U-ri. "Though the Hero was not bound, you have completed your mission, Lady U-ri. Before you leave us, you have the right to name a part of our land."

U-ri led Ash and the Archdevout to the central courtyard of the Hall of All Books. It was as jumbled a place as it had been when she had first seen it, with its bizarrely winding roads and passageways. Yet it was dear and familiar to her all the same. Now, those buildings stood beneath a sky full of stars, their light the nameless land's only ornamentation.

"That," U-ri said, pointing straight up. "Sky told me you call that the heavens here."

"This is true," the Archdevout said, nodding.

"But those aren't just the heavens, that's the sky. The sky of the nameless land." U-ri shook her head. "I wonder if it will ever be blue?"

She could see the stars so clearly. Who could say that the sun wouldn't rise someday soon into a cloudless sky, and the nameless devout who had joined her on her journey would look up, his eyes filled with wonder.

"Very well. From this point on, that which arcs above our heads is Lady U-ri's 'sky.'"

The Archdevout bowed and gently lifted the vestments of protection from U-ri's shoulders.

U-ri's eyes filled with tears, and she put her hands to her face, trying in vain to hold them in.

"You did well," Ash said then. "You and your brother both."

So this is goodbye.

"Farewell."

And that was their word of parting. Brief and to the point.

From Ash, she expected nothing else.

Epilogue

Several days had passed since U-ri returned home and returned to being Yuriko Morisaki.

The memories of her journey were still vivid in her mind, yet strangely, no matter how often she thought of what had happened, the sadness that had left her hollow before refused to show itself. She was protected from it, somehow, shielded in stillness and light, her heart as serene as a boat drifting on a quiet sea under a blue sky.

She had arrived directly from the nameless land to her own room. The first person she met was her double.

Yuriko's double had been sitting at her desk, but when the double saw Yuriko, she stood and greeted her, spreading her arms and smiling in silence to show she knew everything that had happened, and she understood.

Yuriko accepted her embrace, and her double hugged her tight. Her double was warm, despite being made of magic. It seemed like she was there not just to take her place in this region while U-ri traveled through magical lands but to take on Yuriko's emotional burden. The double would carry the lingering hurt so Yuriko didn't have to.

Maybe that was her real purpose all along.

Yuriko was alone in her room. She hadn't even noticed her double leave. It was the middle of the night, so she changed and got into bed. When she awoke, her old daily routine was waiting for her, at least her routine such as it had been since Hiroki's disappearance. Her parents still waited for her brother to return. There was an empty chair at the table and an empty room next to hers.

Yet Yuriko felt different because she knew what had happened. She knew what had become of her brother, and where he was now.

She knew in her heart that she just had to tell her parents what she knew somehow and everything would be better. She felt like U-ri was still there too, inside her, supporting her, though that might have only been her imagination.

I'll be okay.
I think.

An errant breeze tugged at her heart, making her sway, but she soon regained her footing.

No. I will *be okay.*

She started going to school again. There was the occasional uncomfortable silence, the occasional conversation that faltered as she walked by, but things had changed for the better. Time had passed not only for her, but for all her friends as well.

That, or my double was really hard at work putting things right while I was gone.

At home, Yuriko's newfound calm was infectious, and little by little, she could feel her parents relaxing as well. They never forgot Hiroki, of course, not even for a moment. Her mother still cried a lot. There were nights when nobody slept. Yet, like a glyph lighting the darkness, Yuriko was the warm center of the household now, and gradually her family was able to pick itself up off the floor, wipe the dust off its knees, and get back to the business of living.

If they were going to welcome Hiroki back to the family someday, there was no point letting the place fall apart in the meantime. They had to be strong. Yuriko saw it in her parents' faces now and then, a kind of bright resolve, a determination to keep going.

We'll be okay.

I think.

Yuriko put a hand to her chest to still the flutter in her heart.

Yuriko wondered what had become of Ichiro Minochi's cottage and reading room, but it wasn't the easiest thing to ask about. She couldn't decide on the right timing to bring up the subject.

The disappointment her mother had suffered when they went there looking for Hiroki still weighed heavily on her, and she didn't seem eager to talk about the place. And though her father was gradually getting back into life, worrying about how he would split a worthless inheritance from an uncle who wasn't even a blood relation was low on his list.

She could just bring it up, but she was afraid she would be bringing back all those memories of the night they had broken in there, full of hope, searching through the darkened cottage to find only dust. How their hope had changed to despair, and their certainty had been dashed to pieces. Her parents would sink back into the funk she'd found them in, and Yuriko wanted to avoid that if at all possible.

That, and there was a more pressing question on Yuriko's mind. She had never found out whether her parents knew about the girl Michiru Inui. Had

Michiru come to them and told them the truth? Did they know already, and they just weren't letting on? And if they really didn't know, should she tell them?

The police had surely looked into Hiroki's motives and just as surely passed on anything they had learned to her parents. Yuriko wondered how much of the truth they had really been able to uncover. Had the school been successful in keeping its own missteps out of the public eye?

Though if they were all that successful, why would the police have come asking me *questions?*

Yuriko kept to herself when she thought about these things, so her parents wouldn't see something in her face to make them worry. When she had taken all the doubts and questions out of her heart and laid them on the table, examining each of them from every possible angle, she came to a conclusion:

The only people who knew why Hiroki Morisaki had done what he did were Michiru Inui, Ms. Kanehashi, his teacher, and Yuriko. Her parents knew nothing. Neither did the police.

The teachers at school who knew were pretending they didn't. They were keeping their mouths shut. Hiroki's classmates as well, no doubt. It wouldn't surprise her if the school had taken action to make sure no one tattled.

Yet Yuriko's heart still stirred with doubt. She wanted to tell her parents. She wanted to tell them the truth, bitter though it was. She wanted them to see it as she did, to see how Hiroki had sacrificed himself for Michiru, and how close they had been.

But would Hiroki even want that? Would he want me to tattle?

One thing was for sure: If she did tell, there would be casualties. It could only make life more miserable for Michiru. She would blame herself again, just like she did when she had met U-ri the "book-spirit" in the school library. No matter how much her parents might try to console her, try to tell her it wasn't her fault, she would continue to blame herself.

Yet wasn't Yuriko blaming herself already? Poor Michiru was doomed either way.

And there was Ms. Kanehashi. She'd be affected too. She had already tried to take responsibility for the mess in her classroom, and it had done her no good at all. Still, she didn't think her parents would blame Hiroki's teacher for that. Rather, they would thank her for doing what she could to try to help. It might even help take some of the burden of guilt off her shoulders. Yuriko was in a position to help her.

So Yuriko ruminated. Which was the right path?

What would Hiroki want?

To this question she could find no answer. The more she thought about it, the less certain she felt. No observation or reasoning could divine the way out of her conundrum. When the light did shine down upon Yuriko's path, it came from an unexpected direction, on a day in early summer, with vacation not far away.

"They really found a buyer?" Yuriko's mother asked, stopping as she carried a plate in from the kitchen. "Somebody actually wants that dingy old place?"

Her father had come home and sat down at the dinner table that night when he suddenly announced that someone had called wanting to buy Ichiro Minochi's belongings.

"You're getting ahead of yourself, Mother," her father replied. "No one's buying the cottage. A man's come inquiring about those books. Remember the ones in the reading room?"

His brother had called with the news that day at lunch, Yuriko's father explained. "The buyer seemed quite eager. Wanted to make sure that we sold the entire library to him and no one else."

The lawyer they had put in charge of the whole affair said it didn't sound like a bad deal.

Yuriko sat down next to her mother and began to eat, all the while pricking up her ears to catch any scrap of information she could. Her heart was racing.

"Were those books really all that valuable?"

"Seems so. It's difficult though to find a place that can appraise them, seeing as how some of them are downright ancient, and hardly any are in Japanese. Even if we hired an expert to come and do an appraisal, they wouldn't be able to handle all of the books, and the appraisal fee would likely be out of this world."

The lawyer was advising that they take advantage of the opportunity. It was the easiest way to deal with the matter by far.

"But then we'd just be taking whatever this buyer quotes us. What if one or two of those books are really worth something?" Yuriko's mother protested. She was always worried about the bottom line. Not that there was anything wrong with that. Yuriko would rather have her worrying about the family finances than anything else.

"It's certainly a possibility," her father said with a chuckle. "The buyer is a used book salesman himself. And not just any used book salesman." He leaned across the table with an air of importance. "He's the manager of that store in Paris where Mr. Minochi had his heart attack."

The store was located along the Seine. Its name, translated into Japanese, was The Bubbling Spring. The manager was a man of fifty-five by the name of Frans Culeur.

"The lawyer showed my brother a picture of him apparently. He's a handsome old fellow. Looks like Jean Gabin."

Her mother frowned. "Who's Jean Gabin?"

The stirring in Yuriko's chest grew into a realization.

Ichiro Minochi didn't die in that bookstore. He went to the Haetlands, leaving his humanity—and his sanity—behind.

But no one here in the Circle, in Yuri's region, doubted the story that her great-uncle had died in Paris.

Which means there was a very deft cover-up. And the owner of The Bubbling Spring was involved. Handsome old Frans is a wolf—and even if he isn't, he knows about the nameless land and the Circle. How else could he have helped Minochi get away?

And now this conspirator was trying to buy her great-uncle's books.

"Well, I think we should sell them to him," Yuriko said, playing the part of the precocious child. "It would sure make those books happy. I'll bet some of them even came from this Bubbling Spring place."

Her parents looked at each other.

Yuriko went back to eating, chewing her food while she chewed on another thought. If they sold the lot of books, there would be no more reading room. The books would leave the cottage.

Before that happens, I want to visit there again. To say goodbye.

❧

It wasn't difficult. She just had to mix a little bit of untruth in with the truth.

Hey, Mom. All that talk about the cottage last night made me remember something important...

Did you know Hiroki went back, after we visited that one time? With a teacher from school and one of his friends—

He told me to keep it a secret, and I guess I forgot about it. Sorry!

I remember the teacher's name now. Ms. Kanehashi? Maybe she knows who the friend was.

I think it was a girl.

Judging from her mother's reaction, it was clear that she had no idea that Hiroki had been so close to any teacher (nor had Hiroki seen fit to tell her). Even more, the news that there had been a girl Hiroki liked enough to take on a secret summer drive through the mountains hit her like a bolt from the blue.

Things progressed quickly after that.

It had not been but three days since Yuriko's confession when Ms. Kanehashi visited the Morisaki household. Yuriko had pictured the teacher as a slightly dumpy, kindly lady, but when she saw Ms. Kanehashi standing in front of the apartment door, she found she couldn't have been more wrong. Ms. Kanehashi was light and slender and moved with a spring in her step, like a fawn. She was cute too, with freckles across the bridge of her nose.

Yuriko wasn't there when her parents talked to Ms. Kanehashi. She waited in her room, holding her breath and straining her ears to listen. She heard her mother crying a few times, and Ms. Kanehashi crying too.

Hiroki's teacher had left the school before summer vacation. The school administration had made it clear they didn't want her to talk about what had happened. But now that she wasn't working there anymore, all bets were off.

It was another two days before Yuriko's parents went with Ms. Kanehashi to meet Michiru. When they came home that evening, her parents looked exhausted, and her mother's eyes were swollen and red from crying.

"Finally I know what he was going through," Yuriko's mother said after telling her what they had heard. Her mom put one hand to her chest and began to cry again.

"Mom, Dad? Are you mad at her?"

Her father shook his head, but it was her mother who said, "No, we're not angry."

Then she hugged Yuriko to her and whispered, "It's so sad. So sad," over and over.

Finally, they know.

Yuriko felt more peace inside her than she had in a while. She hugged her mother back.

It's now or never.

"There's something I wanted to ask you."

She wanted to go back to the reading room, before the books were taken away. And she wanted to go there with Ms. Kanehashi and Michiru.

On the first weekend of summer vacation, six people piled into two cars. The Morisakis led the way, with Ms. Kanehashi, Michiru, and Michiru's mother in the car behind them. It was a perfect summer day, and they drove out under a blue sky.

When they arrived, Yuriko had her first experience with bushwhacking. The weeds had grown so thick around Minochi's cottage that they had to pull out every cutter and clipper they could find just to get through.

Surprisingly—or perhaps it wasn't surprising at all—Michiru never recognized Yuriko as U-ri, the book-spirit that had visited her. Even in different clothes, and without U-ri's particular speech and tone, Yuriko was sure that her face would give her away, but there was not even a glimmer of recognition in the other girl's eyes.

Her memory had been erased. That day in the library had never happened as far as Michiru was concerned.

Is this another one of the Circle's mechanisms? Yuriko wondered.

"You're Morisaki's little sister, aren't you?" The princess in her damaged tower smiled brightly at Yuriko. "It's so nice to meet you. Morisaki always used to talk about his 'little Yuri.'"

Then her voice choked and she apologized, a tear rolling from one eye. Her mother reached down and wiped it from her cheek.

Somehow, Yuriko knew this—them all being here together—was exactly what Hiroki would have wanted.

They started on the first floor and walked together, examining the different rooms and hallways and talking about the past. They took turns speaking. Or crying. And occasionally even laughing. Until they reached the reading room.

Whether she was scared, or just couldn't bear the weight of her own memories, Michiru didn't want to go into the reading room. No one else spent very long in there either, giving Yuriko plenty of time to herself.

It was dark inside, even in the middle of the day. The dim light leaked in through the small window. Yuriko would have been able to see if any of the books were shining, even faintly, but not a single one glimmered. Nor did any of them speak a word.

The glyph was gone from the middle of the floor. It had been neatly swept away. Yuriko guessed that Ash had been here and seen to that. Still, it hadn't kept her from hoping that were she to stand in the reading room alone, something would change—something miraculous might happen.

There were no miracles today.

The Circle was closed, as was her path to the nameless land.

The only thing coming from the countless old books in that room now was an oppressive silence.

She took a step toward the stepladder she had sat on during her previous visit, when something wrapped around her ankle—the same strip of black cloth she had found when she first came here with Aju.

The way it wrapped around her foot was almost lifelike. With a shiver, she reached down to yank it off, and found it surprisingly heavy in her hands.

What is this thing? Wait—

Even as she held it, one edge of the cloth was turning to black dust. She watched as it spread, until the whole length of it had evaporated into fine particles.

Yuriko suddenly realized what it was, the realization coming not from within but as though someone had thrown it into her mind from the outside.

This is the cloth that Mr. Minochi used to hold the Book of Elem. That's why I found it lying on the floor. Hiroki must have dropped it when he took the book.

It had been so heavy. Perhaps some enchantment was on it. Something to distract the Hero's gaze.

She wondered where the book was now.

Perhaps the Hero, now more and more Kirrick every day, had retrieved it.

How much of his own fragmented body had Kirrick been able to collect?

But all that was happening far, far away in the Haetlands.

"Aju?" she ventured in a tiny voice. "Aju, are you there?"

There was no response. Yuriko had been ready for this, but still, it was another disappointment. She hoped Aju hadn't been injured during their run-in with the Hero.

There was a noise behind her, and Yuriko whirled around, expecting to see the tiny mouse there, his whiskers twitching with pride; or the man with strands of ashen gray hair, the tattered hem of his coat dragging on the floorboards—

Michiru was standing in the doorway, a hand on the frame, staring in at her. "Yuriko?"

Yuriko's heart fell back down into her chest with a thunk.

"Oh, right," Yuriko said, figuring that the girl had come to find her and bring her back to the others. She made to leave, but Michiru was slowly walking into the reading room toward her.

"This place," Michiru whispered, the old books that covered the walls absorbing her voice. "It scared me when I was here last time."

I know, thought Yuriko. You told me.

"Is it still scary?"

"No, I guess not. It seems different now." Michiru smiled at her. "Morisaki liked it here. You should've seen the way his eyes shone the one time we came here together. We…used to talk about books."

"At the library at school?"

"Yeah."

"Did you ever go to the library in town?"

A shadow came over Michiru's eyes. "You mean the public library? Not very much." Then she added in a low voice, "We didn't want to run into anyone from school."

Of course, Yuriko thought. With both of them being on the committee, it wouldn't have been strange to find them in the school library, but if someone saw them together outside of school, that would mean they were really friends and were trying to show it to everyone.

Just the kind of attention Michiru didn't want.

The thought triggered something in Yuriko's memory, and she blurted out, "Did you know that something happened in that library this last spring? One of the books burned, just by itself."

Yuriko knew Hiroki had done it with his magic, but she didn't know why. Maybe she does.

"A book burned?" Michiru looked surprised. "No, I hadn't heard anything like that."

"Yeah, and the funny thing is, the name of the book was Making the Most of Household Cleaners. Who'd burn a book like that—"

Before Yuriko had even finished speaking, Michiru's complexion changed.

In the dim reading room, her face went so pale it seemed to shine like the full moon.

"Who told you that, Yuriko?"

"One of the book—er, a friend at the library."

"Were they mad?"

"No, more like confused."

Michiru put a hand to her throat and took a deep breath. Even in that dusty, dark room, her profile was beautiful.

"I'm sorry."

"For what?"

"I think Morisaki did it. For me," she added quietly. "When all the kids were picking on me at school I got depressed, and I-I thought seriously about killing myself."

Yuriko straightened her posture and listened.

"There are some kinds of household cleaners that you're not supposed to mix together. If you do, it makes poison gas. I...I was going to mix them in the bath."

Finally it made sense. "And that book told you which ones? So you borrowed the book?"

"I did, but that was just around the time that Morisaki started looking out for me."

She had never taken that bath. Her plans for suicide had been shelved.

"I told Morisaki about it later. And then he told me he would get rid of that book, so I wouldn't ever be tempted to do that sort of thing again." Michiru covered her face with her hands and crouched there in the reading room. "And then he got rid of it, I guess."

Yuriko pictured the scene in her mind. Maybe Hiroki hadn't planned on burning the book at first, but once he had the Book of Elem in his hands, and was fully under the Hero's sway, it must have seemed like the perfect target for testing his newfound powers.

He was protecting Michiru again, of course.

He wouldn't regret what he had done, even now. He'd be satisfied. His incomplete self as a nameless devout had been erased, closing the gate and protecting this world, Michiru's world, from the ravages of the King in Yellow.

Yuriko knelt, closing her eyes, letting herself dissolve into the silence of the room. From the bookshelves, the books watched over the girls in the slanting light from the window. Though now they might be pretending to be nothing more than pages bound in leather, Yuriko knew the truth.

Or at least, she hoped they were watching.

Another two weeks passed.

It was a hot afternoon, filled with the buzzing of cicadas in the trees. Yuriko had just gotten back from swimming lessons at the pool, had eaten lunch, and was feeling very ready for a nap. Her mother had gone out to do some grocery shopping.

The news on the television was talking about a war overseas. There were other reports of things happening in her own country—random murders, senseless atrocities. Yuriko knew what it all meant. War was coming. Another age of conflict loomed.

But, recently, she had begun to make her own sort of peace with that. There was a lot of bad news for sure, but it wasn't like the end of the world was at her door, ringing the doorbell just yet.

It wasn't that she didn't care. The realization that there was very little she could do about it had settled on her heart, like the dust collecting on the furniture in Ichiro Minochi's cottage.

A feeling of powerlessness was slowly building up inside her with each passing day, and she found she didn't mind it so much.

The doorbell rang.

Not now! I was just about to drift off—

"Yes?" she called out halfheartedly, and opened the door with the safety chain still on to find a strange man smiling in at her. His broad grin showed a full set of perfect teeth. When he saw Yuriko, he nodded. Even in this heat, he wore a heavy-looking suit with a necktie wrapped tightly around his collar.

"Yuriko Morisaki?"

The way he said her name sounded strange. The intonation was all wrong. *Wait, he's not Japanese?* The man certainly looked Japanese.

"Sorry if I startled you." The man grinned again and bowed. "I am an interpreter. I bring someone who wants to meet you, Yuriko."

"Me?" Yuriko asked, pointing at her nose.

"Yes, you. He is waiting downstairs. He wants to meet only you."

And not my parents? That sounded suspicious.

Yuriko squinted over the chain at the man. "Who is it that wants to meet only me?"

The man replied immediately, "Actually, I'm not sure myself. But he has told me that you would know him were I to introduce him as a friend of the Man of Ash."

✦

Her visitor was waiting in a strange-looking van with high suspension. The sliding door opened, and she could see him looking out at her from the back seat. She knew she should never get into a strange car with a strange man, but this time seemed like an exception. A real exception. Yuriko ran up to the van.

The man was wearing a white shirt, with a brilliantly colored blanket draped over his knees. When he saw Yuriko run up, all out of breath, he smiled merrily.

He has perfect teeth too.

Those white teeth and white eyes and white shirt stood in stark contrast to the man's dark skin.

He was a large man, with broad shoulders. His silver hair was cropped close to his scalp above a smooth forehead.

Yuriko spotted a wheelchair folded in the back of the van.

He's old. An old man.

"This is Yuriko," the interpreter said, running up behind her.

The man beckoned Yuriko to sit in the seat next to him, pointing with one finger to his ear several times. *He's wearing a hearing aid.*

Yuriko got into the van and sat next to him, feeling dwarfed by the man's size. The interpreter closed the sliding door and went around to the front to sit in the driver's seat.

Their eyes met. The old man smiled again, nodding to her two, three times. He began talking rapidly, not even waiting for the interpreter to get settled. Yuriko couldn't make out a single thing he was saying.

"He says 'Hello,'" the interpreter translated, as he wiped the sweat from his brow.

"Hello!" Yuriko said back, bowing her head. "You are a friend of Ash—I mean, the Man of Ash?"

The interpreter spoke again, and the old man answered. She was pretty sure he wasn't speaking English, but other than that, she had no idea what language it was.

"Yes," the interpreter said. "His name is Atali."

Atali. Yuriko had been able to make that word out in the jumble from the old man's mouth.

"It is his 'wolf' name. I am sorry I do not know what that means. Do you know?"

Yuriko swallowed, nodding. She could feel the sweat on the palms of her hands.

"He knows you," the interpreter translated.

The old man's tone was gentler now. He looked directly at Yuriko as he talked, now in broken Japanese. "You are U-ri. *Allcaste* U-ri, yes?"

Yuriko's eyes went wide as she stared back at him. She nodded again.

"I know of your journey. The Man of Ash told me. The other wolves call me 'Atali Silvertooth.'"

That's a cool name, Yuriko thought. A wolf with silver teeth.

"I have known the Man of Ash, Dmitri, for a very long time."

Dmitri. It seemed like years since she had last heard that name.

"Dmitri does not age. But I have grown old. I am an old man." He laughed. "I cannot fight anymore. Nor can I hunt. That is why I now retire."

Here the man returned to speaking his own language so he could speak more quickly. The interpreter, listening to every word and sweating profusely, nodded and occasionally asked questions. Yuriko steadied her own breath and tried to calm her wildly beating heart as she looked between the two.

"You were very brave, U-ri," the interpreter said, turning back to Yuriko. "That is why Atali has come to you. That is why he expects so much of—expects?" The interpreter asked a quick question to Atali, then turned back to her. "Yes, expects."

Yuriko nodded. "I see. But what does he expect?" Her pulse was racing faster now.

"If you would be so inclined, Mr. Atali has something to give you. He wants you to have it."

With a nudge from the interpreter, Atali opened the top few buttons on his shirt, revealing an old yet still muscular chest and a pendant hanging on a chain at his neck, nestled in silver chest hair.

Atali began to remove it, but his fingers did not move as nimbly as he would have liked, and eventually the interpreter had to lean from the driver's seat to help him.

"This is my mark."

The pendant looked small in Atali's large black hand. It glowed a dull silver. Yuriko saw that it was shaped like a fang.

A *wolf's fang*.

"Dmitri does not know. But I have seen it in you. You are strong. Far stronger than you know."

Atali's hand tilted and the pendant chain began to slip. Yuriko quickly reached out to grab it as it fell.

The pendant was warm to the touch. Like it was alive.

With his other hand, the man gently grasped Yuriko's wrist, rotating her palm upward, and placed the chain of the pendant in her hand. Atali smiled. Then he curled her fingers shut until she held the pendant tightly.

"You are strong. You have the makings of a wolf. I retire now, but this fang I pass to you. Will you take it?"

Atali had come a long way for this. He had crossed an ocean. But though his region might be a foreign land to Yuriko, they were both in the same Circle. And wolves roamed everywhere. They had access to all places.

"Where are you from, Atali?"

The man interpreted. For some reason, Atali had to think before he answered. "Homeland," he said.

Yuriko lifted an eyebrow. Was that a country's name?

The man squinted and smiled as though he had expected this reaction. He began to talk rapidly again, making the interpreter rush to keep up.

"Homeland is not a true country's name. It is the name of a district formed a long time ago in the Republic of South Africa. You know in my country there was a thing called apartheid? It means 'apart-ness.' It was discrimination against those with black skin."

"Yes, my brother told me all about apartheid. He saw a movie about it or something."

Atali nodded. "It was in those days, the white people told the black people you must live here, and those places they called *bantustans*, or 'homelands.'"

The interpreter continued, wiping at his face with a handkerchief. "A long time ago, in the Republic of South Africa, there was a story that told the white people they could do what they—what's that? A story?" He turned back to Atali for confirmation. Atali nodded. Yuriko nodded too.

"It was a story, yes. A popular one in those times."

It was a story. People at the time might have thought of it as a philosophy, or perhaps even the simple truth, but it was in fact a story.

"That is when I became a wolf. My desire was to hunt the book that told the story that made one man hate another because of the color of his skin. There are no homelands now. There is no apartheid."

He smiled. "I live in Johannesburg."

But Atali had been born a wolf in his homeland. And he had come from there to give Yuriko his fang.

"I have been searching for a successor for some time now." Atali looked with large eyes at Yuriko. His pupils glinted jet black. They reminded her of somebody else's eyes—the eyes of every brave man she had ever met.

"You would make a good wolf. You will journey again. You want to, yes? When you are older and stronger. You will journey to bind the Hero. I know this. That is why I have come." The old man smiled. "I am glad to have met you. You are exactly as I imagined you to be."

Yuriko's vision blurred. *Why am I still crying after everything I've been through?*

Why am I still such a little crybaby?

But these weren't a child's tears.

"You are strong. You journeyed well. Your journey was hard, but you saved your brother. You saved the Circle. You are strong."

The man's heavy hand rubbed Yuriko's head. Atali smiled. His smile was strong and gentle. "I believe in you. I think Dmitri knows this too. He waits for you. And he will wait a long time, for he will never die. He does not grow old. But you will soon be an adult."

Dmitri the undertaker. The Man of Ash. Ash in his black cloak. *One who is close to the dead.*

He was waiting to meet Yuriko again. Waiting to walk the streets of the Haetlands with her again, where the tragic King Kirrick ruled as the Hero.

And Aju would be there too, for sure, an *aunkaui* dictionary no longer.

The silver fang glinted in Yuriko's palm, reflecting the light in her eyes.
"Thank you."
Yuriko gripped the pendant tightly.
The mark of the wolf, in her hand.

A note on the type

Designed by Jan Tschichold (1902–1974) for both Linotype and Monotype machines, Sabon was named for famed sixteenth century typefounder Jacques Sabon. Sabon was the first to bring Claude Garamond's roman typefaces to Frankfurt, then and now a center of world publishing. When asked to create a font that would work with both Linotype and Monotype by the German masterprinters' association, Tschichold returned to Garamond's original conceptions and spent three years creating the font he named Sabon, which he completed in 1967.

Jan Tschichold was born the son of a signwriter in Leipzig, Germany. A fervent Modernist who came of age during the Weimar Republic, Tschichold was incarcerated by the Nazis for "cultural bolshevism." After the war, he moved to England for two years, embraced some classical notions of design, and for Penguin books created the standard design text *Penguin Composition Rules*. Tschichold spent most of the rest of his life in Switzerland, where he died in 1974.

Now in Paperback
Miyuki Miyabe's Batchelder Award-winning novel
BRAVE STORY!

Alone after his father leaves and his mother attempts suicide, Wataru Mitani ventures from the real world to the land of Vision, where he seeks five magical gemstones representing the qualities of charity, bravery, faith, grace, and the power of light and darkness. With these, perhaps Watari can change his fate and bring his family together again.

$16.99 USA / $23.00 CAN / £12.99 UK ISBN: 978-1-4215-2773-4.
At better bookstores everywhere and www.haikasoru.com

HAIKASORU

THE FUTURE IS JAPANESE

ICO: CASTLE IN THE MIST BY MIYUKI MIYABE

A boy with horns, marked for death. A girl who sleeps in a cage of iron. The Castle in the Mist has called for its sacrifice: a horned child, born once a generation. When, on a single night in his thirteenth year, Ico's horns grow long and curved, he knows his time has come. But why does the Castle in the Mist demand this offering, and what will Ico do with the girl imprisoned within the castle's walls? Delve into the mysteries of Miyuki Miyabe's grand achievement of imagination, inspired by the award-winning game for the PlayStation® 2 computer entertainment system, now remastered for PlayStation® 3.

THE CAGE OF ZEUS BY SAYURI UEDA

The Rounds are humans with the sex organs of both genders. Artificially created to test the limits of the human body in space, they are now a minority, despised and hunted by the terrorist group the Vessel of Life. Aboard Jupiter-I, a space station orbiting the gas giant that shares its name, the Rounds have created their own society with a radically different view of gender and of life itself. Security chief Shirosaki keeps the peace between the Rounds and the typically gendered "Monaurals," but when a terrorist strike hits the station, the balance of power is at risk...and an entire people is targeted for genocide.

MM9 BY HIROSHI YAMAMOTO

Japan is beset by natural disasters all the time: typhoons, earthquakes, and... giant monster attacks. A special anti-monster unit called the Meteorological Agency Counter Anomalous Organism Unit (MCU) has been formed to deal with natural disasters of high "monster magnitude." The work is challenging, the public is hostile, and the monsters are hungry, but the MCU crew has science and teamwork on their side. Together, they can save Japan. From the author of *The Stories of Ibis*.

VISIT US AT WWW.HAIKASORU.COM